**Zoey Gomez** lives and writes  She saw *Romancing the Stone* age and has dreamed of being ever since. She grew up near London, where she studied art and creative writing, and now she sells vintage books and writes novels. A good day is one where she speaks to no one but cats. You can follow her @ZoeyGomezBooks on X and Instagram.

**Rachel Dove** is a writer and teacher, living in West Yorkshire with her husband, their two sons and their animals. In July 2015 she won the *Prima* magazine and Mills & Boon Flirty Fiction competition. She also won the Writers' Bureau Writer of the Year Award in 2016. She has had work published in the UK and overseas in various magazines and newspaper publications.

**Also by Zoey Gomez**

*The Single Dad's Secret
One-Night Reunion with the Vet*

**Also by Rachel Dove**

*How to Resist Your Rival
A Baby to Change Their Lives
Faking It with the Firefighter
One Night to Twin Surprise*

Discover more at millsandboon.co.uk.

# NURSE'S BORA BORA NIGHT

ZOEY GOMEZ

# HATING DR SUNSHINE

RACHEL DOVE

**MILLS & BOON**

All rights reserved including the right of reproduction in whole or in part in any form. This edition is published by arrangement with Harlequin Enterprises ULC.

This is a work of fiction. Names, characters, places, locations and incidents are purely fictional and bear no relationship to any real life individuals, living or dead, or to any actual places, business establishments, locations, events or incidents. Any resemblance is entirely coincidental.

Without limiting the exclusive rights of any author, contributor or the publisher of this publication, any unauthorised use of this publication to train generative artificial intelligence (AI) technologies is expressly prohibited. HarperCollins also exercise their rights under Article 4(3) of the Digital Single Market Directive 2019/790 and expressly reserve this publication from the text and data mining exception.

® and TM are trademarks owned and used by the trademark owner and/or its licensee. Trademarks marked with ® are registered with the United Kingdom Patent Office and/or the Office for Harmonisation in the Internal Market and in other countries.

First published in Great Britain 2026
by Mills & Boon, an imprint of HarperCollins*Publishers* Ltd,
1 London Bridge Street, London, SE1 9GF

www.harpercollins.co.uk

HarperCollins*Publishers* Macken House, 39/40 Mayor Street Upper, Dublin 1, D01 C9W8, Ireland

Nurse's Bora Bora Night © 2026 Zoey Gomez

Hating Dr Sunshine © 2026 Rachel Dove

ISBN: 978-0-263-41983-2

02/26

Printed and Bound in the UK using 100% Renewable Electricity
at CPI Group (UK) Ltd, Croydon, CR0 4YY

# NURSE'S BORA BORA NIGHT

## ZOEY GOMEZ

MILLS & BOON

To Richard D. Thanks for the inspiration.

## CHAPTER ONE

Mina had always loathed Valentine's Day.

It had started from an early age. At her middle-school Valentine's Day party, all her friends' desks had overflowed with anonymous pink and red cards while her desk had sat empty. No ten-year-old boy had wanted to own up to liking the ginger girl whose cheeks were covered in freckles. A few years later, when she'd arrived home from a disaster of a Valentine's disco at sixteen years old, still clutching the pity flower her best friend had given her from the bunch she received, she'd walked in on her parents getting divorced and her dad leaving the country. And then, to cap it off, only a year ago her ex-boyfriend had chosen to dump her on Valentine's Day. The closest thing she'd got to a love letter that day had been an email reminding her she had a week to get her stuff out of his apartment.

She couldn't even escape it at work. She'd have thought hospitals and clinics would be a Valentine's-free space, but there was always some misguided boyfriend bringing a patient a bunch of balloons too big to fit into a ward, or some locum nurse decorating the staff room with tacky pink hearts.

Mina lifted her chin as she strode past a loud red Valentine's display which was covering a coffee shop so thoroughly that the customers could barely get to the counter. Such a waste of time and red balloons. Who needed it? Mina's Valentine's Days were a disaster every year. Which was why it made perfect sense to her that she was spending this 14th February stuck alone in an airport with a four-hour layover until the next plane.

But she was determined not to worry about that when she had an amazing new job to fly to. Looking forward—that was what she was doing now. Leaving her disastrous life behind and making a new one...on a tropical island in the middle of the Pacific, no less.

A thrill of excitement ran through her. She still couldn't believe it was really happening. She, Mina Morgan, the woman who never did anything exciting, was dropping everything and moving alone to Bora Bora to work at one of the most luxurious hotels in the world.

She finally reached the right departure gate for her flight and dumped her bags on the nearest seat, then flung herself down next to them. As she got comfortable and glanced around, she realised that at least fate had chosen the right place to sit for her.

Sat directly opposite her, five feet away across an empty expanse of marble floor, was the most beautiful man she'd ever seen. With dark eyes, thick hair and sharp cheekbones, he looked as if he'd stepped out of a men's style magazine.

There was something refined about the way he held himself. He was immaculately tailored in simple chinos, a woollen jumper and leather boots. But his elegance was softened by the few days of scruff on his jaw and his slightly mussed hair, which made it look as if he'd just woken up. An expensive-looking Italian leather carry-on sat beside him.

There was something else striking about the man. He was the only person in the airport lounge looking at something other than a phone. He was reading a tatty paperback book, half of it folded around so he could hold it in one large hand. She wished the cover was visible so she could see what he was so enraptured by. At that moment, he decided to look up and directly at Mina, and she flushed guiltily but maintained eye contact, a thrill racing up her spine as he gave her a warm smile. She offered back the same smile, then finally looked away. She could feel him staring at her for a long moment before he stopped.

Mina found her mood improving immediately. Flirting with a handsome stranger, however subtly, had given her a little boost. Her life had been so stressful lately that she could barely remember what flirting or having fun felt like.

She'd taken her new job as a direct response to the worst run of bad luck of her life. Her boyfriend and her best friend had betrayed her in the worst way possible only months ago. The thought of it still made her feel nauseous. Then she'd almost immediately lost her flat in London, when her landlord had decided she wanted to move back in herself. Since then, Mina had been desperate to get away from everything. So, when an old healthcare recruiter friend had offered her a job on an island in the middle of the Pacific Ocean, Mina had considered the fact that there was absolutely nothing for her in London any more, made one of the most reckless decisions of her life and said yes.

Finally, things were looking up. She had an exciting new job to look forward to, a new life to discover. After all, she might be stuck in an airport, but at least she was in Los Angeles. It was a place she'd always dreamed of visiting, and it was tempting to stow her bags and just go and explore.

Despite it being February, her weather app said it was warm and sunny outside, and she'd seen flashes of sandy beach and blue ocean right next to the airport as they'd descended. But with her luck she'd miss her connecting flight or get lost in LA. Better to stay put in the airport.

And then, just when she thought she was safe, Mina's Valentine's Day curse struck again. The PA system chimed loudly.

'Due to staffing issues, the following flights will suffer severe delays…'

Mina scrambled for her flight number and dismay set in as she heard it read out among a list of many.

'We will provide updates as soon as we have them. Could all passengers affected please proceed to gate 137 for further information. We apologise for the inconvenience. Thank you so much for your patience and understanding.'

'Thank you so much for nothing,' Mina mumbled sarcastically. She heard a low chuckle from the direction of the handsome man. They shared another smile, and Mina got that same rush of excitement. She got a brief glimpse of breathtaking honey-brown eyes, dark, sultry lashes and the sharpest cheekbones known to man before she started gathering her things to lug them to gate 137 and find out what was going on. Out of the corner of her eye, she noticed the handsome man doing the same thing.

Mina fumbled, nearly dropping her bag, and the handsome man cleared his throat. She looked up at him, bag strap hanging precariously from her fingers.

'Would you like me to watch your bags while you go to the gate?' he asked.

God help her, his voice matched his face; he had the most delicious French accent she'd ever heard.

'Really?' she squeaked.

He shrugged. *He even shrugged sexily.* 'Of course. Then you can do the same for me.'

She tilted her head to stare at him. Did he look like the kind of guy who would steal her bags and run off with them? He looked steadily back at her, waiting patiently for an answer, his book still in his hand. She'd spotted the gate, and it wasn't far; she'd be able to keep an eye on them from there.

She smiled, decision made. This was her week to take chances, and she might as well take another one. 'Thank you. I'd really appreciate that.'

He nodded, smiling, then turned back to his book.

The people at the desk weren't a lot of use. They couldn't share much information, aside from the fact that the delays were likely to be long, and she should wait in or near the airport until they could inform her of her new flight. If the delays were extensive, they said they would be able to offer her a room in a budget hotel, but it all sounded pretty grim and unappealing.

Mina's new employers had paid for her ticket—luckily, since it had cost over a thousand pounds—so she felt she couldn't complain too much. But the extra delay was still frustrating. Now that she'd made the decision to start a new life, she wanted it to begin as soon as possible.

Mina returned to her un-stolen, perfectly safe bags, and then watched the handsome French man take his turn walking to the desk. He was there for longer than she had been, and spoke to two different people. Not that Mina was watching. Her gaze eventually fell on the book he'd left behind, nestled next to his leather carry-on. She twisted sideways to read the upside-down title of the book. It was *Villette* by Charlotte Brontë. *Interesting*. She'd been expecting something more like a spy novel or an autobiography. That would teach her not to prejudge. Evidently he wasn't your typical man.

When he came back, he was smiling.

'Did you get a better result than I did?' Mina asked.

'I have good news and bad news,' he answered.

'What's the bad?'

'None of us are likely to be going anywhere until tomorrow morning.'

'Tomorrow? Oh no, my new job! I start work at…'

He held up his hand with a smile. 'I have good news too.'

'Go on…'

'To compensate us for our inconvenience, I got us two free drinks at the bar, a room each booked at a decent hotel nearby and access to one of the first-class lounges.'

Mina's jaw dropped. 'Wow, good looks really do get you better service.'

The man snorted with laughter, his sophisticated demeanour gone for a split second. It was cute. 'You flatter me. Perhaps the second woman I talked to was in a generous mood. Would you like to go and get that drink together?' He offered his hand to Mina to help her up.

*Oh.* 'Yes, I'd love to.' Mina felt her cheeks flush as she let him wrap his warm, large hand around hers and pull her effortlessly to her feet.

They stowed their bags, and Mina called her contact at the resort to tell them she'd be catching a later flight. She'd already arranged to have a day to settle in before she started work, so she wouldn't miss anything important if she arrived a day later than planned.

'What's the hold-up, anyway?' she asked him. 'They keep saying "staffing issues".'

'I think that may be code for a worker's strike. But they don't usually last for long, just long enough to make a point,' he answered.

'Oh. Then good luck to them.'

'Absolutely. Everything should be back to normal by the morning.'

They took advantage of their access to the first-class lounge. Following the signs, they crossed the large expanse of marble floor and traversed past the lifts and round a corner to it. They were quickly granted access and headed to the bar across a thick geometric carpet which seemed to soak up the echoes and noise outside. Although huge, the bar had a cosy feel with low lighting and oak walls. They made their way past the low tables and armchairs, and ended up at a long glossy bar, almost empty of customers.

The man pulled out a stool for Mina, and waited until she took it before seating himself next to her. His hand accidentally brushed her wrist as he pulled away, and a shiver ran all the way up her arm. The barman gestured that he'd be with them in a moment, and Mina took in the beautiful man beside her. Closer now, she could see tiny freckles across his nose, and long dark eyelashes. When his eyes met hers, a little thrill ran through her again. Who was this man who read classic novels by the Brontës and dressed with such effortless style? She had to know more about him.

'So what do you do?' she asked.

'Small talk,' he murmured softly. 'Do you really care what I do for a living?'

Mina smiled; he had a point. Despite that, she felt a flash of curiosity. She bet he had an embarrassing job that he didn't want to talk about. Or, perhaps more realistically, an incredibly boring job he didn't want to talk about. 'Nothing wrong with being polite. But, I agree, I don't suppose it makes any difference to me what you do.'

He smiled. 'What would you like to drink?'

Mina thought for a moment then opened her mouth, about to ask for her usual white wine.

'Wait, my apologies—what's a drink you've always dreamed of trying but never have?'

The answer came to Mina almost immediately and she laughed. 'I've always wanted to try a Zombie cocktail but I've never been brave enough to order one.'

'Let's do it.' He gestured to the barman and he came over immediately. 'Two of your finest Zombies, please.'

The barman nodded and smiled. 'They're not on the menu but I can certainly whip those up.'

The man turned back to Mina after the barman had left. 'I've never had one either.'

Mina smiled. 'Don't blame me if we hate them.'

'Oh, I will.' He winked at her and she laughed again.

Something suddenly occurred to Mina. 'We don't even know each other's names.'

He shrugged. 'Is that such a bad thing?'

'I suppose not,' Mina said, unsure.

'If you think about it, names are meaningless. Or perhaps I mean arbitrary. Same with jobs, home towns, reality...'

He cast his brown eyes down for a moment and Mina wondered what he was thinking about.

'Maybe I sound ridiculous.'

He looked up with a rueful smile, and Mina shook her head. 'No, go on.'

'We assign value to things like job titles, when truly they mean nothing. Maybe we should try sharing no personal information—see what it's like just getting to know each other as people.'

Mina gazed at him for a moment. Normally she'd have no patience for things like this; she'd be annoyed by any hint of a man playing games or being overly mysterious. But she was never going to see this man again, and she had to admit he was right. It was strangely exciting not knowing anything about him. She could give him any back story she wanted—perhaps he was a model headed home to Paris after a job in LA shooting a fashion ad.

She had to admit it would be refreshing not to introduce herself immediately to someone as a nurse. She was sick of people asking for juicy details about the strangest case she'd treated or the biggest mess she'd had to clean up. Mina would never see this man again and she was on her way to start a new life on a tropical island in the middle of the Pacific Ocean. If she couldn't be a little impulsive now, when could she?

Maybe she'd run into this man for a reason. Maybe he was the perfect way to put a full-stop to her old life, forget all the betrayal and disappointment and start a new chapter. Just this once she could be reckless and silly and, if this was headed in the direction she thought it might be, she could imagine getting very reckless and silly with this man.

'Okay, you have a deal.' Mina held out her hand and he shook it. Apparently her body still hadn't stopped trembling every time he touched her. 'But I have to call you something.' She couldn't continue to call him 'the French man' in her head.

He smiled lazily. 'Dealer's choice. You can call me anything you want.'

She took him all in, from his perfectly styled hair and his beautiful eyes, down to his full lips and wide shoulders, not forgetting his sexy French accent. 'Jean-Paul?'

He laughed shortly and nodded. 'Perfect.'

Before they could invent a false name for Mina, the barman returned with their drinks and a plate covered in baby-pink heart shapes. 'Would you like to try our Valentine's cookies?'

Mina couldn't help her automatic visceral reaction, and winced at the plate. 'No, thank you.'

Jean-Paul turned from the pink cookies to Mina, then back to the barman. 'I'll take one.'

'They're all yours,' he said with a smile and left the plate by their drinks.

'Is it the cookies you don't like or the colour?' he asked Mina.

'The symbolism.'

He picked one up and turned it in his fingers. 'This cookie is symbolic?'

'Of capitalism and crass consumerism.'

'Oh. I just thought it was cute.'

Mina couldn't help but smile. He took a bite of the cookie and chewed it, swallowing before he spoke. 'It tastes good. Ten out of ten; strongly recommend. Are you sure I can't tempt you with one?'

He licked a crumb slowly from his lower lip, and Mina was mesmerised for a moment. The cookie smelled sugary and sweet, and Mina had to admit he made it look good. She rolled her eyes. 'I suppose I could try one. For you.'

A smile spread across his face and he pointed at the plate 'May I?' Mina nodded and watched as he picked out a cookie and passed it to her, their fingers touching briefly for one electric moment. Only when she looked closer did she realise the cookie had words iced onto it in darker pink: *beautiful girl*. She laughed, but felt her cheeks flush.

'Are you flirting with me via baked goods?'

He shrugged. 'It certainly seems that way.'

'I thought French men were supposed to be better at this.'

He took in a breath, mock-offended. 'You mean it's not working?'

It might have been working a bit. The cookie was annoyingly delicious. 'Your flirting is fine, the biscuits are fine. I suppose I'm just not a romantic. I've always hated Valentine's Day. I've never had a good one and I doubt I ever will.'

'What did Saint Valentine ever do to you?'

'Don't ask. I think I'm cursed.'

'I don't think you are. You just need to have a good one for once.' He stared at her thoughtfully. 'Excuse me one moment, I'll be right back.'

He got up from his bar stool and left the bar. Mina assumed he'd gone to find a bathroom, but after a little while he reappeared and handed Mina a pink envelope with a question mark scribbled on it instead of a name.

She stared at it for a moment then burst into laughter as she realised what it was. 'Oh my gosh, this is absurd.' She slid open the envelope and pulled out a Valentine's card.

He laughed too. 'I'm afraid they were all quite obnoxious, so I leaned in and got the worst one I could find.'

Mina nodded. 'It's terrible.' Secretly, she rather liked it: five cartoon kittens holding a red heart. Inside he'd written:

> Dear ?, I promise you the best Valentine's Day you've never had.
> Jean-Paul

Mina set the card on the bar, behind her drink. 'I will treasure it always,' she said, softening the sarcasm with a genuine smile.

'I've never bought a Valentine's card for anyone before. It's not really my thing. But I quite enjoyed it.'

He was probably too cultured to do such things. She really couldn't imagine him strolling into a shop and doing something so mundane as buying a greeting card, although he'd basically just done exactly that for her. What a strange thing to be so flattered by.

'We've got all day…' he said. 'Since you've got time to kill, would you like to eat with me before you check in to your hotel room? More than just a cookie, I mean.'

Mina nodded. She was having a surprisingly wonderful time, so why not continue it?

'I know just the place,' he said. 'I promised you a good Valentine's Day, so we're not just going to eat, we're going to eat romantically.'

Mina laughed and grabbed her card, pushing it into her handbag. 'And what might that entail?'

'You'll see.'

# CHAPTER TWO

THEY CROSSED THE airport concourse and entered a little Italian restaurant tucked away in a corner. It had pretty tiled floors and low ceilings and was quiet after the dinner-time rush. They slipped into a cosy booth.

After checking that Mina wasn't allergic to anything, he convinced her to join him in a lobster dish that was apparently their speciality. But her lingering doubts about airport lobster must have showed on her face, because the man she continued to call Jean-Paul in her head smiled. 'I promise, this place is wonderful. Their lobster is delicious; they ship it in direct from Maine.'

'You must use this airport a lot,' Mina observed. As she spoke, he watched her mouth, and Mina tried not to flush visibly at the attention.

'No details,' he reminded her. 'But, yes, I pass through here regularly.'

He was *so* a model.

She tried to concentrate on ordering her drink from the waitress, but his gaze slipped down her body to her neck and shoulders as she did so. He asked the waitress for a candle and flowers for the table, despite Mina's laughing protests that it wasn't necessary. And, when their legs collided softly under the table, neither of them pulled away. She could feel the heat of his body through her jeans.

It turned out he was right—the lobster was delicious—and afterwards they shared a tiramisu for dessert with two spoons, just to be extra-romantic, he said. Then he pulled a folded napkin out of his pocket and unwrapped it on the table between them, revealing the last few pink heart-shaped cookies.

Mina burst out laughing. 'You stole them?'

'The bartender gave them to us. Think of them as fortune cookies. Maybe they have a message for us. Close your eyes and pick one.'

'You first,' said Mina.

He closed his eyes immediately, his lashes casting a shadow over his cheeks in the low lighting, and picked a cookie. He frowned when he read it, then held it up to Mina. '"Funny Face".' Mina giggled into her hand. 'Should I be offended?' he asked. 'Disparaged by a cookie,' he muttered. 'Your turn. I hope you get a better fortune.'

Mina closed her eyes and carefully chose one. She opened her eyes to read the words '"Come back to mine".' She tilted it towards him, and watched his face as he read it.

'That's quite forward,' he said quietly.

'Yes, it is.' She paused. 'But you can't argue with a fortune cookie. Perhaps it's time we went to the hotel.'

He nodded and held her gaze for a long moment, then smiled warmly.

When Mina excused herself to wash her hands in the restaurant's bathroom, he stood politely. Mina smiled, then realised no one had ever done that for her before.

It wasn't as if she'd missed it; the tradition of standing up when a lady left the table had been left somewhere back in the 1990s, along with shoulder pads and public smoking. Perhaps it was still traditional in France. Or perhaps she'd just happened to come across the most well-mannered man in the world.

She couldn't deny that a small part of her hoped he wasn't so well-mannered in the bedroom. And she wondered for a delicious moment whether she would be lucky enough to find out. In the glossy green-tiled bathroom, she splashed some cold water on her face, careful not to ruin the little make-up she had on, and tried to neaten her wild red curls as much as she could, but as usual they insisted on being unruly.

Despite her long, chaotic day, Mina wasn't tired at all, and she certainly didn't want her time with this man to end. And the heated looks he'd been giving her made her sure he also didn't want the night to end yet.

She couldn't ignore the fact that, if she was right about where this night was going, it would also be a perfect little act of rebellion against her ex. He'd disapproved of one-night stands, fun and recklessness. Quite ironic, now that she thought about how they'd broken up. For someone so judgmental, he'd been strangely comfortable with the idea of sleeping with his girlfriend's best friend behind her back.

Mina sighed. She still missed her best friend. Normally Jodie would be the one Mina would have told about meeting such an exciting man. She felt so hollow inside, knowing that she no longer had a best friend to tell secrets to, or with whom to laugh about things. There was no one she could be her authentic, silliest self with. But clearly none of that had meant anything to Jodie, or she would never have chosen Mina's ex-boyfriend over her.

She took a deep breath. A fun one-night stand, one which didn't hurt anyone, might be the perfect symbolic start of her new life, of moving on and moving forward to fun and freedom with no ties, no commitments and no consequences.

After sharing a short cab ride to the hotel, Jean-Paul spoke to the people on the desk. Mina just had time to admire the hotel foyer's vaulted ceiling, majestic windows and the full-grown trees growing indoors before he returned with two room key-cards, pressing one into Mina's hand.

The hotel was remarkably nice for something the airline was providing them free of charge. But she barely had time to notice that before he pressed his hand lightly on her back to show her where the elevators were.

They got out on the sixth floor and found their rooms which, perfectly innocently, sat right next door to one another. Neither one of them made a move to use their key card.

He opened his mouth to speak, but Mina got there first. 'I have something for you,' she said.

'You do?'

'Yes. Shut your eyes.'

He smiled and shut them with no hesitation.

'Hold out your hand.'

He did so obediently, and Mina took a cookie from her pocket, unwrapped it from its napkin and placed it on his open palm, turning it so that the 'kiss me' written on it in icing faced him.

He opened his eyes slowly and a smile spread over his face as he read the cookie. He reached out for Mina's hand and gently pulled her until she was close enough to feel his breath on her cheek.

'I knew you were a romantic deep down,' he whispered.

'It's just a cookie, not a love poem.'

He leaned down and pulled her closer still, until their lips met softly. She sighed into the kiss, chasing the sweet taste of his lips.

'The night doesn't have to end here, beautiful girl.'

She took a deep breath and tried to recover from the kiss. 'Are you inviting me in for coffee?' He was still being so well-mannered but she was sure they both knew what they wanted.

He held her gaze with hooded eyes. 'I'm inviting you in for whatever you want.'

That was more like it. An irresistible magnetic force pulled Mina's body closer to his. She knew that if she let him walk into his hotel room alone she'd regret it for the rest of her life. He was undeniably the sexiest man she'd ever met. But she also felt as if she'd known him for ever, as if she was safe with him. She needed this. She wanted this. It was perfect. She couldn't be betrayed or hurt by a one-night stand.

She shrugged nonchalantly and smiled. 'I suppose I could stay for a drink.'

'I suggest you stay for a lot more than that,' he said with a sultry smile.

'Oh, really?' she murmured.

'I don't know about you, but I haven't been able to take my eyes off you all day. Every glance, every little touch has driven me closer and closer to distraction. I know we'll never see each other again, but that doesn't mean we can't have one wonderful night together.'

'That's the worst idea I've ever heard in my life.' Mina paused. 'Let's do it.'

He smiled wickedly and pushed his door open, letting her walk in first. She grabbed his shirt and pulled him in after her, then pressed him back against the closed door, kissing him hard.

He kissed her back enthusiastically, running his hands from her shoulders, all the way down her arms to her hands, leaving goosebumps all the way. Then he took her face in his hands and pulled her close, until she could feel his warm breath on her neck. 'You want to do this?' he asked.

Her breath caught at his words; his voice had never sounded deeper or rougher. 'Yes, yes,' she said.

'And you don't mind that we'll never see each other again?'

'That's the best part!' Mina said breathlessly, and they kissed again.

They somehow found their way towards the bed, their hands and eyes more on each other than where they were going. Mina paused, only to catch her breath, and they both noticed at the same time the champagne bucket on the counter, holding a bottle of champagne in ice. 'Does this hotel provide free champagne?' Mina asked in surprise.

The moment was forgotten as he grabbed a rose from the vase on the nightstand and crushed it in his fist, scattering the rose petals on the bed. 'Happy Valentine's Day.'

'You know you can stop being romantic now. I'm literally standing in your bedroom,' Mina said. He smiled but studied her, a faint line of confusion appearing between his eyebrows. Unable to wait any longer, Mina reached for him and tugged his shirt open, revealing a muscular, tanned chest, then pushed him back on to the bed, petals bursting into the air and scattering on to the thick carpet.

As she joined him on the bed, Mina's pulse was suddenly too loud in her ears. His hands found hers in the twisted sheets, and he rolled her on to her back, holding her down as he kissed her hard. She arched her back as his lips grazed the sensitive spot behind her ear and he licked her neck, drawing out a shiver and a soft groan.

Mina lost all track of time as Jean-Paul pressed closer until they were skin on skin, writhing, panting raggedly, his hot breath on her shoulder, his every muscle flexing under her touch. She pressed her lips to his neck, just where his pulse pounded, then his mouth found hers, hot and desperate, and his fingers tightened around hers before the world exploded.

Moments later, still breathing heavily, he kissed his way up her neck. 'Do you like Valentine's Day yet?' he asked, his voice wrecked, before his lips met hers.

Sated and exhausted, Mina hummed happily against his lips, then pulled away fractionally. 'I'm officially a fan,' she whispered. Of Valentines Day, of gorgeous French strangers who might or might not be named Jean-Paul, and of having the best sex of her entire life.

\* \* \*

Mina woke up suddenly, surprised to find she'd been asleep at all. She hadn't meant to stay. But, oh, she was so warm and cosy here. He'd pulled her close at some point, and now she was lying on his chest, extremely comfortable, one arm slung across his waist, her nose nuzzled near his neck. He smelled so good.

But this wasn't meant to happen. She hadn't planned to fall asleep, or stay over. They'd both been pretty clear on what this was: one night of passion and then never seeing each other again, skipping the uncomfortable morning-after goodbyes altogether. She'd planned to make a sophisticated, elegant exit. But now it looked as if she'd have to settle for an awkward extrication from his limbs, and a silent, ungainly hop around the room to find her clothes without waking him.

It was still dark and she could just make out the time on the other side of the room. They could only have slept for an hour, and his gentle snores showed he was still out cold.

She was absolutely fine with never seeing him again, of course she was, but did never have to start so soon? As she lay in his arms, she came to the conclusion that a person could never know true, exquisite bliss until they'd heard a man whisper sweet nothings in French as he removed their clothes piece by agonising piece.

Before she started the extrication, she sighed quietly and let herself enjoy the warmth of his chest for just a moment longer. Eventually, Mina left his bed and managed to get herself, her scattered clothes and her bag out of his room and into hers without waking him. She felt momentarily guilty for her stealth exit, and hoped to God he wouldn't come looking for her any time between now and the next morning, when she'd be leaving for her flight. But then she told herself to get her ego under control. He was just as into the one-time thing as she'd been. He'd be relieved she had gone when he woke up; she was sure of it.

Suddenly exhausted, Mina had a quick shower then changed into her comfy pyjamas and gratefully slipped into the deliciously cool sheets of her luxurious bed. The hotel room really was remarkably nice, and huge. It was a wonder the airline wasn't going bust if they gave out rooms like this for free every time they had a delay. Mina snuggled down into her pillow. Despite the stressful start, this day couldn't have gone more perfectly. One last fling out of the way, now she felt truly ready to face her new life and concentrate on her fabulous new job, where men, sex, romance and all their requisite drama, wouldn't even be a blip on her radar.

Luca Baudelaire woke up alone. Which wouldn't be at all unusual on a normal day, but today he felt bewildered and bereft, until he remembered why. He rubbed the sleep from his eyes and glared at the empty side of the bed. The last time he'd looked, the stunning girl from the airport had still been there, fast asleep, her red curls spread out haphazardly over the white Egyptian cotton pillowcase, her freckled shoulders bare and beautiful above the sheets.

He patted a hand over her side of the bed: cold. He couldn't hear a sound, and he knew immediately that she wasn't in the bathroom. His hotel room was empty apart from him, some crumpled petals and an empty champagne bottle on the floor.

Why was he feeling so flat? This was exactly what he wanted. Things had worked out perfectly: no drama, no regrets, no awkward goodbyes. His phone chimed, and for a split second he hoped it was her. Which was ridiculous; they hadn't even shared names, let alone numbers. It was the airline: his new check-in time was in two hours.

Luca shaved quickly, watching himself in the mirror, cursing the fact that he'd never found out her name. It had seemed so sensible at the time, almost fun, exciting. But, knowing he now had no possible way of ever finding her again made his heart hurt. He frowned. This was a very unfamiliar feeling and he wasn't a fan of it.

He shook himself. Maybe he was coming down with something. Maybe that lobster had been bad after all or, more likely, those heart cookies had given him food poisoning. Speaking of… He finished shaving, wiped off the foam and, still holding the towel, left the bathroom and walked back to the bedside table. The little pink 'kiss me' cookie still sat there, next to his watch and a glass of water. He blinked at it, pushing down the wave of regret that surged inside him, then grabbed it and ate it.

He should be glad that she'd left and gone back to her hotel room. At least the second room he'd paid for hadn't gone to waste. He'd never for a moment thought they'd end up spending the night together when he'd paid for two decent hotel rooms. He hadn't been able to face the idea of staying at the lower quality accommodation the airline had initially offered to deal with their delays, and didn't see why the charming woman he'd just met should have to either. It wasn't as if he couldn't afford it. This hotel was nicer, safer and closer to the airport, so he'd booked it without telling her.

He'd learned a long time ago that good people didn't usually accept favours that involved money, and often felt insulted. And, of course, he hadn't wanted her to think he'd done it to make her feel as though she owed him anything in return. Hopefully she'd enjoyed her room. It would be just like his: same large bedroom, same luxurious bathroom. He would have loved to test out the huge hot tub if he'd had time. As it was, he was going to have to hurry to catch his delayed flight.

Luca left the hotel, resolutely refusing to look at her hotel room door. He didn't even think about her all the way down in the lift and across the foyer. He only let himself exhale when he stepped outside and knew there was no longer any chance of bumping into her. He looked up at the bright-blue winter sky, slipped on his sunglasses and made his way to the airport to catch his flight.

Once Luca was settled in the familiarity of his family's private jet, he pulled his book out of his bag and settled back into the cream leather seat.

'Coffee, Dr Baudelaire?'

Luca looked up at the flight attendant. 'Yes please, lots.'

She smiled. 'Looking forward to getting back to work?'

'Can't wait.'

He was looking forward to it. He loved being a doctor, even if he hated the fact that he worked under his own brother. He certainly hadn't missed his brother, Roman, and he doubted Roman had missed him. Luca's two-week holiday had been spent less on relaxing, and more on taking the chance to work on his personal projects while Roman wasn't there, sticking his nose in and trying to derail them.

If Luca hadn't made a promise to his mother always to look after his brother, he wouldn't have chosen to spend his life on the same continent as him, let alone in each other's pockets. But ifs and buts were meaningless. If his mother hadn't died, there would never have been a promise to keep. If his brother hadn't grown up sickly and weak, hospitalised and babied as a child, he might not have a chip on his shoulder as an adult, however healthy he was now. If his mother and father hadn't hated each other, maybe Luca would have been inclined to commit to more than one night of romance. But happy relationships weren't in his genes. They weren't something that people in his family were capable of.

He checked his messages for the first time in several days. Apparently, a new assistant had been hired in his absence. Hired by Roman, of course; all Luca could hope for was someone vaguely competent.

The flight attendant returned with a steaming cup of coffee and set it down next to him. 'Thank you,' Luca murmured, taking a scalding hot sip immediately. The coffee came with a pink napkin, which Luca used to wipe a drip from the edge of his coffee cup.

He smiled to himself as he remembered his Valentine companion's reaction to anything pink or heart-shaped. She'd seemed to hate all the romance that came with the day. He knew his attempts to show her a romantic evening had been corny, but that had been part of the fun. Luca might not do relationships, but he enjoyed the occasional opportunity to be romantic. He very rarely had the chance. His life, and his job, didn't allow for such distractions. But he could only allow out his true romantic side when he was with someone who didn't know him. It was easy to be vulnerable with someone he'd never see again.

One night with someone so irresistible was all he could allow himself—nothing long term, nothing permanent. He'd let himself care about a woman once before and it had gone spectacularly wrong; Roman had made sure of that., and he had soundly dealt with his brother for it. But Luca wouldn't risk his heart again.

Mina stood on a small wooden dock, waiting for her boat transfer, and stared out at the most beautiful view she'd ever seen in real life. The infinite blue sky, aqua ocean, palm trees and the scent of hibiscus filled her senses.

She had spent most of her flight from LA to Bora Bora's small airport on Motu Mute feeling an equal mixture of nervousness and being pleased with herself. Nervousness about starting a new job and a new life in a place she hadn't had much time to research, and pleased with herself for managing to successfully shake off any self-doubt left over from her turbulent personal life. Due in no small part to the passionate night with her enigmatic French man, she felt good right now for the first time in months, and she was going to make the most of it. She stepped off the dock on to a small, sleek black-and-white boat, helped down into the walnut interior by the friendly captain.

Her new office manager would be meeting her at the other end of the fifteen-minute trip across the water to the resort. Before she'd got this job, she didn't even know that hotel resorts had in-house nurses. But thank God they did because, after the year she'd had, Mina was pretty sure she deserved some time in a luxurious, high-end hotel resort. She found a seat at the back of the boat and tipped her face towards the sun, luxuriating in the heat. Bora Bora was in the Southern Hemisphere, so February was in their summer. Bora Bora's February felt like London's August, given it was their summer.

Mina had spent the last few months feeling worthless, angry and resentful towards the two people closest to her. She'd wasted weeks obsessing over their betrayal but now she was free. She could stop thinking about it, because she no longer cared. That perfect, hot night with Jean-Paul had been a metaphorical 'go to hell' to both of them, and an enthusiastic goodbye to her old life. Now she could well and truly move on, leave romance behind and concentrate on her career, which quite frankly was going wonderfully.

The boat's engine puttered into life and the boat, its captain and a handful of passengers set out slowly into the green-blue lagoon.

Bora Bora was more beautiful than she could ever have imagined. Everywhere she looked there were palm trees and white sands. The water turned a lighter turquoise as they drew closer to Mount Otemanu, which sat in the centre of Bora Bora's lagoon. Fluffy white clouds clung to its peak, above the lush green forest that covered almost all of the mountain. Would this really be her life now? It certainly beat the dingy flat in Ealing she'd left behind.

There were other luxury resorts on the island, but Mina's was located on a coral islet on a barrier reef along the eastern side. As they neared it the boat passed between two wooden walkways, each populated with dozens of beautiful over-water wooden villas on stilts. A family's two young children knelt up on seats inside the boat, enraptured, watching the view through the opened windows.

As the boat slowed, they passed several guests riding neon-yellow jet skis heading out on to the lagoon. Mina watched them weave gently into the distance. The water didn't look real. The clear, vibrant turquoise was a colour Mina wasn't sure she'd ever even seen before, certainly not in nature. She just wanted to sink into it. As the boat slowed further she reached down a hand and trailed it through the cool, fresh water.

The captain guided them into a private dock beside a lobby with a pretty thatched roof and moored next to several boats just the same as theirs, black, white and walnut, each with a different name printed on the hull in gold.

As the guests disembarked, three people came to greet them with a musical Polynesian welcome. A man in a green floral shirt played the ukelele and softly sang as two women welcomed Mina and the other guests off the boat. Mina climbed off last, and had a lei made of sweet-smelling pink flowers placed over her head.

Waiting for her with a warm smile, behind the musician, was Mina's new office manager Rachelle, a woman Mina recognised from their conversations online.

'Hello, Ms Morgan,' said Rachelle.

'Mina, please. It's lovely to meet you in person.'

'Welcome to the resort; I hope your journey was smooth?'

'There was a delay at the airport.' Mina paused, surprised to find herself blushing. 'But I made the best of it.'

'Wonderful!'

Rachelle helped Mina with her luggage and led her through the chic, polished-wood lobby. Apparently everyone travelled around the sprawling resort on golf buggies, and the short trip to her accommodation gave Mina a quick tour of the island. She got passing glimpses of the beautiful pools, the stunning private beaches, the tennis courts, the tall waving palm trees and an endless calm, turquoise ocean.

Mina didn't know what to expect in the way of accommodation. The whole job had been so last minute that details such as where she'd be staying had fallen by the wayside. She knew the resort was providing her with a place to live, and that she was allowed to use some of the facilities for free on her time off, but she knew little beyond that. When she was shown to a beautiful wooden thatched cabin on a small hill overlooking the beach and the ocean, surrounded by the shade of palm trees, she thought there must be some mistake.

'This isn't where I'm staying?'

'Yes!' said Rachelle. 'The staff all live in this wooded area. The more luxurious villas are for the paying guests, of course.'

'Of course,' Mina repeated weakly. She couldn't imagine how much more luxurious they could be. She dropped her luggage in the modestly sized double bedroom with views of the ocean and a large balcony. She got a quick view of a gorgeous bathroom and sitting room with a comfy sofa and a fireplace before Rachelle whisked her off again.

'I'd give you a longer tour, but the resort doctor wants to meet you in the office right away.'

As they passed the larger cabin next to hers, Rachelle gestured at the door. 'That's the doctor's villa.'

Mina wondered who the doctor was. She hoped it was a woman. Most of the doctors at her last clinic had been women and the vibes had been immaculate. If it hadn't been for her ex, she would have been happy to stay there for ever. He'd been the only male doctor at the clinic and he'd broken her heart and ruined her life, so the fewer men she had to work with, the better, in her opinion. She was planning to keep well away from handsome men altogether. Clearly, she was her own worst enemy and couldn't choose the right man to save her life. Staying away from them entirely was the only way to prevent letting a man mess up her job and her life ever again.

They zipped back towards the lobby on the buggy, passing a tiny rustic wedding chapel, climbed a gentle slope right up to the highest point of the resort, past smooth landscaped grass and serene stone sculptures, and finally pulling up at a thatched building labelled 'spa'.

'All the medical facilities are in the far corner of the spa grounds,' Rachelle explained as they climbed off the buggy and went inside. Every surface, wall and floor of the spa's reception was cleanly designed, polished wood with a cathedral-high ceiling and large windows showcasing the beautiful views. Mina followed Rachelle through the reception and along a raised walkway over meticulously maintained tropical gardens.

The medical building was small, and a little more low-key than the spa building, but still beautiful, and had a thatched roof to match the others. They passed a small reception desk. 'I'll show you around after I introduce you to the doctor you'll be working with,' said Rachelle with a smile. Mina smiled back, excited to meet the colleague with whom she'd be spending so much time on the island.

Rachelle knocked quickly on a door and opened it, ushering Mina inside, into a large office with a huge wooden desk and beautiful views of the ocean.

'Mina Morgan, this is our resort doctor, Luca Baudelaire.'

Mina blinked in shock, unable to think, let alone speak. Because her French mystery man, Jean-Paul, was standing right in front of her, looking as shell-shocked as she felt.

The chic, casual clothes were gone. He was now in a dark suit and tie. But it was him: same sultry, honey-brown stare; same long, black eyelashes; same strong jaw; same lips that had tasted every inch of her body.

Mina flexed her fist, shaking her head once as if to force herself not to remember the images flashing through her mind: memories of the night they'd spent together; memories of his broad, muscular chest and strong arms, the smell of his cologne and the rasp of his jaw as he slid his lips down her neck, kissing her sensuously.

Then someone rapped on the door frame behind her and a mirror image of him walked in. How many of this man were there? And which one had she slept with?

'Welcome to the island,' the second man said. 'I'm Roman Baudelaire, the owner of the resort.' Roman held out a large hand and shook hers. There was no spark whatsoever, no recognition in his eyes. And he had rather more facial hair than the doctor. Plus, now that she was closer, his eyes were a flatter brown.

Their body language sealed the deal. One smoothly welcomed her, while the other rearranged items on his desk, blinking furiously.

'Your references were largely impressive,' Roman continued. 'And of course you were available at short notice. I trust you'll be very happy here.'

Mina frowned, not sure how to take those words. But Roman swept out before she could answer, along with Rachelle, leaving Mina alone with Jean-Paul.

Not Jean-Paul—Luca. Or at least she assumed so. For all she knew, there was a third one of him around somewhere, waiting in the corridor to make his appearance.

Luca glared at her, his eyes flashing, before he looked away, pinching the bridge of his nose. 'This is a disaster,' he muttered.

So, it was him.

'You're telling me,' Mina responded, as hurt swelled up inside her. What was he so angry about? This was hardly her fault. She hadn't had any way of knowing who he was. They'd both agreed not to swap names or details. As far as she'd known, he was some French model jetting his way round the world, not a doctor, and certainly not the doctor she'd be forced to work with.

Luca sighed. 'You've made things very difficult.'

'I've made…? The way I remember it, there were two of us involved.'

He stared at her wordlessly, still simmering.

Mina was confused. She didn't know what to think, and had no idea how she could possibly establish a professional relationship with this man. She just wanted to get away from him so she could figure out her next move. It took Mina a moment to gather herself and manage to speak. 'I should go and find Rachelle, complete my induction.'

'Before you go…' Luca said. Mina paused. 'There's something important that you should know, Mina.' Mina tried not to notice how her heart jumped at hearing him say her name for the first time. 'I don't do relationships.' he continued.

'Good. I don't do sleeping with messy, chaotic, commitment-averse men.'

He paused. 'We might have started on the wrong foot. But you will speak to me with respect at work.'

Mina swallowed her response. She needed this job, however rude and arrogant her boss was. She nodded, then left his office.

Mina felt stunned. Where was that sweet, sexy man she'd met at the airport? But she already knew the answer to that. She'd met 'Jean-Paul'; she'd never met Luca. Jean-Paul had never existed; he was just an invention.

And now, not only was she stuck working with a beautiful, arrogant man who in the cold light of day she couldn't stand, she also had to find a way to be professional with him, when she couldn't even look at him without remembering the chills that had run through her entire body when he'd leaned in close, pressed against her and whispered French words hotly in her ear.

Her wonderful new life was slipping through her fingers like sand. She had to snap out of this attraction and keep well away from Luca, or her new life would be as much of a disaster as the one which she'd just upended her entire existence to escape.

# CHAPTER THREE

'So one twin bought a billion-dollar resort, while the other works as a doctor?' Mina asked.

'What of it?' asked Luca.

'You're working shifts like the rest of us, when you could probably afford to buy an island and do nothing. Very noble.'

'I am not my brother,' said Luca firmly.

'Oh, I see.' Perhaps he wasn't as rich as his brother. 'Are you the poor relation?'

'Do you always grill your employers on their financial situation?'

'I'm not sure you count as my employer. That would be your brother, since he manages the resort. But point taken.' He was right, and she would never normally ask such rude questions, but she was disconcerted by this whole situation, and still offended by his earlier words.

Luca looked at her thoughtfully. 'I can certainly see why my brother might have chosen you from all the applicants.'

'What do you mean by that?'

'He would have purposely picked the candidate who would annoy me the most.'

Mina was hurt for a moment, but then remembered

she didn't like Luca and didn't care what he thought of her. She shook her head dismissively. 'I never even spoke to your brother in the whole interview process.'

'No, but he would have seen the videos and transcripts, believe me.'

Rachelle burst back into the room. 'We've had a call. There's been a shark attack down on the east side of the lagoon.'

They grabbed their equipment and were out of the door in under thirty seconds. Mina was barely in the buggy before Luca took off in it down the sandy path. She gripped on tightly, and held her emergency bag to her chest with her free hand, cursing under her breath. The prospect of a shark attack thrilled her and terrified her in equal measure, so she tried to think about something else. Which wasn't difficult, with Luca's tall, solid frame bumping into her every five seconds.

Her fantasy back story of Luca being a model had utterly gone down the drain, but she was doubly disappointed to find he was a doctor. Apparently, she had a type—she was only attracted to obnoxious doctors. Well, not this time. She wasn't going to fall for someone she worked with again, least of all another arrogant doctor who would likely use her and spit her out, just like the last one had. She would never make that mistake again.

She was honestly furious with herself. She might well have messed up her opportunity for a new start before it had even begun. She had to stay focused on her job. It was a miracle that a girl from the wrong side of London had ended up in this paradise of white sands and turquoise seas, when her last flat in Ealing faced a brick wall and some bins. Now she was looking at lush palm trees and views of mystical mountains. She could not risk making a mess of this opportunity.

All that attraction was entirely out of the window—entirely. Absolutely a distant memory. She glanced over at his strong, wide hands as he drove round a corner, and gravity pushed his solid form into hers for a moment, making her smell his cologne and reminding her of that night at the airport. Mina squeezed her eyes shut. She would ignore any sizzling chemistry she might have had with Dr Luca if it killed her, and she felt like it almost might.

Mina couldn't distract herself any longer from what they were about to encounter. 'Are shark attacks common around here?' Mina asked, the breath knocked out of her as they sped over each tiny bump in the road.

'Not remotely. There are hundreds of small sharks around the island but they never bite. It just doesn't happen. It's probably a false alarm.'

'Hundreds of sharks? That doesn't sound too tourist-friendly.'

'They're mostly on the small side, and unaggressive. They're a very popular attraction with the tourists. There are several feeding tours daily; people love it. There are no great whites, just smaller species like stingrays, reef sharks, lemon sharks…'

Lemon sharks? Okay, they didn't sound too scary.

'As long as guests follow the rules, there is no danger at all,' Luca finished.

But when they got to the lagoon there was a visible pool of blood in the water.

'Oh my God. This does not look good.' Mina felt apprehension spike in her stomach.

A boat sat in the middle of the lagoon, by the blood, and a small speed boat was waiting for them at the shoreline, manned by a blond guy in his twenties with green eyes and a pink scar on his chin.

'Jump in, doctor. I'll take you over.'

They both jumped into the boat and Mina grabbed on tightly as the man accelerated across the lagoon. Mina edged away from the side of the boat; the last thing she needed to do right now was fall into beautiful, turquoise, shark-infested water.

'What the hell happened?' asked Luca.

'One of the guests didn't listen to the guide; he wanted to hand-feed the sharks himself. The guests were supposed to stay on board and watch, not jump in holding a fistful of mackerel.'

Mina wondered if they had all the equipment they'd need if the patient was missing a hand.

'Did you see what bit him?' Luca continued.

'It was an eight-foot lemon shark.'

Mina's eyes widened. Luca had said the sharks were small. They docked alongside the larger boat and hopped on quickly.

'Where is the patient? Luca asked.

The guide pointed across the boat. 'He won't get out of the water.'

Luca and Mina ran to the other side of the boat, pushing gently past the gathered crowd of tourists who were crammed against the railing, staring out at the spectacle. There were two sharks swimming lazily in a loose, foreboding figure-eight around the boat, which were joined by a handful of stingrays as Mina watched.

The man stood near the boat, waist-deep in the water,

holding his arm, the blood around him finally dissipating.

'We wrapped a towel around the wound, but he insists he's fine. He still wants to feed the sharks.'

'He'll be providing them a very big meal pretty soon, if he's not careful,' Mina said.

Mina had no knowledge of aquatic creatures, but she'd seen *Jaws*, and if *Jaws* had taught her anything, it was that people shouldn't swim in the ocean alone at night, and that sharks could sense blood from a mile away.

'Sir,' she shouted. 'It's time to come out now. That arm needs treatment.'

The towel was already red, soaked through with blood.

'I'm fine!' he called back.

'He may be in shock,' Mina said.

'Yes,' Luca said. 'And the blood loss is concerning.'

Mina hadn't yet had a chance to ask what the process might be if a patient was in too serious a condition for them to help. Would they call an air ambulance to take them to the mainland? She'd done a quick skim online about Bora Bora on the plane before she'd fallen asleep, so she knew there were no big hospitals on the island.

Luca stepped back from the railings and pushed off his shoes.

'What are you doing?' Mina asked.

'My job.'

He jumped down into the water, cool droplets splashing back against Mina's legs, and started wading quickly over to the man. Mina scanned the water near him for sharks. When Luca was halfway there, the man stumbled back and fell into the water. A woman on board the boat screamed.

'He's lost consciousness, Luca,' Mina called.

'I can see that,' Luca said through gritted teeth. He was there within seconds and pulled the man easily from the water. The patient emerged, coughing and spluttering, and Luca made quick work of walking him back to the boat, half-carrying him all the way. Mina reached down and helped the man up the ladder back on board, Luca supporting him from behind. Someone appeared with large, soft towels and Luca wrapped them both around the patient, not taking one for himself.

'Here, sit down.' Luca guided the patient to a seat. 'We need to take a look at that injury.'

'It's nothing.'

Luca peeled back the blood-soaked towel to reveal the man's forearm. Mina held back a gasp of interest at the tooth marks in his flesh along a clean cut about four inches long in a curved line. She'd never seen a real shark bite before, and was fascinated that it had left such a perfect bite pattern. It was much neater than any dog bite she'd seen.

'What were you thinking, getting in the water?' Mina asked.

Luca glared at her and she shut her mouth. He put a hand on the man's shoulder. 'Never mind that,' Luca said in a soothing, low voice, which just for a second reminded Mina of their night together, when he'd talked lowly and softly to her like that in very different circumstances. 'We're going to get you back to the health clinic and get you fixed up,' Luca continued.

Mina tried to clear her head and battle the unwelcome memories. 'That's going to need stitches,' she said.

'Yes. I would say so,' said Luca.

'But I have tickets to the dolphin-watching tour in an hour,' said the patient, sounding put out.

Mina frowned. Was the patient's odd behaviour due to shock or was he always like this?

'How long is this nonsense going to take?' he asked, sounding annoyed.

Mina plastered a smile on her face and looked at Luca, trying to gauge his reaction to the patient. If the man didn't want to waste precious time getting treated, maybe he should have followed the rules and stayed in the boat. She wouldn't dream of saying that out loud, but no one could stop her thinking it.

As the boat took off, Mina started disinfecting the wound and taping and bandaging it temporarily until they could get him back to the health clinic. She was quick and efficient and was finished in the few minutes it took the boat to reach the shore of the lagoon.

Once the patient was safely off the boat, Luca spoke to Mina in a low voice. 'In future, please address me as Dr Baudelaire in front of the guests.'

Mina frowned. 'What did I call you?'

He sighed wearily. 'You called me Luca.'

A memory flashed through Mina's head of her calling out his name when the patient had passed out. 'Sorry, Dr Baudelaire. Luca was just quicker.'

Luca nodded shortly. Frankly, he was lucky she hadn't shouted 'Jean-Paul'. 'Can you manage the walk to the buggy, sir?' Mina offered her hand to help the patient walk.

'Yes,' he snapped, pushing away Mina's hands. She smiled and moved back as Luca stepped smoothly in between the patient and her.

'This way,' he said shortly. Perhaps the patient's behaviour was finally getting to Luca too. Once the patient was seated in the buggy for the ride back, Luca and Mina climbed in and Luca sped them back to the health clinic.

'Was it really a shark bite?' Rachelle asked as she welcomed them back inside.

'Seems to have been. First one in ten years,' answered Luca.

'What on earth happened?'

Mina went ahead and showed the patient to the exam room as Luca and Rachelle spoke briefly, but she faintly heard Luca whisper to Rachelle as she left through the door. 'I wouldn't blame the shark, put it that way.'

The patient hadn't lost as much blood as Mina had feared, however dramatic the blood in the lagoon had looked. They wanted to keep him under observation for a few hours, but even after Luca had expertly sewn up the wound and bandaged it, and Mina had told the patient how to keep it dry, he was still sighing in annoyance and behaving like all this fuss had been unnecessary.

'You know, the shark was probably attracted to your watch,' said Luca. 'They are tempted by shiny objects in the water.'

The patient grunted, and didn't seem interested in that fact.

'Really?' asked Mina, fascinated.

Luca smiled, but his face quickly returned to normal. 'An attack is extremely rare. Some tour guides do allow guests in the water with the sharks, even children. But they are very closely monitored, with the guide in the water with them, so they can head off any danger.'

'Personally, I will not be doing that while I'm here,'

said Mina as she got the needle ready for the patient's tetanus shot. 'I like to admire nature from afar. Especially when it has teeth the size of a kitchen knife.'

Luca glared at her again and gestured at the patient.

'Sorry,' said Mina. But the patient was ignoring them, more interested in looking at his phone. Perhaps he was scared of needles and was trying to distract himself with the phone, which would be entirely understandable.

'I have a safari excursion booked soon; I'd like to at least make one of my bookings today,' he said pointedly, as though it was their fault he'd been bitten rather than his own.

'You can do that,' said Luca. 'But if you feel light-headed or short of breath at all, you must call us immediately. And you must come back tomorrow to get that dressing changed.'

'Fine.'

After the patient left, with some pain medication and a card with the health clinic's number on it, Mina looked at Luca. 'You're soaked through.'

He looked down at himself, apparently surprised at his wet state. 'I'll have to run home and get changed. I only keep a spare shirt at work, in case of… Well, you know what it's like.'

Mina did. It wasn't exactly unusual as a nurse to get dirty at work but to get every piece of clothing soaked wasn't something anyone planned for. 'I can keep an eye on things while you're gone, don't worry.'

He passed Mina awkwardly, as if making sure not to touch her. 'Thank you,' he said stiltedly. 'That's surprisingly kind of you.'

'I'm actually very competent.'

\* \* \*

It took Luca all of five minutes to arrive back at work, clothes changed, slightly out of breath.

'You really didn't have to rush, I had it under control,' said Mina.

'Didn't rush,' he said, still breathing heavily.

'Did you expect me to have burned the place down?'

'No, but it is your first day here. You don't know how we do things yet.'

'On that note, can I ask a question?' Luca nodded somewhat reluctantly. 'You didn't give that patient much of a telling off,' Mina continued.

'We're not here to tell the patients off, Nurse Morgan.'

'I've always been of the mindset that, if you don't tell people, they won't learn.'

'Our job is to treat them as quickly and thoroughly as possible, so they can get back to enjoying their holiday and having a wonderful time.'

'Of course. But he needed to be told that what he did was idiotic and dangerous, or he might do it again.'

'They're paying guests. You can't talk to them like that.'

'Some people need telling.' Mina said obstinately.

Luca sighed. 'I don't know how you behaved at your last job, but here we don't tell our patients they're idiots.'

Mina could think of one or two times in her career she had done just that—specifically at the end of a long overnight shift at an A&E in west London. But she saw Luca's point. That environment was very different from where she was now. People had paid in her opinion an exorbitant amount of money to relax in paradise.

'But, for what it's worth, I agree,' Luca said, surprising Mina. 'That patient in particular was idiotic. I hate it when people abuse the island or its nature, as if it's there solely to entertain them.'

Mina stared at Luca. This was a side of him that she could get on board with.

'But ultimately,' he continued, 'We are here to provide a service, and get the guests back on track as quickly and efficiently as possible. We want them to spend as little time as possible in the health clinic, and as much time as possible on the paradise beach holiday they've probably been planning for months.'

'And paid a normal person's yearly wage for.'

'Well, quite.'

Not that Luca would know, she thought. Despite his insistence that he wasn't like his millionaire brother, Mina couldn't imagine that he was the type of person who'd ever had to worry about where next month's rent was coming from.

Rachelle swooped through, her arms full of paperwork, and Luca held out a hand to get her attention. 'Could I have a word?'

'Of course,' Rachelle trilled without slowing down for a second. 'Follow me to my office,' she joked, headed for Luca's office.

They both disappeared inside, and the look he gave Mina as he closed the door behind them made her think she was about to be the topic of discussion—not ideal. But, whatever they thought of her, she was going to keep her head down, be as good a nurse as she knew how and keep this job.

# CHAPTER FOUR

Rachelle crossed to the filing cabinet where they kept physical copies of certain records and started filing things away efficiently, her back to Luca. 'Well?' she prodded.

He stopped in front of the window near Rachelle, and stared out at the glistening ocean and the yachts beyond, keeping his voice low as he spoke.

'I'm not sure the new nurse is a good fit. She doesn't know how to deal with the guests.'

'That's why she's here—to learn.'

'No, the reason she's here is because Roman handpicked her to get on my nerves.'

'He knew that a beautiful, feisty woman with her own opinions would annoy you? If that is true, maybe you should have a period of self-reflection.'

'Rachelle! That's not what I mean. She's rude and abrupt.'

'She probably thinks the same about you.'

He glared at Rachelle's back.

'Don't give me that look, Luca,' warned Rachelle with a smile in her voice. She closed the drawer and turned round. 'Anyway, your brother isn't as sneaky and all-controlling as he likes to think he is. He didn't hand-pick Mina at all. I did the interviews. She's the one I wanted. And, after I'd made my decision, I did what I had to do to make him think he was choosing her out of the shortlist I gave him.'

Luca raised his eyebrows. Rachelle never stopped surprising him. The truth was, he was embarrassed that Mina was here, and Luca didn't embarrass easily. He found Mina fascinating. He'd never met anyone quite like her. She was stunning, fiery, remarkable. Everything he'd said and done when they'd met at the airport had been real.

But he didn't understand why he couldn't stop thinking about her. Luca didn't believe in love. How could he when he'd never seen a relationship work? His parents' relationship had ended up being a loveless financial arrangement more than a marriage. In which his mother had made investments and done a modicum of parenting, and his father had been devoted only to his obsession with music. Luca didn't have a single, solitary friend or relative who'd managed to stay in love longer than a few years. They'd all had just endless loveless, joyless marriages. Maybe some people out there could make it work; some lucky, mystical couple might truly be soulmates and live happily ever after. But certainly no one in his family. The Baudelaires weren't capable of it. Happy relationships weren't in his genes. So Luca had never let himself want it. Long term romance wasn't something he'd ever factored into his life.

His grandparents' and parents' marriage problems had proven that a Baudelaire man could either have a big passion project or a happy relationship, not both. Luca's father's obsession had been music. He'd composed operas for the Opéra de Paris, and he'd been trying to finish his magnum opus his whole life. He'd put it above his marriage and his children, and he still never finished it. Well, Luca had his own passion project, and it was much more important than some delusional yearning for love.

And that reminded him—he wanted to take some papers home overnight to get a better look at them somewhere he could concentrate. He grabbed a folder and tucked it inside his bag.

It wasn't that he'd never tried to believe in love. He'd lived all his adult life knowing that there was no such thing, but then a year ago he'd met Claudia—someone who'd somehow got under his skin and made him believe he might be wrong. She'd been so convincing and so perfect for him. He'd let himself stop the cynicism, stop the stories he told himself that he wasn't capable. And then she'd betrayed him in the worst way possible. She'd hurt him more than anyone else ever had. And he'd let it happen. It was his own fault; it was karma. He'd been right all along: long-term love wasn't for him.

But there was something he allowed himself. Occasionally if the situation presented itself, if he met a woman he was attracted to and the feeling was mutual, he would spend the night with her. As long as they both knew it was just for one night, it meant he could experience the fun part: the attraction, the chase, the flirting, the adrenaline rush, the physical side. But no one could get hurt. He only ever let the romantic side of himself out when it was safe.

But now those two worlds had collided. Every time he looked at Mina, he was mortified. She'd seen the vulnerable, romantic side he only showed to strangers, the parts of him that he very deliberately never showed to people who were in his every-day life. Now he found himself hiding beneath an outer shell. One in which he apparently couldn't help being arrogant and rude any time he was around Mina, when she reminded him just how attracted to her he was.

'If she's not as well versed in guest etiquette as you want her to be, then I suggest that she shadows you for the day. She can attend any calls you get along with you, and you can show her how it's done.'

Before Luca could explain at great length exactly why that was a terrible idea, Rachelle continued firmly, 'Today looks like it'll be a slow day, until this afternoon, when you're both due to supervise the big event on the beach. So there's no problem if you both stick together for a while.'

He knew Rachelle well enough to know she'd be like a dog with a bone until he agreed to whatever she'd planned. He took a deep breath, and then the phone rang.

Rachelle picked up the phone on his desk, greeted Reception and listened for a moment. She pointed at the receiver and mouthed, 'First job of the day.' She spoke in French, thanking whoever was on reception that day, then put down the phone.

'Well?' Luca asked. 'Where are we going?'

Rachelle smiled, understanding the tacit agreement to her plan in his words. 'There's a guest in villa twelve whose young son has a rash.'

Luca nodded wearily and left his office to find Mina. 'Normally I would attend the calls alone, but Rachelle suggested you shadow me on a call or two,' he informed her when he saw her.

'Sounds great,' Mina said with a fixed smile. But it looked as if she'd rather be anywhere else than with him at the moment. The feeling was mutual. 'What's the call? More sharks?'

'The child of a guest has a rash. We're going to the villa to check up on him.'

Mina nodded. 'Should be a simple one, then. We used to get a lot of new parents coming into A&E with children with rashes. It's usually nothing, but people worry, especially when it's their first child.'

He could just imagine her saying something insensitive to the mother when they got to the villa. 'Listen, I'd appreciate it if you took a back seat on this one. Let me do the talking.'

Mina stopped. She blinked at him, and looked as if she was having some sort of battle inside her head. She inhaled, pasted on that smile again and carried on walking until they reached the buggy outside. 'No problem, Dr Baudelaire.'

After a short drive, Mina followed him down the wooden jetty over the water to villa twelve, and stopped just behind him as he knocked gently on the door. She hadn't said a word since they'd got on the buggy, and he was starting to worry that he'd offended her. Not that he should care.

A woman answered the door, smiling but looking stressed. 'Thank you for coming so quickly, doctor.'

'No problem at all.' He thought he detected a German accent. 'Would you prefer to converse in German?'

She laughed. 'Oh, no, English is fine, but thank you so much for offering.'

He was fairly fluent in several languages, so he always offered to speak in a guest's own language when he could. They often gave much more accurate reports of their symptoms in their own language.

'He's lying on the sofa,' she said. She led them into the lounge, where she'd shut the curtains and switched on the fan. A young boy was lying on top of a blanket, head on some pillows, holding a stuffed bear. Luca had a moment of unwelcome nostalgia. The image reminded him of his brother when they'd both been children. In complete contrast to now, Roman had been a sickly child, always ill, tired and sad, always lying alone in a bed in a room with the curtains closed. Luca had never been allowed in to play with him.

'Hello, young man,' Luca said to the boy. 'What's your name?'

'Benji,' the boy said. He seemed cheerful enough. 'Can I go outside and swim now?'

'You're sick,' his mother said. 'You should be resting.'

'But I feel fine.'

Luca smiled. 'What can we do for you? What are the symptoms?' Luca asked the boy's mother.

'He has a rash on his hands.'

Luca gently took a look at the boy's hands. A red rash was indeed covering the pads of his fingers.

'Have you touched anything hot, Benji?'

'No.'

'Does your son have any allergies?'

'No, none.'

'It could be a reaction to a new soap or detergent—

perhaps one he's not used before, one that's provided here in the villa.'

'I hope you don't think I sound odd, doctor, but I brought my own soaps from home. I think it's very important to use organic products that are good for the environment, even on holiday. He hasn't used anything new.'

Luca nodded, slightly nonplussed, but at least that information narrowed it down further. 'Very commendable.' He examined the boy further, checking the rest of his body for rashes.

'The rash is limited to the hands. It looks like contact dermatitis. Have your hands been itchy, Benji?'

Benji nodded.

Mina cleared her throat. 'Could I ask you something?'

Luca tried to get her to meet his eyes, but she was focused on the mother. His whole body went tense, waiting for her to say something insensitive.

'That plant on the kitchen windowsill—has Benji been near it or touched it at all?'

'No, he's not been near the sink. I don't think he could even reach it up there.'

'There isn't another one anywhere in the villa, is there?'

Where was she going with this? 'What is that plant, Ms Morgan?' Luca asked.

She threw him a raised eyebrow, probably in response to the formal address.

'Oh my goodness, his bedroom.' The mother ran to the bedroom and shouted. 'There's one in here too.'

Mina nodded. 'I believe that's a ficus elastica. It's rare, but a small percentage of people can have an allergic reaction to touching the sap from its leaves.'

'Oh my word.' The mother put her hand to her heart and quickly returned to her son's side. 'Did you touch the plant in your room, sweetie?'

He nodded. 'The leaves were sticky.'

His mother grabbed a wet cloth and wiped at his hands gently. 'Is he going to be okay, doctor?'

'I think so.' Luca smiled at the boy. 'We'll get you some medicine and your hands should be feeling all better soon.' He turned to his mother. 'I'd like to treat him with some antihistamines, and of course prevent any further exposure to the plant. You might want to get some allergy tests with your family doctor when you get home. And of course, if his symptoms continue while you're here, call me.'

She nodded.

'We'll get rid of the plants for you. And we'll make sure to remove them from any other villas and public spaces too. We'll tighten the checks on all the approved plants with head office.'

'Don't worry, we're not going to sue you or anything,' the mother laughed. 'I'm just relieved to know what was causing it.'

Luca had to admit he was relieved to hear they weren't planning to be litigious but his main focus was to make her feel comfortable and her son healthy. He found Mina already watching him. 'If you could remove the two plants, we'll put them in the buggy,' he said.

'I'll double-check the rest of the rooms too, if that's okay,' she said to the mother.

'Of course, of course. Thank you so much.'

As they left the villa and walked back up the jetty

side by side, holding one plant each, Mina looked at him with a wry smile. 'Am I allowed to talk on calls now?'

Lucas rolled his eyes, but couldn't help the smile that crossed his lips. 'I suppose we could allow it. How do you know so much about plants?'

A shadow crossed her features, and Luca wished he could take the question back.

'My best friend...well, someone I used to know... she was a botanist. She had some really rare plants too, ones that don't normally survive in England—certainly not in cold, rainy London. She had to make them little heat lamps. She looked after those plants better than she looked after herself.' A little wistful smile appeared for a moment, before she cleared her expression again, and Luca frowned, wondering what more there was to that story that she hadn't said.

# CHAPTER FIVE

Occasionally there were events held at the resort that guests might find strenuous, or at which someone could feasibly get injured, and Luca would often be dispatched to supervise in order to make sure everyone stayed healthy and there were no accidents. This time, with the objective of Luca showing her the ropes, Rachelle had insisted Mina tag along.

This afternoon a local company was having its bi-annual parasailing demonstration, letting guests at the resort try a short parasail session along the edge of the beach free of charge. It was always a popular event, and lasted several hours. But it meant that dozens of people who wouldn't normally try such an activity, and who weren't used to high-octane pastimes, would spontaneously decide to have a go. Particularly older guests, who got drawn in by the free offer, family pressure or the general excitement of the day. Which meant the resort needed medics present in case there were any injuries, heart problems, or panic attacks.

'Must be an amazing view from up there,' Mina murmured.

'I'm sure.'

'Haven't you ever tried it?'

'Me? No. It's not my sort of thing.'
'What is your sort of thing?'
'Being in contact with the ground.'

Mina snorted a quiet laugh. Luca paused. 'You could always have a go,' he suggested. Mina shook her head, smiling. 'Go on; I can cover you for ten minutes while you go up and check out the view.'

Mina's peal of laughter made Luca feel unmoored. 'No, I've changed my mind. Leave me alone.'

Every time Mina and he were alone, Luca was sure she was going to bring up the night they'd spent together. He'd been desperately hoping she wouldn't all day, but suddenly he was starting to wonder why she hadn't. In a moment of weakness, which was very unlike him, he found himself having doubts. Had she had a bad time? Was it an unpleasant memory she was happy to forget? Was this what it was like to feel insecure?

The next few hours were filled with assisting the parasailing crew with helping the guests in and out of the harness, bringing water to thirsty guests, giving people a place to sit and recover from the excitement under the shade of an umbrella and chatting to people waiting for their partners to come back down from the wide, blue Bora Bora skies. Luca was surprised to find that Mina was very popular with the guests. They seemed to be receptive to her friendly smile and frank way of talking.

Eventually the staff opened up the doors to the Tiki bar, and started setting out the free food and drink being provided after the parasailing event. Roman swept in, holding a glass of champagne, dressed in a light suit. Luca wasn't surprised he could look so cool and composed in so many layers on such a warm day, but it was annoying. 'Luca; Nurse Morgan. Lovely to see you here.'

'Of course we're here. We've been overseeing the event all afternoon,' said Luca flatly.

Roman continued as though he hadn't heard the tone in Luca's voice. 'I assume you'll be staying for the after-party.'

Luca sighed. 'We've just worked a full shift, but yes, I'm sure we can stay on for a while.'

'Make sure you do. The guests want to get to know their doctor and nurse!' Roman raised his glass at someone behind them and marched off to chat to a group of people.

'There's always a social event after things like this,' Luca explained to Mina. 'It's mostly for the guests, but Roman likes all the staff to stay on and mingle. I usually just stay for half an hour.'

Rachelle appeared and pulled Mina into a discussion. A while later, Mina noticed Luca at the bar, nursing what looked like a coffee. She tried to listen to what Rachelle was saying, but was distracted by Luca. He looked so sad and contemplative. What was he thinking about?

She nodded at a question Rachelle had asked, but got distracted again when Luca stood and walked over to a girl at the bar. Her heart sank as she noticed the girl's age. She was way too young for Luca; she looked like she was still in her teens. Surely he wasn't that kind of guy? Luca and the girl spoke for a moment as Mina's heart sank further, then Luca reached over and plucked a glass of wine from the girl's hand. The girl flushed and looked down, then Luca patted her on the shoulder once and passed the full wine glass back to the barman. He beckoned the barman off to the side, and Mina watched as they had a very tense looking back and forth. Even Rachelle was watching them now.

Luca spotted Rachelle and came over to join them. Rachelle slid over and he sat down next to her. Mina could smell his cologne across the table, and his knee knocked into hers as he made himself comfortable. An electric shock passed through her body and she flushed and took a sip of her water.

'I'm going to have a word with Roman, and we're letting that barman go. He served a sixteen-year-old alcohol, and I doubt it's the first time.'

So Luca absolutely wasn't that kind of guy. He was in fact a very honourable guy. Mina felt a thrill go up her spine at how protective and sweet he was.

Luca got up to make a phone call, presumably about the barman, but on his way back he was accosted by a very glamorous older lady. She had perfectly groomed hair and wore the highest heels Mina had ever seen. She strutted up to Luca, making serious eye contact, and asked him for a light. She was standing way too close to him for polite conversation. In fact, she looked as if she wanted to devour him.

'It's lovely to see you here, doctor.'

She stepped even further into his personal space, and he smoothly stepped back a little, disguising it as reaching behind the bar for some matches. She leaned in again, holding her cigarette, and he quickly lit it for her.

He let her run a hand up and down his bicep, but then he took her hand, clasped it smoothly as a goodbye and removed himself. 'I have work I must get back to, but do enjoy your evening.'

He headed Mina's way, looking relieved to escape, and Mina smiled. He had clearly had to do that many times before.

As Luca approached Mina, she grabbed two glasses of champagne from a passing waiter's tray. 'We're off the clock, aren't we?'

'You are, yes,' said Luca.

She held the second glass out to him, but Luca refused. 'I'm actually on call this evening.'

'I'm not. I guess I'll have both.'

But before she could even take a sip there was a shout from further down the beach. Jude, one of the staff from the hotel came running through the sand, out of breath, and came to a stop with one hand on Luca's arm. 'They need a medic down past the rocks.'

'We're on our way.' Luca turned to grab his medical bag, but Roman appeared as if from nowhere and stopped him with one hand. 'How far past the rocks?' he asked Jude.

'At the next cove.'

'That's not our resort; that's the next hotel's property.'

'So?' asked Mina. But Luca knew exactly what Roman was getting at.

'Not our guests, not our problem,' said Roman firmly.

'Are you joking?' asked Mina.

Luca held both his hands out to calm the situation, and hopefully stop Mina saying anything else. 'Fine, Roman. I'll call the other hotel.'

Roman nodded. 'Make sure you do. I've warned you

about this before. You're needed here, ready at all times to aid our guests. If you go running about the island to everyone, you can't very well do your job here, can you?'

Luca stared at Roman until he backed off. 'I need to get back to our guests.' Roman said, as he backed away and rejoined the crowd further up the beach. Luca turned back to Mina, who was clearly about to blow a fuse, and grabbed his bag. 'Let's go.'

Mina grinned at him, and they ran off towards the rocks with Jude. 'God, how can you stand him?'

'Roman?' asked Luca.

'Yes. I can't believe how vile and heartless he can be.'

'Well, he had a point.' Luca found himself almost reflexively defending his brother. 'He's not responsible for guests who aren't his.'

Mina glared at him in disbelief. 'Legally maybe, but not morally.'

Before Luca could agree with her, Mina continued, 'If this is what money does to you people, you can keep it. I've never come across such entitlement and lack of care.'

Luca bit his tongue hard. It looked as if she was lumping Luca in with Roman in her talk of entitled people, and that hurt. He'd fought so hard against that label all his life. He'd strived to help everyone and do everything he could with the good fortune and opportunities he'd been born into.

They clambered over the rocks, Luca keeping half an eye on Mina. She was from London; the run across sand would have already been exhausting, as sand was notoriously difficult to run on, and he didn't want her breaking a leg on the rocks now because she was rushing to keep up with him. But she kept up impressively well, in fact pulling ahead of him as they jumped down onto the wet sand on the other side.

They found a young girl lying on her back on the sand. A woman was kneeling by her side, holding her hand tightly. She looked up at Luca and took in his shirt, tie and medical bag. 'Doctor, thank goodness,' she said in Spanish.

'What's happened?' Luca asked, also in Spanish.

'My daughter was climbing on the rocks. Her leg got tangled in a fishing net and she fell all the way down.'

The girl had thin blue strings wrapped around her legs. Luca couldn't imagine how they'd managed to get tangled up so badly, but they had. It looked like the nets fishermen left out to catch mahi-mahi. They shouldn't have ended up on the rocks on this beach, but somehow they had. Perhaps some kids had pulled the net out of the sea and left it there when they'd got bored with it.

'It's okay, we'll get you good as new in no time,' he said to the girl, smiling.

She smiled back around the thumb stuck in her mouth. That was a good sign; hopefully she wasn't too badly hurt. Luca gently checked her vitals and made sure she could wiggle all her fingers and move her feet with no pain.

'Where does it hurt?' Luca asked.

They eventually settled on the fact that her elbow and wrist hurt, and that they were probably what she'd landed on. He applied a bandage to her arm.

'That's her wrist wrapped up, but it's just a sprain. No broken bones! Next, though, we need to get all this off your legs.' Luca got her to sit up comfortably. 'Nurse, scissors please.' Luca held out his hand without looking, as he was busy trying to make the little girl laugh by making faces at her. Mina had been poised above the medical bag ready to help ever since they'd arrived, and she quickly whipped out the scissors and held them out to him, point first.

'Damn!' He retracted his hand, immediately in pain, and checked his nicked finger. A tiny bead of blood appeared and he sucked it angrily. Mina gasped and turned the colour of a tomato. 'A different pair of scissors, please, if you can manage to hand them to me without slicing a finger off,' he instructed through gritted teeth.

She dropped the used scissors into the bag and grabbed another pair, this time holding them out carefully, handle first. 'Sorry,' she mouthed at him silently.

Luca snipped away the netting carefully and made sure to put them into the medical bag so they wouldn't be a trip hazard for anyone else. 'If her pain gets worse, or you have any worries at all, call the health clinic and ask for me—Dr Baudelaire. Don't worry that we're at a different resort.' Luca reached into his pocket and pulled out one of their cards, handing it to the girl's mother.

'Thank you, doctor.'

As they left, climbing back over the rocks, Mina touched his arm hesitantly.

'Is your finger okay?'

'It's fine,' Luca answered shortly and moved his arm away. If he was honest, he was worried that she could do something so amateurish as to hand him something sharp-end first. She was supposed to be a professional nurse with several years of experience. But, on the other hand, it was a minor mistake and there was no harm done.

It was the equivalent of a papercut if anything. His professional instinct was to reprimand her but his emotional instinct was to reassure. He wasn't used to having emotional instincts in the workplace, certainly not with staff.

She sighed. 'I don't know why you're being such a baby about it. I apologised.'

Luca stopped walking. 'Excuse me?'

She stopped too, her expression suggesting she hadn't meant to speak to him quite so casually. That seemed to be a habit with her, speaking before thinking. That could be dangerous around his patients. He still wasn't sure if she was quite the right fit for this environment when they needed to be there to smooth situations at the resort, not disturb them.

He shook his head. 'I don't think this is going to work.'

He didn't say it to hurt her feelings, but it looked as if that was what he'd done. Her lips momentarily parted in shock, and a flash of hurt crossed her face, then disappeared.

Her eyes flickered with anger. 'Lucky I'm here to convince you, then, isn't it?' she said, grabbing the bag from his hand and stalking off back to the health clinic as best she could on the uneven sand.

He had never met anyone like her. He was fairly sure they'd just argued, so why was his bloodstream flooded with adrenaline, and why was his first instinct to run after her and kiss her until that angry look turned into something far happier?

He could never quite manage to say what he meant around her. Perhaps, unless it was necessary for the job, it was safer not to talk to her at all.

\* \* \*

Luca strode through the reception door a few seconds after Mina, and Rachelle tutted at how hard he pushed the door. It slammed shut behind him loudly.

'What is wrong with you two?' Rachelle asked.

'Ask him,' Mina muttered, still angry, but not entirely sure why. Was she angry at Luca for being the rude, arrogant pig she now knew he was, or was she angry at herself for making such a stupid, novice mistake? Luca glared at her—again. That seemed to be his go-to expression around her.

'Just go home, get some sleep and try not to stab me tomorrow. Your job is supposed to be healing injuries, not causing them.'

Before Mina could open her mouth to angrily retort, Luca had stormed into his office, the door slamming closed decisively behind him. Perhaps it was best. Mina simmered as she glared out of the reception window and tried to gather herself.

Rachelle cleared her throat delicately behind Mina, and Mina whirled round. 'I forgot you were in here,' she said.

'That seems to happen a lot around you two.'

'What's that supposed to mean?'

'Oh, nothing. Just that you tend to get each other a little hot around the collar.'

'He's just really annoying.'

'I know. I work for him too.'

'I don't work for him, I work *with* him,' Mina mumbled.

'He's just a little—brittle around the edges. He hasn't

been the same since last year, when he broke up with his ex-girlfriend.'

'He has an ex?'

'Have you seen him? Of course he does.'

'No, I mean, obviously. He's very handsome, and tall, if you like that sort of thing; I'm sure he's had lots of women.'

Mina's stomach swooped as she felt an unwelcome and frankly ridiculous wave of jealousy for all those other women, plus some embarrassment that she'd been one of them—probably one in a very long line. She knew all too well how confident and attractive he could be when he turned on the charm. How he made her feel special when he paid so much attention to her, and tried so hard to make her laugh, as if he'd chosen her—as if, despite everything, she were the most attractive woman in the world.

But that had been 'Jean-Paul', not Luca at all. In reality, Luca was just an arrogant, rude man who could have whatever he wanted, whenever he wanted, and he didn't want her any more—if he ever had. Of course he'd had countless other women. He probably bedded a new one every time he passed through an airport.

'Well I don't know about that,' said Rachelle. 'He doesn't kiss and tell. I just happen to know there was one special woman, and let's just say it ended very badly.'

As disgusted with Luca in general as she was, Mina desperately wished she could ask for more details, but she wasn't supposed to be interested. Plus, it really wasn't any of her business.

Rachelle stepped closer. 'You'll never guess who she kissed behind Luca's back.'

The thought of Luca being cheated on sent a painful jolt through her heart as it brought back a flood of memories of her own past. Not to mention that, however frustrating Luca was, Mina felt guilty talking about him behind his back. But at the same time a small part of her was grateful she worked with such a gossip. 'Who?'

'Roman.'

Mina gasped. 'His own brother?'

Rachelle nodded sadly.

'And they still work together?' Mina asked.

'I don't think Luca's ever forgiven him. But there's always been bad blood between them, this is nothing new. It's strange; Luca's no pushover but somehow, whatever Roman does to him, he always ends up sticking around.'

If nothing else, Mina knew exactly how it felt when two people who were supposed to care the most about her betrayed her. She sighed. Maybe that explained the sad, distant look she sometimes noticed in Luca's eyes. Betrayal wasn't something a person got over fast, if ever. Suddenly she found herself feeling sorry for Luca. 'I assumed he and Roman were close. I mean, they're twins.'

'Doesn't mean they have to like each other.'

'I suppose not.'

Rachelle carried on sorting through paperwork.

'I thought he had it so good here, living in paradise with family around, able to get time off whenever he wants it.' Or anytime he wanted to bed a new random airport woman, Mina reminded herself. 'Able to run to the boss and get anyone he doesn't like fired.'

'Oh, there's no love lost between them at all. Roman

would be more likely to fire someone if he knew Luca *did* like them.'

'Lucky he hates me, then.'

'Whatever you say, Mina.'

'What does that mean?'

Rachelle didn't answer, just smiled smugly.

'Luca's not the only infuriating one around here,' muttered Mina.

Rachelle laughed. 'I'm just saying. You could cut the tension between you with a knife. You either hate each other or love each other; I can't decide. And I don't know how you've managed to create such levels of tension so quickly!'

'It's one of my many talents.'

Mina felt uncomfortable lying to Rachelle, at least by omission, about the fact that she and Luca had already met. But telling anyone the truth about that would be too mortifying even to contemplate. If only because she'd done the one thing she'd come out here to avoid; the exact thing she was running away from and had vowed never to repeat. She'd somehow managed to sleep with a colleague before she'd even started the job. It was outstanding, actually. Almost impressive.

She thought wistfully of the two champagnes she'd swiped but never got to drink. At least a champagne or two might make it easier to ignore the mess her new life was already in. Mina decided to walk home rather than drive a buggy. They were dotted around in various places, with charging stations for free use, but the evening was so beautiful she just wanted to enjoy the fresh breeze.

Once again, she delighted in the fact that this was her

commute now. Birds sang in the trees, their birdsong unfamiliar to her. The sweet scent of jasmine hung in the air and the evening sun was still warm on her face. She'd almost managed to forget that Luca's villa was next door to hers until she rounded the corner and saw it. She had to walk past his bungalow to reach her own, and she purposely didn't look in the windows to see if he was home yet. He was probably busy somewhere doing something important or dastardly. Or on a date with his next conquest.

She walked between the two palm trees that bookended her little path up to the front door. She hadn't even unpacked everything yet, but that could wait until later. Right now, she was starving, and her heart sank as she realised she should have brought food back with her. But when she opened her fridge and cupboards, she found them fully stocked. This job really was too good to be true. As her evening had been saved by the kitchen fairy, or more likely Rachelle, she decided to prepare something quickly and enjoy it out on the balcony to watch the sunset.

After eating, she grabbed her sketchbook from her suitcase and curled up on the comfy cushions on her balcony. A view like this made her hands itch to draw it. She almost hadn't packed her sketchbook, thinking she wouldn't have time for indulging in hobbies like this, but at the last minute she'd reminded herself that that was the old Mina: busy all the time, working every waking minute. The new Mina did have time for enjoying herself. She would make time.

Now that she was on her balcony, it really sank in how close it was to Luca's. Each was framed by wooden railings at waist height, and Mina stared over, contemplating the twelve inches of air between them with a drop down on to the grass. And of course, that was the moment that Luca's back door opened and he came out on to his balcony.

Mina inwardly groaned and shifted in her seat so that she was facing out at the ocean again. It took him a moment to notice her and he froze, holding a drink in one hand and a folder of papers in the other. He turned back towards his door.

'Hey, don't run away from me,' said Mina.

'I'm not,' he sulked. Clearly, he was.

'If you want to sit on your balcony, sit on your balcony. Enjoy the sunset. I promise I won't ruin it for you.'

He grumbled under his breath and sat down in a chair on the far side of his balcony. But she was still close enough that she could tell he was drinking beer from the glass. As if he could hear what she was thinking, he raised the glass in her direction and pointed at it. 'Dr Kai took the on-call shift tonight. He wanted me to cover him next weekend.'

Luca settled down, setting his drink on the table. Sitting back on his chair, he sipped his drink, and they both sat in silence. The sunset was just starting to take shape; the clouds had a slight tinge of orange and the sky was beginning to darken a little. After a few minutes, Mina cleared her throat. 'I am sorry about what I did. I honestly don't know what I was thinking. I know how to medically assist, I promise you.'

Luca paused for a moment. 'I'm sorry if I overreacted. I believe you that you wouldn't normally do that. It's probably jetlag.'

*Huh.* Mina hadn't even thought of that. Maybe that was exactly what it had been. She'd tried to downplay what she'd done afterwards, and found herself deflecting, acting as if Luca was in the wrong for being upset. But he was right to be, and deep down it had worried her. She was never sloppy when she was with a patient.

'It must have been,' Luca continued. 'After all, even toddlers know not to hand scissors to someone sharp-end first.'

Mina rolled her eyes. Apparently, Luca's moment of being nice was already over. Every time she thought she saw a flash of the sweet guy he'd been at the airport, every time she thought she'd drawn the old Jean-Paul out for a moment, he disappeared. It was frustrating. 'How about we try sitting in silence?' she suggested.

'Sounds wonderful.'

Luca disappeared inside and returned with another beer. The silence felt oppressive at first, but after a few minutes Mina found herself relaxing. The sounds of the waves lapping at the beach below blended peacefully with the few birds still singing. Luca was busy reading whatever papers he'd brought out with him, occasionally making a note with a pen. She wondered what they were. Was he the type to take work home with him, or was it something unrelated to the day job? What did he even do aside from being a doctor, anyway? She had no idea.

She turned quietly to a new page in her sketchbook and, almost before she noticed it, she found herself sketching Luca. It was still the golden hour, when the red evening sun shone gently over everything and made it beautiful. The light made Luca's skin glow warmly, and highlighted his thick, dark hair. Her soft graphite pencil made dark charcoal-black lines on the paper, defining the angles of his jaw, the fullness of his mouth and the dark shadow of his eyelashes.

It was almost torture, spending so much time with someone she was drawn to but couldn't have. She knew she had to resist her attraction. It was the only way to avoid being sucked in by another commitment-phobic doctor and heading down the path of ruining another wonderful job. There certainly couldn't be any gazing at Luca across a crowded waiting-room at work. But no one could stop her gazing at him, if it was only to practise her drawing skills. And he really was beautiful. It would be a crime not to get him down on paper.

He had a flawless profile and she couldn't help herself sketching it several times over. She worked on his body for a moment, trying to get the shape of his muscular arm and strong forearm just right, the way the light lit the soft hairs on his arm, then his hands and the elegant fingers holding the papers he was reading. She lost herself for a while, as often happened when she drew, and when she came back to herself, she realised that Luca had moved his head and was now looking over in her direction, watching her. She blinked and closed her sketchbook.

Surprisingly, he didn't ask her what she was doing; in fact he didn't say anything. Mina tucked her sketchbook and pencil down into the cushions of her bench seat and turned back to the sunset.

The clouds were purple and pink now; she'd missed a huge chunk of the changing colours while she'd been busy drawing Luca, and she gazed out at the huge, all-encompassing sky, feeling almost dizzy, trying to take it all in.

'Beautiful, isn't it?'

Mina smiled. 'It's not bad. Not bad at all.' She thought about the small strip of sky she could see from the window of her old flat, just enough to see if it was clear or cloudy and try to guess whether she should wear her big coat or her small coat. Not that the weather in London was ever predictable. It could hail one minute and be boiling hot the next. She was willing to bet that Bora Bora was at least going to be a little more predictable in its weather.

Since Luca had tried to open up conversation a bit, and even though that was probably the two beers he'd had loosening him up, she felt she should make an effort too. Without really thinking about it, she asked the question she'd been wondering about earlier. 'What are you working on?'

He looked at her, suddenly flustered, and paused as if he wasn't sure what she meant.

Mina pointed at his folder. 'Your papers.'

He held them up briefly. 'These?'

'Yeah. You looked like you were making some pretty serious notes.' When he held them up, she saw a quick flash of the top page: some kind of architectural diagram. 'Are they plans?'

Luca hesitated. 'Er...' He hesitated again.

'Sorry. I didn't mean to pry.'

Mina knew how embarrassed she would be if someone looked inside her sketchbook, even if they just saw her landscapes. They were personal, something she wasn't yet ready to share with the world, let alone her drawings of Luca. If he were to see those, she might just expire from mortification. She searched her mind for something to say to change the subject and take the focus off something he clearly didn't want to share, but he spoke before she could think of anything.

'Actually, they are plans.' He paused. 'For what good it'll do,' he said quietly, almost talking to himself, but, in the quiet of the evening, Mina could hear him perfectly. The despondence in those few words pulled at Mina's heart. What was he so sad about?

'Plans for what?'

He looked over at her and stared for a moment. Then, seeming to come to some sort of decision, he stood and crossed the width of his balcony, coming to a stop at the railing where his balcony almost met hers. He passed the folder over to Mina and held it out until she took it. 'Did you know Bora Bora has no hospital?'

'Actually, I did.'

'There are ten thousand people living in Bora Bora full-time. Half of those live in Vaitape, the city on the western side of the main island. No big hospital; if they need specialist care, or there's an emergency, they have to be evacuated by plane or helicopter to the general hospital in Tahiti. That's over 150 miles away.' Luca's eyes were bright and passionate and he gestured animatedly as he spoke.

'So the only specialist medical facilities on the island are in the fancy hotels? The locals get nothing?'

'Exactly.' Luca stared at her in wonder, as if he'd finally found someone who understood.

It was refreshing to find someone as rich as Luca who noticed people less fortunate than himself, let alone cared about them enough to get as passionate as Luca seemed to be about this.

'So what are the plans?'

He shrugged, suddenly losing steam. 'It's just an architectural drawing of a small hospital. Something that would work for the island.'

'And you're going to build it?'

'Someone should. I never said me.'

Mina looked at the plans. They were of a fairly large, one-storey building, with plenty of treatment rooms and two operating theatres. It seemed perfect for a population of ten thousand. There was a drawing of the exterior too; it even had the ubiquitous thatched roof to make it fit in with most of the other buildings she'd seen so far.

'You contacted an architect for it; seems like you're pretty serious about it being you.'

He looked away. 'I just asked a friend of mine to draw up some preliminary plans; they studied architecture at university.'

Why was he playing this down all of a sudden? He'd seemed so enthused when he was describing the idea to her. It had been nice to see a flash of the passionate man she'd met at the airport. And it was delightful to discover that he might not be the arrogant, spoiled man she'd feared he was.

'Why not you? Could you afford to build this?'

'Yes, of course.'

'So why not?'

Luca paused. 'I have other responsibilities.'

Maybe she was wrong. Maybe this was just for show. Maybe that was why he was only excited about the plans and not the execution—enjoying the dream more than the hard work.

'Why would you want to do this anyway—spending your own money to help strangers?' She could tell he'd sensed the cynical tone of her voice by the determined angle of his jaw as he answered.

'They're not strangers. They're my neighbours.'

They stared at each other for a moment, then Luca sighed and, for no reason that Mina could identify, he started opening up. 'My mother died several years ago.'

Before Mina could offer her condolences, Luca continued.

'Apart from a few charities, Roman and I were the only beneficiaries. There was a lot of money. Roman bought the resort with his, but I want to do something more useful with mine. Roman and I are just two more people who have come to this island, and are using up its resources for fancy hotels and millionaire getaways, I have to give back something useful.'

'Were you close to your mother?'

'Before she died, I promised her that, despite our difficult relationships, I would always put family first. I would always look out for Roman and keep him close.'

Mina almost felt guilty for listening to something so personal. But, for whatever reason, he'd decided to open up, and now she didn't know how to stop him. Maybe it was the alcohol loosening him up, or maybe it was Mina's gentle encouragement. She didn't believe that he felt he had to prove something to some new, fairly infuriating nurse who'd just rocked up from Ealing and had already annoyed the hell out of him, according to Luca. So maybe he just needed to talk, and didn't care to whom.

He sat a lot closer to Mina when he returned from his kitchen with his third beer, and now only the railings separated them. 'Would you like one?' he offered.

Mina shook her head. It certainly seemed as if Luca

could handle his drink. He was still walking straight and steady; the only sign of change in him was how comfortable and loose-limbed he looked, leaning back in his seat, his head tipped back on to the cushions. And of course, the fact that he'd turned into such a chatty Cathy all of a sudden. It was quite endearing. He looked happier, too. He was smiling at her now, his brown eyes twinkling.

'How are you and Roman so different?' she wondered out loud. What made Luca care about people when Roman didn't? What could have happened to make the twins, who'd had the same childhood, so dissimilar? For a moment, she wondered if they shouldn't be talking about Roman at all. After what Rachelle had revealed to her, maybe Roman was the last thing Luca wanted to talk about.

But he answered almost immediately. 'We are different. Roman's never really had a purpose or a passion, like mine for medicine. Roman's always owned land, and he owns even more now. But I've never wanted to be a land owner. I've had to be the responsible one all my life, so now I like my freedom. Which is why I'm probably not the right person to build and manage this hospital.'

'Maybe you've changed.'

Luca scoffed quietly and didn't speak for a while. 'You wouldn't believe what Roman was like when we were kids.'

It looked as if story time wasn't over yet, after all. 'What was he like?' Mina asked with a smile.

'Roman's healthy now, but he grew up very sickly and weak, and spent a lot of time in hospital. We didn't know what was wrong with him at first but, once they diagnosed him, he got it treated eventually. I used to visit him in hospital with our parents. I hated going. But one day I met another kid our age in the hospital—Gabriel. His family weren't wealthy like ours, and they couldn't afford access to the kind of care Roman was getting.' Luca sipped his drink. 'Gabriel and I became very close friends; I saw him all the time. But he was slowly getting worse. I begged my mother to pay for his care, but she wouldn't. They said it wasn't possible, it was too complicated, but I was a kid and I didn't get it.'

Luca took a long swig of his beer. 'Gabriel died, two weeks after his twelfth birthday. That was the first time I was confronted by the unfairness of life; the first time I realised that money can be the difference between life and death.'

'I'm sorry,' said Mina, her heart breaking for the younger version of Luca.

'Roman never understood my friendship with Gabriel. And he never understood what I learned about life back then. It was hard for him, being so sick, but that's no excuse. He's always been entitled and ignorant. I'm not sure he knows how to care about other people. We were twins, but because he was sick everyone expected me to take a much 'older brother' role, to protect him, keep him safe, and I did. And he hates that. He thinks it makes him weak, so now he over-compensates. But, despite his bravado, he's actually quite vulnerable deep down.'

It all made so much sense. There was clearly a lot more to both of them than Mina had imagined.

'I can see now why you don't live together. Where does Roman live?'

'Not here. He's on a private island to the east of Bora Bora. The rest of the year, he has a place in Paris.'

That led Mina to another question. 'Why do you live in a villa like mine? Shouldn't you be living on a luxury private island like him? Or in some luxurious villa built on top of the mountain, like a Bond villain?'

Luca stared at Mina. 'If I wanted to, I suppose I could live on a private island, but it sounds like a waste of money to me.'

'Well, me too, but I'm normal.'

'Thanks.'

'I mean, I'm not as rich as Croesus.'

Luca shrugged. 'This villa is perfectly acceptable. It has everything I need, and is close enough to everyone that I can rush to an emergency anywhere on the resort.'

Mina nodded. 'That makes sense.'

'Glad to hear it.'

Mina paused. 'Sorry I said you weren't normal.'

Luca laughed. 'You're forgiven.' He stared at Mina for a long moment in the growing moonlight. She tracked his eyes moving up to her hair, and slowly down her face, to her lips. 'You really are exquisite, Mina,' he breathed.

Her lips parted as she gasped quietly, not sure how to respond. Before she could say anything, Luca stood, seeming unsteady on his feet for the first time that night. He blinked down at her. 'I'm sorry. I should get some sleep. Good evening.'

He climbed awkwardly between the table and chairs on his balcony and headed into his villa. Mina still hadn't spoken, and simply watched as he pulled the door firmly closed behind him.

# CHAPTER SIX

THE NEXT MORNING, as soon as Mina arrived at work, Luca opened his office door and called her in. 'Could I speak with you a moment?'

'Of course.' Mina went into his office and he closed the door firmly behind her.

'About last night...' Luca began.

Mina laughed shortly. 'It's a little late for that conversation, isn't it?'

Luca frowned, confused, then blushed slightly as he realised what she meant. 'Not that night—last night. I'm afraid I over-indulged on my night off. The thing is, I get very talkative when I drink.'

'Yes, I noticed.'

He looked up at her, worriedly. 'I don't really remember what I might have...' he adjusted a pen on his desk '...said to you.'

Mina felt sorry for him. He clearly hadn't meant to share as much personal information as he had. She smiled. 'Don't worry about it, it was nothing untoward. It's all forgotten.'

He looked doubtful. 'Either way, I'd ask you not to bring it up again. Or discuss it with anyone.'

And now Luca was back to being cold again, as if a wall had gone back up between them.

'I wasn't exactly planning on yapping about our conversation to Rachelle at the coffee machine, Dr Baudelaire.'

He blinked at her. 'As long as we're on the same page.'

Mina nodded before leaving his office as fast as she could. It looked as if they were back to square one again. They were only colleagues, not friends, and certainly nothing more. Thank goodness she'd sworn off men.

Mina sipped her tea as Rachelle sat at the reception desk sorting through the post.

'I believe I have you to thank for me not going hungry last night,' Mina said.

'Oh! I guessed you wouldn't have time to get yourself any food.'

'You guessed right. Thank you; you're already my new favourite person.'

Rachelle laughed.

'So, question…' Mina continued. 'The other day Roman mentioned I was hired at short notice. Why did you need someone so quickly?'

'The nurse you're replacing left,' Luca said, making Mina jump. She hadn't known he was there.

Mina waited for him to continue, but clearly that was all he was willing to share. 'You're full of scintillating details.'

'You want more? Very well; they were fired by Roman for annoying him. You'd do well to take note of that.'

'I don't annoy people. I'm charming.'

Luca snorted. 'There's very little evidence of that so far.'

'Children, children,' Rachelle said, holding up her hands as she carried on sorting the post. 'Don't make me split you two up, I'm too busy.'

Luca grabbed a file and cleared his throat. 'I'll be in my office.'

Mina was sure she noticed a pink flush on his face before he disappeared through the dark-wood double door of his office, leaving it slightly ajar behind him.

'Is he always this annoying?' Mina whispered.

'Yes,' Rachelle answered bluntly. 'But that's why we love him.'

Mina hummed dubiously in reply. The jury was out on that one. She jumped when Rachelle suddenly waggled an envelope in the air.

'You got another one, Luca!' she called out loudly.

Mina watched as Luca reappeared to pluck the envelope from Rachelle's hand and tear it open. He took out a card and read it, then nodded. 'It's from the coral-reef rash.'

'From last week?' asked Rachelle. 'The honeymooners?'

Luca nodded once and headed back to where he'd come from. Mina looked at Rachelle quizzically.

'He gets a lot of thank-you cards.'

*Ah.* Mina watched Luca disappear into his office, presumably to throw it straight in the bin. Mina couldn't imagine that sweet thank-you notes were his sort of thing. Mina's clinic used to get a few of those, usually from new mothers with a picture of the baby. They were appreciated and kept in a drawer.

'Follow him,' Rachelle said.

'What?'

'Follow him to his office and see what he's doing.'
'Are you crazy?'
'Just do it!'

Mina rolled her eyes but dutifully followed Luca's route across the reception and approached his office door, where she stood, hesitantly, and peered into the room. She found Luca with his back to the door, pinning the thank-you card to a huge cork noticeboard on the wall. It covered half the space, and was crammed full of what had to be every thank-you note he'd ever received. There were letters, cards, photographs and what looked an awful lot like poems. Mina slipped away before he saw her. Maybe there was more to this man than she'd thought.

When Rachelle informed Mina she was due an afternoon off, Mina didn't know what to do with herself. She was struck once more by how different this job was to any other she'd ever had and how incredibly lucky she was to have it. Her first instinct was relief that she could spend a few hours on her own to clear her head. Her second instinct was to refuse it and stay at the clinic anyway, but Rachelle had insisted she take the time. And, after all, one of her aims in coming here was to try to stop being such a workaholic.

'Go home and sleep if nothing else!' said Rachelle. 'But I would suggest there are better things to do.'

'Like what?'

'Mina, you are living on one of the most luxurious resorts in the world. For the love of God, enjoy it. Go and get a hot-stone massage, an oxygen facial, walk on the white, sandy beaches; swim in the infinity pool.'

Rachelle had a point.

So, that afternoon, Mina found herself dressed in her bikini by the side of the most beautiful pool she'd ever seen. She untied her sarong, sprayed on some sunscreen and settled back into a cushioned sun lounger. All she'd brought out with her were her sunglasses, a book and her phone, but she would leave that in her bag. She ordered a watermelon and lime mocktail from the bar and set her mind on relaxing. She watched four people quietly doing yoga on the beach, and listened to the waves lapping, the breeze in the leaves and the quiet sounds of people playing tennis somewhere behind the trees.

A while later she realised she'd read the same paragraph three times and set down the book. Relaxing was harder than it seemed. She couldn't get Luca out of her head and doubts were swirling. There were moments when she wondered if he might have feelings for her, but was she kidding herself? How could a man like him be interested in her? Sure, there was a physical attraction that clearly went both ways, but could there really be anything more? Everyone lost interest and betrayed her in the end, and she couldn't see why Luca would be any different.

Mina heard a yelp from the direction of the tennis courts, then a clatter, and the unmistakeable thud of a body hitting the ground.

'Sir, are you okay?' called a deep, panicked voice from the same direction. Mina jumped to her feet and ran towards a gap in the hedge signposting the entrance to the tennis courts. When she got there, she found a middle-aged man lying on the artificial grass court, grabbing his chest, and a tennis coach dressed all in white crouching over him.

'I'm a nurse, can I help?'

The coach looked her up and down in surprise, and Mina remembered she was only wearing her bikini. 'Off-duty nurse,' she smiled briefly, and he gestured her over.

'He just collapsed,' he said quietly. 'He's not having a heart attack, is he?'

The coach stood and pulled off his own shirt, rolling it up quickly and tucking it under the man's head, leaving himself topless. He was blond, tanned and muscular, and looked like the type of guy who was constantly on the lookout for reasons to take his clothes off and show off his body.

Mina ignored him and focused on the patient. 'I'm a nurse; can you tell me your name?'

'Isn't there a doctor?' the man asked.

'Not right this second.' She smiled. The man looked reluctant. 'Your name?' she nudged.

He sighed. 'Quentin.'

Mina pressed a hand to Quentin's forehead to gauge his temperature, but it felt normal. Then she took his pulse: also normal. Now that he'd stopped playing tennis, he wasn't sweating or short of breath.

'My chest feels like it's burning.'

'Okay, can you try to relax for me? Breathe in slowly, then breathe out slowly.' She pressed a hand flat to his chest and breathed with him, nodding when he followed her lead. 'Can you sit up?' She took his hands and helped him sit up. 'Have you eaten anything this morning?'

'Yes, I just had a large cooked breakfast at the restaurant.'

'Do you happen to have a sour taste in your mouth?'

He frowned. 'Yes, I do.'

'Okay, I think you're suffering from heartburn.'

'Oh.' The man took a deep breath and seemed to relax.

'But we can take you to the clinic, check you over more there.'

'No, I actually feel much better now.'

Mina nodded. The patient was looking a little self-conscious. 'No need to feel embarrassed; heartburn can be very painful. I can get you some antacids for the pain.'

'No, I think my wife has some back at the villa. She has heartburn all the time, I just never realised how painful it was.'

*Maybe you should consider listening to your wife a bit more, then*, Mina thought. But she thought of Luca and kept her mouth shut. She smiled and helped the man up.

'If you have any doubts at all or feel unwell, come and see us at the health clinic.'

'I will. Thank you.' She walked with him to the edge of the courts and he shook her off. 'I'm really fine now, thank you.'

She returned to the coach, picked up his shirt from the court where it still lay and threw it to him. He caught it easily. 'Wow, you were amazing,' he said. 'I was about to panic. I can't be killing any more clients.' He winked. 'That was a joke.'

Mina couldn't help but laugh. 'I got it.'

'Are you a guest here?'

'I work here,' said Mina. 'I'm new at the health clinic.'

'Oh, wow. My name's Anders, tennis coach. Super-pleased to meet you.'

Mina shook his hand. 'Nurse Morgan.'

He nodded, grinning, and still didn't put on his shirt. Mina mentally rolled her eyes. He was ridiculous, but harmless.

'Mina?'

Mina turned. 'Luca!'

'A guest phoned reception,' he called across the court. 'Someone was injured on the tennis courts?'

'Hey, doc, no need to panic. Your nurse saved the day.'

'Thank you, Anders,' he said dismissively. 'Mina?'

'Just a bad case of heartburn.'

'Looked like a heart attack. Don't know what I would have done without her, doc.' Anders stepped closer to Mina and slung an arm around her shoulders.

She stepped away gracefully and smiled. 'Just doing my job.'

'How about we keep our hands to ourselves, Anders?' Luca ground out, glowering. 'And get dressed, you're working.'

'Oh, sorry. No offence meant,' Anders said to Mina, holding up both hands, then pulling his shirt on over his head.

'None taken,' Mina answered, distracted. She'd never seen a jealous Luca before and, although she knew perhaps it shouldn't, it sent an undeniable thrill up her spine.

The smile fell from her face. It didn't matter how thrilling his possessive streak might be, when that was exactly the sort of thing she needed to ignore. She had to protect her heart; she had to take a step back if she didn't want to get hurt.

# CHAPTER SEVEN

RACHELLE HAD MENTIONED to Mina that the waterfront restaurant was the best place to get breakfast. They opened early for staff, earlier than the advertised opening time for guests, and apparently it was always quiet in there first thing. So Mina set her alarm a little earlier, woke up and swung open the doors to the balcony to get ready with the sound of waves lapping on the shore, and a gentle warm breeze. Then she enjoyed a pleasant walk up to the restaurant.

The restaurant had no walls, just wooden pillars topped by a huge domed thatched roof. Where the walls would have been, there was instead a view of glistening ocean, palm trees and beaches almost blindingly white in the early-morning sun. The restaurant was empty, but there was food laid out along the buffet tables, and it all looked so fresh and delicious. She grabbed a plate and piled it ridiculously high with fresh mango and watermelon, and chose a kiwi and strawberry smoothie. She took it to a table in the corner out of the way, and sat down, slipping her sunglasses on to combat the glare reflected from the water.

She exhaled, letting herself relax into the comfortable cream cushioned seat of her wicker chair. Rachelle was a genius; this was a wonderful way to start a work day. Much better than standing in her villa's mini-kitchen inhaling a bowl of cereal, which was what she'd have planned otherwise.

And then, of course, Luca had to appear and ruin it. He strode into the empty restaurant carrying a newspaper, dressed in his usual work clothes but without the tie. His shirt was unbuttoned at the top, revealing a glimpse of tantalisingly tanned collarbone that Mina absolutely didn't stare at. He hadn't noticed her yet, and she watched as he took a plate and grabbed a croissant and a small black coffee.

He turned to choose a table, and finally caught sight of Mina. She smiled to herself when he froze, indecision clear on his face for a long moment. Would he come over to join her or sit somewhere else? She was fairly sure he would prefer to sit alone, but his manners might just win out. She looked out at the ocean, leaving him to make his decision.

A shadow fell over her table.

'Good morning, Mina.'

Why did his voice have to be so deep and deliciously rough first thing in the morning? And why did it sound so unutterably exquisite saying her name? She glanced at his plate. 'Very French.'

He stared at her breakfast. 'Are you planning to open your own fruit shop?'

'It's called healthy eating. Some doctors swear by it.'

'Actually, too much fruit can overdose you with natural sugars. It can be quite unhealthy.'

'Better than pink heart-shaped cookies.'

Luca's head shot up as he sat down and Mina blushed

as he stared at her across the rather small table. Aside from the first time they'd seen each other in Luca's office, this was the first time either of them had made any reference to the night they'd spent together. Mina cursed herself for saying anything about those stupid pink cookies. 'Anything interesting in the paper?' she asked, desperate to change the subject.

'It's just the local paper. Well, Tahitian; it's the closest one. Would you like it after me?'

'It's in French.'

'Ah, yes. *Désolé*.'

Unless she needed to ask where the library or swimming pool were, or tell someone that her name was Mina and she had two sisters, her mostly forgotten school French wasn't going to get her very far. There was a circle drawn in red pen around a listing on the page Luca was looking at.

'You buying a second-hand sofa?' she joked.

He looked at her, then followed her gaze down. 'Ah, no. There's a plot of land for sale on the island.'

It clicked. 'That land wouldn't happen to be hospital-shaped?'

He smiled briefly, his eyes crinkling at the corners. Mina liked that look on him. 'It could be.' He shrugged and the smile disappeared. 'But it's not the right time.'

'Maybe you should snap it up before someone else does.'

'There's no rush. The land has sat empty for five years.'

'Maybe it's waiting for you, then.'

He smiled but shook his head dismissively and folded up the newspaper, tossing it to the side. He took a bite of his croissant and closed his eyes, unconsciously letting out a small moan of pleasure. Mina shifted in her seat. He had no business making noises like that. He quickly licked a crumb from his finger. 'This is delicious. Can I get you one?'

'No, no, I'm good.'

Mina took a long swallow of her cold smoothie, and held the icy glass to her neck.

'Hot?'

'Little bit.'

'It's pretty hot here year-round.'

'I noticed. I'm not a big fan of hot weather, to be honest, but I'll be fine. Every room in this place has air conditioning.'

'Perhaps you would have been better off with a job in Antarctica.'

Mina smiled sarcastically, and he grinned. She pushed her plate away, after she'd forced down what felt like a week's worth of her five-a-day. Her stomach had been full about half-way through, but she couldn't leave any fruit on the plate and risk making Luca think he was right about something.

'Well done, you made it,' Luca teased.

'Thank you.' Mina delicately dabbed at her mouth with her cotton napkin.

The chef at the waterfront restaurant was French. Roman had poached him from a three-Michelin-starred restaurant in Paris. The food was the best of the best, and Mina had only eaten plain fruit. It was infuriating. Luca wasn't too bothered about Michelin stars and where the chef had trained, but he did love good food. Good food could make the difference between an ordinary day and a wonderful one. Luca's morning croissant had not been just a croissant, it was an award-winning croissant that had taken chef Pierre years to perfect, injected with pistachio cream and dusted with crushed pistachios.

He'd overheard Mina talking to Rachelle yesterday about buying boxed cereal, of all things. He found himself planning to show her all the wonderful food she had at her disposal. He shook his head at himself. There would be none of that. She was only his nurse. It shouldn't matter to him what his nurse ate and drank and whether she was enjoying the local cuisine. This woman was dangerous. Why couldn't he just ignore her beautiful red curls and the way the sunlight reflected in her deep-blue eyes?

Luca knew how it was. He could either have a career, a passion project, or a personal life; he couldn't have all three. He couldn't even have two without one failing. That was why he was concentrating on his career for now; his passion project could come later, if at all. The personal life was never going to happen. He had his hands plenty full right now.

Luca still remembered his mother's exact words when she had made him promise to look after Roman. *'Stay in his orbit, don't go your separate ways. Once you do that, he'll be lost to you forever, just as my sisters were to me. It's so easy—you blink and suddenly you haven't spoken to your family in twenty years.'* So that was exactly what he was doing. Just as when he'd been a kid, he was protecting his brother. Only this time his brother didn't know he was doing it.

Roman had a history of misusing alcohol and prescription drugs. It made some sort of sense, with his history of physical pain, but he was healthy now—physically in any case; his mental wellness was an issue between Roman and his therapist. Roman had no need for prescription drugs any longer, and as far as Luca could tell he wasn't misusing them. But, when he did, Luca knew from bitter experience that everything around Roman would go downhill fast. His mother was right—Roman needed him—but, by God, it was a thankless task. Luca supposed that was what big brothers were for. And he was three minutes older.

Every now and again, Luca would find Roman in his office and, instead of Roman's usual snarkiness or confrontation, he would be quiet and hesitant. Luca would ask the right questions and eventually establish the fact that he needed Luca's input on something to do with the running of the resort. Roman never explicitly asked, but Luca knew he needed him around, even if Roman would rather die than admit it.

Luca would check over the books, look into the incomings, outgoings and business decisions Roman was making and make sure the resort was working as it should, making a profit and running smoothly. Generally, he was making sure his mother's inheritance wasn't being wasted.

So not only was Luca working full-time as a doctor, he was also helping run the business. He had no time for building a hospital. Mina could drop as many hints as she wanted, but he didn't live in a fairytale world where he could do whatever he wanted. He had responsibilities.

Yesterday, at the tennis courts, Mina had looked like some kind of stunning Amazon, tending to the patient, taking care of business and doing a perfect job, even though she'd had no medical equipment and had been dressed in only a bikini. She really was a breathtaking human, and much too good for him.

And it clearly wasn't only Luca who thought so. The tennis coach hadn't been able to take his eyes off her. A small part of Luca couldn't blame him; she was a force of nature. But most of him had wanted to rip the guy's head off.

That was the problem. This was exactly what he'd been scared of. He could either let his entire being become overwhelmed by the most beautiful, bewitching woman he'd ever met, and give her everything she deserved, or he could have the ability to carry out his lifelong plans. The dream he'd had since he'd been eleven years old, when he'd first met Gabriel. Luca refused to turn into his father. His father had achieved his dreams but had left his neglected wife by the wayside, alone and eventually turned bitter by constant, endless rejection. The idea that Mina could ever be forced to end up like that was unbearable.

As Luca arrived at work, a huge butterfly fluttered in through the reception doors along with him and crossed reception, heading straight into the kitchen. Luca sighed and followed it, planning to open the window and shoo it out. It was already clattering its wings against the glass when he got to it. 'Hold on, *papillon*, I'm on my way.'

He pushed a chair to the side which jostled the table and knocked someone's bag on to the floor, but he stepped over the bag and pushed the window open. He used one hand to gently nudge the butterfly out of the open window and watched it flutter away into the trees.

Good deed done for the day, he picked up the bag from the floor to set it back on the table. As he picked it up, a book dislodged itself and fell to the floor, landing open on the tiles.

As he bent down to retrieve it, he realised it was a sketchbook. And the page he was looking at had several pencil drawings of a familiar face: his.

He frowned and carefully picked it up, standing to look at it in the light. He flipped to the front cover and found a gold *M.M.* monogrammed on the front. Mina Morgan? He suddenly remembered their evening on their respective balconies. She'd been scribbling away in her notebook the whole time. He'd thought she was writing. He suddenly felt guilty. He shouldn't be looking at this. He obviously wasn't meant to see it. But he couldn't resist turning the page, just to check what was there: more pictures of his face. Did he really look like that? The drawings were so beautiful. But he could recognise his hair, his mouth, his eyes…

He knew he was an okay-looking guy. Sometimes people stared. He'd had his share of people approaching him and trying to get to know him better. But it always felt as if they wanted something from him. No one had ever looked at him like this before—seen something worth recording, something worth depicting on paper. No one had made him into art before.

There was nothing he wanted to do more than look at the rest of her art, turn all the pages and see what else she'd drawn. What else had she made this beautiful? What else had she noticed and found special enough to record? There were plenty of beautiful things on Bora

Bora, and he suddenly, desperately, wanted to see them through her eyes.

But the guilt was too strong now. He reluctantly closed the book and placed it carefully back into her bag. But he couldn't stop thinking about it for the rest of the day. What did the drawings mean? Did they mean anything? Was she in the habit of drawing things she hated? Or did she only draw things she loved?

# CHAPTER EIGHT

Mina and Luca came off their shifts at the same time, and Mina hung back to let him leave first. Luca leaned on the reception desk, talking to Rachelle. 'Did Malo's meds get delivered?'

'Yes,' Rachelle answered. 'They came this morning. They're in the drug cupboard.' She took the key from her pocket and disappeared to fetch them. When she came back, she handed Luca a paper bag that rattled with the sound of pills. 'Here you go.'

'Thanks. I'll take them up to him now.'

'Say hello from us!' Rachelle said, smiling.

'Who's Malo?' asked Mina.

'He's an old friend of ours,' replied Rachelle. 'He used to work at the resort, but he's taken early retirement. Now he lives near Vaitape with his wife, half way up the hill.'

'Oh, you're going through Vaitape? Could I come? I'd love to see the town. I've not had a chance to look around yet.' All Mina had seen so far was the inside of the resort. And, as beautiful as that was, she was itching to get out and see the real island, and maybe meet some more islanders. She'd met Rachelle, and a handful of locals who worked at the resort, and so far they'd been some of the kindest, friendliest people she'd ever known.

On top of that, as apprehensive as she was about spending more time with Luca, it might be a good idea to try to spend some time alone with him, outside of the work environment—somewhere more on his own turf; somewhere he might be more relaxed and more himself. Part of her still wondered whether she could draw some of Jean-Paul out of him, or whether she should just give him up as an anomaly, something that was never going to happen. Another part of her simply wanted to improve their professional relationship. Taking a short walk with him might be a great way to do that and mend some bridges.

And, if all of that turned out to be a bad idea, well, they couldn't be going far. A trip to this Malo's house and back wouldn't take long, so the outing would be over before she knew it.

'So can I come? I'd love to see more of the island.'

Luca hesitated.

'Yes, let her go with you, Luca. Cardinal can handle it.'

Rachelle's sly smile made Mina nervous. She wasn't sure who Cardinal was but, after Luca sighed and walked out, he held open the door for Mina, and she took that as a yes, dutifully following Luca outside.

They took a quick boat ride from the resort dock to the main island, a reverse of the trip Mina had taken from the airport when she'd first arrived. She still couldn't stop staring at the beautiful, unearthly green-blue of the lagoon. Would she ever get used to that colour?

They disembarked and Mina paused for a second

to get used to standing on solid ground again. 'Are we walking from here?' she asked.

'No,' said Luca.

'Oh, are we taking a scooter?' There were several people on scooters leaving the dock.

'No.'

'A car?' Mina was running out of suggestions. Before she'd arrived in Bora Bora, she hadn't expected to see many cars on such a small, idyllic island, but she'd seen plenty so far. She knew locals drove around between their homes and workplaces, or down to the small town centre she still hadn't yet seen. She was excited to experience it.

She followed Luca across a road and down a side alley towards a wooden gate. He unlatched it then knocked on the door of someone's fenced-off back garden beyond.

Were they at Malo's house already?

He spoke quietly to the man who answered his knock, then the man disappeared and reappeared moments later leading a horse by the reins. The large, light-brown horse clip-clopped on to the path and, as Luca reached up to stroke its nose the man passed him the reins. Mina's eyes widened.

Luca turned back to Mina with a smile. 'Hop on, then.'

A laugh burst out of Mina's mouth. 'Are you serious?'

'You wanted to know our method of transportation to Malo's house.'

'A horse?'

'Nothing gets past you. This is Cardinal.'

Now Rachelle's comment made sense. Mina looked behind the horse towards the open door. 'Just one horse?'

'Yes. We'll have to share. Have you ridden before?'

'Not really; I rode a horse a couple of times as a kid, sitting in on a couple of my friend's lessons, but they're not exactly a common sight on the streets of Ealing.'

'Are you up for it?'

Mina tucked her hair behind her ears and took a deep breath. 'I am.'

Luca gave her a slow smile, which Mina thought she could almost identify as a little proud, before he turned to face the horse. He held the reins in one hand, and fisted the other hand into the horse's mane, then jumped up on to the horse's back. It was a pretty impressive, smooth move, and the horse barely even blinked. Mina exhaled, then noticed something.

'Wait, there's no saddle.'

'Cardinal prefers not to wear one. He finds them uncomfortable.'

'Can he even handle both our weights?'

'He's carried a lot heavier. He'll be fine, I promise.' Luca patted Cardinal's neck and squeezed his sides with his legs, and the horse walked over to a thick log, which lay on the ground along the wall of the nearest house. Luca nodded at the log. 'Hop on to that and I'll help you get up behind me.'

It suddenly struck Mina that she was going to have to sit extremely close to Luca, and her face flushed. Whatever had possessed her to volunteer for this trip? She just hoped she'd be able to mount the horse without falling off the other side or making some other absolute show of herself.

She stepped up on to the log, and Luca nudged the horse closer. It snorted and swung its head, its tail swishing to swat away flies. Once she had the added height of the log, the horse looked a little less intimidatingly tall, and when Luca held out his hand Mina took it, jumped carefully and somehow managed to launch herself up on the horse behind Luca, her hands on Luca's sides.

'Perfect,' Luca said. 'Well done.'

She exhaled, happy to have made it on board, and then squirmed, trying to get comfy. 'You're sure this isn't hurting Cardinal?'

'Positive. Come on, let's go.' Luca clicked his tongue and the horse set off towards the road. Once Mina got used to the back and forth movement beneath her, she settled into a comfortable position.

'Allow your hips to move with the horse's gait, and hold on to me. You'll be fine.'

Part of Mina wanted to wrap her arms around Luca's waist and hold on tight, but she was trying to be professional. So she gripped the edges of his shirt loosely, and held on, trying to keep a respectful amount of distance between their bodies. After all, they were work colleagues on a trip for work, delivering medication to a patient.

As they walked down the road, Cardinal's hooves clattering on the tarmac, Mina let her hands settle gently on Luca's sides. He leaned back, settling closer to her and she smelled his cologne as he turned his head to check for cars. He waved a slowing car past them with one hand and she felt his hard muscles moving under her hands.

She cleared her throat. 'So you do this a lot?'

'Riding? I used to ride a lot in France. We had a stable full of horses. Now I rarely get the chance to spend time on one. Only when I borrow Cardinal to visit Malo.' He patted Cardinal's neck affectionately. 'Malo's meds get delivered to the resort along with our medication delivery from the pharmacy. I arrange them for him personally. Then I take them up to him. He can't get out easily to pick them up. The lanes are too narrow for most cars, and it's quicker by horse to cut straight across up the hill.'

Mina didn't know if it was the physical proximity, but she was feeling rather fond of Luca at this moment. It was very sweet of him to take the time to do all this for a friend.

'Sometimes Malo needs to visit the accident and emergency over in Tahiti, and that's a nightmare too. It'd be a little easier if he moved down here to the coast, to a house with easier access, but the house he lives in now is his dream house. He built it with his wife, when their children were small.' Mina could hear the smile in Luca's voice. 'There's no way anyone would have a chance of getting him to leave that place.'

Mina tapped Luca's side with one finger. 'So, Malo is one of the locals who would benefit from a hospital on the island?'

Luca twisted in place to smile back at Mina and, as ever, a grin from Luca that close up took Mina's breath away.

'Yes, he would. He has regular treatments he has to travel to Tahiti for, as well as any emergencies. A closer hospital would be wonderful.'

It all made sense. It was nice to see first-hand why Luca was so personally involved and enthusiastic about the hospital, and why he so badly wanted to build it.

Mina wondered what Roman thought about Luca spending time on a patient who wasn't a guest at the resort. Maybe that was why they were making this trek after work hours. It was good of Luca to take all this on his own back and go out of his way to help Malo, and outside of work hours. Mina was sure, if Luca had wanted to, he could have easily hired someone to deliver the meds, however out of the way Malo's house was.

As shops started to appear, the street grew a little busier and vibrant with people.

'This is the centre of Vaitape,' said Luca.

Tourists and locals walked the sandy pavements and the occasional car drove past, followed by kids riding bikes. The horse picked its way around a happily sleeping dog, and walked on past a man selling fresh fish at the side of the road, hung horizontally from a frame. The food smells floating from the cafés were delicious, and there were several places selling fruit and vegetables that made Mina wish she could jump off the horse and buy something.

Every minute or two someone recognised Luca and shouted hello to him, greeting him warmly and asking how he was. He had a nod and a smile for everyone. He was clearly very well-known and respected around Vaitape. It wasn't the tourists; it seemed to be mostly local people working in the shops and on the stalls.

'How does everyone know the doctor from a hotel resort?' Mina murmured, close to his ear.

She felt him shrug. 'I do a few local outreach things when I have extra time.'

Mina nodded. Very interesting. There was definitely a lot more to this man than she had originally thought.

They passed a lemon-yellow church with a tall steeple and red roof, then some souvenir shops and several jewellery stores selling black pearls.

'They cultivate black pearls here on the island,' Luca explained.

As they reached the end of the busy road, the palm trees that lined the streets grew thicker and wilder, and Mina saw a scattering of beautiful houses with red tiled rooves perched on the foot of the lush green mountain.

Mina gazed up at Mount Otemanu, which had grown ever bigger as they'd gone on their way. Luca finally directed Cardinal off the road and on to a narrow sandy pathway that soon turned into grass, and they headed up the hill.

The angle grew steadily steeper, but the horse had no trouble making his way up, and Mina felt safe on his back. Fifteen minutes later, they passed through some thick trees, light branches swatting Cardinal's flanks. Luca held a few branches back to stop them whipping Mina's face, and they suddenly emerged into a sunny clearing, where a modest but beautiful house sat.

Luca came to a stop and turned back to Mina. 'You'll have to dismount first; do you want any help?'

'No. I'm good.'

Mina swung her right leg over the horse then slid down slowly, dropping to the ground. She patted his flank as she stepped away, relieved she'd managed to dismount fairly gracefully. Luca, of course, jumped down like a professional, and hitched Cardinal's lead rope around a post at the edge of the property.

# CHAPTER NINE

THE WOODEN CABIN, clearly made by hand and a few decades old, was patched up here and there with mismatched wood and pieces of corrugated metal, but it still looked homey and charming. It was surrounded by coconut and mango trees, growing close to the house and casting their precious shade over it. It looked like an oasis of cool and calm, which must be such a relief in the hotter months. A tiny white cat ran up to them and Mina immediately bent down to make friends with it.

A smiling woman came out to meet them. 'Doctor, it's so lovely to see you.'

Luca gave her a quick hug hello. 'Lani, when will you start calling me Luca?'

Mina straightened up from greeting a cat, and Luca introduced her as his colleague, then she got a warm hug too. A man Mina assumed to be Malo came out next, walking with the help of two walking sticks. He shook both their hands warmly, then collapsed back on to a porch swing, beaming at them. 'Join me, please.'

Luca handed Lani the paper bag containing Malo's meds and she took them inside. When she reappeared, she came armed with four glasses of lemonade. Luca and Mina took theirs gratefully and Luca sat down on one of the mismatched porch chairs. When Lani went back inside, Mina followed her and stood politely in the doorway. The kitchen smelled delicious. 'Can I help with anything?' Mina asked.

'You're very sweet. I was just getting a bucket of water for the horse. He must be thirsty.'

'Oh of course, how thoughtful!' Mina felt guilty for not having thought of it herself. When Lani passed her a lime-green bucket, she gestured at the kitchen sink. 'Should I fill it here?'

Lani nodded and Mina ran the cold water tap, then carried the heavy bucket out of the door. She was met by Luca, who gave her a wink as he took the bucket from her. Mina ignored the butterflies in her tummy that fluttered after that wink, and took a seat by Malo while she watched Luca carry the bucket, as if it weighed nothing, and deposit it by Cardinal. The horse gave him an appreciative snort.

'So, how are you feeling, Malo?' Luca asked, returning and taking a long swallow of lemonade. He wiped the condensation off the glass on to his forehead, and sank down next to Mina, his thigh a warm line against hers.

'I can't complain,' said Malo.

'You can to me, I'm a doctor.'

Malo laughed and shook his head. 'I'm still having the occasional dizzy spell, but nothing's worse than it was since my last check up. The meds help.'

'I'm glad to hear it. But you have my number, and you know I mean it when I say you can call me day or night if anything feels wrong. I'm usually up all hours anyway, so you won't be waking me.'

'Thanks, doc.'

Luca turned to Malo's wife. 'I mean it, Lani.'

Lani nodded. 'I won't be scared to bother you, doctor. Now, who's hungry? I want to feed you all up.'

Mina and Luca exchanged a glance. 'Actually,' said Mina. 'Seeing all the delicious fish and vegetables for sale on the way here did give me an appetite.'

Luca smiled. 'I never say no to your cooking, Lani.'

'Wonderful. I already have something on the stove, so it won't be long.'

'While Lani is cooking, could I show you both around?' Malo asked Mina.

Mina wasn't sure she should accept, since the man needed two sticks to move. But Luca finished his lemonade and stood up. 'Lead on.'

They wandered slowly around the idyllic property. Mina was relieved to find that Malo seemed perfectly happy walking, as long as they went at a slow pace. He led them through a grassy garden filled with fruit trees. 'This is what I like to call my vineyard.'

They were far enough away from the roads that there wasn't any traffic noise. All Mina could hear were birds, bees and the distant sound of waves crashing on the rocks somewhere down the hill. Then Malo showed them his dahlia and rose garden, full to bursting with every colour possible.

'I'm so glad I came,' said Mina. 'This is beautiful.' The real Bora Bora was so much more breathtaking than the perfectly manicured lawns and landscaped beaches of the resort.

Suddenly all Mina could think about was living

somewhere like this. Maybe one day she could; there would be nothing stopping her. She couldn't think of anything better than having a huge, rambling garden like Malo's, and maybe even her own vineyard.

She got distracted by the sight of a huge bumblebee burrowing its way into a rose and, the next thing she knew, Luca was calling out her name in desperation. She darted around the rosebush, to find Luca just barely managing to hold up an unconscious Malo. The man's eyes had rolled back in his head and he was taking both himself and Luca to the ground. Mina rushed over to take some of Malo's weight, and together they slowly helped him onto the grass. 'What happened?' she asked.

'He's just having one of his turns, as he calls them,' Luca said calmly.

Mina took off her cardigan and folded it up then handed it to Luca. It was too small and thin to really make a decent cushion, but Luca wasn't wearing any layers he could take off, and it was better than nothing. Luca tucked it underneath Malo's head. 'He's epileptic. The seizure will just last a minute.'

Luca gently undid the top few buttons on Malo's shirt and rested a hand on his shoulder as he fitted. Just as Luca had predicted, the convulsions stopped in under a minute, and he and Mina carefully turned Malo on his side.

Mina gathered his two sticks from where they'd fallen, one in a rose bush and one on the grass, and brought them back to him. Malo's eyes fluttered open.

'How are you doing?' Luca asked.

'Oh.' He blinked as he came to, and sat up a little. 'I had a feeling I might get one today.'

Luca smiled softly. 'You know what I'm going to say, Malo.'

'I do, and the answer's still no. I won't be moving closer to the town. I'm happy up here, Luca.'

'I know.'

They sat with him on the ground for a few minutes until he felt better.

'Do you need anything?' asked Mina as they both helped him up.

'Just a nap.' Malo chuckled. 'Which I planned to have anyway after Lani's delicious beef stew.'

The stew was indeed delicious. Lani had made it with paprika and pineapple, and served it with coconut rice, and Mina couldn't stop thinking about it all the way home.

Now that it was Mina's second time on the horse, she felt a little more used to it. 'It's actually quite fun being this high up.'

'Maybe you can do this more often. I'm sure my friend will let you borrow Cardinal if you want to.'

'Let's not get ahead of ourselves. I'm just saying this was a lot of fun.'

Luca paused before answering. 'I'm glad.'

'Apart from poor Malo, of course,' Mina added, not wanting it to sound as if she'd enjoyed that element of the visit.

'I worry about him living all the way up here,' said Luca. 'He really needs a closer hospital.'

Luca sounded melancholy. He'd had a pretty rough afternoon, dragging Mina half way across the island with no warning, and looking after his friend suffering a seizure. Mina wished she could give him a hug. Then she realised she could. In fact, she couldn't be in a more perfect position to. She reached her arms around his waist and squeezed his rib cage tightly for a moment. 'He's lucky to have you.'

Luca patted her hand in thanks, and she drew back, wishing she could have stayed in that position all the way home, and wondering vaguely whether Lani had put some sort of alcohol in that stew or whether she was just feeling a little reckless.

But she really didn't feel as if she needed to leave a respectful gap between them any more. On balance, this little trip had been a success. She did feel a little closer to Luca now. There was less awkwardness between them, and she felt that she might even know him a little better. She certainly understood his reasons for wanting to build his hospital on a more personal level.

The horse made a misstep and stumbled as they reached a particularly steep incline, and Mina panicked, grabbing Luca tightly. But Cardinal righted himself almost immediately and carried on as if nothing had happened. Luca grabbed her hand, laughing. 'You're okay, Mina. Cardinal's a pro on this terrain.' He didn't let go of her hand for a long moment.

As Luca turned the horse back onto the main street towards the shops, Mina got an idea.

'Luca…'

'Yes?' he asked, already sounding dubious in response to her tone.

'Could we stop at the shops? I need to buy some of those vegetables. And maybe a pineapple.'

'You're still hungry after Lani's stew?'

'Not hungry, inspired. I know mine will pale into insignificance next to Lani's, but I'm going to need to try to recreate that stew some time this week.'

Luca laughed. 'I'll stop if you let me taste some when you make it.'

'Deal.'

Luca pointed the horse in the direction of the greengrocer, then came to a stop and let Mina jump down. 'I'll stay with Cardinal. Unless you need me?' he said.

'No, I'll be fine. Back in a minute.'

Mina passed the beautiful display of perfectly stacked lemons and limes with their leaves intact, and a barrel of giant oranges. Inside, the place smelled of bananas and mangos, and she took her time browsing the aisles of the small shop.

A few moments later, a man walked into the shop. Immediately Mina felt a twinge of uneasiness, and she subtly watched him out of the corner of her eye for a minute.

He looked at the mangoes, and picked one up as if to squeeze it, testing for ripeness. Maybe Mina was imagining things. He seemed to be acting pretty normally. Her instincts might be off, being in a new country. Infinitesimal things that subconsciously triggered thoughts of danger in England might be different here. She wasn't even in the same hemisphere any more, after all. So maybe she was off-balance. She couldn't blame herself for getting it wrong.

But she wasn't wrong.

While Mina was hidden from view behind a pillar, she heard the man speak in a low voice. 'Empty the cash register.'

She frowned as she recognised the English accent.

Her instincts had clearly been right after all. The woman behind the till gasped audibly and said something Mina couldn't understand.

Mina's pulse sped and her body tensed. How dared this man come in here and scare a lone woman just trying to work for a living? She tried to peer round the pillar without being spotted. If the man had no weapon, she was almost angry enough to confront him. And if he did have a weapon, at the very least she'd be able to give a decent description of the man.

He had short black hair and was wearing a light jacket and shorts. Was he a tourist? What kind of person went on holiday just to commit a robbery? Maybe he lived locally, or worked on one of the goods boats, or perhaps he was staying on one of the other islands.

The woman was moving around behind the counter and the man seemed to be getting impatient. 'Faster. Put it in the bag.' There was a small holdall on the counter, into which the woman was putting cash with shaking hands. Mina couldn't see any evidence of a weapon, and the man didn't look all that big. If she acted now, she'd have the element of surprise. She was pretty sure the man wasn't aware that she was even still in the shop, let alone watching it all from the back. If she didn't hurry, she'd be too late.

But suddenly someone rushed into the shop, as if from nowhere, and grabbed the man. Mina bolted out from behind the pillar to help and found Luca holding the man's arms behind his back, twisting his wrist to make him let go of the knife he was holding. Mina stared at the knife as it clattered to the tiled floor. It looked like a fruit knife, but it was still three inches of sharp steel that could have done some damage if she'd confronted him as she'd planned to.

Luca twisted the man's arm up behind him until he moaned in pain, then kicked at the man's ankles, forcing him down on his knees. He pushed him neatly down to the floor until he was lying on his stomach and then sat on his back, keeping him pinned to the floor. 'Mina?'

'Yes?' she asked, still slightly stunned and feeling as if sound was muffled and everything was happening in slow motion.

'Call the police.'

'Oh, of course.' She snapped out of it in a split second, and everything was sharp and loud again. She ran to the woman's side and reached one arm around her shoulders. 'Are you okay?'

The woman nodded, then shouted in Tahitian at the man on the floor. She grabbed a tin from a small display on her counter and threw it at him, hitting him squarely on the leg, causing him to grunt in pain.

Mina couldn't agree more, but tried to distract her. She didn't want her accidentally to hit Luca with anything. 'Do you have a phone?'

The woman stopped in her tracks, and grabbed a landline from underneath the counter. Mina was embarrassed to realise she didn't know the number for police in Bora Bora, or if they even had police on the island. The woman dialled an eight-digit number and got through to the local police. She spoke for a moment then hung up. 'They'll be here soon. They're only down the road.'

Once two police officers arrived and arrested the man, hauling him off to the island police station, Mina remembered to buy her fruit and vegetables. The shopkeeper let them have them for free, thanks to Luca's quick actions.

'I feel guilty,' said Mina as they left the shop. 'I got a free pineapple and I didn't even do anything.'

'I'm glad you didn't. I can do without treating you for stab wounds, thank you very much.'

Mina tucked her arm through Luca's for a moment as they walked. 'You were very brave. Where did you even come from?'

'I only came in because you were taking so long. Then I saw what was happening and took him by surprise. He didn't exactly plan the robbery very carefully. Anyone could have come in and caught him in the act.'

'I feel weirdly guilty, on behalf of my countrymen; I wish he hadn't been English.'

'I'm sure she won't hold it against you. She gave you free fruit.'

'That's true.'

'So, am I invited over when you make this stew?'

'Of course. You're the man of the moment. But you'll have to wait until tomorrow; even heroes can't eat two stews in one day.'

## CHAPTER TEN

Mina rushed across the walkway and headed up the hill towards Roman's office. Rachelle had called Mina to inform her that Roman wanted to meet for an informal chat about how she was settling in. As she approached the building next to Roman's, Mina was sure she could hear Luca talking to someone around the corner. She couldn't discern any words, but his tone was very affectionate. That didn't sound like Luca at all; he didn't talk like that to anyone.

Unless—of course; he must be talking to a woman. Mina's cheeks flushed with embarrassment, and a weird spike of jealousy lodged itself through her chest. But she was too close to the corner now. She had to go this way and, as she was about to turn it at any moment and see just who Luca was whispering so passionately to, there was nothing she could do about it. They would both have heard her footsteps growing closer on the wooden walkway. Nothing for it but to grin and bear the awkwardness of interrupting them in the middle of God knew what.

Mina reluctantly turned the corner to find Luca swaying back and forth on the walkway, holding a tiny, grey fluffy cat close to his face and murmuring things into its ear as he cuddled it.

Mina melted inside and put a hand over her mouth to stop herself making any noise. She couldn't interrupt this. Luca somehow hadn't noticed her yet and was still talking to the cat, who was purring like a motor. He was mostly speaking in French, but Mina distinctly heard the words 'fluffy' and 'cute'. She bit her lip, but couldn't stay quiet any longer. 'Who's your friend?' she asked quietly, so as not to startle the cat.

Luca whipped round, saw it was Mina and smiled ruefully. 'She's a stray; they live here and there under the villas. We feed them and put water down.'

'She's so cute.' Mina stepped closer and Luca held out the cat so she could tickle her under the chin. 'Can't you take her in?'

'I tried but they prefer living outside. It's not like it ever gets particularly cold here. They like food and some strokes, though.'

'Adorable.' Mina gazed at Luca. She'd never felt envious of a cat before. 'Well, I'd better get going.'

Luca nodded. 'Good luck.'

'Have fun with Rachelle,' said Mina.

'It would be more fun with you there,' Luca said. 'You know all they'll be doing is gossiping with each other about the resort staff and getting tipsy.'

Mina felt her cheeks grow hot and smiled, waving goodbye, and rushed to make her way up the path before he could notice his effect on her. Annoyingly, the meeting was scheduled at the same time as Rachelle and the rest of the health clinic were shutting up shop for a couple of hours to go and celebrate Rachelle's birthday. It was the only time they could all get away, while still being on call for emergencies, and Mina was devastated to be missing it. She still felt very much like the new girl, but they'd all been so welcoming to her that she already felt as if she was at home on the island.

Mina couldn't have done it without Rachelle in particular; the woman was a godsend. Mina planned to try to follow them on when this meeting finally ended, but she suspected she'd have missed most of it by then.

Mina waited inside Roman's huge office. She didn't feel comfortable sitting down in the empty room while she waited for Roman to turn up, so she stood near his large bookshelf, having a look along the shelves, checking out what sort of thing Roman read. Or perhaps, more accurately, which books Roman wanted people to think he read.

Rachelle had warned her that Roman would be late, as some sort of power play. Apparently, he did it as a matter of course to everyone with whom he had a meeting. Although why he should think he needed to demonstrate how much power he had over the resort nurse, she didn't know. Rich men were odd. She thought of Luca…some rich men. Typical of Roman to have his office in the only building on site that went higher than the ground floor. They were near the highest point on their part of the island and his huge windows looked out over everything; as if he were a proper Lord of the Manor.

The rumour, at least according to Rachelle, was that Roman didn't spend all that much time at the resort. That he spent weeks away all year round doing his thing, socialising with other wealthy people and hanging out on yachts. He described it as networking, apparently.

But, when he was here, he liked to at least act like he was across everything. Hence the meeting.

Mina checked the time and sighed. They'd probably have left by now. Luca, Rachelle and Dr Kai would be jumping on one of the little boats and jetting across the lagoon and out to the coral reefs. Rachelle wanted to dive down to the coral garden and see all the beautiful fish, and Luca had got sick of hearing her talk about it and booked her a boat.

It was a shame. Mina wasn't sure if everyone was planning to dive or just Rachelle, but she'd worn a bikini under her clothes today just in case. Not that she'd probably need it now, she thought sadly. Suddenly Roman's office window slid up, making her jump.

'Mina,' she heard a deep voice behind her.

'What the heck?' She ran over to the window, only to find Luca outside in a T-shirt and shorts.

'Luca! How are you out here? This is the second floor.'

'I climbed. Listen, you can't expect me to go on a trip with those people without you.'

He reached out to help her climb through the window, realised the angle was difficult and ended up grabbing her gently around the waist and lifting her easily out and on to the fire escape. She straightened her shirt and tried to recover from being lifted by his strong, gentle hands as if she weighed nothing.

'Those people are your trusted colleagues and friends,' Mina said, still trying to catch her breath.

'And they'll be a nightmare. I need someone normal if I'm to survive it.'

Mina laughed. 'What about the meeting?'

'You were here for it on time, he wasn't; that's his fault. Come on.' Luca held out a hand and waited until she took it before leading her down the steep fire-escape steps. They jogged across the grass away from Roman's office and towards the dock, Mina feeling like a giggling schoolgirl skipping class, and found their colleagues waiting in a small boat. They both cheered as she and Luca jumped on board.

The four of them plus the pilot of the boat sped off across the blue water. Rachelle produced a cake from her bag, and cut it into pieces carefully, holding the knife tight as the boat bumped over the water, and handed out one to each of them, including the pilot.

'Shall we sing Happy Birthday?' asked Mina.

'Absolutely not,' said Rachelle.

Mina had given Rachelle a plant for her desk earlier, since she had expected to miss this, but Luca presented Rachelle with a mini-hamper and a magnum of champagne. 'That's just for you. I brought some substandard rubbish for us to share on the boat.'

He took a bottle and some glasses out of the cupboard under the seats and poured each of them a glass of champagne. He poured Dr Kai a fresh orange juice, since he was on call, and they all toasted Rachelle.

The boat came to a stop once they reached the coral reefs, and the pilot, who was evidently also a diving instructor, got his equipment ready. Rachelle disappeared into the boat to change and came out wearing a wetsuit.

The pale pink of Luca's t-shirt made his arms look even more deliciously tanned. The sleeves clung to the muscles in his upper arms, bulging slightly as he helped

Rachelle climb over the edge of the boat on to the step. There wasn't much gear involved, just a mini-scuba tank that could put be put in the mouth and swum with. They were only going down a few metres, and the ocean was so clear that the people on the boat would see everything that was happening under water.

Mina leaned over the railing and watched Rachelle having the time of her life. It was easy to see the larger fish gliding around Rachelle, but tiny spots of colour darted around her too, impossible to focus on from this distance. She couldn't help but remember the sharks from the lagoon but, as if he could hear what she was thinking, Luca leaned on the railing next to her. 'Don't worry, there won't be any sharks. And if there are, the pilot knows how to see them off.'

They enjoyed the sun and champagne for a while, and when Rachelle came up her face was shining. She shook the water out of her hair and pulled herself up until she was sitting on the edge of the boat. 'Doesn't anyone else want a go? It's fantastic down there!'

'Not me,' said Dr Kai. 'I'm having a lovely time staying dry.'

'I don't have anything to change into on the boat,' said Luca.

'Mina?' Half of Mina wanted to get down there and join her, but no one else was getting in, and there was absolutely no way she was going to be the only one in a bikini while everyone else was fully clothed. Even Rachelle was covered neck to toe in neoprene.

Mina grinned. 'Maybe next time. Get back down there and see some fish.'

A slightly bigger boat had been slowly getting closer

for some time, and when it reached them a man onboard shouted a greeting to Luca, who got up and threw a rope over to them.

'That's my boat,' said Luca.

'It is?'

'Yeah.' Luca suddenly looked slightly uncomfortable. 'I was wondering if you'd like to come and see it.'

'We're going to head back soon,' Rachelle said, smiling.

'I'm on call anyway,' said Dr Kai.

'So we'll just take this boat back to the shore if you're going onboard Luca's boat,' continued Rachelle.

'Wonderful,' said Luca. 'Mina?'

Mina paused for a second. 'Of course. I'd love to see it.' Suddenly it felt as if everyone else was aware of a plan that she wasn't. Or maybe she was over-thinking it. Either way, she was suddenly very curious to see Luca's boat. She hadn't pictured him having one. It seemed too much of an obvious show of wealth for him. But she supposed, living in a place like this, surrounded by ocean in every direction, it was only natural to have one.

They climbed on board Luca's boat, and its pilot swapped on to the smaller boat, leaving Mina and Luca alone. They waved at Rachelle and Dr Kai until their boat was too far away to see.

'Rachelle's the best,' said Mina.

'Yes, she's the one who's really in charge. Couldn't do my job without her. Now, first of all,' Luca began. 'Do you want to take a dive? I could see your face while you were hanging over the rail watching Rachelle down there.'

Mina laughed, a little embarrassed to have been so seen. 'You caught me. I wouldn't mind, but only if you go in too.'

'I will if you will. I have swim shorts in my room.' He gestured over his shoulder with his hand. 'I also have something on board for you to wear, in case you didn't bring anything.'

'Oh, well, actually…' Mina stood and peeled off her top to reveal her aqua-green bikini.

She couldn't miss his gaze dropping quickly to take in her body before he smiled. 'You came prepared.'

'I did. Very kind of you to offer me a swimsuit, though. You shouldn't be so sweet, it could give a girl ideas.'

His eyes darkened and he stepped closer. 'What kind of ideas?'

Mina lost her breath. 'Romantic ones.'

He stepped closer still and took her hand in his. 'Is it working?' he asked quietly.

She gasped as he ran his fingers lightly all the way up her arm, then brushed a lock of hair off her forehead.

'I think it might be,' she breathed.

He glanced down at her lips, then took a breath and backed away. 'I'll just get changed.'

Mina sat down on the side of the boat, suffering slightly from emotional whiplash. She dangled her legs in the beautifully warm water, waiting for Luca to get back. Now that she was about to get in the water herself, she got a surge of nerves. She tried to remember what one was supposed to do in case of an attack. *If the bear is brown lie down, if the bear is black fight back, if you see a shark punch it on the nose*. Could that be right?

She scanned the surrounding clear water. No sharks in sight; it'd probably be fine.

This was the first bit of real down-time she'd had since she'd started her new job, sitting on her balcony after work notwithstanding, and it was the first time she'd had a chance to really reflect on how she felt now that she was on the island. The pace of life really was slower. She didn't feel on edge all the time. She was still busy, still working hard—just how she liked it—but there was true relaxation time too. And here, that time could apparently be spent with tiny colourful fish and Luca wearing shorts.

Luca returned, now dressed in even smaller shorts. Mina tried not to stare, but her breath was taken away by the acres of tanned skin and firm muscle. He made sure Mina knew how to use the scuba tank, just like the one Rachelle had used, and then he smiled kindly. 'You want to go down together?' he asked.

And have another pair of eyes to watch out for any approaching fish big enough to eat her? 'Yes, please.'

He nodded. 'Ready?'

She grinned and dove down under the water. The sea was only a couple of metres deep and she soon reached the sandy ocean floor. Bright, buttery shadows danced over the sand there constantly, reflecting the light on the surface. Rocks and corals were scattered beneath her in every direction as far as she could see. She momentarily had the strange feeling she was swimming inside a huge fish tank. She swam straight towards a group of tiny fish, so bright blue she could hardly believe they were real, and they scattered as soon as she reached them. She looked around for Luca, who was watching her and smiling. He threw her a thumbs-up and she did the same back. Fish of all sizes and shapes dashed across the red and lilac corals.

The water deepened to dark blue in the distance, and she peered into it curiously, but there was nothing sinister hiding in the shadows. Luca beckoned her over to a large coral and, when she reached close to him, he pointed out an octopus hiding underneath a ledge.

After a while they'd both had enough and they returned to the surface and swam back to the boat. They both clung to the edge of the boat for a moment, getting their breath back. Luca's arm was pressed against Mina's, and she could feel the heat from his body seeping into hers. Luca shook his head, water droplets scattering everywhere, including onto Mina's shoulders. 'You want to go down again, or are you done?'

His face really was stunning this close up. Water droplets ran down his temple from his hair to his jaw, and dripped on to his chest. His skin pebbled against the cool breeze. There was a pink flush on his cheeks from the exertion of swimming, and water droplets clung to his long black eyelashes. His eyes were a bright honey-brown in the sunlight.

Mina pulled her gaze away and cocked her head, thinking about his question, and trying to remember what he'd asked her. 'I'm done, for today. That was amazing, though. I can't believe all that life is down there the whole time, and we're up here, oblivious.'

Luca pulled himself out in one smooth movement, then leaned down to help Mina on to the boat. He came close and wrapped a white, fluffy towel around her shoulders. 'It's very beautiful,' he said. 'I thought on the way back I could take you to see something.'

'See what?'

'Do you remember that piece of land I circled?'

'For the hospital?'

'Yes, I wanted to take a better look at it in person, and you seem almost more enthusiastic about it than I am. You can be my second opinion.'

'I would love to see it.'

Dried off, and dressed again, Luca drove the boat back to the island and right round to the other side. He parked in a quiet dock and they stepped out.

'Unfortunately, the owner of this land is Roman,' Luca explained. 'So, I'm working on getting him to agree to sell it to me. I'm having to play the long game, as I'm sure you can imagine.'

'I can indeed.' No wonder Luca hadn't seemed as enthused as she'd thought he should. Roman's involvement would put a massive spanner in the works. She could just imagine him holding it over Luca endlessly.

'He's changed his mind several times already. He might sell, or he might lease it to me instead. He threatens not to sell every time I do something that annoys him. It's all quite tiresome and rather pathetic. I'm humouring him for now. But I'm getting very close to losing my patience.'

'I don't know why you put up with him.'

Luca shrugged. 'I have my reasons. He's not quite as bad as people think.'

'I just don't understand why you're willing to put

your whole life on hold for your brother when he treats you so badly.'

'Sometimes there are things that outsiders don't know.'

It hurt a little to be called an outsider, but she reached out a hand and touched Luca's arm. 'I know. I just don't think it's good for you.' She paused. 'All I can say is, you have a lot more patience than I do.'

'I know.'

He gave her the side-eye, and she laughed, slapping his arm with the back of her hand. 'Shut up.'

It was a short walk through overgrown grasses and trees, then out into a clearing. A deserted stretch of beach lay to their left, and to their right there was a slight incline. They climbed the hill and Luca stopped. 'This is it.'

Mina turned in a circle. It was a large, empty, flat patch of land that was in the middle of nowhere. No other buildings were visible through the trees that surrounded them, and down the hill all they could see was the empty beach and ocean. The only civilisation visible was the island on the other side of the lagoon. Mount Otemanu rose up behind them.

'What do you think?' asked Luca.

'It's beautiful. So hidden away!'

'Almost seems a shame to build something here.'

'I think a hospital's a pretty good reason, though. I guess you'd have to build a road too.'

'Only a short length. There's a road over the back of the hill it could meet up with, although it's hard to believe since it's so quiet.'

All Mina could hear were birds and the lapping waves

at the bottom of the slope. She was flattered that he was even asking her opinion. What did she know about building hospitals? 'Why do you care what I think anyway?'

Luca looked at her. 'You're a nurse; you've worked in hospitals.'

'Exactly. I don't know anything about construction, or business. Don't you have any fancy investment pals to ask for their opinions?'

He frowned in consternation. 'I guess all my fancy investment pals are busy.' He reached out a hand and playfully pulled her closer. 'I wanted to know what you thought.'

Oh. She smiled and looked down shyly. 'Well, I like it. I think it's perfect.' A breeze blew towards Mina from the sea and Mina smelled a sweet, fragrant scent. 'What is that delicious smell?'

Luca turned and pointed down the slope. 'Honeysuckle. It's actually pretty rare to find it here. We had it everywhere at home, where I grew up.'

'In France?'

'Just outside Paris. In the countryside. Hey, do you want to taste it?'

'The honeysuckle?' Mina asked, confused.

'Yes. It's delicious. Come with me, I'll show you.' Luca took Mina's hand and led her down the slope closer to the beach and over to the flowers. The bush was taller than Mina and covered in pretty yellow blooms. Luca reached a hand into the leaves and carefully picked out a flower, which he brought closer to Mina, pressed his thumb into the stem, then pulled out the style, revealing a drop of nectar. He placed the nectar on his tongue, closing his eyes briefly against the sun, and Mina held her breath as he swallowed. He smiled, then went back to pick another one for Mina.

He held out the bloom. 'Here, you try it.'

She took it with a slightly shaking hand and tried to copy what Luca had done. She cut the stem with her thumbnail and pulled on the style. The nectar dripped on to her finger and she quickly brought it to her mouth, so as not to lose it. The sweet taste blossomed on her tongue, and she laughed, surprised it was so delicious. Luca was already watching her intently when she met his gaze.

He reached out a hand and traced his fingertips softly across her cheek, touching a finger to her lips. She kissed it and it tasted sweet like the honeysuckle. Her heart started to race. This was finally happening.

He stepped in and pulled her closer, holding her tightly to his body as they sank down to the ground, hidden in the tall grasses. His kisses tasted exquisitely of nectar and of Luca.

'Speak to me,' she pleaded.

Luca smiled fondly, and whispered beautiful words she didn't understand as he gently unbuttoned her shirt.

She tugged him closer, relishing the soft moan he breathed into her ear. Mina battled with his shirt, desperate to feel the heat of his bare skin against hers, and when she finally pulled it free Luca moaned again, his fingers buried in Mina's hair. The heat between them had sweat forming in the small of her back, and Luca kissed the salt off Mina's skin. Mina gasped as Luca deepened the kiss, and licked possessively into her mouth. He rolled her, pressing her into the soft ground beneath, his weight a grounding presence keeping her safe and protected.

It was easy and familiar, the way their bodies fitted together. And their quiet, desperate noises as they finally made love again went unheard, obscured from the world in their secluded hideaway.

Afterwards, Mina never wanted to leave, and they stayed together wrapped in one another's arms, watching the ocean, and the sun setting. The skies streaked with pink and purple before Luca finally got to his feet and pulled her up to join him with a kiss.

# CHAPTER ELEVEN

Despite wanting to stay cocooned with Mina for ever, Luca couldn't ignore the need to eat any longer. Luca couldn't speak for Mina, but he'd certainly worked up an appetite. In Bora Bora there was never a big change in temperature in the transformation from day to night, but tonight there was a cool breeze coming in from the sea, and he noticed Mina shiver.

'Let's get you back to the boat. I have something warm you can put on.'

'How many women's clothes do you keep stored away on this boat? You've offered me a swimsuit and a top so far. What's next—do you have a ball gown squirrelled away?'

Luca snorted a laugh. 'I was offering you a wetsuit earlier, size small, which belongs to one of my little cousins, and I'm now offering you one of my hoodies.'

'Oh,' said Mina. 'Yes, I'd like to wear one of your hoodies, please.'

Luca didn't let go of Mina's hand all the way down the hill and through the trees back to where they'd moored the boat. He helped her jump on board, and then brought her inside while he grabbed his favourite old hoodie from a shelf in the sleeping quarters. 'Here, that should warm you up.'

'Thanks. It gets chilly on the water. I didn't realise. It's actually quite pleasant to feel cold for once this week.'

Luca smiled as she pulled it on over her head and then warmed her hands inside the sleeves. 'Are you missing home?' he asked.

She tilted her head in the way she did while she thought about things. 'Not really. Not yet. Do you ever miss Paris?'

'Sometimes. I'm not sure I ever really felt completely at home there. I've felt more myself since I came to Bora Bora.'

'That sounds nice.' Luca thought he could detect a wistful tone in Mina's voice. Luca pulled in the mooring rope, and started the boat. He sat on the bench seat behind the steering wheel and patted the seat beside him. Mina hopped up on to it and snuggled into his side. The water grew dark, as did the sky above it. Their destination across the lagoon was lit with hundreds of spots of light, and the few boats still out were lit orange in the dusk.

'Sometimes people come here for the sun and the palm trees, sometimes they come to start a new life and sometimes they're running away from something,' said Luca, wanting Mina to share more if she was up to it.

'And sometimes they come because their brother buys a hotel and they're too nice to let him be alone and self-destruct.'

*Touché.*' Luca smiled and wrapped his arm around her shoulders, pulling her even closer. 'Which one are you?' he asked.

'Can I be more than one?'

Luca nodded softly.

'I came here to start a new life, but the reason I wanted to do that was because I was running away.'

'From what?'

'From whom.'

'Ah.'

'It's weird. I haven't really thought about him since I got here. Before I left, I thought about his stupid face every day.'

'You missed him.'

'I didn't miss him; I was imagining creative new ways to end him.'

'Sounds good. I'll help.'

'Thank you.'

Luca looked down at her, and played with a lock of her curly red hair in his fingers. 'Seriously, who could ever want to hurt you?'

Mina met his eyes and smiled, then looked away. 'Apparently lots of people. Well, at least two.'

He stroked his thumb over her shoulder, hoping she'd continue with her story, but not wanting to force her. At least she'd stopped shivering now.

'At one point, I thought he might be the one, you know? Seems ridiculous now. But that's the trajectory I thought we were on. When I was a kid, I never fantasised about things like marriage and weddings, but when we first got together he started talking about marriage right from the start. I told him he was crazy; it was too soon. But after six months I started trying to find a way I could get used to the idea, because I thought marriage was important to him, and I did it. I figured out a way

I could be comfortable with all those traditional things like a white dress, speeches, dances…all that stuff I'd never even thought about. That was a big deal for me. And then…'

'Then?' he prompted gently.

'Then he slept with my best friend.'

'Damn,' he whispered.

'Quite.'

'I'm so sorry he did that. That's brutal.'

'Yeah. That's a good word for it.'

'How are things between you now?'

'He's dead to me now. I don't speak to him at all.'

'Sorry, I meant between you and your best friend.'

'Oh. We haven't spoken since. She did try, many times. But I couldn't ever call her back.'

'I'm sorry.'

'The worst part of it was we worked together, he and I. Actually, he was a doctor.'

She looked up at Luca and he nodded sympathetically. 'So, he took your future, your best friend and your job from you.'

She looked up at him and made eye contact, nodding. 'Yes, exactly. You get it.'

'I do get it.' Was he really going to talk about this? 'A similar thing happened to me.'

Apparently, he was. He'd never talked about this to anyone. He'd thought he never would. He'd thought he'd dealt with it perfectly well by himself. But maybe there was more to deal with after all. Or maybe he just wanted Mina to know she wasn't alone. That she wasn't stupid to have let this happen to her. That it wasn't her fault.

'I never thought I was going to marry my ex, but I

loved her, I think. My brother, he has a habit of trying to assert his dominance in certain ways. It's become a habit for him to, I guess, try and ruin any relationship I might find myself in. He says that he's doing it to prove that those women aren't good enough for me, that they don't deserve me. I think sometimes he even believes that's why he does it. I don't know. I can't even get that angry. He never actually sleeps with them, just flirts with them, then comes running to me with the evidence that they're willing to cheat.'

Luca steered carefully between some buoys, lit by the boat's lights. 'Anyway, most of the time they meant little to me so I didn't care. But my ex; I never thought she'd fall for it. I thought she was different, I thought I'd found something special. I was wrong.'

Mina shifted in her seat and held her arms out for a hug. And suddenly Luca wanted one more than anything in the world. He slowed their speed and kept an eye on the water ahead of the boat, but accepted her hug and wrapped his arms around her shoulders. She squeezed him tightly. 'I'm sorry they did that to you. You didn't deserve it,' she whispered.

He squeezed her back, shocked by how emotional he felt all of a sudden. He took in a deep breath and, when the hug ended, he put both hands on the wheel, gripping it tightly to keep himself grounded. Mina rubbed a hand over his forearm and then thankfully changed the subject.

'Just for the record, I think Roman's a prat.'

'Is that your way of reassuring me it won't happen with you?'

She laughed suddenly, as if he'd surprised the laugh

out of her. 'Yes. I mean, plus the fact that I'm nice and I wouldn't do that to someone.' She paused. 'But mainly because he's a prat.' She smiled, and Luca couldn't help but laugh.

'Seriously, though,' she continued. 'As agonising as it is, I'd almost rather be left than have to be the one leaving someone—at least someone I cared about. I can't imagine how terrible I would feel every time I thought about them. How do you live with that?'

When they reached shore, he moored the boat at the resort, then walked Mina to her villa door. She turned and stood in the doorway.

'Would you like to spend the night together or do you need some time to decompress?' Luca asked.

Mina paused for a moment. 'Both! I'm exhausted and I need a shower to wash the sea water off.'

Luca smiled. 'Understood.'

'But I'd love to see you after that.'

'Of course. Come over to mine whenever you're ready.'

'I'm dreading finding out what your flaws are, because right now I think you might be perfect,' Mina said.

Luca smiled. 'See you soon, *ma chérie.*'

He leaned forward for a kiss, expecting a quick peck, but was so thoroughly kissed he almost felt dizzy afterwards. She closed the door with a sweet smile, and he walked the short distance to his own door in a daze. He was still on a high from sleeping with Mina again. It had been every bit as mind-blowing as he remembered, and even better. Everything had been familiar and exciting at the same time. Was it really possible that he could have this? Everything with Mina felt so easy.

He knew exactly what his mother would have said about her. But Mina certainly wasn't interested in his family's money. She never mentioned the stuff, and he'd detected a definite disdain for people with too much of it, which he could understand entirely. He knew his fair share of fellow ultra-wealthy people and he was in full agreement with her on that.

She even understood exactly why he wanted to build his hospital, why he wanted to give something back to Bora Bora, when people like him had taken so much from it. He hadn't even had to explain that to her. Anyone else who'd got wind of his dream over the years had pointed out all the flaws at best and poured scorn over it at worst—his brother especially.

Speaking of his brother… As much as part of Luca wanted everyone to know what was happening between himself and Mina, he couldn't risk making it public. Not because he was worried that Mina would be seduced by Roman. However she did or didn't feel about Luca, he believed with all his heart that she thought Roman was a prat, as she'd succinctly put it. He knew perfectly well that Roman would try, though. And he didn't take rejection well. Luca wasn't going to risk Mina's happiness at work, or perhaps even the security of her job. When she rejected Roman, and when she most likely gave him a mouthful of righteous anger, Roman might well try to fire her, or worse, make her life so unbearable that she quit.

Roman had a long history of interfering in his love life. When they'd been younger, as soon as Luca had shown an interest in a woman, his brother had stepped in and tried to seduce her first. And, if that hadn't worked, he'd ruined it for Luca in some other way. Roman was no different now. If his brother spotted that Luca had any interest at all in Mina, she'd be out of a job and sent back to London within the week. And Luca couldn't do that to her.

Obviously, Luca would do whatever was necessary to stop that happening, or to protect Mina from his brother's idiocy. But it would be smarter to avoid it happening altogether. Roman was already under the impression that he and Mina didn't get on. Luca had been focusing so much on everything he found frustrating about Mina—all the better when one was in denial about how much you liked someone—he'd almost convinced himself, let alone Roman. All Luca had to do was let Roman continue to think he and Mina were clashing. Or at the very least avoiding each other.

It would be difficult, as Roman's personal assistant, Louie, always kept a close eye on the rest of the staff, always ready to send any gossip or discord back to the boss. Most of the staff were of the same opinion as Mina about Roman, if Luca was honest. But Louie was loyal to him. Without him, Roman would know little about the intimate ins and outs of the resort. He went from spending weeks at a time at the resort to disappearing for weeks at a time on his various work trips, which seemed to consist of socialising with all the wealthiest people he could find. Roman called it networking; their mother had affectionately called it hedonism.

It was amazing what the golden child could get away with, when the older twin had always been held to such exacting standards of behaviour: *look after your brother, keep him safe, don't waste your time socialising, work hard…* While Roman could do what he wanted.

Luca made himself a black coffee and poured sugar into it. That was his version of a night-time drink: to make it sweet. It always sent him off to sleep, anyhow. He didn't want to waste his night thinking of his family. He was still on a high from his afternoon and evening spent with Mina.

There was a soft knock at the door, and Luca beamed. He was already so excited to see Mina again. It felt like coming home.

# CHAPTER TWELVE

Mina woke up with a shaft of sunlight in her eyes. She moaned and rolled over on to her stomach, hiding her face in the pillow. The pillow that smelled delightfully of Luca. She popped up her head and peered around her. This wasn't her bedroom. She smiled as everything that had happened yesterday rushed back to her.

Last night after her shower she'd found herself more giggly and nervous than she'd been since her teens. She'd managed to get it under control before she made it next door to Luca's, but as soon as he'd opened the door and she'd laid eyes on his gorgeous face again her heart had started fluttering. His golden-brown eyes had grown dark and he'd pulled her close, crowding her against the door once it clicked shut behind her. And, as he'd buried his fingers in her hair and kissed her deeply, any remaining laughter had died in her throat as she'd been fully overwhelmed by his strong, capable hands.

But where was Luca now? Mina sat up, brushing her hair out of her face, and looked around properly. She'd only seen this room in the dark last night. His bedroom was similar to her own, but looked more lived-in and surprisingly homey. Green leafy plants lined the window sill, and there were several low bookshelves full of books.

'Luca?' she called out. *Nothing.*

There was no note on the bedside table or on Luca's pillow. She checked her phone: no message. Had he ghosted her in his own home? This was a new low, being abandoned in someone else's bedroom. She was being silly. Perhaps he'd had a call from Rachelle and had had to rush to see a patient. Maybe she should get going herself, and see what the emergency was.

'Hey, what are you doing up?' Luca swept in through the French doors to his bedroom, carrying a silver tray. 'I wanted to get back while you were still sleeping,' he murmured, placing the tray on the bedside table and sitting down gently beside her on the bed. The mattress dipped and tipped her gently towards him. He caught her deftly, leaned in and kissed her on the mouth.

'Where did you go?' Mina smiled and whispered into his lips, unable to look away from his face. He still looked adorably sleepy and heavy-eyed. Most unlike the perfectly groomed, well-dressed Luca he normally showed to the world.

'I got you breakfast in bed, *ma chérie.*'

Mina looked at the tray properly for the first time. It was piled high with small delicate pastries, a small cafetière, two cups and some fruit.

'I sneaked in early before anyone else and had the chef make you all the best things. Some of them aren't even on the menu.'

He fed her bites of the most delicious, melt-in-the-mouth chocolate pastry, and between each bite gave her a sweet kiss.

'I could get so used to this,' murmured Mina.

Luca's phone rang just as they shared the final delicacy, and his eyes met Mina's as he listened. 'It's Rachelle. We're needed.'

Luca and Mina rushed to one of the over-water villas on the jetty and met one of the staff from reception as they arrived. 'We had a call from the guest next door complaining about noise—said it sounds like someone's in pain—but they couldn't get in because the door's locked.' He rushed ahead of them with a key and opened the door. Luca rushed in. 'Hello? Does anyone need help?'

'Here!' shouted a woman from another room, followed by a groan of pain.

'I'm a doctor, can I come in?'

'Come in, for God's sake,' the voice shouted.

Luca pushed open the bedroom door to find the room dark, all the curtains drawn, and a woman lying on the bed. 'Ms Villiers?'

'I think it's contractions,' she bit out.

Mina ran to her side and knelt down. 'When is your due date?'

'Not for another month. This was supposed to be our last fun holiday before it was too late.'

'Is your partner on the resort?'

'He left early and went to Tahiti for the day to play stupid golf.' She threw the phone she was holding in the general direction of the bedside table and it fell on the floor. 'My phone has no signal.'

'We're going to contact him and try to get him back for you,' said Luca. 'But for now we're going to make sure you and the baby are both okay.'

Mina pulled on her exam gloves and checked the patient's temperature, pulse, blood pressure and respiration rate. 'Everything's looking good. I need to check your cervical dilation now, is that okay?'

The patient nodded, and a few moments later Mina stood, smiling, and pulled off her gloves.

'My husband's not going to make it back in time, is he?' the patient asked

Mina shook her head. 'I don't think so. The baby's well on its way.'

The patient grunted in pain, or perhaps frustration. 'I can't believe this is happening. The one day we've spent apart this whole holiday.'

'He'd only be in the way,' Luca said, winking kindly at the woman, who managed to laugh tiredly.

Between contractions, Luca pulled Mina into the kitchen area to have a quick whispered conversation. 'We have a little more monitoring equipment at the clinic. I'd like to get her there to give birth.'

Mina shook her head. 'There's no time. That baby's coming out any minute.'

Luca cursed under his breath.

'We can do this,' said Mina.

'I know we can. I'll arrange for a helicopter to take her and the baby to the hospital in Tahiti, then her partner can meet her there. When we eventually get hold of him.'

While Mina took care of the patient, Luca called Rachelle. 'The guest is pregnant; the baby's coming now.'

'Oh my goodness, how wonderful. Is everything okay?'

'It's a month premature, but Mina's on top of everything. The baby's father is playing golf in Tahiti. We need to get hold of him. There's only one golf course there, but if he's not at that one, try the course on Moorea, the island next door. Can you call them and get hold of Mr Villiers? Get them to send someone running all over the course in person if you have to. I need a helicopter to take her to Tahiti after she's given birth, and he's to meet her there.'

'Got it. I'll take care of everything. You concentrate on the baby.'

Luca smiled as he hung up. Rachelle really was the best. Once his hospital was up and running, he might have to poach her. But there'd be no need for helicopters, as they'd be able to take care of a premature birth right there on the island.

He paused, shocked. That was the first time he'd thought of the hospital as a foregone conclusion, rather than just a vague dream of the future. Mina's enthusiasm was really starting to have an effect on him.

Luca had never been happier to feel more like a spare part. He was present but stayed out of Mina's way and watched her take complete control. She helped the patient smoothly, quelling every worry, solving every problem. Watching her move around the room as she assisted the patient was almost like a dance. All Luca did was pass Mina anything she asked for, cool the patient down with a cold cloth on her forehead and regularly cross to the kitchen to pour the patient another glass of iced water.

Several contractions later, they didn't seem to be getting very far. Mina and Luca shared a look.

'Things aren't progressing as fast as I would have expected, so I'm going to take a closer look,' said Luca. He pulled on his gloves and examined the patient. 'Okay, I see the problem. The baby's in the occipito-lateral position,' Luca whispered to Mina.

'What the heck does that mean?' whimpered the patient.

'It means your baby is facing to one side,' said Mina. She rummaged through her medical bag and pulled out a pair of forceps.

'What's happening?'

'Everything's fine. But you're going to need an assisted delivery.'

'What does that mean?'

'Your baby is in a slightly awkward position, so we're going to use forceps to help guide them out. But try not to worry, this is quite common. Do we have your consent for the procedure?'

'Of course. Just do it.'

Luca gave the patient a local anaesthetic to numb the area, then picked up the forceps. 'I should do it,' he said to Mina.

'How many assisted deliveries have you performed using forceps?' Mina asked.

Luca hesitated. 'None since training.'

'I've done four in the last year. I'd like to do it.'

Luca nodded and handed her the forceps.

'I know these can look a little scary,' Mina said to the patient. 'But I promise they're safe, and I'm going to be very gentle with them.'

Mina carefully positioned the forceps around the baby's head. 'Okay, during your next contraction I want you to push, and at the same time I'm going to gently ease the baby out.'

As the next contraction hit, the patient started pushing, and Mina turned the forceps gently and slowly. The baby immediately started moving, and Luca heard Mina exhale in relief. 'Thank goodness,' she whispered. 'There won't be any need for an episiotomy.'

Labour was over in no time after that, and Mina handed the brand-new baby to Luca. Luca checked the baby's head: not a mark or bruise in sight. Mina was incredibly skilled.

'Is she okay?' the patient asked exhaustedly.

'She's perfect,' he said as he gently cleared the baby's mouth and nose with a suction bulb. The newborn was then able to take a breath and make a loud, clear cry. The patient laughed in relief and Luca couldn't help but join her.

'Beautiful, healthy lungs.' He cleaned the baby off quickly; he wanted to get her to her mother as swiftly as possible. He gently gave the baby to her mother and laid her on the mother's chest as Mina cut the cord. 'Congratulations,' said Luca. 'You did a wonderful job.'

Once the mother safely had her baby, Luca stepped back and put an arm around Mina's shoulders. 'So did you,' he whispered.

Mina leaned her head back and exhaled. 'That was a rush.'

Luca suddenly found himself imagining Mina holding her own baby—their baby. Good grief, where had that thought come from? He'd never once imagined what it would be like to have children with anyone. Only, the more he sat with the idea, the more he liked it. He had no idea if Mina was even interested in having kids some day, but it was certainly a wonderful thought to keep close to his heart.

Luca's phone rang and he listened for a moment, then hung up. 'The helicopter's ready, and Reception have brought a wheelchair to get you both there.' He smiled at the patient 'We've located your husband and he will be waiting for you at the hospital.'

They got the patient safely and quickly to the helicopter, and stood well back as it took off. Mina waved with one hand as it retreated off across the ocean towards Tahiti, her other hand still holding the patient's glass of water.

'That went well.' She smiled up at Luca, and he pulled her closer.

'That went spectacularly.' He couldn't help but kiss her.

Mina pulled away, smiling. 'I'm all gross. I need a shower.'

He took in her rumpled clothes, messy hair and red cheeks. 'You're perfect.'

As the helicopter finally disappeared into the distance, they turned round as one to walk back to the clinic. Only to find Roman's assistant, Louie, staring at them across the helipad. How much of that had he seen? If he'd seen the kiss, he was bound to go running straight to Roman. And if he reported back to Roman, then Mina could be in trouble.

He stepped away from her, making more space between them as subtly as he could. He crossed his arms in front of his body and glared down at her, she stared back in confusion until she noticed Roman's assistant for herself.

'Right, Dr Baudelaire. I'll get back to the clinic.'

'See that you do. And I expect you to be more on the ball in future,' he said sternly, loudly enough for Roman's assistant to hear. 'No more mistakes.'

'Yes, doctor.'

She gave him a conspiratorial smile, which he couldn't return, as Roman's assistant was still staring, then twirled round and stalked off. He forced himself not to watch her leave, and took a different route back to the clinic.

Luca managed to get back before Mina, and Rachelle met him at the door. 'I heard the helicopter leaving; did it all go well?'

'Mother and baby left us healthy and well. Thanks for finding the husband.'

'No problem. That's what I'm here for.' She paused. 'So, how was it?'

'How was what?'

'Last night! You and Mina.'

Luca had been planning to be subtle, and keep his cards close to his chest, but the smile that spread across his face from ear to ear as soon as Rachelle asked the question rather gave the game away. Rachelle giggled. 'That good, huh?'

Luca pressed a finger to his mouth and took a second to try and wipe the grin from his face. 'We had a lovely evening together, thank you for asking.' And an even lovelier morning. He remembered Mina's face as she'd enjoyed the treats he'd brought her from the chef. He'd known she'd love them and it made him so happy that she had.

'I bet you did. You know I'll just ask Mina what happened if you don't tell me.'

'That's your prerogative. I, on the other hand, have to get on with some work.'

Rachelle stared at him. 'You really like her, don't you?'

Luca stared back. He really hadn't meant to answer, but found he was suddenly speaking without his own permission. 'She feels right.' Luca rolled his eyes when Rachelle squealed in pleasure.

He went into his office, but left the door open. He put his bag by his desk, and started to get on with some work, trying to pretend to himself that he wasn't listening out for Mina to arrive. She was taking a while getting back. But perhaps she'd dashed home for a shower; she'd mentioned wanting one. He knew she'd probably use her own shower, but he liked the idea of her in his place, using his things. He loved the idea that he might smell his shampoo in her hair when she got back to work.

# CHAPTER THIRTEEN

'Luca?' Rachelle popped her head into Luca's office. 'Could I have a word?'

'Of course.' Luca blinked down at the paperwork he was holding; he was still daydreaming about Mina and wasn't even sure he could remember what he'd started reading. He dropped the paper on his desk and focused on Rachelle as she closed his office door and sat down opposite him. 'What's wrong?' he asked when she seemed to hesitate.

'It's no big deal. I just wondered if perhaps you might have made a mistake on this prescription.' She held out a page from his prescription pad and he grabbed it. It was for an elderly female patient he'd seen the day before who needed treatment for a bacterial skin infection. He read through what he'd written in his neat, printed handwriting, and his heart froze. 'Damn it.'

Rachelle grimaced.

He took a pen and scribbled out ferociously the word 'melperone, replacing it with 'meropenem'.

'It's an easy mistake,' Rachelle said soothingly.

'No, it isn't,' he snapped. It was a horrible mistake—potentially life threatening.

'We caught it in time,' she continued.

'You caught it,' he said curtly. A doctor couldn't make a mistake like that. One mistake could kill a patient.

Rachelle took the corrected prescription and opened his door.

'Rachelle.'

She paused and turned around. 'Thank you,' Luca said. 'Really. I'm sorry I snapped at you.'

'I know.'

Luca's heart sank as he sat back in his chair. Perhaps it was just as he'd feared. He'd really started to believe that he could have everything: his career, his grand hospital plans and maybe even love. But he'd been stupid. As soon as he got distracted by one thing, he failed at another. He'd been too busy daydreaming about Mina to pay attention to his work, and he could have killed someone…

Mina was hurrying back to the clinic, her hair still damp from the shower, when Roman approached her out of nowhere.

*Oh, here it comes*, thought Mina. Roman's assistant had seen them after all, and he'd run straight to Daddy and told on them. If Luca's predictions were right, Roman was going to flirt with her now. She steeled herself.

'Hello, Nurse Morgan.'

She nodded. 'Mr Baudelaire.'

'We never got a chance to have our catch-up.'

He was right. Luca had stolen her away from his office to celebrate Rachelle's birthday on the boat, and they'd never rescheduled.

'How about we remedy that now?' he asked smoothly.

Mina felt trapped, but agreed. 'Why not?' Better to get it over with.

'Walk with me,' said Roman.

They walked the path along the edge of the beach, under the swaying palm trees. It was strange to be with someone who looked so much like Luca, who even spoke with the same beautiful accent, but who exuded such a different aura. In every way that Luca was warm and responsive, Roman was cold and sharp.

'How are you enjoying the job so far?' he asked.

'I love it. You have a beautiful resort, and the clinic is wonderful.'

'And how are you finding your work colleagues?'

'They're wonderful too.'

He nodded thoughtfully. 'That's good. You know, if you encounter any problems you can come to me in full confidence.'

Mina looked over at him, but he was wearing sunglasses and appeared to be watching the ocean as they walked.

'Problems?' she asked.

He shrugged one shoulder. 'I don't want to talk out of turn, but I will just say that my brother... He can have a way of getting too close to people.'

Mina hummed a noncommittal response.

'I am not one to talk behind his back,' Roman said, and Mina forced herself not to roll her eyes. 'But,' he continued, 'He has many women in his past. I would not want you to become just another name on his list, used and discarded.'

Mina frowned. This man was unbelievable. 'I can assure you nothing untoward has happened on Dr Baudelaire's part.'

'Of course, you wouldn't be just another name,' Roman said as though Mina hadn't spoken. 'You are a little different from the many women that came before you. He normally goes for models, actresses or successful businesswomen. You are none of those things.'

*Right.* This was where he was going with this. He wasn't going to flirt with her and try to steal her from Luca. He was going to try and target her insecurities and try to see her off in a different way. And the most frustrating part of it was, even though she knew exactly what he was doing, something about what he said was getting under her skin. She could feel his words working, just a little.

A cold stream of insecurity ran through her heart. She and Luca really didn't have much in common. He had probably dated models and actresses: beautiful, rich, powerful women; women nothing like her.

He'd said he only ever dated women once. He'd only tried one serious relationship. Of all the other women he'd dated, none of them had tempted him into staying with them. What on earth made her any different? What could be so special about her, of all people, that would inspire him to stay?

'He's a doctor, of course, and women love that. He's very wealthy. And without wanting to sound egotistical—' Roman gestured to his own face '—he's a very attractive man. He's used to being able to have anyone.'

Mina raised an eyebrow and said nothing.

'But that shouldn't extend to colleagues. I like to

keep things professional at the resort. Do you understand?'

Roman might be full of hot air—he might be lying about Luca's past, and he was certainly rude and passive aggressive—but he did have a point. It wasn't uncommon for bosses to discourage workplace relationships. And, if that was the deal here, then Mina could get fired or at least relocated for being with Luca. And she did need this job. She hadn't been lying to Roman; she loved the job, loved the resort and loved her new life here. She couldn't wreck this—not again, not over a man. She'd somehow forgotten that, getting caught up in the whirlwind of falling for Luca.

'Absolutely,' said Mina. 'I understand completely.'

They parted as the path ended and turned into the road. Roman stepped into a waiting black car, and Mina continued on her way to work, feeling unmoored. Should she really risk her job like this? Roman had made it clear he knew or seriously suspected something was going on between them. And what was she risking it for? Could she really hold Luca's interest for much longer? Everyone else had always lost interest and betrayed her. Why would Luca be any different?

Luca appeared at the coffee machine as Mina was making one. 'Would you like a coffee?' she asked.

'Black. Thank you.'

Mina pasted a much more cheerful smile than came naturally, but there was a strange, stilted silence between them.

'Sorry about earlier,' Luca said. 'At the helipad. I didn't want Roman's assistant to get the wrong idea.'

'You mean the right idea.'

Luca smiled. 'I hope I didn't confuse you with the fake argument.'

'No, I understood what you were doing as soon as I spotted him. You were lucky I didn't go full soap-opera; you could have got the remainder of the patient's glass of water thrown in your face.'

He smiled again. 'Do you think it worked?'

Mina scratched her nose and tucked her hair behind her ear. She didn't want to lie to Luca, but she also didn't want to make him angry with his brother, or cause any fallout between them. She wanted to be sensible, and think about her job. Roman had made her feel uneasy about a lot of things. Her head was filled with doubts, and she didn't feel ready to talk about any of them yet.

'We can only hope.'

# CHAPTER FOURTEEN

That night Luca took Mina on a date they'd already arranged, an evening hike part-way up Mount Otemanu.

The first time they'd watched the sunset together was before they'd even admitted how they felt about one another. It already seemed so long ago. And Luca could feel the shift between them now. Things had changed and he wasn't sure how, or whether, they were rectifiable.

'Aren't we going to the top?' Mina asked.

'I thought you wanted a gentle hike. It would take six hours to reach the summit.'

'Wow, it's bigger than I thought. Part-way up is good.'

They hiked up the hill through long grasses and bracken. There was a path to follow, but much of it was overgrown and a battle to get through. Luca reached back to help pull Mina up through the steepest parts.

They walked for half an hour, and eventually reached the spot Luca was aiming for. It was high enough to have stunning views of the whole island and the ocean beyond. They sat down in the clearing, leaning their backs against a smooth rock, and shared the water and snacks that Luca had packed.

Some of the stars were already out in the inky sky above them, and the clouds on the horizon were orange and red. As the sun sank further towards the sea the twinkling lights of the resorts turned on one by one, and tiny dots of light started to appear on every boat.

'There's something I have to tell you,' said Mina.

Luca's heart felt as if it had stopped for a moment.

'I spoke to Roman.'

Luca had flashbacks of all the other women he'd been with over the years being lured away by Roman, especially his ex. He felt a cold sense of acceptance wash over him. If it was happening again, he'd deal with it. 'Did he try to seduce you?' *And did he succeed?* he managed not to add.

'No, he actually didn't.'

Luca frowned. It almost sounded as if Mina was trying to defend Roman.

'So what did he say?'

Mina sighed. 'He made some unexpectedly good points.'

Luca's head snapped up to look at Mina. 'Excuse me if I find that less than believable.'

'I don't know. He just made me think. You know what's happened to me, you know what's happened in my past. I never wanted to meet someone here, Luca. I came here dead set on giving this job everything, on finding a new life. And now, the exact thing I wanted to avoid, I've done. I've fallen for a doctor. A doctor who could ruin everything I've worked so hard for. If this all went wrong again, I don't think I could survive that a second time.'

Roman was clever, Luca would give him that. Instead of taking the route of trying to seduce her, he'd realised that wouldn't work with Mina, and he'd manipulated her in a different way.

'Why would I ruin anything? I would never hurt you.'

'You can't say that, Luca. No one thinks they'll hurt you until they do.'

She looked down at her hands and took a deep breath. 'And I know that, because—'

'Wait. Don't.'

He knew exactly what Mina was about to do. She was about to break up with him, and for good reason. He knew he wasn't good enough for her, he brought too much baggage with him, but he remembered what Mina had said to him before: that she couldn't imagine the guilt of having to hurt someone she cared about by leaving them. And he knew she cared about him; that was his cross to bear. He had to break up with her first and save her the guilt.

And she was right, anyway. There were so many reasons he was bad for Mina. If things went badly between them, she could lose her job, her new home, her whole life. He would never send her away, or make things difficult for her, but she might not want to stick around either way. She might feel forced to leave.

'If I'm nothing else,' he said carefully, 'I'm a Baudelaire man. And Baudelaire men have a fatal flaw.'

'I know you think that, but it's not true.'

Luca took her hand. 'Please let me say this,' he said gently.

She nodded, and gripped his fingers in hers.

'I know how it sounds, but it goes back generations. We're obsessive; we can only pursue one thing at the expense of all others. Roman's is money. My father's was his music.'

'And what's yours?' she asked, looking as if she didn't want to hear the answer.

It was kinder to set her free before she fell for him any more deeply, he reminded himself. 'If I can only do one thing with my life,' he started. 'I have to choose building my hospital.'

'What are you saying?' Mina frowned, moving away from him, and Luca felt part of his heart break as she pulled her hand away. What if she never touched him again? What if this was the very last time? He almost crumbled and almost took it back. But he steeled himself, took a deep breath and forced himself to meet her eyes.

'I don't have time for a relationship.'

He watched as shock crossed her face momentarily, then a wall came down as her chin tilted up. 'I see,' she said quietly.

*No, you don't*, he thought. Luca almost changed his mind. He almost reached out for her. He couldn't bear the thought of never holding her warm hands in his again. But it was better this way. He was no good for her.

Mina stood. 'I think you've said everything that needs to be said.'

Luca stood too, but she held up a hand, as if to keep him away. 'I'd like to walk back alone. Please stay here.'

Luca nodded. He felt his heart fall to pieces as she walked away from him. He waited until she was out of sight, then followed her down the mountain at a distance, making sure he was far back enough that she wouldn't see him, but close enough to know she wasn't in any trouble.

She knew the idiot was behind her. He wasn't anywhere near as subtle as he thought he was.

She vibrated with anger as she picked her way down

the mountain. She felt stupid and humiliated. All she'd wanted to do was discuss things with him, share her fears about their relationship, maybe get some reassurance and move forward together. But that was all irrelevant now. Apparently, he'd only taken her on a hike up the mountain to break up with her somewhere pretty. He hadn't even wanted to talk about it; he certainly hadn't been interested in fighting for their relationship. He didn't even seem angry at his brother for interfering.

She should have known better than to trust someone. Luca had chosen his hospital over her. He'd betrayed her, just as everyone she'd ever cared about had done.

## CHAPTER FIFTEEN

RACHELLE KNOCKED ON Luca's office door and, although he didn't tell her to come in or even turn around, he could see her in the reflection of the window, and she didn't hesitate to walk right in.

'You've started shutting your office door again.'

'And yet it's not keeping anyone out.'

'You're in very early,' Rachelle said, ignoring him.

Luca would rather be at work than at home, wondering what Mina was doing only a few feet away in her own villa. He'd heard her go out onto her balcony just before sunrise that morning, and he couldn't cope with knowing she was right there. So he'd left, quietly, and walked to the clinic, ignoring the fact that, once they got to work, she would be just as close, just in a different location. But getting to work so early at least gave him an hour or so of separation.

His hospital architectural plans were laid out on his desk. It was a bigger, more detailed plan now, incorporating some of Mina's clever suggestions and ideas. He should be happy, excited that now he could throw all of himself into making concrete plans to build his hospital. That was what all this had been for. But he just felt empty.

He tired of looking at them and turned to look out at the island through the window, staring at Mount Otemanu, staring at the place where it had happened—where he'd lost Mina. What was the point of it all without Mina by his side?

She was gone for good now. Now he could never tell her he loved her. And what a time to realise that he did, when it was too late to say it.

Rachelle cleared her throat, startling Luca.

'Sorry, I forgot you were there.'

'None taken,' she said dryly, coaxing a rueful smile from Luca.

'What can I do for you?' Luca asked, turning to face her.

'I just wanted to see if you were all right.'

He broke eye contact. Somehow, as usual, Rachelle seemed to know exactly what was going on even though he certainly hadn't told her, and the genuine sympathy in her eyes was too difficult to see. 'Any calls?'

'Not yet. And no appointments until later this morning.'

Great, nothing to distract himself. He might as well have stayed at home, obsessing about what Mina was doing on the other side of the wall.

'You've done something stupid, haven't you?'

'I beg your pardon?' he asked, confused.

'You know, I've never in my life seen you as happy as you've been since Mina came here.'

Luca turned back to the window. The sun had risen further now, and it was almost full daylight, but things were still quiet out there. Most of the guests would still be sleeping, but the staff were out, making the most of the remaining cool air and starting to make their way to their posts.

'Don't ignore me, Luca.'

'I'm listening.'

'Hmm. Have you done something stupid?'

'No. I did the sensible thing.'

'The sensible thing would be marrying that girl the first chance you get.'

'Rachelle…'

'I'm serious. What has that cursed brother of yours done now?'

Luca whirled round, suddenly keen to protect Mina's reputation and defend her character. 'He hasn't done *that*.'

'I know he hasn't, Luca. Mina would never fall for that sort of foolishness, or treat you so horribly.'

He nodded, glad to know they were on the same page about that.

'But that doesn't mean Roman hasn't done something equally underhanded. He's like a child that can't stand to see someone else with a new toy. He has to take it or destroy it.'

Luca snorted humourlessly. He hadn't realised it was so obvious to everyone else what Roman was like.

'So, what's he done?'

'Nothing, really. Just got inside her head. Magnified her own insecurities. Made her think we're not right for each other.'

'I would have thought she was too clever for that.'

'It's not really about her. I'm the one at fault.'

'How's that?'

'I ended things.'

'What on earth for?'

He'd asked himself the same question. Suddenly all the reasons he'd been so convinced by before seemed utterly ridiculous. Rachelle was right—he'd done all this to himself.

'Luca, do you know what people want in a partner?' Rachelle asked.

Various words ran through his head, possible answers as to what someone could want from him. Security? Safety? Companionship? 'I have absolutely no idea.'

'They want someone who loves them so much that they'll fight to keep them.'

*Oh.*

'That's all. It's as simple as that. Have you fought to keep her, Luca?'

*No.* Luca frowned. No, he hadn't. He'd let her go at the first sign of trouble like some sort of martyr. He'd ended it so that she didn't have to. He'd convinced himself she was better off without him, that things might not work out between them, so it was better and easier just not to try.

Baudelaire men might not be able to have it all. But, if Luca wanted it enough, he could change what being a Baudelaire man meant. And he couldn't want Mina more. Maybe he'd be the first Baudelaire man to try.

# CHAPTER SIXTEEN

ROMAN SWANNED INTO Luca's office without knocking, and Rachelle left, but not before she'd levelled a pointed look at Luca. 'Fix this.'

Luca nodded.

'Fix what?' Roman asked.

'What do you want, Roman? I'm busy.'

'I'm having a little get-together for some investors. I'd really like to impress them, so I'm taking out the largest yacht tonight and showing them a good time.'

'The one that's in the boat yard right now, getting maintenance?'

'It was finished yesterday, it's good as new.'

'How many investors?'

'Around twenty.'

'That yacht only allows twelve guests,' Luca said.

'I'm sure a thirty-million-dollar yacht can handle one or two extra billionaires.'

'It's illegal, Roman.'

'Who's going to know?'

'Everyone on the yacht who can count. Those rules are there for a reason. There are only enough life jackets for twelve guests and eight crew.'

'Who says the crew get any?'

Luca sighed at Roman's attempt to be humorous. 'I won't allow you to endanger peoples' lives.'

'What do you care?'

'It's literally my job to keep people safe.'

Roman rolled his eyes. 'Always so full of your own importance.' Roman gave him a glare, then left to make a phone call and returned, looking even more smug than usual. 'I spoke to the captain; he's allowing more guests.'

Luca narrowed his eyes. 'Under what circumstances?'

'We can have anything up to fifty guests if we stay in port.'

Luca shrugged. If the captain was fine with it, then Luca was too.

'One more thing,' said Roman, just as Luca was about to usher him out of the room. 'I need a favour.'

'I'm in no mood to do you any favours right now.'

'I need my favourite little doctor and nurse team on the yacht with me to impress the investors.'

'Not happening. You've done your best to cause a rift between us and now you expect us to fawn over your friends for you?'

'Come on, surely you feel better now everything's more clear and professional between you and little nurse Mina?'

Luca slammed his hand on the desk and loomed over Roman. 'I don't even want to hear her name out of your mouth.'

Roman smiled, but stopped. 'I need you on the yacht, regardless.'

'The answer's no, Roman.'

'We'll see.'

\* \* \*

The rest of the day was busy with wall-to-wall call outs. Unfortunately, none of them were jobs Luca and Mina could attend together. Luca was busy with a sprained ankle, an allergic reaction to a jellyfish sting and a coral rash. Whereas Mina was kept occupied by a string of cold and flu symptoms in children that had seemingly spread like wildfire after a kids' mini-golf play day.

Luca didn't even get to speak to Mina, or see her more than in passing all day. Whenever they were in the same building, Mina refused even to look his way. Which was entirely understandable, if utterly heart destroying.

That night, at dusk, Luca knocked on Mina's door, but got no response, so he parked himself on his balcony with a drink and a book and waited patiently for her to come home. They needed to talk. And, if she was even slightly open to letting him anywhere near her, there were things he needed to say to her.

A firework exploding over the water made him jump and he frowned at the gold and red sparkles as they slowly glittered back down. He peered through the trees and saw another firework shoot up into the evening sky; it seemed to be coming from the location of a large white yacht in the centre of the lagoon.

'Is that Roman's yacht?' he whispered to himself in disbelief.

He had agreed to keep it in port. And there looked to be twice as many people on there than there should be. Luca stood up, took a quick video of the yacht on his phone, then swiftly played it back and zoomed in. He scanned the deck. There was clearly more than the twenty guests Roman had stated. It looked more like forty people. That was dangerously over-capacity. What was that idiot thinking?

He called his brother's mobile as he started making his way down to the dock by way of the clinic. But, as expected, Roman didn't pick up. Luca fired off a quick angry message, and shoved his phone in his pocket.

And that was when the fireworks started in earnest. Luca glared through the trees as he jogged to the dock. Roman had got someone to rig up some kind of raft that was being pulled behind the yacht, from where the fireworks were being set off. Luca sighed. He bet Roman hadn't got any health and safety checks done on that before implementing it either. He'd probably come up with it an hour ago and paid someone whatever it took to set it up—that was his usual MO.

Luca reached the health clinic just in time to catch Rachelle closing up the office. 'Can I use your phone to call Roman? I doubt he'll answer you either, but it's worth a try.'

'Are you telling him about that party boat?'

Now that Luca was on the edge of the lagoon, the boat was much louder. They were playing loud music, and the guests were shouting and laughing. Somehow Roman's billionaire investors transformed into a college party once they were given champagne and fireworks.

'He *is* the party boat,' Luca said wryly.

'Oh my.'

They both leaned on the railings and gazed out at the boat all lit up in the middle of the water. Luca tried Roman on Rachelle's phone, fruitlessly. As he hung up, he wondered where Mina was. She clearly wasn't here at the clinic and he hadn't passed her on the way down.

Suddenly there was a series of loud popping sounds. Luca and Rachelle both instinctively ducked then stared out at the yacht. Too many fireworks were going off at once, and they were exploding in all directions, some twisting off randomly across the water, then some shooting off horizontally, one directly at the yacht.

Luca swore as he heard screams across the still water, and within seconds flames became visible through the lower windows of the yacht.

'Rachelle, call the fire crew, alert the helicopter pilots that we might need emergency trips to the hospital in Tahiti and call in Mina and Dr Kai.'

Rachelle ran back to unlock the clinic door and rushed inside to use the phones. By the time Luca turned back, the flames on the yacht had already grown. The raft was on fire, and fireworks were still randomly shooting off, whistling into the night sky. Luca tilted his head and stared hard at the yacht. It was difficult to see in the dark through the smoke and flames, but he was sure the yacht had started listing to one side.

The hull must have been breached somehow by stray fireworks. Luca swore again and ran to the clinic door; he leaned inside, until he spotted Rachelle already on the phone. 'We need as many boats out there as possible to pick up passengers from the water!' he shouted. 'God knows how many casualties there might be. I think the yacht's going down.' As soon as she answered in the affirmative, Luca took off down to the dock.

He grabbed any staff he could find on the way, and found several standing and watching already at the water's edge. Luca joined the staff already jumping into boats to go out and help.

Luca grabbed a small resort speedboat and sped off towards the yacht. Now that he was on the water, he could see people huddled up at one end of the yacht, and watched as some of them jumped into the water. None of them seemed to be wearing life jackets. Luca slammed his fist on to the control panel. Damn Roman. This was exactly why Luca had told him not to overload the boat, and why the captain had ordered them to stay in port. There were only a certain number of lifejackets on there.

His phone buzzed in his pocket—finally. Maybe it was Roman. He grabbed it and found Rachelle on the other end. 'Luca, Mina's on the yacht.'

His blood ran cold as he came to a stop near the boat. Roman must have convinced Mina to go alone without him. He stared desperately at the people on the boat, and the people in the water, trying to spot Mina's face, or anyone with red hair. Flames were now reaching up twenty feet in the air, and smoke was billowing up from the other side. The yacht was seriously listing now. Luca had to get on board. He directed his boat as close as he could, and shouted to get one of the crew member's attention. 'Tie me up!'

The crew member nodded and caught Luca's mooring line. Now tethered to the yacht, Luca grabbed the five life jackets from the speedboat and threw them up on to the deck, then ran up the ladder on the side of the yacht. He quickly helped hand out the life jackets to the nearest passengers, and told the crew member to get them and anyone else he could down on to the speedboat. 'Take it back to land then return for more people if you can.' The crew member nodded and turned to go, but Luca grabbed his arm.

'Where's Mina Morgan, the nurse?'

'I think she was on the other side, near the fire.'

Luca's heart dropped and he climbed over fallen tables and chairs, forcing his way to the other side of the boat. Everything was at an angle, and moving anywhere without losing his footing and shooting straight into the water was almost impossible.

His heart soared as he spotted Mina, alive, well and soaking wet. She was braced up against an open door, helping the people inside the yacht to climb out on to the deck and escape.

'Mina!' Luca grabbed her slippery wet arm. 'We're going, now.'

'No, these people need help!' she shouted over the noise of the flames.

Luca cursed. He checked the fire. It hadn't quite reached them yet, although he could feel the heat on his skin. At least the fireworks had stopped exploding. Luca helped pull several people out of the yacht with Mina, then Mina gasped and pointed to the last person in the room. It was Roman—and he was lying unconscious under a table that had slid to the back of the room.

'Stay here,' Luca said to Mina. 'I'll go in and get him.'

He climbed into the room and slid closer to Roman. The yacht was listing much more deeply now, and the floor felt as if it was at a 45-degree angle. His heartbeat quickened as he got closer. Roman wasn't moving at all. 'Roman?'

Luca took a deep breath and reached out to check Roman's pulse. As much as he hated his twin right now, he couldn't even bear to think of how it would feel to lose him. They'd been friends once, even if it was so far back he could barely remember it. He felt a faint pulse and exhaled in relief.

'He's alive,' he called back to Mina. Now he just had to get him out of here.

The yacht creaked loudly around them, and Mina told him to hurry. The last thing they needed was for the yacht to tip over fully into the water and start sinking while they were trapped onboard. There was blood on Roman's face, which Luca could see was coming from a gash on his temple. He must have fallen in the rush to get out, or something had fallen on his head. Either way, he just had to hope that was his only injury. There was no time to be careful moving him. Luca reached down, grabbed his brother under each arm and pulled as hard as he could. It was unnervingly like lifting a dead weight, and he pulled himself and Roman across the floor, up towards Mina.

As soon as she could reach, she grabbed Roman's shoulders, and together, they managed to yank him up and out of the doorway on to the deck, where Roman suddenly opened his eyes and started groaning. 'Of course, you wait to wake up until we've done all the hard work,' Luca mumbled.

Luca tried to pull Roman's eyes open so he could take a look at his pupils, but Roman slapped his hands away. 'Get off me.'

Luca couldn't help but be relieved to hear Roman's voice but now was not the time to talk. 'We have to get off this boat.'

One on each side, Luca and Mina helped Roman limp along the deck past the scorchingly hot flames to find the railing. There was one boat still floating near the yacht; all the others had moved back away from the fire. Luca sent Roman down the ladder first, helped on to the boat by staff members, then Mina went down. 'Is everyone accounted for?' Luca yelled to the boat below.

'We think we have everyone,' the crew member shouted back.

Luca took one more look around him. He couldn't see anything but overturned furniture, broken champagne bottles, dropped handbags and crackling flames. He climbed down the ladder, the last one off the yacht, and stepped onboard, pulling himself into Mina's arms.

She held him for a moment as they drew away from the yacht. The only positive was that it was listing towards the fire. If it went over, at least the flames might go out. They watched it slowly capsize, tipping into the water, then start to sink. Its descent was shockingly rapid. In moments the entire thing disappeared below the water; the only evidence that it had existed was the bubbles bursting on the surface.

Still in shock, both Luca and Mina turned away and checked over the other passengers. Most were soaking wet, some with various injuries that needed to be seen to. Back on the dock, the scene was chaotic. Dozens of passengers sat around in various states of shock, bedraggled. Many had been treated by first aiders, but all needed to be properly checked over by Luca and Mina.

'Mina, your arm.' Mina had a shallow cut on her forearm.

'It's nothing, I can't even feel it.'

'Come here,' Luca said gently. She might not be able to feel it now, with the adrenaline in her bloodstream and the cold of the water numbing her body, but she'd feel it soon. He grabbed a first-aid kit and cleaned off the cut. Then he bandaged it up, securing it neatly, and lifted her arm to his lips. He kissed it gently.

'Thank you,' she whispered.

'Well, isn't this romantic?'

Roman. Luca stood swiftly, anger taking over, and grabbed him. 'You'd better have an exact passenger list with the number of people who were on board that yacht so we can check if we've pulled every one of them from this water.'

'I do, I do. There are eight crew and thirty-three guests.'

Luca let him go. 'I'll inform the fire crew. Get yourself seen by one of the first-aiders. The coast guard will have to contain and clean up any fuel that spilled into the water from that yacht; you'd better hope no wildlife are harmed because of your actions.'

'I've got bigger problems than wildlife.'

'I bet you have. I'm sure all your investors are really impressed, you jackass.' Luca pushed him away, and Roman pushed him back.

'Roman,' Mina said sharply, stopping them in their tracks. 'Someone's been teaching me recently to keep my mouth shut, hold my tongue and stop speaking with no filter. But that time has well and truly passed. You are a real piece of work. Luca just saved your damn life. You would be dead if it weren't for him, probably several times over. You'd certainly still be trapped inside that yacht on the bottom of the lagoon right now if he hadn't bodily hauled you out single-handed. He loves you, despite everything, despite how cruel you are to him. He rises above it over and over again, and you haven't even thanked him.'

'He's only here because of a promise he made years ago and has probably regretted ever since. Thank him for what?'

'For saving your life, not ten minutes ago.'

Roman looked abashed for a moment, but then seemed to remember himself. 'I don't know who you think you are, but just because you're cosying up to my brother doesn't mean you can talk to a superior like this. I can have you on a plane back to London within hours.'

'If telling the truth gets me fired, so be it. Or maybe you could just listen for once and be man enough to do something about it.'

Roman sneered at her and turned to Luca. 'Are you going to let her talk to me like this? Our mother would have been disappointed in you, Luca—choosing someone like this over family.'

Luca held his hands up; he'd finally had enough. 'I can't do this any more.' He stepped closer to Roman and, despite his injury, hauled him away. 'I beat you to a pulp once before and, damn it, I will do it again.'

'I didn't touch your girlfriend this time,' Roman said, defensively.

Luca pushed him away; he couldn't bear to touch him any longer. 'I don't care if you won't sell me the land, or give me permission to build. I'll find some other way to do it, or I won't do it at all. I'm not going to let you cast this shadow over my life any longer. I promised our mother I would do everything I could to look after you, and I've done that. But I don't think this is how it should be done any more. I can't teach you how to have empathy for other people, or to care, or to be mature enough not to throw a damn party on a boat and almost kill all the guests. You don't need me running around after you trying to fix all your mistakes and put out all your fires. You need to learn how to look after yourself—or not. I don't care any more. I'm done.'

'You can't be done. You work for me—I'm your boss.'

'Not any more. I quit. You could have killed Mina, Roman. You could have killed all these people. You could have killed yourself.'

As much as he hated Roman now, his voice broke on the final word. Looking at Roman, wet and dishevelled, his head bleeding, just reminded him too much of him as his little twin brother, three minutes younger, lying in bed in that hospital in Paris, never able to play, always stuck alone. He used to look at Luca just like this: resentment mixed with sadness, but always tinged with anger. Nothing had changed…except Luca.

'I know what you think of me,' snapped Roman. 'I've been a burden to you all your life. I know you think that everything I do is some attempt to further antagonise you and get in your way. But have you ever thought for one second that maybe—'

'Maybe what?'

'Maybe the reason I don't want you to have that land isn't because I have an inbuilt urge to arbitrarily stand in your way? It's because I don't want you to go.' All the fight seemed to drain out of him. 'I like having you here.' He looked down. 'You're the only one I have.'

Luca's heart sank in sympathy. He took two steps

forward and put his arms around Roman's shoulders, pulling him easily to his chest. His shirt rapidly grew wet from the sea water drenching his brother, but he didn't let go. It was the first time he could remember them ever hugging. Roman held himself stiffly at first, then relaxed into Luca all at once, gripping the back of his shirt in his fist and holding tight.

Luca should have seen it himself—of course Roman would never ask him to stay outright. Of course he'd find some ridiculously over-complicated way to try and manipulate him into staying instead. Roman had a lot to learn, but Luca would just have to figure out a way to help him realise that he wasn't planning to move to the other side of the world, only to the other side of the island.

Luca would never stop feeling the compulsion to protect his brother. But now he knew that there was the possibility of something else out there for him, something better. Something bright and true: Mina.

# CHAPTER SEVENTEEN

AFTER THE CHAOS was finally over and everyone was safe, dry and treated, Luca had checked on Mina's injury and taken her home. He'd tucked her into his bed and told her to sleep as long as she needed to.

He'd watched her there for a long time, just enjoying the simple rise and fall of her chest. She was alive and well, and safe again. Those moments when she hadn't been had been the worst of his life, and he just needed to be with her for a while, to convince himself that the danger had passed. When the adrenaline and remnants of panic had finally drained away and Luca could breathe normally himself, he got up, took one last look at Mina and left the villa. There was something he needed to do.

An hour later, Luca walked back into his bedroom. He smiled as he looked down at Mina lying in his bed, still sleeping, her bandaged arm resting on top of the covers. He carefully set down the tray he was carrying on the bedside table, not making a sound, and knelt down on the floor by her side. He kissed her feather-softly on the head and smiled. Her hair smelled of his shampoo.

A recovery diver had been down to look at the yacht. The initial report was that a firework had smashed a porthole and the yacht had started taking on water, then the fireworks had started a fire onboard. Roman had bribed the first officer to take the yacht out against captain's orders.

Everyone had been rescued from the water and all had been treated. There were cuts and bruises, minor coral scrapes. Only one patient had needed to be flown to hospital in Tahiti, with minor burns. He would fully recover. Roman had been very, very lucky. Of course, that probably wouldn't stop several of his billionaire guests and their very skilled, well-paid lawyers from attempting to sue him. But that was well and truly Roman's problem, not Luca's. Not any more.

But, strangely, even Roman seemed to have had some sort of reaction to last night's disaster. Perhaps, against all expectations, something one of them had said had got through to him. Early this morning Luca had found pushed through his door a contract for the sale of the land, already signed by Roman, just waiting for Luca's signature. It looked as if Luca might build that hospital after all.

And, if the worst came to the worst, and Roman somehow lost the whole resort, maybe there would be a job opening available at Luca's hospital for him as a porter. Luca smiled. He knew it wouldn't come to that. Roman always seemed to have the ability to come out on top of any situation, and Luca was sure he'd find a way to worm his way out of this one too. He just had to hope he might worm his way out as a slightly better man. Miracles did happen.

\* \* \*

Mina woke up, stretching and smiling up at Luca. 'Hello, you.'

Luca kissed her again. 'Hello,' he whispered.

'I guess I've lost my job, then.'

Luca shrugged. 'It frees you up for other opportunities.'

'Like what?' she asked, yawning.

'You wouldn't want to be equal partners in the building of a brand-new hospital on a gorgeous South Pacific island, would you?'

'Sure, do you know of one going?'

'It'll be a lot of work. I don't know if I can do it alone. But I can do anything with you.'

She sat up and looked at him seriously. 'You're not your father, or your brother. You can believe in a Baudelaire curse if you want, but you can break it. You're better than them. And you have one thing they didn't.'

'What?'

'Me.'

Luca grinned happily. 'I can't argue with that. Now, are you hungry?'

'Starving! What have you got? More of those delicious pastries?'

'How would you feel about a cookie?' He revealed a tray, which held a plate of heart-shaped cookies covered in pink icing.

She looked down at them, frozen still for a moment, then laughed in surprise. The sound of her delight filled Luca with pure happiness. 'I had the chef make them especially for you. They're as accurate as I could make them from memory. Would you like me to choose one for you?'

She nodded, smiling. 'Go for it.'

Luca carefully picked one out and held it out to her, holding his breath: *Marry me?* was iced on to it in white letters.

Mina gasped. 'Do you mean it?'

Luca nodded. 'Of course.'

Mina took the cookie, then grabbed Luca by the collar, pulling him down on top of her. 'Yes, yes, yes,' she said against his lips, before kissing him softly. The rest of the pink heart-shaped cookies scattered across the bed and on to their bedroom carpet.

# EPILOGUE

*A year later...*

MINA BREATHED IN the scent of the honeysuckle bush—the same yellow honeysuckle they'd tasted together just over a year ago. Luca had been very careful to keep it protected all through the building work. And now it grew surrounded by a patch of neatly landscaped grass just down the slope from the entrance to the hospital.

She smiled as Luca appeared with two glasses of champagne. He handed her one and joined her, sitting on the soft grass.

'The last of the builders have left. It's just us here now.'

Mina took the glass and held it out to Luca, toasting him. 'Congratulations!'

'For what? Getting Henri to stop chatting and finally go home for the day?'

'No,' she said softly. 'For finally finishing your hospital.'

'Our hospital,' he corrected, smiling. Luca exhaled and leaned back on his hand, to admire the view of the newly finished building. 'It is pretty great, isn't it?'

'It's perfect.'

It was beautiful. It was as if the plans Luca had drawn up over a year ago had come to life. Now, it was pristine and empty. Soon it would officially open and be full of people; full of staff, patients and noise. It would never be quiet like this again a day in its life.

Things had moved pretty quickly once Roman had granted Luca the land. Luca's plans had been finalised, the plans perfected, the hospital enlarged in size a little to incorporate a specialised children's wing and a few extra services for the island.

Local nurses and doctors had been hired. Local people had been hired as technicians, porters, receptionists and admin staff. Luca didn't just want to serve the local community for its patients, he wanted to provide extra jobs for them too and make the hospital an integral part of the community.

Luca had been so touched, and thrown, by Roman's sudden attack of generosity in allowing him the land that he'd offered to name one of the hospital wings after him. But Roman had suggested they name it after their mother instead, and Luca had agreed. The children's ward had been christened the Gabriel Beaumont Children's Wing after Luca's childhood friend who, as Luca had often said, was the one who had inspired this whole project right from the beginning.

The build hadn't been without its problems, but the work had been completed even quicker than Mina had expected. Apparently piles of money could get things moving. Who knew?

Of course, with all the building work to oversee, they hadn't yet had a moment free to get married. Luca had been keen for it to happen as soon as possible, but Mina had been happy to wait until she could give it her full attention.

Not that it would take much planning. She wanted something small and simple. If she was honest, she'd have been ecstatic to elope, just Luca and her. But there were plenty of family and friends who couldn't wait to celebrate with them—including Rachelle, who was desperate to be maid of honour; Roman, who in a surprising turn of events Luca had asked to be best man; and a certain ex-friend of Mina's from home who had recently come back into her life. Along with a multitude of repentance and a dozen apology plants, which were still arriving thick and fast.

Jodie had called, and for the first time Mina had felt capable of picking up the phone and talking to her. What had followed was a sincere, heartfelt apology and months of Jodie trying to make things up to Mina. And it had worked. Apparently, surprising no one, the relationship between Jodie and Mina's dastardly ex had only lasted a few weeks before he'd done the same to her, and Jodie had realised what an absolute idiot she'd been. Now, Mina couldn't wait for her to come to Bora Bora for the wedding, and to see the life she had made for herself.

Roman had further surprised them both with the gift of another small piece of land. Just up the hill and round the corner from the hospital, not all that far from Malo's and Lani's house, there was a quiet, secluded space big enough on which to build a cosy little house. It would be bigger than their two villas but just the right size for them, with the most beautiful view imaginable.

Although, that was debatable. The most beautiful

view might be Luca, sitting in the grass next to Mina, looking happy, carefree and contented.

They'd healed something in each other, something that had helped them each become the person they needed to be. Now they were both ready to move on from their past, welcome in the people who deserved to share their future and be strong enough to forgive them.

Luca took Mina's hand, laid his head in her lap and offered her a honeysuckle bloom. She had Luca, and that was everything.

* * * * *

*If you enjoyed this story,
check out these other great reads
from Zoey Gomez*

One-Night Reunion with the Vet
The Single Dad's Secret

*Both available now!*

# HATING DR SUNSHINE

## RACHEL DOVE

MILLS & BOON

For Dave Thompson

# CHAPTER ONE

*You have got to be kidding me. Seriously. What's going on in this hospital? This is supposed to be one of the leading ER departments in the country, and I just walked into a circus. Literally.*

"Ah, Doctor! Just who I was looking for!"

Natalia, the perky woman from HR, was positively bouncing on the balls of her feet at Lauren's side, but all she could do was stand there in the stark white corridor like the Queen of Doom. From the way her scar tissue was pinching, she was also pretty sure that her default facial expression had plumbed new depths of scowl. What was the source of her discomfort?

Mr. Chirpy. Or Dr. Chirpy, to be more accurate. The ER doctor she was going to be running the department with was currently sporting a clown's red nose and huge fake brogues that added at least five sizes to his feet. And the red wig? She wasn't even going to comment on that. He looked like Ronald McDonald on happy pills. *This cannot be my new counterpart. Surely not?*

"Hi, Natalia! Have you come to join in the…fun?" The second the white-coat-wearing clown spotted Lauren, his sentence spluttered to a stop. Pulling off his wig, he ran a hand through his locks, trying and failing to sort out his unruly dark hair. All the while, his eyes never left hers.

In return, her own felt like they were pinned to his intent gaze. The second she looked into them, she wasn't standing in the hall anymore. She was enveloped in the dark of that night, her terrified gaze clinging to a pair of eyes that were so similar to this man's that it took her breath away.

*It...can't be. It's just not possible.* He couldn't be the person who'd helped her on the night of the car crash. Was she seeing him everywhere now? Was his face really going to stick in her head forever, so that anyone with a resemblance froze her on the spot?

Seattle wasn't some tiny one-horse town. She had thought she was safe from bumping into him, but now?

She tried to reconcile the two men, looking him up and down to determine if it was the guy who'd run to her wrecked car and saved her life. The whole thing was already so confusing in her head that having him here, in her new workplace, would short-circuit her already frazzled wires. Both men were tall and strong-looking; she couldn't see anything notable that would put her fears to rest.

It had been so dark that night, the lighting on the street skewed by shadows and blood. Too many details were lost to her, others replaying with glaring clarity.

Damn face paint. If only she could see his face, she could quell the pending panic attack she was fending off with every tattered scrap of strength she had left.

*It's not him, Lauren. You'll see. The Nolans are out of your life, just as swiftly as they arrived and wrecked it.* Meeting his eyes again on a deep breath, he was still staring back, scanning her intently. But she saw no hint of recognition in his gaze. *See? Not him. Get it together!*

She fixed her expression to something akin to neutral. A mask of bored nonchalance, but he didn't move an inch. Was he looking at her scar? *Look away, bozo.* Seriously.

Did this guy not get the memo that a staring clown was a bit scary? People didn't like things out of place; anything different was unnerving. She'd found that out for herself over the last few months, and she was unlikely to forget it. Her days of melting into the background were over, but this guy? He was Mr. Front and Center.

Even dressed as he was, he was still looking at her like she was the one with the issues. Entirely too inquisitive for her liking. This was just one of the many reasons she'd resolved never to bother with the opposite sex again. What was he looking for, a label?

And why in the name of holy heck did he have to have the same eyes as her rescuer? She hardly needed another reminder of her accident, stabbing her at every turn. If she had to work in the same hospital as this man, she'd need to start wearing blinkers like a darn horse.

She turned to Natalia, painfully aware that she had to show off her gnarly, scarred side profile to Dr. Doofus. Her return to medicine was not the quiet reintroduction she'd longed for. She needed to take back some control.

"If you don't mind, I would like to start seeing patients." She motioned around them, pointing out the very full waiting room and nurses speedwalking the corridors carrying out various tasks. "I noticed the patient wait time you have listed for this department is over five hours. I think that's a problem. A little less clowning around, perhaps?"

She could see a couple of nurses raise their eyes at her words but didn't bother to take her eyes away from Coco.

She saw his brows lift. Not hard to miss, since they were thick, black and painted on. She waited for him to bite back, but no. The grin was back. *Jack Nicholson, eat your heart out.* The effort was oddly charming even if it should be creepy.

"Well noticed, Doctor…"

"Basso. Lauren Basso."

*Did he just suck in a breath? Had he heard about her? Was that what the stare fest was about just now?*

"I knew it."

"Knew what?" she snapped.

He dropped his gaze pretty quickly. "Er…nothing. Doctor Basso, it's nice to have you on board. I was actually just coming back from the children's ward. Their entertainer came down with Covid last minute, so I offered to fill in. As for the wait times, that's why you're here. As you probably know, Seattle isn't the driest place on the planet. With all this rain, I figure that some of these patients are just a little scared about the weather warnings. People need people. And now I have another doctor to work with, I figure we can cut those times right down. So?" Turning his irksome grin to Natalia, he motioned to the papers in her hands. "Is our new doctor all signed off?"

"Yes." Natalia positively preened at him. "All ready, I just came down to do the introductions. What do you say, Doctor, you ready to jump in?"

Giving her new work colleague another hard once-over, Lauren drew a deep breath of her own and even managed to flash Natalia a tight smile that landed nowhere near sincere. She resolved right then and there to ice this guy out. After Oscar, she was never going to let a man get close again, in any capacity. No matter how annoyingly happy this guy was, she wasn't going to fall at his feet like the rest of the staff seemed to. No, sirree. She was here to busy herself with work. Anything else, especially haunting eyes, was firmly off her radar.

"Of course. It's why I'm here."

"Great!" Natalia waved one of the lingering nurses over.

"Well, you know where I am if you need anything, Doctor. Welcome to Seattle General!"

As the nurse came over, tablet in hand, Lauren's eyes flicked back down the corridor, but it was now clown-free.

Over the next couple of hours, Lauren discovered that Seattle General was a lot busier than her old position at Seattle Presbyterian. For one thing, General had a level-one trauma center, which meant lots of patients from all over Seattle with a myriad of symptoms and injuries. Like the man currently writhing on his gurney, refusing treatment despite the fact blood was dripping down his nose and his shoulder was sloped down at a very uncomfortable-looking angle.

"My camera, man, I need my camera! I have to upload that footage. That news crew showed up just as I was getting stuffed into the ambo! They're going to scoop me!"

Lauren clenched her teeth and held her hands out in a placatory manner. *I was never this bad when I was a patient, and I was in much worse shape.* "I know, sir, but your camera is with the police right now, and I need to treat your arm. Once we have your shoulder popped back in and treat your lacerations, they want to speak to you, so you can take it up with them."

"No way," he huffed, throwing his arms out. She winced. The second he tried to move his dislocated arm; a high-pitched scream burst from his lips. "That hurts! Can't you give me some more pain relief or something?"

She checked his chart with a shake of her head. "Sorry, you maxed out on morphine on the way here, but the pain will be alleviated once your joint is back in place." She stepped closer. "Now, just follow my instructions and let's get you sorted."

The second her hand went near his shoulder, his whole demeanor changed. She saw a flash of movement, and the second before his fist connected with her face, something hard pressed against her back and blocked it. Before she heard his words, she felt the rumble of a broad chest reverberate through her.

"Don't you dare touch her," the voice growled. A hand gripped her patient's uninjured arm tightly.

"Ow, man! You can't do that! I'm the patient here, but she's not listening to me! Do you know who I am? I'm Johnny Danger! I have two million followers!"

Lauren felt an arm come around her, shielding her as the person gripping Johnny's arm leaned in closer. She took a step back, awestruck that someone had come to her aid so swiftly. And that she was allowing it to happen.

"I don't care how many followers you have spending their time watching you hurl yourself off buildings like a flying squirrel. You're in our hospital now, and you will not touch her. Ever. You understand me?"

Johnny's eyes widened as he took in the man's face. Whatever he saw there made him shrink into himself. He practically deflated into the mattress. "Okay," he stuttered.

"Apologize."

"There's no need," Lauren cut in. "I'm fine. Thank you..."

When her rescuer turned to face her, she felt her heart screech to a halt. Those eyes again.

She thought of the clown in the corridor earlier. The way his gaze zeroed in on hers, and how it had jolted a memory of something. *Someone.* She thought she'd never forget their intensity, the tiny flecks of dark night contained within them, but she hadn't wanted to believe it in the hallway earlier. She'd become such a pro at hiding her feelings since the accident, schooling her features into a hardened mask.

Now, seeing his face without the clown paint, every nerve ending was screaming, *I told you so. It's him. It's definitely him. He's here. How is he here?*

Dr. Mickey Nolan. The man who'd come to her aid when a drug-impaired driver had crashed into her car. The brother of the man behind the wheel, Denny Nolan.

"You're the clown."

He nodded, but she could still see the tension in his shoulders, the way he was still glaring at Johnny.

"I don't hear that apology. Quicker you do, the faster we can get to treating you." He jerked his head toward the curtain behind them. "As you can see, we have a lot of people needing medical attention today, and they're not all causing trouble. The police are in the lobby, waiting to speak to you. I don't think you want to add attempted assault to the charge sheet, right?"

Johnny's face paled so much his skin went translucent. Probably considering his followers and what they would make of him trying to hit a doctor for doing her job. "Right. I'm sorry. I just… The camera footage is important for my job, but I shouldn't have taken my frustration out on you, Doc." He dipped his chin. "I'm ready for you to fix my arm now." Another pitiful whimper left his quivering lips. "It does hurt a lot."

Lauren barely heard him. She was too busy trying not to throw up. She should have known. Should have listened to that first jolt when their eyes met. Should have checked into him and where he worked before she took this job.

She knew Denny Nolan's brother was a doctor. Mickey had told her himself that night, but she'd never considered that she would end up working alongside him. Doctors held a lot of different positions. She knew it was in medicine, given his knowledge and the way he never flinched at her injuries, but still.

An ER doctor was just a little too tragic to be funny, though. He was part of the past she was trying to shake, not rub up against. She was grateful to him, sure—but she was no damsel in distress. He might have been there that night when she was lying in the wreckage of her car, he might have stayed by her side till she went into surgery, but she knew the whole truth now. Of what had happened that night and why. How she was in the wrong place at the wrong time and had the scars to prove it—both physical and mental.

Coming around from surgery and having to deal with all those twists and turns had changed her forever, and this man with his kind, worried eyes was right at the center of it.

She had planned never to see him again. Now he was here, helping her out again—and she was furious. This hospital, this job was supposed to be the start of her new life, and it had been hijacked all over again. Along with the control she was finally taking back on the reins of her life. In this guy's presence, she felt like she was riding a wild horse all over again. Blindfolded and without a saddle to cling to.

"Good," she told Johnny. "Well, I have it from here. Thank you."

She went to move past her savior, but his arm shot out, searing her upper arm through her doctor's coat. Her stupid body locked up on her, and she could see in his eyes that he'd clocked it. His grip faded to the lightest touch, but he didn't remove it entirely.

"Are you sure you're okay? I can deal with this if you need to step out."

With a clench of her jaw, she wrenched her arm from his grasp. "It's my job. Thanks for your help, but I don't need it. Not now, nor ever." She narrowed her eyes, wanting him to know that she knew just who he was.

Her scars were like a calling card to him, she knew. Any doctor there that night could have picked her out of a lineup blindfolded. His eyes gave him away.

She couldn't bear to look into them for a second longer than she had to. She didn't want to be reminded of the darkest time of her life. Her time of being a vulnerable patient was over, in the past. She just wanted to feel like herself again. Or whatever the new version of her was, at least. "I don't need anything from anyone. Especially not from you."

She didn't allow his look of surprised hurt to register in her own swirl of emotions. He might be here, and she had to work with him, but no way in Hades was she going to give him more than the time of day. She didn't need a rescuer. She was already lost, and Mickey Nolan wasn't going to be the one riding in on a white horse again.

"Now." She forced her voice to be strong, the authority of her medical training carrying her through as she felt the swish of the curtain, signalling his departure. "Let's get that arm set, shall we?"

The crunch of Johnny's bone joint dropping back into place was eclipsed by his scream as she rotated his arm and set it back into place. Once his limb was strapped up, and she was satisfied that his lacerations from sliding down the side of a low building in a failed parkour attempt were free from debris and superficial, she called for a nurse.

When Erin came in, she was practically bursting with questions. "Did Dr. Nolan really shout at the patient?" she inquired in a feverish whisper.

"Er...well. I wouldn't exactly say that." *Hmm. Maybe a little.*

"Jarvis said he went all alpha on the guy."

"Jarvis?" Lauren asked, wondering why the staff here had enough time on their hands to gossip.

"The porter," Erin added. "You've seen him. Big guy, bushy eyebrows. Anyway, he said that Dr. Nolan got all growly and everything. So unlike him! I didn't even know the man knew how to scowl. I wish I'd seen it."

"Well, I don't know about all that."

"Oh, I do. The guy is a total retriever."

"Retriever?" Lauren had no idea what that meant.

"Yeah! You know, like the dog, the golden retriever? He's always so happy, like a bouncy pet."

"A pet. Right." *I am so done with this conversation.* It did give her a tiny bit of satisfaction to hear that Mickey was ruffled, though. The thought that he might just be rattled that they had to work together almost made her situation bearable.

Erin was still talking about...something, but Lauren cut her off. "I've finished here and updated his patient record. Once his wounds are dressed he can be discharged, but the police need to speak to him first."

"No problem," Erin beamed, faltering only momentarily at her dismissal. "I'll get right on it!"

"Thank you," Lauren said, turning on her heel before Erin started talking about dogs again.

She was back at the front desk, hand on the next patient file when a strong voice called her name.

"We need to talk," Mickey said, reaching for the file in her hands. "Our office."

*Wait, what?* "We share an office?" she asked as he strode off down the corridor.

He didn't answer, staying silent till she begrudgingly followed him into a room, and he closed the door behind them.

It was a small space, two desks in the center of the room facing each other. Filing cabinets and a huge bookshelf filled the back wall. Next to the door, a small couch was wedged under the blind-covered window. It was cozy, at best.

Stifling at its worst. She was really supposed to share an office with him, as well as an ER department? When she heard of the post a few weeks ago, she'd been thrilled at the challenge. The ER was getting busier all the time, and patient waiting times were at an all-time high. Even with patient satisfaction and outcomes being one of the best in Seattle, it was clear that the department was stretched. Which begged the question, how had Mickey been running the department alone?

She wasn't entirely immune to what he must have gone through eight months ago. After all, his brother was now in prison for causing the crash. Working the hours they did, with the pressure of being in charge of staff members who described him like some kind of excited puppy? It didn't compute. Was he even human?

*Oh God, I can't breathe. The air in this office—it feels like I'm standing on a mountaintop. Focus, Lauren, he's just a person. You'll have to work with him. Somehow.*

She was still taking in her surroundings when he came to stand before her. She caught a hint of his cologne and closed off her nostrils to quell the butterflies it provoked in her gut. She might not want to be in this man's orbit, but she wasn't dead below the waist, either. Of course her new nemesis had to be hot, right? The universe couldn't have had her rescuer be butt-ugly. That would have been far too kind, and not at all on trend for her life this past year.

The truth was, she'd thought about Mickey Nolan a lot

over her months of recovery. When she'd first woken up, bruised and battered and sore from surgery, she'd asked for him, but the nurses had been tight-lipped. She'd wanted to see him again, to thank him, but then she'd learned the truth… Why he'd been there that night, so concerned for her. It wasn't just because he'd been passing by, a good Samaritan jumping into the fray.

He'd been there trying to stop his brother from hurting someone. He probably saw the whole thing happen. Had chosen to stay when his brother hadn't.

Of course, he wasn't at her bedside when she woke up, why would he be? The news was full of the Nolan family. She was a statistic, a byline. A victim.

Being in his presence now, she had so many questions she would never ask. Around him, her whole body felt like it was on fire. Like she was on show, and he could see through her like a pane of glass. It was unnerving, seeing all the pieces of him and wondering how they all fit together to make the man.

Before seeing him again, she had thought that her pain and delirium had exaggerated her rescuer's attributes in her traumatized mind, but she was fast realizing that if anything her memory had downplayed things. The man was fine with a capital F. Over six feet tall, dark hair and angled jaw handsome. The clown getup had definitely hidden his looks, if not his eyes.

Ones that were looking right at her now as he dipped his head to meet hers. "I think you know who I am."

*Getting right to it then.* That voice, too. She'd thought of that so many times since, as well. Wished in secret that she could hear it again, even after she knew everything. Like it or not, she'd always associated that timbre with safety. Not feeling alone. She'd been so alone ever since she awoke in the hospital. The voice was another part of him that had been hard to shake from her memory.

Now, she wished she could close her stupid ears to block him out. After Oscar, she was never going to let another man in. Especially this man. It would unravel her at the core, and she was already playing at being all stitched back together as it was.

"You do, don't you?" he said again, softly. "Remember me?"

"I do," she said, her words clipped. "Did you know I was coming to work here?"

"No." His lips thinned.

*Great. Now I'm looking at his lips. Eyes, lips. What am I supposed to focus on?* Choosing a spot just to the left of his head, she set up camp.

"We needed another department head, so I knew someone was starting," he went on. "Not who. HR never gave me a name. I didn't even know you were looking for another job."

The hackles rising along her shoulder blades could give a werewolf a run for their money. As if he knew about her life. What she'd been through. "Why would you? It's not like we know each other."

"No, but you did your residency at Pres."

"How would you know about that?"

His mouth opened. Closed. "I...just know people there."

Of course he did. She'd heard about the mighty Nolan family. The news coverage had focused more on the scandal than they had on the fact that an innocent person had been hurt by one of the family.

"I just figured since you'd stayed there after completing your residency, you would go back to it when you... returned to work," he finished awkwardly.

*From sick leave*, she added in her head petulantly. *Hardly a break from work when you go from doctor to patient.* Seattle Presbyterian had been tainted by more than memories of learning her dream job now, sadly. She'd seen too much behind the curtain to be clear minded walking those corridors. The people he'd mentioned knowing there had behaved differently toward her since the crash. She couldn't stand the pitying looks, the way they hadn't treated her like a fellow doctor when discussing her injuries. She couldn't stay there, not after that.

"Yeah, well you figured wrong. I needed a fresh start." *Stop talking. You don't owe him a catchup chat.* "How did you know where I worked, really? Was it honestly someone from Pres that told you or the tabloids?"

He shrugged, looking away.

"Right," she sneered. "The press. Figures. They wrote everything else about me before they got bored real quick. Vultures. What else do you know? Should I write you a quiz, test you on all things Basso? Keep you occupied while you wait for clown college to start?"

She was deliberately goading him now and she didn't care. She *was* a werewolf, and he was the moon she wanted to howl at. She didn't want him to know her, she didn't want anyone to. Oscar had known her better than anyone, and he'd walked away all the same once he saw her injuries.

"I know that you took some time off after the accident."

"It wasn't an accident," she spat back. "A drug-impaired driver smashed into me while I was on my way home from a twelve-hour shift. Oh, and then he drove off, leaving me bleeding and terrified, trapped in my own car. After that, it was just one big party. My boyfriend took one look at me and left, my parents were traveling and I didn't want to burden them, and even though the press largely left me alone after the first few days, it was too late. I had strangers knowing about the worst time in my life, and I couldn't do a thing about it. Happy now? Know enough?"

Her voice was cracking, and she despised her throat for giving out on her. The fact her body seemed to be defective when Mickey was in her vicinity pushed her anger to white-hot frustrated rage.

"I'm fine," she managed, "and in case you didn't read this when you did your little deep dive into me—which is beyond creepy by the way—it's none of your damn business. Are we done here? I have work to do."

He got to the door before her hand wrapped around the handle. "No, we're not done. I'm sorry… I wasn't trying to upset you. I would never want that."

She felt him behind her, but there was no way she was turning to face him. She wanted to disappear. To be back at her place, in her sweats, watching ridiculous thriller movies and ignoring the world. If she'd known her first day was going to be like this, she never would have left her couch. "I'm here to work, not to discuss the past."

"If we are going to work together, we have to, Lauren. You must realize that. It's unavoidable."

"No!" She turned on him. "You are unavoidable. All day you've been watching me, and sticking your nose into the Johnny thing—"

"He was going to hit you!"

"So what? You think a patient's never taken a swing at me before? I don't need your help, so don't bother trying to smooth-talk me."

"Smooth-talk you? I just want to make sure you're okay! You moved to a new job, your boyfriend left you, and you had a major trauma—"

"Caused by *your* brother!" She was shouting now, and she wanted to stop but her anger had finally boiled over. It was hissing and fizzing out of her, and when he reached his hand out to her she slapped it away. "Your addict brother ran into me, and I lost everything! My confidence, my identity! My privacy! People were writing about me on the internet for days, talking about my scars, my injuries. Even about Oscar leaving me! I know you're thinking I'm going to air our dirty laundry at work and diss the Nolan family name, but my guess is that everyone here already knows. I don't plan on telling anyone a thing about my personal life or about my injuries. But anyone not living under a rock knows what happened to me."

Pinching the bridge of her nose against the looming tears she felt pricking at her eyes, she tried and failed to keep her voice even. What came out was a strangled sob, wrapped in words of desperation. "I just want to work and feel normal!"

"Hey, it's okay—"

He reached for her again, but she shrank back farther, halting him.

"It's not okay. None of this is okay. Today, this job—it was supposed to be my first good day. So no, I don't want to talk about it. Any of it!"

"Okay. Okay, but people talking…" He ran his hand through his hair, not seeming to care when it stuck up at odd angles. "That won't happen, not with me around. That's not what I'm worried about, Lauren."

"Dr. Basso," she snapped. "It's Dr. Basso to you, and I don't care what you're worried about. I don't care about Oscar or your stupid deadbeat brother. I just want to get on with trying to be normal. Don't you get it? I was broken. I lost my confidence, my sense of safety. My colleagues all treated me differently. My only friends were the people I worked with. When I got discharged, I had to start over. With everything. A new place, no friends to fall back on. My parents meant well, but they couldn't deal with my volatile emotions. I was so angry." She clenched her fists by her sides. "It's all I have to get me out of bed in the morning. Can you fix any of that? Can you fix what stares back at me in the mirror every morning? No, you can't, so don't bother trying. I am fine alone. I'm used to it by now. I want nothing from you, so stay the hell away from me!"

He stepped back, face stricken and the second his hand was off the door, she was out of there. Slamming the office door behind her, she almost took Erin off her feet.

"Oof!" Erin reached for the files she'd dropped. "Dr. Basso, are you okay?" Her eyes shot from her to the office door, and Lauren willed her face to look akin to something professional.

"I'm fine, Erin," she assured her.

"I heard shouting, are you sure?" Erin was looking at the door as if she could see Mickey behind it.

Lauren knew that if he came out of that door, her grip on her act would be sunk. "Yes. I was just talking to an insurance company for one of my patients. They were denying coverage."

"Oh." Erin smiled, not looking entirely convinced. "I get it. They do love their loopholes."

"Yep." Lauren laughed, but it came out shrill and hollow, which was a weird kind of achievement she never wanted a trophy for. "People always look out for themselves, no matter what." Ignoring the frown Erin shot back, she tapped the files in her hands. "If they are my next patients, I'm ready to work."

# CHAPTER TWO

CLICKING HIS APARTMENT door shut with a sigh, Mickey heard the telltale teeny thumps across the wood floor.

"Hey, Tripod. You hungry, little fella?" Throwing his keys into the glass bowl on the side table, Mickey scooped up his furry roommate and headed for the kitchen. The cleaning service had been by that morning, so he knew that the squawking from Tripod was him trying it on. Ever since he'd seen the bedraggled bundle at the side of the road one night, leg broken and bloody, Mickey had been wrapped around the little tom cat's claws. Someone had bagged the poor thing up and shoved him out of a car window with his feet tied together. The fact the bag had torn open had been the only thing to save Tripod's life.

As soon as he'd spotted those bright green eyes peeking out from the plastic, Mickey couldn't just leave him there. Besides, he was used to trying to clean up other people's mistakes, right? What was one more, in a cute little mewling package?

At least this rescue hadn't left him and didn't despise him on sight. It had been good for him, a month after Lauren's accident. Someone to pour his concern and care into over the last eight months. Care and concern that he couldn't put into Lauren, the woman his brother had hurt and the one he couldn't forget.

Her face haunted his dreams, and now she was here. Hating him, lashing out at the world. He'd had no idea that she was so damaged, so filled with rage.

*I should have tried harder to see her after, at the hospital. Maybe I could have helped.*

Hearing that her boyfriend had left her over this infuriated him. What a coward. She was all alone, and Mickey had been here nursing a cat back to health. Burying himself in work, doing damage control for the family, for her. He'd seen what the press had said about her, about Denny and even himself. He'd been hailed as some kind of hero angel to his brother's dark devil. She was a footnote in her own accident compared to the exposure the Nolan family had received, but it was still too much.

What he'd found out about her had been bad, but nothing compared to the reality of what she'd told him with her own mouth. He'd done his best for her that night, but the urge to look out for her hadn't left him. Doctorly instinct? Guilt? He didn't know himself; the only thing he was sure of was that Lauren Basso was still in his head, and there was no chance of that changing any time soon.

If anything, he wanted to protect her more. To show her that she was stronger than she thought.

"I should have told her that," he said to Tripod, who gave a little meow as if he understood perfectly. "She's the strongest person I've ever met." Tripod rubbed his face against his palm, making him smile. "Just like you're the strongest little furball."

After three surgeries and a hefty bill, Tripod had come home to live with Mickey and now ruled the roost. Putting him down next to his already full dish, Mickey shot the cat a knowing look and reached into the fridge for a beer. "Nice try, bud. No chicken after dark, remember? I know Teresa will have given you a treat today."

Just like Mickey, Teresa was a sucker for the black-and-white terror on three legs. He still couldn't shake her well-meaning words when she'd first found out about Tripod. She was being nice, he got that, but it had cut him to the bone.

*Oh, Mickey, bless you. You're such a good boy, cleaning up other people's horrors.*

Was that what this thing was, the connection to Lauren he felt at the core of him? He did feel guilty... Of course he did. His brother had driven away on Mickey's watch. He'd not been able to stop him or make it right after.

Leaning back against his kitchen island, he drank half the beer in silence. The only noises were Tripod smacking his lips on the food, and the hum of the refrigerator.

*Other people's horrors.* Teresa had a point. It was a huge part of him, this drive to help others, being what they needed him to be. The clown, the protector, the punching bag for verbal frustrations. Even in his job, he patched people up. Shootings, car accidents, kitchen incidents. Illnesses and disease. Domestic violence, family disputes. Gang wars. People were always taking chunks out of each other in one way or another, and he was getting a little tired of being the only seemingly sensible one in a sea of idiots. It was hard to keep smiling sometimes.

Today had been awful, and he was still reeling from seeing Lauren at work. He'd thought about her often since the day of the accident, but the woman he'd encountered today was vastly different from the picture he'd made in his head after researching her. She was colder, cut off. The light in her eyes dimmer than in the photos he'd seen online, as if hope itself had been drained right out of them.

It broke him in half the first time he saw it. The urge to help, to go to her side, was overwhelming. But she was just like a frightened cat in a bag, unable to bear the touch of helping hands, and he still felt the sting of her claws.

The whole department had felt it. He'd seen the looks the staff shot them both as they studiously worked together without exchanging so much as a personal word. The only thing going for them for the rest of the day was the fact that as a doctor, she was amazing.

Sure, they were very different doctors. Her bedside manner was slightly standoffish but still caring. Johnny was the exception, of course, but Mickey himself had wanted to shove his camera somewhere a proctologist would need to retrieve it. He'd walked in just in time to see the patient raise his hand to Lauren, and he'd acted. He'd barreled right into her back, his arm shooting up before he could think. He'd just leaped right for her. The fierceness of his own words had shocked him, but not as much as wrapping himself around her had.

He was protective of her, he already knew that. He'd run interference with the media as much as he could behind the scenes, but it hadn't been enough. He wasn't fast enough to quash the entire news frenzy in those early hours and days after. He'd had to pull in a few favors as it was, to manage what he could to protect her.

He knew now that this wasn't just about helping his brother or allaying his own guilt over the crash. It was more than that. He saw something in her, saw the parts that were missing that he somehow just knew were hiding underneath the hurt and pain and walls she'd built around herself.

Not for the first time, he felt the shame and pressure his family name brought with it.

Another aspect of her crossing his family's path was the public nature of it all. Their family name was well-known, for both bad and good reasons, due to him and his brother being young bachelors with a powerful CEO for a father. Nolan Industries was a tech company that regularly hit the business pages, and the notoriety had followed both brothers—and anyone involved with them.

After the accident, the press had been gleeful about Denny's fall from grace. His parents were heartbroken, and then there was Denny, facing a trial for drug-impaired driving, hurting an innocent woman and leaving her for dead in his panic.

On the other hand was Mickey, the good son, the doctor who made his own money and never dipped into the family coffers. The man who wanted to help people and smile doing it. He'd known from an early age that he wanted to be a good man, one who cared for everyone and made the world brighter, and not because of the Nolan name. Often it was in spite of it and the expectations of his parents and society in general.

Mickey wasn't made for the world of business. He would choke to death in some stuffy office. It simply wasn't his path.

In that way, the brothers were similar. Denny had always struggled to fit into the mold set for him at birth, too. Denny had always been the one who got the attention, even though most of it was negative. All Mickey had known was that his brother was behaving badly. Fighting at school, hanging with the wrong crowd. Between work and his brother, the attention of his parents was never really on Mickey.

He'd tried to be the perfect, happy child for them. He was always the one who made them laugh or smile when they needed it. He'd looked after Denny, tried to curb his impulses or anticipate them. Not that it had worked. Being the brother and son everyone relied on and never worried about had meant nothing in the end.

Mickey couldn't control Denny. Not when his demons were driving his emotions. That night, he'd been terrified that it would be the end for Denny, that he'd kill himself on that road. What happened to Lauren was something he could never have foreseen. Or forgive.

For the first time in his life, he'd been tough on Denny. Far tougher than before, and he'd gone against his parents to make sure that Denny made it right, as far as he could. It was his price for not walking away from his sibling, but it came with a price for him, too. Being stuck slap bang in the middle, not wanting to dishonor his family but unwilling to write his brother off, either. He was the only bridge keeping their family together, but that bridge was pretty rickety. Held together by vague threats, quiet judgment and deafening disappointment.

Even after everything, though, Mickey couldn't cut his brother out of his life, especially when their parents dropped him like a hot potato. So he'd had to make peace with losing his parents, too, in a way—and his brother wasn't going to be home for a long time. Denny had pled guilty for causing the accident and leaving the scene, but his family had tried to make a deal. In the end, Denny finally had to face the consequences of his actions. Agreeing to rehab had lessened his sentence, but even the family influence couldn't save Denny from spending some time in prison. It was only right, and Mickey had encouraged him to take responsibility. Another thing that his parents couldn't quite come to terms with.

Mickey didn't care. Denny could have killed Lauren

that night, and some things could never be taken back or brushed under a rug, no matter how plush the weave.

And then there was Lauren Basso herself, the woman in the other car that night, the innocent person Denny had almost killed. He'd not been able to stop thinking about her since that night, for many reasons. He figured that she'd recovered, but seeing her in the ER corridor today, his throat had closed up.

She was thinner than he remembered, her pretty features sharper. The scar on her face cut right across her cheek, the bridge of her nose and ended above her brow. She'd covered it with makeup, but the mark was still there. The mark the Nolan family had left on her forever. Her legs were the same, he knew. She'd been pinned in that car, upside down. The mangled wreckage had torn through her skin and muscle like a knife through butter. She was lucky to have survived with broken bones and ripped flesh.

Mickey had tried his best to keep something this awful from happening. Before the accident, he'd gotten Denny into rehab, but he kept leaving. Desperate, Mickey had taken him in. Forced him to be his houseguest so he could help him detox from all the drugs in his system, the addiction screaming for its next fix. It had been working, to an extent, but it was exhausting.

Working at the ER and taking care of his brother, Mickey had been wiped out that night. He'd fallen asleep, and Denny had taken his damn car and scored. Within half an hour, he was driving around Seattle as high as a kite.

Mickey had tracked him down, but too late. When he'd first come upon the crash site as he tried to chase down his idiot brother, he'd thought with his heart in his throat that surely there would be a body in that car. However, Lauren had been beyond lucky and had not only survived but recovered well enough to return to work. To walk and move around with such grace it made his whole body tingle.

That night, she'd been so strong, even terrified and stricken with pain. She hadn't seemed the type of woman who would just give up, but now he wasn't so sure he'd been fully right on that one.

She obviously didn't see her recovery as amazing, not that he blamed her. From the second Denny's car had barreled into hers, she'd been a casualty of addiction and a pawn for the press.

Mickey could still remember how that young reporter had hounded the hospital corridors, desperate for a money shot of her post surgery. If the hospital security guard hadn't arrived, Mickey would have killed the leech himself. As it was, the family lawyer had to convince the guy that a black eye and destroyed camera was nothing to what the family's money and influence could do to him if he pressed charges. Not that Mickey had cared at the time. It would have been worth it.

After that and the strings Mickey pulled, the press had left her alone for the most part. He couldn't be seen at the hospital after she'd woken up. The one time he'd tried, Oscar had been by her bedside. So Mickey had retreated and kept tabs on her progress as best he could, thinking she had someone…when she hadn't.

When things had died down, he hadn't wanted to pry in case it stirred things up again. She'd recovered, and he'd thought she would go back to her life and heal. But she clearly hadn't. Instead, she'd had to make a whole new life for herself, and she'd gotten through that, too. Then, she'd finally felt safe enough to return to work and walked right into being his new colleague. Which, he now knew, she hated with everything she had.

He, on the other hand, didn't know how to feel about it yet. The looks she'd flashed him had cut him to the quick, and all he wanted to do was apologize for what his brother had done and for not being there afterward. Hell, for not stopping his brother from getting behind the wheel in the first place.

Mickey would have done anything he could to make it better. Who had cared for her, when he couldn't? The press would have had a field day, and what would he have said anyway?

He'd let her think he was just there by chance that night. He couldn't imagine how she felt when she learned the truth about him being Denny's brother. She hadn't talked to the press, she hadn't said anything. Stopped permitting visitors, he'd heard, but still—he'd thought she had Oscar. He should have been enough, if he'd been a man with a damn backbone.

Lauren had shut down on any attempt at an apology from Mickey, though. The bitter exchange in his office was still ringing in his ears. What the holy heck was he going to say to her during their next shift? How could he turn the anger fueling her into a different kind of fire, one that would put the light back in her eyes?

Reaching for another beer, he clicked on his usual delivery app and ordered sushi for the fourth time that week before heading for a shower. Anything to work out the knots in his body from the tension of the day.

But hours later, he was still tossing and turning. Thinking of a bloodied face in the dark and a cold, wet hand dwarfed in his, clinging to life.

Two and some hours into their shift the next day, the battle lines had well and truly been drawn. Mickey, turning up to their joint office early, donuts and coffee in hand, had been met with a stony silence. When he put the cup on her desk, she'd poured it out into the sink in the corner and muttered about the cup not being recyclable before shooting it viciously into the corner bin. He'd left a caramel-filled donut on her desk sitting on a napkin and came back at break time to see it had been put back on his desk, a very prominent side fist imprint on its oozing surface.

*Better than my head*, I suppose, he'd thought with a despondent sigh.

On the ER floor, things weren't much better. Oh, she was professional, efficient—but whenever she saw him, she either used words as if they were in dire shortage or headed the other way altogether. Communication came through their work phones' messaging app or via a nurse.

Whenever she had to speak to him directly, she was concise, to the point. Cool, icy, professional. It was driving him crazy, because he knew from her outburst in his office that behind her facade, she was still struggling. And now, so was he.

He hadn't really cottoned on to just how much time he'd spent thinking about the woman till she was right there working with him. It was unhealthy to say the least, and Mickey did what he always did when he was in his feelings. He shined brighter, so annoyingly bright that it chased the darkness away. Which, of course, seemed to drive the cause of his turmoil absolutely insane.

He left her alone for a whole hour before he went to check on her again. She was in trauma bay one when he found her, with a little boy who'd fallen out of a tree in the park.

"I'm afraid it's looking like a fracture, Riley. We'll get an X-ray to confirm," she told the child, a softness in her voice that had Mickey stepping closer to hear better.

*If only she'd use that tone with me*, he caught himself thinking as he lingered there like some kind of secret protector.

"If it's a clean break, which means right across the bone in a straight line like this..." she laid a finger over her own forearm, patiently waiting for the ten-year-old to nod back "...then we should be able to get away with a splinted removable cast, but I'll wait for the results of the X-ray to confirm fully, and then the orthopedic surgeon will come to see you."

His mother sighed with relief in the chair by his bed. "So, no surgery?"

Lauren turned to face the mother, her small smile faltering when she saw Mickey standing there. One slow blink, then she ignored him, her face going from stony to soft again in a flicker. Perhaps she had a switch in that defense mechanism of hers. He kind of hoped she did, because that meant he just had to find that sucker and turn it off. *Or yank out the wires altogether.*

Riley spotted him over her shoulder, his eyes lighting up. "Dr. Nolan!"

Lauren's shoulders shot up around her ears, and he braced himself.

"Hey, Riley Roo! Back again, eh? You'll be getting your next time here free, you know. That loyalty card of yours must be punched out by now."

"Don't even joke," Mrs. Maddison said, rolling her eyes and suppressing a laugh of her own. "I turned my back for one second to take a work call, and he decided to do his best Spider-Man impression out of the biggest tree in the park."

Riley flashed him a sheepish look. "I almost made the landing. I would have if that stupid branch hadn't flipped me."

"Ouch." Mickey glanced across at Lauren, who was busy writing up notes on her tablet. It heartened him to see the ghost of a grin play across her lips, however momentarily. He took the opportunity to push her. "Dr. Basso's pretty great, though, huh?"

Riley turned his attention to her, and Mickey saw the look of curiosity on his face.

*Oh no*, Mickey winced as he saw Riley take in her appearance. *Don't say it, little man. Do me a solid.*

"What happened to you?" Riley asked her, unaware of Mickey's silent pleas. "Did you fall out of a tree, too?"

Lauren's fingers stilled on the screen, and Mickey held his breath.

"Riley," his mother warned, but Lauren waved her off.

"No, it's okay." To Mickey's surprise, she took a seat on Riley's bed and leaned in a little closer. "Don't tell anyone," she said, her voice turning into a soft stage whisper. "But I'm a bit of a superhero, too, in my spare time." Riley's eyes widened as she looked over her shoulder, studiously ignoring Mickey as if she was searching for some dastardly caped avenger. Clenching her fist, she turned back to Riley. "And if you see Wolverine, tell him next time I am going to win, and his adamantium butt is mine."

Riley's jaw practically dropped to the hospital sheets as his little eyes narrowed. "I will," he whispered, bringing his own clenched fist up to bump hers. "I hate his sideburns."

Then a sound came out of Lauren that made Mickey's gut clench. She laughed. Head thrown back, blond hair shining under the hospital lights, patting Riley on his shoulder affectionately.

"Me, too, pal," she tinkled.

Yeah, her voice was pure tinkling bells, and Mickey

could do nothing but stand there, drinking it in. *This is the real her. The before version.* He liked it. "Jarvis will be along soon to take you to X-ray."

Mickey was grinning at her when she turned around, but it took effort to keep it on his face when she looked right at him and scowled.

"Checking up on me, doctor?" she asked, a tense expression on her features that he knew she was trying to pass off as bored nonchalance. Her stomach rumbled as she passed him, and his hand closed around her wrist before he could stop himself.

She wrenched it away like his hand held hot coals. "Stop bothering me." She glowered up at him. "Stop talking to me, stop—"

Gloria, one of their best ER nurses, came barreling up behind them. She frowned as she noted their tension before she flicked back into nurse mode. "Doctors, gunshot victim coming in via ambulance. ETA three minutes."

Lauren started running, but he was hot on her heels. Bursting into the main ER department the same minute the ambulance crew came zooming through, they spoke at the same time.

"Trauma room one! Let's get some blood ordered, trauma kits. GSW protocols in place!"

The victim was barely an adult. He still had peach fuzz on his face, for the love of God. His dark, thick lashes fluttered against his pale skin as he groaned when being transferred from the gurney to the bed. Lauren cut through his blood-soaked T-shirt with her scissors, and Mickey rounded the bed at the other side as nurses hooked the youth up to various monitors.

"We need to—"

"Turn him," Mickey finished, and together they rolled

his body, back facing Lauren. She relaxed, just a little, as her keen eyes and able hands assessed him. "Through and through, right?"

"Yes," she confirmed. "But he's still torn up in there."

Mickey frowned, already thinking the same thing. "Portable ultrasound?"

She nodded, and Erin dashed off to grab it.

"It must have gone straight through his liver, right? Call the OR!" Lauren called out as their team came together like worker bees in a hive. Fluids were put up, blood crosschecked and ordered as they both peered at his wounds, one on each side. "Blood is still free flowing, but he's got a pulse. Can I get more gauze, please! Breathing on his own, let's pack him and get him up there."

"Dr. Reilly is up there today," Mickey told her. Dr. Reilly was one of the best, and he would be needed if they were going to try and save this guy's organ. "More gauze, stat!"

The patient came to with a start, and his terrified, pained shouts filled the room.

"Hey, hey." Mickey bent down to meet his eyes, then glanced up at Lauren who gave him a look he immediately understood. He nodded at her, and she got to work, packing the wound to stop the bleeding while they made the dash up to the OR on the floor above. "We've got you, okay? Dr. Basso is packing your wounds, but we need you to stay still. We are giving you blood to counteract the loss. There's a lot of damage from where the bullet passed through your body. You need surgery, and—"

A commotion broke out behind them. Jarvis stepped into the room, but he was immediately shoved aside.

"Kaleb!" a man shouted. His expression was feral as he

raised something silver, aiming it straight at the patient. "What? Are you not dead yet, you fu—"

"Gun! Get down!" Mickey heard himself yell, reaching across the patient to grab for Lauren as the nurses screamed, some running from the room, others hitting the deck. But not the object of his frustration. Oh no, that would be too easy, right?

No, this woman jumped onto the bed, knees bent and supporting the patient's back as she damn well folded herself over him.

"No!" she yelled, her hand reaching out toward the gunman. "Don't shoot!"

The shooter looked as shocked as Mickey felt. He saw the moment of hesitation, and that was all it took. Grabbing one of the metal kidney dishes from the side table, Mickey swung it at his hand, knocking it away as the gun went off.

It missed Lauren by mere inches, the wall behind them exploding into chips of plaster as the bullet burrowed into the brick.

The gunman, enraged, went to raise his gun again, until a security guard shoved a barrel into the back of his neck.

"Freeze! Put the gun down!"

Another officer yanked his free hand behind his back, and within seconds, the gunman was disarmed and on the floor, screaming pure vitriol at everyone around him.

The whole area was chaos. Patients shouting in the corridors, nurses holding each other, and all Mickey could see was Lauren. She jumped off the bed, blood covering the whole front of her scrubs. She had a thick streak of red across her face, almost running parallel to her scar, and it made the blood in his veins freeze.

Her lips opened, and she said something, looking right at him.

"Huh?" was all he got out, not able to stop seeing her in that car all over again. Bleeding, the red life force leaking right out of her body and down her nose, onto the asphalt below.

"Mickey, we're okay. Snap out of it! We need to move!" she boomed, just as his hearing decided to work again. "He's bleeding out!"

That snapped him out of his stupor, and his hands were on the bed, gripping, pulling and finally moving. Jarvis took the head, and between the three of them, they passed the melee of bodies outside the trauma room. Feet and heart pounding, Mickey matched them step for step, right for the elevator. They didn't stop till they hit the OR floor.

Dr. Reilly raised his eyebrows, doing a double take when he saw Lauren. "Dr. Basso, are you hurt?"

"What?" she asked, impatience in her voice even now. "No, it's not my blood. His liver is lacerated from the bullet. We didn't have time for a scan, but it's a through-and-through."

She rattled off the patient's stats and the medication and interventions they had already administered. She didn't look Mickey's way till the OR doors swished closed in front of them.

Mickey was about to chew her out for being so reckless with her own life but one look at her pale face, and he was dashing to her side as her feet went out from under her.

"I've got you, it's okay. I'm here. I've got you." Catching her in his arms as she pitched forward, he slowly lowered her to the floor.

# CHAPTER THREE

"Hey! Hey, are you okay?" Mickey was on his knees in front of her, his hands on her face before she could stop him. "Talk to me, Lauren."

"I'm good," she managed to croak out. Her hands were shaking so much she couldn't even reach up to bat his away.

She'd surprised herself, acting like that in the ER. She'd read so much information after the accident about trauma and the responses it provoked. She already knew that shutting herself off wasn't entirely her choice, and neither was the anger she felt. It was just what she had to work with, so she'd clung to it. She figured anything that got her out of bed had to be something, even if it wasn't the healthiest way to deal with things.

When that gun came out, she had dealt with it. She hadn't crumbled or rolled into a ball. She'd acted. In the moment, her doctor's instincts had kicked in to protect the patient, to save that life.

Now, all she could sense was her racing heart. The way the red sticky blood clung to her, staining her. "It's not my blood. It's not my blood. Not mine."

His hands flexed on her cheeks, and she registered his touch. He was here, with her. The blood and him, it all mingled into one but this time, she wasn't trapped in a twisted metal cage. His touch was sure, warm and safe.

*His damn hands.* She'd thought about them more than once since the car crash. The way he'd run them over her body, assessing the damage. How he'd stroked her cheek, the one that wasn't torn flesh. His fingers wrapped in between hers as he'd held her hand in his huge grip. She shouldn't like it so much. When she met his eye, he looked just like that night. His gorgeous dark eyes were so intense, concern etched within them.

She needed to get away, breathe. Remember the reality of their strange relationship and get back to her safe place of not needing anyone.

"You can get off me now." *I can't take the way you're looking at me. Like you care.* It felt too good, and she needed to shut that down real fast.

When he didn't move an inch, she unsheathed her claws. "I don't need you clucking over me like some mother hen."

"Oh, it's like that, huh? Still, Lauren, really?" He swallowed. Hard. She felt it in every fiber of her being. "Fine. Have it your way." His face hardened into irritation.

She high-fived herself internally, till he dipped down lower and scooped her right off the floor. "What are you doing? Put me down, jackass!"

He ignored her, carrying her like a darn baby as he headed down the corridor. In the opposite direction of the elevator.

"Where the hell are you going? Mickey!"

He kicked the door open to the stairwell and didn't miss a step as he headed down the stairs. When she tried again to get free of him, his grip tightened.

"Stop it. Your legs are like jelly, so don't pretend you can walk."

"I can," she shot back, to which his only answer was a raised brow.

"Oh yeah? I can feel your whole body shaking. It's called shock, Lauren, in case you've forgotten your basic trauma training."

"Don't call me Lauren," she tried to grit out, but her teeth betrayed her, chattering together. "I don't like you," she managed to get out.

He chuckled, the rumble of it reverberating around her. "Tell me something I don't know, Basso. Still not putting you down. I'm taking you to the washroom next to our office. You look like a damn extra from a horror movie."

Looking down at herself, she fully registered the blood for the first time. She was covered in it, and she knew it was all over her face. She'd felt it as she lunged to cover her patient, the feel of it triggering memories from that night all over again now the rush of adrenaline was fading away. Making her shake anew.

Mickey had sensed it, of course, but when didn't he sense her? The man seemed to have some kind of instruction manual to her she hadn't written, let alone divulged to anyone. It was the most annoying thing about him.

"I…" She tried to say she was okay, but her body was not in the mood to cooperate. In fact, it was a downright needy traitor. Her arms had slid up and were holding onto him, the only thing stopping her from vibrating right out of his firm grip.

"You're okay," he said, his voice barely there. "I've got you, Laur—"

He cut himself off before he spoke her name in full, but she frowned anyway.

"No one calls me Lor," she muttered, her panicked brain finally catching up with her and knocking her tongue loose.

Of course, the cocky knowing smile he shot back proved that her retort was like catnip to him. Or whatever the equivalent would be for the golden retriever currently cradling her to him. Chirpy Erin was spot on in her assessment.

Lauren found herself wondering what animal Erin would compare her to. A wild animal, probably. A panther, a cobra even. Always ready to strike at anyone stupid enough to try to get close.

"Ever? Not even Oscar?"

What did Oscar have to do with this? They weren't the type of couple to have pet names for each other. They never did any of that cutesy rubbish. "Especially not him," she muttered. "We weren't like that."

"Noted," Mickey replied, and she thought she saw another little smile cross his face. She couldn't be sure, though.

The blood was drying on her face now, feeling like a chalky facemask. Which meant that her makeup would be ruined too, and her cover-up kit was in her office. Great.

They reached the door to the floor below, and he paused. "Do you think you can walk to the washroom? I can carry you, but there are people out there."

She would rather die than let their colleagues see him carry her. The washroom was at this end of the corridor anyway, not far. She nodded, and he let her down, tucking her behind him. She froze when his hand came back and slipped through hers.

Turning his head to the side, he didn't look at her. "Just to steady you. I'll walk in front, stop people rubbernecking. Ready?"

"Ready."

He pulled her after him through the doors, pulling his big hand closer to his body, which forced her to tuck into his back. He walked straight to the washroom doors, head held high, but they needn't have bothered.

The department was in full-on control mode, Gloria the only person spotting them.

"Mickey!" Peeking over the side of his arm, Lauren could see the look of concerned relief flash across the nurse's dark features. When she saw Lauren, her eyes widened but she didn't comment. "Are you both okay?"

"We're fine," he replied, reaching the washroom and opening the door so Lauren could slip through. "We'll need a minute, though. You got everything covered here?"

Lauren peered into the washroom, which was essentially a mini one-room apartment for the doctors and nurses. It had a couch and a metal bunk bed in one corner for the staff who needed to pull all-nighters. Next to a small kitchenette was a little circular dining table with uncomfortable but functional-looking dining chairs. In the opposite corner was a small shower room complete with stark white tiles, a toilet and a sink.

Mickey's hand was still holding hers, and she realized she didn't want to lose that contact right now. She stood and listened as Gloria relayed the ER situation.

The police had taken the gunman away, and he wasn't getting out of their clutches any time soon. The rest of the staff were scrambling to treat the patients and calm them all down after the drama.

"Okay, call HR," Mickey said, taking charge. "Tell them we're going to need some cover. Dr Ferguson might be available."

Gloria left, and Lauren let Mickey lead her into the room. Spotting the mirror, she took a deep breath and, dropping his hand, stood in front of it to assess the damage.

The shaking returned as she took in her appearance. Her face was a mess, blood covering most of her scar like some cruel joke from where she'd pressed her face to her patient's front to try to shield as much of his body as she could.

"That was pretty crazy, what you did back there."

She met Mickey's gaze in the mirror but couldn't hold it. Reaching for one of the washcloths on the shelf, she set about wetting it with warm water. "Stupid, you mean, right?"

"No. Well. Maybe. Brave is more what comes to mind. What if he'd shot you?"

Wringing out the cloth, she started to wipe off the blood, careful not to uncover her scar in front of him. She never let anyone see the real her.

"Then I'd be shot," she sassed back.

"Exactly. A risky move. Some might even say reckless."

"Yeah, well, I didn't see you hitting the floor, either. You were lunging for him, too."

"I was lunging for you," he refuted, his eyes lasering onto her through the mirror. She was glad the mirror was between his gaze on her, because even that degree of separation felt like too much to take in. It was like looking into the sun. "The patient just happened to be there."

"Playing the hero again, huh? Aren't you bored of that yet?"

He swallowed, finally looking away. "Obviously not," he murmured, something in his voice she didn't want to acknowledge, let alone analyze. "Stay here. I'll go get you some clothes. You can't go home like that."

"Go home? Why would I go home?"

Mickey's face fell into a frown. "Well, after what we've been through, I'm pretty sure HR will be sending us both home. I thought you might want to go."

"Are you going?"

"Well, no…but—"

"I'm not, either. I'm fine." She thought of what awaited her at home. It wasn't like she could go out with friends or distract herself. All that waited for her at home were those familiar walls. She didn't relish the thought of being alone any longer than she had to. "I have nothing waiting for me. If I go home, I'll only think about it."

"Okay." His smile was soft, but his eyes were ever assessing. *How does he do that? Look at me like he's trying to read my mind?* "Then we'll both stay. I'll leave you to it."

He was almost out of the door when she swallowed her pride and called after him. "Mickey?"

"Yes, Lor?"

*Geez, that's less annoying than it should be.* She brushed the feeling off, steeling herself to ask this man for a favor. "I need something, from my desk. My, er… makeup bag. It's in the bottom drawer. Could you please bring it to me?"

He nodded as he turned back to the door. "Of course. I'll flick the sign to Occupied so you're not bothered."

"Thank you," she called after him.

Pulling off her clothes, she winced at the bloodstains. They were all over her, and she wondered how her patient was doing. Even the blood loss could make surgery difficult, not to mention the stress of being accosted by a gunman as he lay injured. Whatever he was involved with, no one deserved that.

He wasn't the first gunshot victim she'd treated, but it was the first case when the shooter had come into the hospital to finish the job. Security would have to be increased now. She hoped that the press wouldn't spot her leaving if they decided to camp out at the hospital. That was the last thing she needed, on top of everything else.

She was out of the shower and sitting at the table in a towel when the door opened again.

Mickey's head popped around tentatively, his pupils dilating as he saw her sitting there. She saw his gaze flick down to her legs, but he didn't linger on her scars. Her face was free of makeup and blood now, and she forced herself not to look away as he assessed her facial scarring. And he was assessing; she could see him scrutinizing the lines on her face.

"Coming in," he said a moment later, his arms filled with clothes and a couple of take-out boxes. "I brought us some food, too. We missed lunch." Putting the clothes down first, he slid the boxes across the small table. "I can leave, if you like."

Her first instinct was to tell him yes, but something in his hopeful eyes stopped her. Shrugging instead, she reached for the clothes and headed to the bathroom. The makeup bag was on top, so she got to work, dressing quickly and applying the concealer to her face. Working till she was satisfied that her scars were covered, she was about to zip up the bag again when her eyes fell on the lip gloss she never used. She'd bought it on a whim one night when ordering her usual makeup online. Ignoring her own head asking her what the heavens she was doing, she slicked some across her lips and shoved her ruined clothing in a biohazard bag from under the sink.

Placing it all by the main door, she returned to her seat.

Without a word, he pushed the other box of food toward her.

As she opened it up, she noticed some scratches running along his corded forearm and leaned closer. *Did he get hurt earlier?* A wave of unease rattled through her till she saw that they were scabbed over. A few days old, at least.

She felt his eyes on her, and feeling more confident with her mask back in place, she raised her brow at him.

"I have a cat, a rescue."

Digging into warm chicken salad, she couldn't help the smile that battled to be freed. "You rescued a cat?" Who was this guy, Dr. Dolittle on his days off?

"Yep." He shrugged as if all life-saving hot doctors rescued animals in their spare time. "Tripod. Found the little thing at the side of the road, tied up and dumped in a bag."

"Tripod? A male cat then?"

He chuckled, and to her horror, she joined him. "Dr. Basso, that was oddly risqué of you. I like it."

She filled her mouth with a forkful of salad to hold back her sassy retort.

"He lost a leg, hence his name. He's still a kitten, just barely. Loves a good scrap. Usually when I'm trying to sleep."

"You kept him? At your place?"

Another tiny shrug of his broad shoulders. "Well, we'd already kind of bonded. Figured he'd been through enough, and I have the room."

"Didn't your…" oh God, she was not going to ask that question. She did not care. Not in the slightest "…roommate mind?"

And there it was. That cocky smirk. "Roommate? I don't have a roommate, besides him." A beat passed. "No girlfriend, either, if you were asking."

"I wasn't."

"Fine. What about you?"

She finished another mouthful. "What about me?"

"Do you have a…*roommate*?"

"Nope. No roommate." Her lips twisted to the side, and his eyes flashed.

"No one else, since Oscar?"

She bristled at the name. What the hell were they doing here? What was this, some kind of weird date? *You're colleagues, nothing more. You don't like him, remember?* "You seem pretty obsessed with my ex-boyfriend, Dr. Nolan."

She didn't miss the wince her words elicited, but he recovered quickly. "Not obsessed. I just didn't like the guy, and I wanted to know if you had anyone else in your corner."

"I hold my own corner."

"Really?"

"Really. I'm fine."

"You don't seem to eat properly. You look exhausted a lot of the time, and—"

Her hackles woke up again, stretching from their little nap. "And a boyfriend would solve that problem, right? Tell me, Mickey, how is my personal life any of your business? Because I had a boyfriend, and he left when it mattered, so I don't think some new man is going to come along on his white horse and make all my boo-boos better. My diet, sleep schedule—all of it—are not your concern. As long as I'm doing my job, it doesn't matter how I look after myself."

"Having some support would help. We all need someone. At least someone who will make sure you eat and get some sleep. You've looked tired every day you've been here."

"Great." She threw her fork into her box of food. "So I'm too thin, and I look tired. Anything else you want to pick on me for?"

He placed his own fork on the table with a sigh. "I never said that you were too thin. There's nothing wrong with your body. That came out wrong, Lor. I was just looking out for you—as a colleague."

"My name is not Lor." *Nothing wrong with my body? Does he really not see my scars? He never looks at them, and the number of times he stares at my face, that just can't be true.*

"So you keep saying. I'm sorry, it…just slipped out. I… get flustered sometimes, around you."

"Flustered? You?"

The twitch of his lips made her almost smile. Almost, because she tamped that down real quick. "Yes. Me. You get under my skin. That can't be news to you." He flashed her a defiant smile. "I'm pretty sure it's not one-sided, either."

She let her pout answer for her. He did get under her skin, in more ways than one.

"As for the other stuff, I wasn't being unkind. I just want you to look after yourself. This job is hard, and with your time off and recovery, it's easy to neglect yourself." He pushed her food a little closer. "We have time. Finish your food. Please."

*And there he goes again. Trying to look after me. I can't afford to get used to this or rely on it. He'll leave eventually, like everyone else. I know it. Once the reality of seeing who I am sets in, the dark melancholy that follows me, he won't stick around.*

"No." She went to stand, and he came with her. *Of course he did. He's never going to let up unless you shut this down.* Whatever this thing was between them, it wasn't healthy. She was not going to be some pitiful thing he worked his savior magic on. "I don't need you to prompt me to eat, Mickey. I can look after myself. Have done for a heck of a long time. If you have a problem with the way I work, then take it to HR. Other than that, my lack of a personal life is nothing to do with you. I'm fine on my own. I am fully recovered from what your brother did to me and—"

"Are you?" He rounded the table, but she sidestepped him and headed for the door. "Because I see a glimpse of the real Lauren now and again, but the rest of the time, you're like a ghost."

"A ghost?" She whirled to face him, but he was closer than she thought, and it unnerved her in more ways than one.

He was so handsome, so hot standing there. The way his eyes pinned hers. She had never seen him look like that at anyone but her, which royally ticked her off and thrilled her in equal measure. Something deep within her wanted to reach out to this man, to let him bring her food and save her from bullets. It felt so…primal, this thing between them.

She shouldn't have watched so much *Vampire Diaries* while she was holed up in her apartment. It was the only thing she'd been able to stomach, the rest being true crime and medical shows that felt far too much like real life. And boy had her guilty binge-watching backfired—she was turning into a lovesick teenager, not a hardened ER doctor who couldn't quite remember that the gorgeous, too happy man in front of her was related to the very person who had made her like this in the damn first place. "How would you know the real Lauren, huh? You never met her."

"I did!" he shouted, but the second the words left his lips, he bit at them. "That night, you were different."

"Different? Are you kidding me? I was terrified!"

"I didn't mean it like…oh God, Lor. I always say the wrong things around you. I meant that you're so closed off. So shut down. You look like you've lost your light, or something… I don't know. I know you were scared that night. I was too. Petrified. I wanted to lift that car off you with my bare hands."

"Yeah," she snorted, feeling like she was going to vomit. Her emotions were all fighting their own battles in the pit of her stomach, bouncing around while they fought for supremacy. She pushed down into her default, anger, before nausea got the chance to decide for her. "So your brother wouldn't get punished."

"What?" His fists clenched by his sides. "No. I have never tried to protect my brother from what he did. I was there that night to stop him from hurting someone, and I failed. That's on me, but I don't make excuses for Denny, either. He was messed up, and he hurt you. I will never forgive him for that. You were injured so badly, and I was so scared you wouldn't pull through. If Denny had killed you that night…" His eyes closed as if the pain of keeping them open was too much. "I just wish I'd gotten there sooner. You experienced such a horrible thing. Look at you now, though, Lauren. You've taken your life back, as much as you think you're failing. You got out of there alive."

"I know that, Captain Obvious," she scoffed. "I was the one in the damn wreck."

He took a step forward. "Do you? Because sometimes I think you still feel trapped under that car, and all I want to do is remind you that you are not alone and that you survived. You're still here. The accident can't define your life unless you let it. You are so much more than that."

He moved closer, as if he wanted to press the words right into her. "I know that I am the last person you probably want to hear that from, and it's easy for me to wax lyrical about something I never went through. I have no right to comment on any of this or even get involved. I get all that, and I'm sorry if what I'm trying to say comes off wrong. I… I'm just in awe of you, for surviving what you did. For everything you went through. I know you feel like you're probably drowning. I just want to remind you, somehow, to come up for air."

For a moment, she couldn't speak. The lump in her throat choked off her words as she processed his. She had survived. She'd clawed herself back to the point of being able to work, and she was good at her job. She loved helping people, the medicine of it all, but it wasn't enough to fix her—and then along came Mickey.

Riding in on his white horse, he saw her vulnerability through her carefully closed off persona. It was driving her crazy. She knew he meant well, but hearing all this from him? She didn't want to feel vulnerable ever again. She wouldn't survive a second time if it all went wrong again. He was too close, too knowing. Somehow, her broken parts stood out to Mickey like they did for no one else.

Not for the first time, she wished it had been anyone else but him who had come to her rescue that night. That the man before her wasn't in her life, trying to save her over and over again. She couldn't—wouldn't have it. "God, you are so full of it."

Mickey's head couldn't have snapped back any harder if she'd slapped him. "What?"

"Do you even hear yourself? What did you do, take a course in therapy in between rescuing damsels? You think you can be the one to save me. Again. Right? Save me from the accident, from myself, from some gunman?"

"Well, I did save you from getting shot today after you recklessly offered yourself up as bullet fodder. That counts for something, right?"

"Counts, toward what? You trying to score points for

something? Need me to fan your hero complex for you, is that it? You're not your brother. You don't need to make anything up to me. I am not your problem or your concern."

He laughed, but it came out hollow. "I don't need you to do anything for me. I want you to do it for yourself. I'm not playing the hero here." He looked away, as if he wasn't entirely convinced himself. "I know that my brother is at fault, that's not in question. We…colleagues, and I just want to help, that's all. I want you to realize that you still have a life to live."

"Oh!" She threw her hands in the air, resisting the urge to strangle him. "You're infuriating. What doesn't kill you makes you stronger, right?"

"Well, yeah," he started, his words dying when she laughed in his face.

"Aww, Mickey. That's perfect. Maybe instead of moonlighting as an unpaid therapist you should print your own T-shirts. Get your own website—mrsunshinedoesitagain dot com!"

He gave a nonchalant shrug, as though he was pretending to consider it, but his shoulders were tense. His features taut. His eyes were nearly black as he watched her unravel in front of him, which just made her worse. "Mr. Sunshine has a nice ring to it. Maybe I should patent that," he said.

"Of course it does, Dr. Perfect! Ever since I got here, I've been waiting for rainbows to shoot out of your backside! Do you want to know something, Mickey?"

"I'm pretty used to you speaking your mind by now. Have at it, I can take it, Basso. Bring it on."

"At least I *have* a mind!"

"What is that supposed to mean?" She went to pull

away, but he blocked her exit, caging her in. His brooding presence dominated every single sense she possessed. "Come on, Lauren. Say what you mean, for once. My sarcasm-decoding skills are a little fried lately."

"I mean that the world is not all cake and stupid rainbows, Mickey! You walk around this place like everything is great, and everyone is happy, and it's all a load of bull—"

"Oh, so just because I choose to look on the bright side of things means I'm some joke, right? Well, what about you?"

Bunching her fists by her sides, she got closer to his face to give him her best stink eye. "What about me? I'm a realist, I see—"

He let out a hearty snort. "Realist, right. And Dracula was a Boy Scout. In fact, are you sure you two aren't related? Because you kind of rock the whole Princess of Darkness persona. Isn't it exhausting, being so miserable? So guarded all the darn time? I'm surprised you have any teeth left with the amount of grinding you do! So tell me how trying to see life as a good thing is so bad, especially with the jobs we do. Shock me, Lor. Prove my rainbow-shooting ass wrong, I beg you! Because I swear, if I ever see a real, genuinely happy smile on that pretty face of yours, I will back right off."

Their faces were so close their noses brushed against each other.

She could feel the sting of his words like a slap on her skin and felt the onslaught of tears burning her eyes. "Well, that might just be worth the effort! You are so damn annoying—and saying I'm pretty?" Her voice broke. "That's just low, Nolan."

His hands were on her cheeks before she even registered

his movement. "Stop that," he growled. "I wasn't being nasty, Lauren. I wouldn't joke about that, either. You are pretty. With makeup or without."

She could scarcely draw breath to answer. His stupid entrancing eyes were right there, looking right at her, and she didn't miss it when his gaze dropped to her lips. "Don't pity me," she breathed. "Don't you dare. I don't need it, especially from you."

He'd already seen her at her worst. Broken, terrified. Bleeding. She'd thought about his face so often since that night. His strong voice, speaking with such urgent conviction that she wasn't alone, that he was right there with her, that she was going to be okay.

But she wasn't. Sometimes, she felt like she'd never be okay again. Going through the motions was hard enough. The effort of pretending she was still functioning was exhausting.

"Pity you? Never." Mickey pulled her right out of her head, until all she could feel was him. His thumbs brushed along her cheekbones, and it took everything in her not to let her eyes roll back in her head.

What was it, this thing between them? Not quite hate, but...something. When she caught glimpses of the man who'd held her hand that night, it did things to her. Confusing things that she wanted nothing more than to run from.

"You *are* pretty, Lauren Basso," he reiterated, his voice softer now. "In fact, I think you're beautiful. So utterly breathtaking that I can't get you out of my happy little mind."

His grip tightened, and before she could stop herself, her lips were on his.

She felt the jolt between them as their lips connected. His tiny little flinch of surprise before he slipped one hand behind her neck and pulled her closer, tilting her head to deepen the kiss. And oh…what a kiss! He kissed her like he'd been born to do it, and his mouth felt like heaven on hers.

Of course, the mouthy golden retriever that was Dr. Mickey Nolan could kiss.

His arms came around her, and she wrapped her legs around him tight as he pushed them both back to the wall. His hands slid under her thighs to grip her body to his. His hard length pressed up against her as he cradled her to him, breathy pants in her ear.

"We shouldn't be doing this," she managed to breathe out between furious kisses.

"Probably not," he rumbled, nipping at her earlobe and letting out a groan. "We're doing it anyway. God, you smell amazing."

"It's just anger," she muttered, trying to stifle the moan that threatened to rip through her when his mouth moved down her neck. "This…thing between us." The moan that chased her denial gave away her lies.

"Yep," he agreed, sucking at the spot above her collarbone. He'd nuzzled her clothing out of the way like a hungry bear. "All riled up right now, that's for sure. Take your anger out on me, Lor. I can take whatever you've got."

"I don't even like you," she grumbled as his lips came back to meet hers. She didn't stop her tongue peeking out to taste his, regardless.

"Yeah?" He raised a brow as he pulled back just a fraction, his eyes dropping to her shirt and back up again. "Tell that to your hard nipples, Lor."

She growled, which only made him smirk.

He robbed another kiss and pulled away. "That's okay. I think I made my point."

Disheveled, clothes askew, he set her back on her feet. He looked so gorgeous standing there, a satisfied smirk on his face that she wanted to slap off and kiss some more all at the same time. His chest was rising just as rapidly as hers, and she didn't miss the way he pulled his white coat straight to cover his arousal.

"Point?" she asked, gasping for breath, knowing that he wanted her to ask but unable to pretend she didn't care. "What point was that?"

"That I find you beautiful and sexy." He gently ran his thumb right along her scar, and she willed herself not to flinch. "Every single inch of you."

"That it?" she challenged, wishing her heart would stop trying to jump out of her rib cage.

"Nope. I also find you intensely annoying, argumentative, and you definitely have the air of a know-it-all about you."

"You're a pig," she spat, but the heat behind her words was lukewarm at best.

He knew it, too, judging from his satisfied grin.

Which was the exact opposite of what she was feeling in that moment. She was still vibrating from their encounter, wondering what the hell had just happened. And why she wanted to drag him back to her and do the whole thing all over again.

"Oink, oink," he quipped. "Now finish your food like a good little doctor and come find me when you're ready." He was just a head in the door as he scooped up her dirty clothes and shot her a wink. "For kissing or shouting. It's up to you, Lor, but I'm here for both."

And he left her leaning against the wall, alone with her racing thoughts and the sound of her heavy breathing.

# CHAPTER FOUR

Two whole weeks. To be exact, she'd been working at Seattle General for seventeen days since they'd mauled each other in the breakroom, and Mickey was annoying with his attention. He didn't try to kiss her again, but he was always there. That cocky smile, his eyes roving over her when no one else was watching. His ridiculously upbeat greetings, the jokes he cracked to try to make her break and smile. He was everywhere. What made it worse, was that she was *paying* him attention.

Since that kiss—and his words—she couldn't stop watching him. He really was perky, like, all the time. She'd thought it had to be an act, but nope. The man was so happy he probably woke up with a smile on his face and a spring in his step. Which just wasn't sustainable for a human.

It made her feel even worse when her moods dipped. Three times this week, a patient had commented on her face, and one of the nurses on the peds floor had read all about her and Mickey's brother and asked how things were going, working together. It was annoying to say the least, and the comment on working with Mickey had only served to remind her that she'd kissed the enemy. Or the kin of the enemy, at least.

She knew Mickey wasn't to blame for the accident. He'd

tried to stop it, in fact, and stayed to help, but that didn't make it any better. The fact was, the only man to set her whole being on fire was wrapped up in the worst time of her life, and it was getting more and more confusing that she couldn't separate the two as time went on. Billions of men on the planet, and she found herself wanting the one man she definitely shouldn't. It went against everything she had promised herself in the aftermath of the pain she had suffered.

When Oscar had left her without so much as a backward screw-you, she'd made an oath never to be in that position again. Her ex had taken one look at her damaged body and scarpered. They might not have been love's young dream, but it had still hurt that someone she had shared her life with could walk away from her so easily. Could be so unmoved by seeing their partner like that. She was better off alone, and kissing her work colleague was definitely not part of the plan.

Especially this colleague. He should be the last man on earth she would ever want.

Mickey Nolan was the distraction from her simple solitary life, the complication she never could have foreseen. All in a joyful, six-foot-odd package, wrapped in abs and muscles that quite frankly no man had any business hiding under a white coat. He was haunting her with his hot, protective ways, and she was crumbling quickly.

*I really need to stop binging TV in the early hours, too. Maybe even pop one of those sleeping tablets my doctor prescribed. My new life is all about work and being a strong, independent woman.*

So she threw herself into work, which was pretty easy. Seattle was still the busy city she remembered, and people were still getting ill. They'd had the usual asthma attacks, minor burns and scrapes, rashes and fevers. Chest pains, stroke symptoms. A wave of children all from the same school with a fast-moving and very concerning stomach bug.

And of course, the darker side of ER life. People hurting each other and making silly mistakes. Just this week, she'd had two gunshot victims, one that didn't make it despite her and Mickey's best efforts. Another time, they'd worked together on a patient who'd fallen from low-level scaffolding while catcalling a woman down below. Mickey, when hearing this, had not only helped treat his shattered legs and other injuries but had also given him a stern talking-to about not treating women like objects for his own amusement.

The nurses around them had practically swooned, and Lauren even found herself a little weak in the knees. He was…something else, and knowing what he felt like now, to hold, to kiss? It was…confusing.

After Oscar, she'd vowed never to bother with the opposite sex. The thought of getting naked in front of a new man had left her cold, but now? That resolve suddenly wasn't so clear in her head. Given that she'd had more than one dirty thought about him since their argument-turned-make-out session in the washroom, she was struggling to keep her anger sharp around him. Sometimes it morphed into something else just as vivid.

Red-hot lust.

It was the worst thing that had happened since the crash. Things felt…unpredictable around Mickey. She felt unpredictable around him, and that was not on her post-accident checklist. Being around him was even worse now she was so hyperaware of him. Noticing little things about him that she committed to memory like some kind of groupie, in her *I heart Doctor Nolan* file. It was crazy how much she'd learned about the man she was supposed to be avoiding like a deadly disease. Of all the men she'd sworn off for life, he had to be the worst pick possible. Was her libido seriously this twisted? Since when was trauma bonding this cruel?

*How do you get under my skin? Let me count the ways.*

Mickey Nolan had a secret smile, for a start. She noticed it whenever she caught him looking, or to be more accurate, when he caught her looking. They were like teenagers crushing on each other. She was still closed off and confident in her work—medicine brought that out in her—but when he was around, she noticed him. Was flustered by him, even. She had to concentrate on her own body when he was nearby, to stop her from floundering around the place like a startled gazelle. Worse still, he seemed to know it, thrive on it and demand more.

She knew that the nurses had noticed. Erin wasn't one to stay quiet on the subject. On any subject, Lauren was fast coming to realize about one of her hardest working nurses. She didn't miss a trick and wasn't shy in citing her sources, either.

"So," Erin said, sidling up to the main ER desk. Lauren was typing up the notes on the last patient, a lovely woman in her fifties who'd gone out on a date not realizing that the sauce her food was served in was made with lobster puree. Her shellfish allergy had kicked in, causing her to balloon up and struggle with breathing right there in the middle of the fancy restaurant. Lauren had treated her quickly, and her date hadn't left her side the whole time, holding her hand. "It looks like they're going to have a hell of a second date. I swear, he was acting like she hung the moon. It was so romantic."

Lauren's eyes flitted across to the couple as they headed

through the ER doors, his arm holding her tight to him as he guided her out. "Yep. Probably."

Erin gave her the look Lauren had come to recognize as wanting more of a response. *Sigh.* She looked back at the couple, seeing the tender forehead kiss the man dropped on his date as the doors closed behind them. "They were pretty cute."

"Who's pretty cute?" a familiar voice sang behind her.

"No one," Lauren huffed, right as Erin said, "The couple Lauren just treated. Allergic reaction on a first date. Ha!" Erin giggled. "A lobster found them their lobster, get it?"

Lauren repressed a groan. "I get it. Funny."

"That exciting, huh?" Mickey beamed. "Sorry I missed it. I love a little bit of romance in the ER. Makes everything that bit sweeter, right, Dr. Basso?"

Erin's head was watching the two of them like a tennis match.

Lauren wished she could cut the blood flow to her cheeks to stop the blush spreading across them. *Good Lord, he's sure of himself.* So infuriatingly hot she wanted to bite back. Or bite him. One of the two.

"I wouldn't know, Dr. Nolan." She bared her teeth at him, but he only smiled wider. "I focus on the medicine, not some crush." *Damn it.*

"Crush?" His brows hit his hairline, his stupidly handsome face lighting up to a megawatt level. "Who has a crush? I never mentioned anything like that. Did you hear me mention a crush, Erin?"

Lauren looked at Erin for help, but the traitorous nurse was nearly vibrating with excitement. She was enjoying their latest round of banter, and as Lauren glanced around, she saw Erin wasn't the only one. Gloria whispered something to Jarvis as he wheeled past with a patient in a wheelchair, and Jarvis nodded as his gaze slid over to them.

All eyes were on her, and she hated it. Being around Mickey was changing her. Changing how people saw her. No, scratch that, it made people see her, and that wasn't what she wanted. Not at all.

Witnessing Oscar's reaction to her accident had been testament to that. The second he'd seen her face, her legs, knew what her recovery would entail—he'd changed. She'd never been needy with Oscar, they'd never had that kind of desperate can't-live-without-the-other type of love, but she'd needed him then. The bare minimum would have been to tell her that everything was going to be okay, even if it wasn't. To tell her that he would stick by her, see her through this.

If it had been Oscar under that car, she would have done it for him. She would have helped him with whatever he needed, taken time off work. Oscar acted like the whole thing was her problem, an inconvenience to the easy life they'd been living. So she'd watched him leave and didn't put up a fight. There was nothing to save, and she didn't have the energy to even try. If he couldn't stick around, she reasoned, then no man ever would. And she would never give them the chance.

In those early weeks, she couldn't bear to look in her mirror. Her face had been altered so much that she didn't recognize herself anymore. They'd gotten the best plastic surgeons to work on her at Pres, but the scar was still there. A mark of what had happened, and she couldn't even hide it. She would never be able to fade into the background. People would always look, do double takes when they saw her. It was human nature when someone looked different.

Even after all of her surgeries and post-op care, she would never see the old her in a mirror ever again.

Her face felt hot, like her scar was burning, and she stood up so fast the chair beneath her rattled into the wall behind. "I—I…"

Mickey noticed, and he was rounding the desk before she could stop him. "Hey, hey," he said, his voice so low she knew it was only for her. "I was just kidding, I didn't mean to—"

"It's fine. I have work to do."

His hand closed over her wrist, him looking as surprised as her that they'd made contact in front of everyone. "I didn't mean to embarrass you, Lor."

"You didn't." She flushed, something about that stupid pet name of his uncurling something inside her. "I just don't like being on show. Everyone's watching us."

His face softened, and she couldn't stand the tender, protective look he was giving her.

The nurses had all seemingly sensed the tension, heading back to work, but the frisson of emotions in her stomach escalated, if anything, as their audience dispersed. Her phone rang in her pocket, but she made no move to answer it. Not with his hand still cuffing her wrist like a burning brand.

"Lauren, I—"

"Incoming!" Julio yelled. "RTA, two casualties. Multiple injuries. Coming in hot!"

"Clear trauma rooms one and two!" Mickey shouted as the pair of them sprang apart and into action.

"We're going to need blood, trauma kits and all non-essential personnel dealing with the patients waiting," Lauren boomed as the two of them washed up, grabbing gloves and aprons. In silent tandem, he tied her plastic apron, and she turned to tie his.

"You good?" he asked when he turned back to face her. His way of asking if her head was in the game.

"I'm good," she told him. "Let's go, you take trauma one."

He held out a fist, and she bumped it before they both ran to meet the gurneys the ambulance crew were rolling through.

"Anna, what've we got?" Mickey called to the paramedic who was busy bagging a female patient.

"Passenger of the car, Grace Score. Twenty-eight. She was thrown through the windshield when the car hit the streetlight. Left pupil is blown, she's not been conscious since. Pulse is thready and weak. No response to stimulus."

Lauren looked down at the patient, her head cut to ribbons, and for a second, all she could see was herself lying there.

"We got her breathing through CPR, but…"

She didn't need to say it. Lauren could see on the monitors that her barely there vitals were fading. If she wasn't being bagged, she wouldn't be breathing. Her body had been through a catastrophic event. This amount of trauma wasn't survivable.

"Trauma one. I'll take her," Lauren said, earning a look from Mickey. She was half expecting him to argue, knowing that he could see what she could, but he clenched his jaw and gave her a nod before running to the other gurney.

His patient was cut up, too, but he was also screaming for his passenger. Screaming meant life in their line of work. It was the silent patients who were the most vulnerable, the closest to death's cold grip.

"Grace! I'm so sorry! Grace! Help her, please!" He went back to groaning in pain as Mickey took him into trauma room two. Lauren could hear him trying to calm the guy down as she worked on Grace.

"Both pupils are blown," she called to the nurses working around her. "Massive head trauma."

"We need the portable CT in here, now!" Erin shouted, but as Lauren listened in at her chest, she shook her head. The scan would have to wait. Grace was already dying.

"Have it on standby, we've lost her again. Defib!"

While one of the other nurses, Bonnie, readied the machine, and Gloria breathed for the patient with the Ambu bag, Lauren racked her mind for a way to save this woman. There must be something she wasn't thinking of, right? She couldn't just let this woman die, when her fate was so similar to hers. It was like admitting defeat all over again.

"Ready!" Bonnie called, and Lauren grabbed for the paddles.

"Three hundred. Clear!"

Grace's body jolted as the shock hit her chest, but the heart monitor flatlined again.

"Adrenaline!" Lauren instructed, and Gloria was there with a needle in milliseconds, driving into the patient's IV that the paramedics had already used for the first dose. "Prep for three-fifty."

Lauren listened again, but the heart in Grace's chest wasn't beating.

The patient next door was screaming and crying, calling her name as Mickey's soothing but firm voice spoke to him as he tended to his less severe injuries right in the next trauma room. When Lauren shone the pen light into Grace's eyes, prying open her lids, they were fixed and dilated. No response. The trauma to her head had already wreaked havoc from the moment of impact. They weren't getting her back. Not in any real way.

"Patient records, does she have any directives?"

What they were doing was already extraordinary measures, but with no DNR in place, they were doing what they could, until there was nothing left to try.

"She's not an organ donor," Julio called out over her shoulder. "No other directives in place."

Lauren nodded, raising the paddles again. "Clear!"

*Zap.* Nothing.

The whole room was silent other than the sound of the bag's rhythm as it pumped air into Grace's chest and the continuous death knell beep of the monitor.

"Charge again," Lauren called, but Erin shook her head. "Doctor, she's down. She's been down a long time."

Lauren clenched her jaw. "Charge again!" She met Erin's eye. "One more time."

She knew that the Grace that had gotten into the car that day would never be back. Even if they got her heart beating again, even if her brain trauma was operable, she would be a husk of the person she had been that morning.

As Lauren waited for the charge to ready, taking in the pretty necklace around Grace's neck, she wondered what sort of woman she'd been. Whether she'd been happy with her life before the crash, like Lauren had thought she'd been.

"Ready," Erin said, giving her an encouraging look that told her she agreed with this one last try. Trauma doctors and nurses were the elite, and they didn't stop trying to punch death in the face even if they knew a loss in the ring was right around the corner.

"Clear!" Lauren called again and held her breath as the whole room watched the monitor.

# CHAPTER FIVE

SHE WAS ALMOST to her office when Erin caught up with her later that day. "You made the right call with Grace. If we could have saved her, something good might have come out of it."

Lauren dipped her head, feeling the flash of pain in her shoulders from the exhaustion and effort of the day. "I didn't do it because of what I went through."

"I know," Erin said quickly. "You wanted to save her, despite the odds. I get it." Her gaze flicked over Lauren's scar. "I wanted to see if you were okay. I know it might have brought some things up."

Lauren's default here would have been to snarl and shut down, but she surprised herself by placing her hand on Erin's. "It did, but actually not as bad as you're probably thinking." She bit on her lip. "I feel bad, but also kind of guilty for feeling lucky. Thanks for checking on me, Erin. I know I've been pretty difficult since I started." She laughed at Erin's face. "Don't try to be nice. I know I have. It's been…a lot, to say the least."

"I bet. Mickey told us you might need a minute."

*What? What had he told these people?* "Mickey told you?"

Erin's face blanched. "No specifics, but we put two and two together. The media coverage and all, we knew the patient was a doctor, just not the details of you, per se. When a couple of us put it together the first day, Mickey went to HR and organized a bit of a briefing for the ER staff."

"HR briefed you about me? Wow, that doesn't make me feel like a charity case at all."

"It wasn't like that. He just… I guess he didn't want you to leave. He wasn't talking about you, he just pointed out that your personal life was not part of the job. That you were here to run the department and that you deserved respect. You're not angry with him, are you?"

"I…er. No, I'm not. I am here to work. He's right there."

So much made sense now. Why everyone in the ER had been so nice and normal, why none of the ER staff had mentioned Denny or the crash. Why no one had batted an eyelid at her scars, even when she'd changed in the locker room that time and she knew Gloria had seen the damage to her legs.

He'd been looking out for her, all this time. Not for his family but for her. She found herself wondering how far his reach was, given the media intrusion tapering off so suddenly after the frenzy in those dark early days. Maybe he'd been looking out for her this whole time.

*You need someone in your corner.* His words came back to her. She should be angry about people talking about her, but he'd sorted it out. Given her space to settle into the hospital. Without even being asked, he'd looked out for her. She didn't know quite how to feel about it.

Erin's voice brought Lauren back to the corridor with a bump.

"If you don't mind me asking," she ventured just as Lauren's phone rang again. It had been ringing on and off all day, but she'd ignored it. "Why did you stay after you found out Mickey worked here, too? It must be…difficult."

She'd asked herself that question so many times over the last few weeks. She was still in her probationary period; she could easily have left with minimal notice. None probably, given the circumstances, but she was still here. Her phone stopped ringing and then immediately started up again.

"I guess I'm getting tired of hiding from it," she told Erin. "I didn't want to lose anything else." She thought of her first day, the way Mickey had been. The way she'd reacted to him. "Mickey, too, I guess. He annoyed me so much, I guess I wanted to stay just to keep fighting with him." It was maybe too honest, but it had been a factor. Mickey had brought out her fighting spirit and stoked the old fires within her. In more ways than one, it seemed lately. She couldn't walk past the washroom without blushing. "Keep this conversation to yourself, though, please."

It was Erin's turn now to give her a comforting squeeze. "No problem. For what it's worth, I think you're good for each other. I'm here if you need anything, okay?"

Lauren left her to walk the rest of the corridor alone, digesting Erin's words. *We might be good for each other, but it doesn't mean we can be anything else.* It was all so exhausting; her inner monologue alone made her feel like she'd been through the wringer. Today was not the day for soul searching. Days like today, being alive and well was a gift.

Once she was in their shared office, she closed the door behind her and settled onto one corner of the couch. Her shift was almost over, but the ER was thankfully quiet so she could grab a few minutes. Her pager would alert her if they needed her. She'd not seen Mickey for the rest of the shift, having been pulled into one trauma after the other since they declared time of death on Grace. Unable to restart her heart, they'd had to let her go.

Lauren herself had made the call to next of kin, and she could still hear Grace's mother's cries of anguish as she'd told her the news that her daughter had passed away. Wondering how her own parents back in Florida would have taken that call.

She'd kept them away, even though they were close. Asked them not to visit her while she was in hospital. At the time she couldn't bear to have them look at her lying there like that, watching the media storm about the accident swirling around her. Now, she wondered whether her parents would have cared about any of that. If Grace had pulled through, Lauren was pretty sure her parents would have dashed to her bedside, as they had done to say their goodbyes before their child was sent down to the morgue.

As she pulled out her phone, it started ringing again, and she saw her landlord Earl's number pop up. She hadn't lived there that long; she'd rented the place pretty much unseen from her hospital bed and had shipped her stuff from Oscar's place there after he left. After his hasty retreat, she didn't want to enter his apartment ever again. Or see him again, or watch how he looked at her now, with pity and something akin to revulsion. It wasn't her home anymore, and she had no wish to see it ever again. Not that she'd ever thought of Oscar's place as home, really. It was just somewhere to store their things and sleep, occasionally making time for each other when their demanding jobs allowed. The fact that she'd never even missed her home with Oscar hadn't come as a surprise to her at the time, but the fact she didn't miss Oscar had.

Almost losing your life had a pretty good side effect to it. It shook loose the bull you were going along with. Made you realize that the things you thought were okay maybe were never enough.

*That the face and body you saw in the mirror every day wasn't that imperfect, after all?*

"Hello?"

Mickey's shift was long over, but he was in no mood to go home. He was vibrating with too many feelings to unleash them on anyone, and as he walked into his office, they were rapidly unraveling.

The second the door closed behind him, he couldn't breathe. Ripping off his stethoscope, he pulled off his coat, threw it to the floor, sank down into his office chair and burst into tears. Not Hollywood, one-solitary-drop-down-the-cheek tears, either. These were full-on sobs, ripping his chest open as he heaved them out.

His fists clenched and unclenched on the table as he replayed the image of Grace's broken body in his head all over again. How he'd felt when Erin told him that Lauren had battled to save her in vain. Another life gone, wasted, thrown away. Yet he'd saved his patient. Oh yeah, Finn, Grace's boyfriend, was just fine and dandy, despite driving under the influence of drugs. He'd gotten lacerations from the glass, broken a kneecap, smashed his femur and lost a couple of teeth from smashing into the console, but a couple of nights in the hospital, and he'd be back out into the world.

*Not quite*, the rational wisps still ruling Mickey's brain chipped in. *He lost his girlfriend. All he has now is jail to look forward to. Guilt and grief will be his cellmates.*

But it wasn't enough to quell his frustrated rage. Another drug-impaired driver, another bloodied and broken woman. It was too much to take, and he hadn't even gotten a chance to check on Lauren before she'd gone home. He could only spend the night wondering what the hell she was going through, and then wait till next shift to find out. He didn't have her personal number, and contacting her on her work phone out of business hours, especially as the moon shone high in the office window, just seemed the wrong thing to do.

Maybe she was sleeping or seeking comfort somewhere. *With someone*, his helpful little mind offered. And that thought made him feel all kinds of things. He hoped she had someone in her corner outside of the hospital just as much as he hoped that she didn't. If only because that kiss had fueled his dreams about her. And now, tonight, when he got home, he had the image of poor Grace to add to his own personal horror reel. Right along with Finn's face falling when the police came to tell him that his girlfriend was dead because he'd been too high to have any business getting behind the wheel in the first place.

Mickey thought of Grace again, and her face morphed into Lauren's, pinned under that car, begging him to stay with her. As if he'd want to be anywhere else.

"Damn it!" he cursed, his voice a low growl as he slammed his fist onto his desk.

A startled squeak came from the couch, and his furious eyes zeroed in on Lauren's startled ones. She was lying on the couch, her hair tousled from sleep, a blanket wrapped around her.

"What are you doing here?" It came out as an angry snarl that he wanted to take back the second it ripped out of him. Especially when he saw her sleepy shock turn into something else. *Fear? No.* He never wanted to see that from her. He wanted to be the one person who chased it away for her.

"Geez, snap much?" She yanked the blanket up, and he saw that she was in joggers and a sweatshirt with Seattle Wildcats across it. "It's my office, too, remember? You scared the hell out of me." She glared at him, but the longer she took him in, the more the scowl faded away. "What's wrong, Mickey? This isn't like you."

"No. I know. I'm sorry. I didn't mean to shout like that, I'm just… Today was hard."

She wrapped the blanket up with a heavy sigh he felt in his gut, pushing her feet back into a pair of sneakers she must have tucked under the sofa. "I know. Grace was already gone when she got here. We did everything we could. I tried to save her, but it was already too late. At least her boyfriend made it, though. You saved him, right?"

The reality of that statement should feel good, not like a punch to the gut. "Yeah, I saved him."

"Well, that's something, at least."

"Except he was the one doing the harm, Lor. He killed his girlfriend, and I patched him up. Right while you were trying to save Grace in the next room."

"He killed her? What do you mean?"

He was up and pacing, but when he passed where she was sitting, she grabbed his wrist.

"Sit down," she commanded, her voice strong. Her *don't mess with me* doctor voice. "Tell me what's wrong with you. What do you mean, he killed her? You're not making any sense. It was an accident, wasn't it?"

"He was high." Just saying the words made Mickey sink to the back of the couch, deflating him entirely. It was so late, and the exhaustion was kicking in big time. He was so sick of dealing with other people and their problems. Of never being able to help in any real way. As hard as he tried, he was always a step behind. Always there after the fact, trying to mop up the damage. "Never should have been behind the wheel, but he did it anyway, and she suffered for it. He killed her, Lauren. It was his fault, and he got to walk away. He made a choice, and she paid the price with her life."

"Her tox screen was clear," Lauren said after the longest time. She sagged into the cushions beside him, her fingers running along the fringed edge of the blanket. Up and down, like she was trying to hold onto something to soothe herself. "She wasn't high. There was nothing in her system, I checked. He was really intoxicated?"

Intoxicated wasn't the word. Mickey didn't even know how Finn had managed to start the car, given his levels. Seeing a patient like that, all he could think of was his brother. How it could have ended that way for him, for the woman trying to comfort him right now. He felt so angry, so frustrated and impotent. Like he'd felt that night. Scared and powerless, as though even with all his medical training, he was still just a bystander, watching the horrors unfold and not being able to stop them.

*Denny.* That name floated between them like a specter whenever things like this came up, and it kept playing on repeat in his head. It was driving him crazy, thinking of Lauren ending up like Grace.

"Yeah. I could tell the second I started to treat him. Did the blood draw myself. The police will take him when he's well enough to be discharged. I sent him to another ward, so you won't have to see him again."

"He's a patient, like any other. I can handle it."

Mickey huffed out an exhausted breath. "I know you can. It's me that can't. I can't be as objective with things like this. It affects me. I know you don't need me barging in like some white knight, but I don't know… I just don't like the thought of you getting upset."

She didn't miss a beat, which almost shocked him more than her words. "Me, upset? I'm more rattled by this moody bear side of you."

Her reaction was the opposite of what he was expecting. Was she really not broken by this?

When his jaw dropped, she laughed like she'd been trying to hold it in. "I thought you were going to break the desk."

"Yeah, well, I was mad. I don't get that way easily, I can assure you. It takes a lot to rile me like that."

"I know, it's just weird to see, that's all." The tiny little smile she gave him was like seeing the sun rise for the first time. "I assumed you were more Winnie the Pooh than grizzly."

That got him smiling. "Sorry. I can't always be Mr. Sunshine on command." He sighed, leaning in a little closer as he turned to look at her. "I can't be that for everyone all the time. Are you sure you're really okay? Seeing Grace like that and hearing what happened, it rattled me, and I didn't go through it like you did."

He waited for her rebuttal, but she just stared right back at him. "I'm glad I didn't know about Finn when I was treating Grace. I don't know if I could have concentrated, to be honest. I guess now, knowing how upset he was, hearing him shout for her, it's different somehow. I know he'll feel that pain. My anger won't be worse than that."

"You're still entitled to feel it, all the same." Lauren needed that anger, he knew. It was the thing that had kept her together all this time. It had filled in the cracks the accident left her with and stopped her from shattering altogether. "It must have felt a little too close to home."

"I saw myself, you know? When I first looked at Grace, it was me on that gurney, just for a second." Her eyes welled with tears. "Do you think she knew, before she died? What he did?"

Mickey shook his head. "I don't know anyone sober who would get into a car with someone that high, but I guess that's something we'll never know."

"But he'll know," she said, her voice colder than before. "He has to live with it now, knowing what he did. He'll have to pay for his mistakes. Live with them."

The unspoken passed between them as they looked at each other. It was always there, this gulf between them, Mickey realized with a pang. Perhaps in another life, they could have been more than friends. If he'd seen her in a bar, he wouldn't have hesitated to go over to her. Ask to buy her a drink, a coffee, a meal. If they had just been colleagues, even, he would have been stupid not to make an attempt to date her.

But his brother hung between them, the aftermath keeping them stuck like magnets, both repelling and attracting each other. He felt it now, that push and pull he felt deep in his chest. He longed to know if she felt it, too, but it wasn't the time to open that door. He wasn't strong enough to hear the answer.

"What were you doing in here, anyway?" he asked, changing the subject before he let his tongue get too loose. "I thought you'd gone home ages ago."

She went back to playing with the corner of her blanket, her body tensing. "Nope. Landlord called, my place is flooded. Well, the living room, anyway. Something about my upstairs neighbor leaving a tap running. It took out the electrics, caused some damage. I can't get in there till it's all repaired and dried out, so I thought I'd crash here for tonight. Figure it out tomorrow."

*Not a chance.* She wasn't sleeping on some office

couch. "Don't you have a friend you can call, with a spare bed for the night?"

She fiddled more with the blanket, not meeting his eye. "I'm fine. My friends were mostly work colleagues, I guess, or mutual ones with Oscar. We lost touch, pretty much."

"You pushed them away after the accident, didn't you." He wasn't asking; he knew this woman and how she worked. He didn't even need to press her for an answer. "I have a spare room. Stay with me."

"What? Oh no. No need. I'm fine here."

"I know you're fine here, but the offer's there. I'm just going to grab some food on the way home and pass out when I get there." He knew the second he asked that she wouldn't say yes, but he still wanted her to. Desperately. After today, it felt right somehow, them being together. The urge to take care of her surged to a level that scared even him. "And it's your day off tomorrow, but I picked up a shift. It's just a room, Lauren, and it's better than hanging around the office all day with your sad little blankie." He flashed her a cheeky grin, his mood lightening back to his sunny default, even as his heart beat in his throat waiting for her answer.

"It's not a blankie," she scoffed, shoving his elbow with hers. "I got it from my car, jackass. I can go out tomorrow, find somewhere to hang out."

"All day and all night?"

That clearly got her thinking. She started biting her lip, a telltale sign that she thought he was making sense.

"I'll be gone first thing," he went on. "You can have the place to yourself tomorrow. I'll leave you a key so you can go meet your landlord, and at least then you won't have to haunt the halls of this place like an evil spirit." He laughed out loud when she shoved his shoulder this time. "We can go back to being enemies when you get your crypt fixed, Dracula. Quit being stubborn."

She clenched her jaw. He figured it was time to cut his losses, but then she stood with him and dropped the blanket onto the couch behind her.

"Fine," she said, sounding like she'd just agreed to a root canal without anesthesia. "But I pay for the food on the way home."

Mickey couldn't answer till he wrestled his grin for control of his mouth. "Deal, Morticia. I'll drive. I can bring you back for your car tomorrow on my break if you need it."

No way was she driving tonight. The only way she was going anywhere was with him behind the wheel.

# CHAPTER SIX

WAKING UP IN Mickey Nolan's spare room, Lauren felt rested. That was a sentence she never thought she'd think, but it was the truth.

They'd jumped into Mickey's black SUV and picked up Chinese food on the way to his apartment. He'd been nothing but an attentive host, showing her the spare room and where the towels were in the main bathroom of his rather large place. Then they ate at his kitchen island in a not entirely uncomfortable silence. Tripod had made an appearance, and Mickey had fed him before taking him to sleep in his room for the night.

They were obviously the closest of buddies, and the three-legged cat was quite friendly for an animal who'd been through such trauma. She'd expected a hissing, spitting ball of angry fur, but the little black-and-white cutie was anyone's for a bit of shrimp wonton.

Just as they were cleaning away the take-out containers, Mickey got called back to the hospital. She offered to go with him, but he'd waved her off, telling her to make herself at home and that he would just sleep at the hospital after.

When she'd settled down under the fresh, clean covers in the guest room, her eyes beginning to droop, she couldn't help but think about how Mickey was there for her again. Seeing him so distressed in their office when he'd thought he was alone had startled her. He'd been hurting, but she knew that her seeing that had been an accident rather than by design. His mask was well and truly on the rest of time. Not unlike hers, except while his was a smiling, happy face, hers was all hard lines and glares.

She'd slept till ten the next morning, a first for her. Normally, she was up early no matter what, her body conditioned to be an early riser. Even during her recovery, she'd wake before the time when her alarm for work would have gone off. The difference was that today, she felt... oddly settled.

*It's the change of environment*, she told herself. That was it. Her apartment was associated with pain and recovery now. After losing Grace yesterday, waking up in her old flat alone would have probably sent her into a tailspin, but being at Mickey's? She was...surprisingly relaxed.

Mickey's place was spacious and neat. Too neat. The man had a serious cleaning problem, judging from the lack of dust and everything being in its place. The living room had a comforting, homey feel to it, and nothing aside from the take-out menus stacked neatly on top of the fridge screamed bachelor pad. It was strange, seeing his inner sanctum. She had half expected to see clown portraits on the wall. Maybe a ball pit in the lounge or something. A race car bed, not that she'd ventured anywhere near his bedroom to check.

Seeing his home added another layer to knowing him, though. Another piece of him to analyze. The man was just so—bouncy, but his home was all man. One who was starting to really confuse everything in her life, everything she'd clung to after the crash.

Mickey was fast becoming someone who took the pain

away, giving her something else to overthink. A sparring partner at work, and now this other side of their dynamic with the moments alone, the tenderness and the selfless care he so readily gave to her.

Like now, when he'd given her a space to be in when her place was out of action. She shouldn't be here, but the moment he'd asked, she knew it made sense. If only for a night. She couldn't be here too long. It would give another of her secrets away, and he was already rooting out the core of her too easily for her liking. This was not part of the plan, and with Mickey of all people? It was too hard, too complicated.

Did he still see her in that wreck? Did he feel the urge of protective instinct because he truly cared about her or purely from some sense of duty? What if this thing between them faded when he realized the truth? Her new life would be over. She couldn't start again, not now. No, she needed to stay steadfast. Stand on her own two feet and not rely on anyone.

The trouble was, whether she liked it or not, Mickey Nolan was in her head.

She had the place to herself for now at least, so instead of trying to plan her immediate escape she decided to sit with her feelings, just for the day. Use the time to reset herself and not work or wallow for once. She ordered food from one of the many take-out menus, watched some TV on Mickey's huge gray couch, and even had a good nosy through his bookshelf. The man was a reader, that was for sure. She couldn't imagine him sitting still enough to read a book, but he'd surprised her all over again.

She picked one she'd always meant to read from the shelf, settling in for the afternoon as the sun shone low through his floor-to-ceiling windows.

The next time her head lifted, it was to a familiar voice. "I could get used to this, you know."

She looked up from his couch, surprised to see him standing there. Freshly showered, judging by his still damp hair. She'd been so engrossed in her book she hadn't heard him come in. Hadn't noticed the Seattle skyline turning to the blackest of night.

"Used to what?" She looked around. Tripod had been absent most of the day, but in the last few hours he'd sneaked onto her lap. He was still half asleep now, a lazy purr vibrating through her warmed thighs.

"Coming home to you, sitting on my couch like this."

"Seriously?" She raised a skeptical brow. "I'm not sure whether you're talking to me or the cat."

He flicked a switch on the wall, and the brushed metal reading lamp behind her lit the room with a warm glow. "Well, it's better than coming home to Tripod licking his butt. You two look comfy."

It was weird, but she was comfortable here. More so than at her place. Home had been a place to hide, but this afternoon, she'd felt like herself again. Not that she was about to admit that to him. "Well, your couch is bigger than mine, for a start. How's your patient from last night?"

"Stable. I thought we'd have to pull an all-nighter, but his stats improved. He should be able to go to surgery tomorrow if things keep improving."

"That's great news. I could have come with you to help. Thanks again for letting me come here, but I could have found a room somewhere at the hospital."

He was already shaking his head as he sat next to her on the couch. "That's stupid. We spend enough time in that place without staying there. The couch in our office is like sleeping on a bed of nails, anyway." He rolled his neck, and she knew he'd slept there at some point during the night. While she slept here, in his home. "Did they say when the plumbing and electric were going to be fixed at your place?"

She groaned, remembering the call from her landlord earlier. "Well, my reliable-as-ever landlord was pretty vague on the phone, but my neighbor texted me to say that the plumber hadn't even been round yet." *Oh, God. And he came home to still find me here. I didn't even think about tonight.* "Actually," she said quickly, almost falling over his feet as she scrambled to get up, "I should be going."

Mickey's head snapped back. "Going where? Wait!" His huge hand caught her by the wrist.

"I lost track of time," she mumbled, angry at herself for spending the afternoon reading instead of finding a place to sleep. "I'll get a hotel room."

She felt the heat from his skin as he covered her hand with his. "Lauren, there's no need. Really. Stay here as long as you want. You like the spare room, right? There's plenty of space."

She broke the connection between their hands, unable to bear it any longer, and folded her arms. *He's doing that hero thing again.* "I'll be fine at a hotel." Anyone would think he liked her being here.

He laughed, his cheeks pinking up in an adorable way. "Right. Forgot." Running a hand over his scruff, he shook his head. She didn't miss the wry look he shot her. "You know, it's okay to lean on people sometimes. It won't kill you."

She sat back down on the couch, processing his words. "I never said it would. I'm just used to taking care of myself, is all."

"Like when you were injured?"

Her breath hitched, but the usual snarky bite back didn't come. "Yeah. Then, too."

"When did your boyfriend leave? How soon after the accident?"

"Oscar? Oh, he left pretty much the second he saw me in that hospital bed. He stayed in the waiting room till I woke up, though, to tell me that he couldn't do it, so that was nice. Better than a Dear Jane letter."

He didn't laugh. In fact, he looked furious. "You're kidding, right? Couldn't do what exactly?"

She chuckled, seeing the funny side now through the darkness. "He said he couldn't be there for me through my recovery. He'd just got a big promotion at the firm he was working at, and he'd been working more hours. A lot more, and with my hours, I guess we weren't in the best place when it happened. Oscar is the opposite of us. He never could cope with sick people."

"I don't know about that, but I do know that he never deserved you. A man who walks away when things get tough is not worth anything, Lauren. Especially not to someone like you."

"Someone who has an acid tongue and a chip on her shoulder? Yeah, I'm a real catch, and I wasn't this cheerful after I got hurt. Believe me, he would have been in for a tough time. It was probably safer for him to bail when he did."

He moved closer, gripping her chin between forefinger and thumb to pull her attention to him.

*Is it hot in here?* She felt like he'd lit her on fire.

"Anyone would have struggled, going through what you did, and you did it alone. I swear, sometimes I think you forget that fighting spirit you have. You're probably the strongest, most infuriatingly independent woman I've ever met. If he hadn't had left, it wouldn't have worked out anyway."

"Right," she breathed, willing her body to stop vibrating. "And you know that how?"

"Because anyone who truly saw you would never have thought about leaving, Lor. I wouldn't have left your side if I'd been given the choice. I think you're amazing, and all I want to do is get to know you. All sides of you."

She felt the coarseness of his thumb when he ran it along her bottom lip. The tension between them…

She needed to get out of here. Now. She needed to find a hotel and hole up away from all this. Away from how she felt when Mickey said these nice things to her. Away from the shadow of Denny that hung between them like a dark fog. Away from his damn kissable lips, because if he didn't stop touching her like this, making her feel beautiful, she was going to jump on him and devour his gorgeously irritating face.

Another huge problem. Her body was different now, altered forever, and she hadn't even made peace with it. How could she get naked with him, let him see the consequences of that night with those haunting eyes of his? The fear of rejection loomed large, taking her breath away. He'd told her she was beautiful, but would he truly still think that when they were naked together?

Clearly unaware of her spiraling thoughts, he hadn't taken his attention from her for one second. He made another pass over her lip with his thumb, his eyes dark with intent.

Swallowing, she was just starting to close her eyes, lean in, when…

"I'm going to take a shower. Have you eaten?" He was up off the couch before she could react.

Her lip still tingling, she sat up straight, trying to pull herself together. *What the hell was that? And why did I like him saying it?* If he'd closed the distance then, she would have let him. *Stupid. So stupid. Mickey is the last man on earth I should be feeling this for.*

"Lauren? Did you hear me?" When her head snapped to his, she saw that secret smile of his before he hid it away. Was he…smirking? "Did you eat? I can order in."

"Er, no. Not since lunch."

"Pizza okay? There's a pretty good place that delivers. Menu's on the fridge. Do you need to shower first?"

"No. I'm good. I don't have anything clean to sleep in, though." She only had a spare change of clothes with her at the hospital, and getting into her place was not an option. She'd used her only spare top last night as a nightshirt.

He paused, turning on his way to the bathroom. "I have some spare clothes you can wear. I'll put them on your bed. Order anything you want, I'll pay. Just no pineapple."

"Shudder at the thought," she tried to joke, but the tension in his shoulders didn't drop. What was wrong with him? He'd pulled away, but she didn't want to ask him why. It was for the best, right?

The next thing she heard was the bathroom door closing. Whatever that little moment was, it was gone now. She would eat and then get into that spare room and keep away from him. It was only for one more night. She'd buy some clothes tomorrow if she had to, then find a hotel. The sooner her apartment was ready, the better.

"No. No!"

Mickey bolted upright, his bedroom dark and still. *What the hell was that?*

"Help me. Please, somebody, help me!"

*Lor.*

He heard her call out again, and then he was running for her door. It was pitch-black in there, the only light coming through the slits in the blinds. "Lauren?"

She was tangled in the sheets on the spare bed, thrashing and mumbling, her hands trying to claw away an invisible threat.

*A nightmare? She has nightmares?* "Lauren! You're okay, it's okay." Rounding the bed, he yanked the covers away and pulled her onto him. His hammering heart wouldn't accept anything less.

Her skin was slick with sweat, her hair wet when he ran his hand over it. Cradling her in his lap, he leaned against the headboard and held her tight. "Lauren, I'm here. You're not alone, baby."

She let out a pained squeak, and then those gorgeous eyes of hers flashed open. The pain and shock he saw there made him want to change his last name. Denounce his whole damn birthright. Anything. He would do anything to be the one man she could trust, the damn port she came to in the middle of her storm.

"Mickey?" she whimpered.

"Yeah, baby, it's me." *The man who just called you baby twice and doesn't want to take it back.* How many times had he thought of this over the last few months? Holding her in his arms, trying to piece her back together. Back then, that night, he couldn't get to her. He remembered every touch, though, every moment. The way her warm, wet blood covered his hands. The smell of the gasoline and burnt rubber in the air. His anger that Denny had done this and how he'd been powerless to stop it.

Maybe if he hadn't been chasing Denny that night, trying to get him to stop driving while he was high and go to rehab, the crash wouldn't have happened. But then he wouldn't know *her*. He felt like a monster for even thinking it. He pulled her tighter into his arms.

"What happened?" she asked him, confusion clouding her beautiful, sweat-streaked face.

"Nothing, just a dream. That's all. I'm here. You're okay."

"I got out?" she asked, and he realized she was still there somehow. Trapped in that mangled wreckage. Part of her had probably never left.

Next time he saw Denny, he was going to punch him so hard in the face. Clenching his fist where she couldn't see, he stroked her face with the other. Tender one side, concealed rage the other. Two halves of him, like the two sides of her. Maybe between them, they made a whole.

"Yes, ba—you got out, Lor. You're safe. I got you. I'm here."

She searched his face for the longest time as they clung to each other in the dark. He let her look her fill. It meant that he got to watch her, too. It felt like all he did was watch her and worry about her. It wasn't just obligation that drove him. Or the burden of family guilt. If he was honest with himself, he'd never take his eyes off Lauren Basso again, if she allowed it.

"I'm... I'm sorry," she started, reality settling in.

He held it at bay, although he couldn't say for who. He just needed to keep her close, somehow. "This isn't the first time, is it? You've had these nightmares before."

For a split second, he saw that mask of control slip over her face, but he refused to let her lock herself away from him. He was done with not being helpful. He was done with not being there for her.

"I know it isn't. It's why you don't want to stay here,

right? Why you don't take naps at work?" His lips twitched when she frowned at his question. "The staff talk. Every other doctor grabs a nap from time to time. You don't." He moved a stray lock of hair from her cheek and allowed himself one brush of her skin with his index finger. No more. Having her in his arms, feeling her muscles slowly unlock, was enough. "You're staying here till your place gets fixed. No hotels."

He waited for her reasons why she couldn't, wouldn't, agree, but she shocked the hell out of him by dipping her chin once.

"Thank you," he told her, earning himself a quirk of her brow.

"Shouldn't that be my line?" *That's it, baby. Come back to me.* "This is your thing, right? Being Mr. Annoyingly Helpful."

He gave a nonchalant shrug, making sure his grip on her didn't falter an inch in case he broke the spell they were both wrapped in. She must still be delirious, agreeing so readily. He wasn't about to give her the chance to clam up again. He was going to play this just right. He sometimes pushed the wrong buttons on this woman, but he was a mighty fast learner.

"I'll sleep better this way. Hotels are not ideal for a woman alone." He felt the doubt creeping into her and headed it off at the pass. "Look, we're colleagues. If you're all exhausted and burnt out at work, then life's harder for me." Her eyes narrowed at him, and it took everything in him not to break character and laugh. "Plus, my neighbors might think I'm a player if they hear a woman screaming every night. I have a pretty boring reputation around here."

She giggled but covered it with an eye roll and a tap on his shoulder. "See, total pig."

He wiggled his nose, making a snorting sound. Finally, he forced his arms to release her. She was going to stay. "I'll leave you to sleep. You know where I am if you need me, okay?"

Pulling the covers back around her, she watched him walk backward to the doorway. "Mickey," she called at the last minute.

"Yeah?" *Don't shut down on me now. Please.*

"Thank you. For being there."

He flashed her an easy grin. "Sleep tight." He didn't miss the small smile as she settled back against her pillow.

Once the door was closed behind him, he leaned against the wall and took a deep gulp of air. She was okay. She was letting him in, healing. He'd been able to comfort her, calm her down. And the irrefutable truth of it was that he wanted to be that for Lauren Basso for as long as she'd let him.

## CHAPTER SEVEN

Seattle Down was fast becoming her favorite coffee shop. Two blocks from the hospital, it was a bright, bookish place that allowed people like her to slide in unnoticed. The man who ran the place with his wife was an amputee, and the first time she walked in and saw his metal prosthetic under his shorts, she'd relaxed. Even more so when he and his wife didn't even look twice at her scar like others did. His left arm was damaged, too, yet the exposed muscle and gnarled skin was never hidden away under long sleeves.

She felt at home here, and after the last few days, all her thoughts seemed to be about the comfort she craved in her new life. She was fast realizing that Mickey was unique to anyone she'd ever met, both pre-accident and now as her trauma-scarred self.

He had made breakfast for them both earlier that morning. She'd emerged in another one of his T-shirts and basketball shorts she'd had to cinch together around her middle, and she'd been startled to see him there at the kitchen table. *Am I getting comfortable with him without even realizing it?* Usually she wore stockings with dresses or long trousers, aware that her legs were visibly scarred. Worse than the one on her face, they were bad enough to give coffee shop guy a run for his money.

She'd tensed the second she saw Mickey's eyes running over her body, his fork raised halfway to his mouth. *This is it. This is the moment he shows his discomfort.* She was still fighting the urge to turn tail and run back to the spare room when he spoke.

"Wow. You look so much prettier in my clothes than I do. Hungry?"

Feeling herself blush at his easy compliment, she headed straight for the chair he pushed out for her, noting that he kept his eyes on her face. *Did he even register the mess my legs are in?* She pushed the stray thought out of her head as she settled at the table. He was an ER doctor. He'd seen worse. They both had. That was all it was. He was desensitized to the ugly, right?

"I'm starving, actually. Did you really make all this?"

On the table was juice, a coffeepot, pancakes, cut fruit and syrup in a little glass jug. She reached for a couple pieces of bacon with her fork, spearing them together and placing them on the plate he'd laid out for her.

"Yep. Well, I didn't really know what you'd like. You eat like a mouse at work."

"A mouse?" He put two pancakes next to her bacon, and she reached for the syrup.

"Yep. You're a nibbler."

"Am not," she refuted, before she remembered that he'd seen her lunch more than once. "Well, not always. I have been known to grab the odd burger or two."

"Good to know, because kale salad is not enough to sustain a body doing our shifts. I'm surprised you haven't passed out yet." He reached for the bowl of cut fruit, pushing it closer. "Now eat up. I'll make dinner tonight after our shift."

And she'd agreed. Readily. No fight. Even when he

refused to let her help clean up breakfast, she didn't bite back or tell him off.

It had taken her a moment to realize it herself—she was actually starting to let this man in. He had this way about him. The happy-go-lucky persona that was Mickey was drawing her in, making her forget her hard shell was supposed to be impervious. It was dangerous, but inch by inch, that shell was cracking. And now here she was, about to go to work and see him again.

She'd drawn the line at him taking her to work, though. Turning up in the same car in the morning was too risky. People might read into things. Things that would just shine more light on her, and she didn't want that.

Whatever was in those pancakes, it had worked. She felt…happy. Which was terrible, because her plan to go back to work and life a quiet life on her own was the total opposite of what she was doing: lusting after and living with the brother of the man who'd turned her ordered life into a smoldering wreck in the first place.

She should probably wise up. Remember how it had felt when Oscar had coldly cut her off, how her friends had gone from treating her like a respected boss and peer to a patient in need of kid-glove treatment. Opening up to people, especially with the shared history that Mickey and she had, was too hard. She'd survived all that once and was in no hurry to endure anything akin to it ever again.

Work was safe. Being alone was safe. Wasn't that all she had hoped for, all those months stuck in a hospital bed? As soon as her apartment was ready again, she would be gone. In the meantime, she was going to repay him. She wouldn't owe him a damn thing. They could go back to snapping at each other like a couple of pugs. Normality would be restored. She could get over this stupid attraction she was feeling.

Just because he'd been there for her a few times didn't mean a thing. He was like that with everyone, and she wasn't going to be anyone's pity project. He felt guilty for what his brother did. Whatever they could have been to each other in another life, they were living in this one.

"Any lunch for you today, honey? I have a kale salad prepped." The owner's wife beamed at her from behind the bar at Seattle Down.

"Er, no. Could I actually get two ham salads and a couple of lattes to go? I have to get to work."

"Sure thing." She tapped the order into the cash register, flashing her a knowing look. "I hope you don't mind me saying, sugar, but it's nice to see you smile." She sashayed off after dropping her kindness bomb. *Nice to see you smile.*

Lauren had been coming here for a few months now, using it as a place to test being out in public before she'd started at Seattle General. Had she really been that bad, that a relative stranger commented on the fact that she'd smiled for once? She had been closed off for a long time. Maybe too long. The old her would have been happier, right? She didn't remember being discontented. Tired, overworked, sure. But the old her hadn't given up on life.

Somewhere along the way, Lauren had lost a bit of the rage burning inside her. The thing that scared her most was the thought of what lay latent under that rage. Without it, what would be left?

"What's with you?"

"Huh?" Mickey was standing in the middle of the ER, staring at the door but pretending to focus on the board. It was quiet for the usual early morning rush, which probably meant that they were due a tsunami of patients any time now. "What did you say?"

"She'll be here. You were here early, remember?" Dr. Rossi smirked. "So, it's true. She's really working here?"

Mickey felt himself bristle. "What did you hear? I told HR to shut that stuff down."

Doug Rossi raised a brow. "Oh, they did, but I was there, remember? I know what you were like after everything went down."

"We're just colleagues, and she doesn't like people speculating about her story, or staring at her, for that matter. Shouldn't you be leaving, anyway? You're not even on shift."

Laughing, Doug slapped him on the arm. "Calm down. I came in to get some research done, and I kind of wanted to see it for myself. The nurses are all talking about Dr. Nolan and Dr. Basso and the spats you two keep having. Sexual tension is off the charts, apparently."

"Really?" Mickey asked. "They really said that?" *So, it's not just me who's noticed this spark.* Seeing her at the breakfast table that morning, so embarrassed about her legs, he'd wanted nothing more than to scoop her up onto that table and show her just how sexy and perfect she was. He wanted to touch and kiss every scar she had and prove to her she didn't need to hide from him. From anyone.

"Yeah, and she's quite the looker, apparently. Even with—"

Mickey stepped into his space. "Don't finish that sentence, Doug. She's our colleague, so let's keep it professional, shall we? She's not someone to ogle."

"Okay." Doug nodded. "Sorry, man." He must have seen something on Mickey's face, as a look of recognition dawned. "You like her, don't you?"

Mickey winced that he'd almost shown his cards. "My opinion of my colleague is irrelevant. We're here to save lives, not gossip. If I hear anything from anyone about Dr. Basso—"

"What about me?"

Mickey closed his eyes, pulling back to see her standing there, a take-out bag and two coffees in hand.

"Nothing, I was just discussing—"

"Me," she cut in, her eyes moving from Rossi and back to his. The look in her eyes almost felled him. It was so cold, so guarded. Every little bit of light he'd coaxed out of her was gone, shoved back under the mask she'd worn from the beginning. "Dr. Rossi, did you have something to say to me?" She noticed people watching, her cheeks reddening. "Does anyone have something to say about me? Because we are here to work. My personal life is off-limits. If anyone has any questions for me, kindly direct them to HR." She swallowed hard. "I'll be in my office if I'm needed. I have paperwork."

Mickey made himself wait a beat before following her. It was enough time to address the elephant in the room. "You heard what Dr. Basso said," he boomed. "This is a hospital, not a high school. Keep your gossip to yourself and get on with your work."

A muted chorus of "yes, Doctor" followed him as he strode past Doug, heading straight to their shared office.

She'd barely closed the door when he reached for the handle, not giving her the chance to lock it behind her.

"Lauren," he started, but she was all ice queen as she placed the bag and coffees on her desk.

"Dr. Basso to you." Leaning back in her chair, he watched as her shaking hand reached for the cup with her name on it. Next to it, on the other cup, was scrawled Nolan.

"You got me a coffee?"

Her eyes flitted to his so quickly, the daggers they

threw almost took his head off. "The coffee shop around the corner knew your order."

"So, you got me a coffee. Because I didn't place a coffee order today." He matched her movements, taking the cup and leaning back to face her in his own chair. He took a sip, slow and deliberate. "Latte. Perfect. Thank you."

"I didn't want to owe you for breakfast."

His teeth gritted in his mouth under the weight of his jaw clenching. "Okay. What's in the bag?"

She kept her eyes on his, running her tongue along her front teeth. "Lunch. Same answer."

"That wasn't what you thought, you know."

"So people weren't talking about me? Is that what you're saying?"

He didn't answer. He didn't want to have to lie.

"I'm used to people discussing me by now, Dr. Nolan."

"Mickey, Lauren. My name is Mickey to you."

"Whatever your name is, you don't have to protect me. I don't need anyone."

"You don't?" he challenged, remembering how she'd clung to him last night when he went to comfort her. "Never, huh? What was last night then?"

"A nightmare, Nolan." *Still annoyed then.* "Children get them, and they survive."

"Yeah, because their parents comfort them, Lor." He was pushing her now, and he knew it.

"My parents are in Florida," she shot back. "A bit far to travel, but I'm fine on my own. I survive."

"Surviving is not living, and you know it. Dr. Rossi was out of line, saying what he did."

Her carefully closed-off expression gave way, just a bit. "And what was that?"

He couldn't tell her that Doug was going to mention her

scars. It would only hurt her, and Doug was wrong anyway. He didn't see the real her. Scars didn't matter. Nothing could take away from her beauty. "He said you were pretty."

Her jaw dropped. "That's it? Why would that bother you?" Her hand came up to cover her scar, something she did without registering far too much. Her question hung in the air, and he grabbed for it.

"I didn't like it." Her hand lowered, just a bit, and the thrill that ran through him spurred him on. "I don't know, it just…bothered me. I made that clear."

"He's not interested in me. I've barely crossed paths with him."

"Doesn't matter," Mickey said, keeping her eyes on his as long as he could. "Are you home for dinner tonight? I'm cooking."

Her pager went off. She took a long pull on her coffee and was heading for the door before he could think of anything else to say.

"No pineapple," she said in a soft voice half a second before the door closed behind her.

A meaningless throwaway line to anyone else, but between them? It meant that she was finally opening up. When things got tough, she wasn't lashing out like before. Their banter was something she reached for instead of her usual default emotion.

That was when he knew that even in this weird situation, there was something there to explore.

For the next week, they settled into a routine of working and living together. They took their own cars to work, but he still made breakfast every morning. She brought lunch. One night, when he'd stayed late at work, he'd come home to a homemade curry.

"It was my turn." She shrugged when she saw his happy expression. "Only fair. I bought groceries, too."

"You didn't have to."

"Just paying my way till my place is fixed. Landlord said it shouldn't be too long now."

"Good," he lied. "There's no rush, though. Stay as long as you need to."

She kept doing it. Meeting him move for move. Every time he ordered take-out or cooked a meal, she matched him. Every coffee he bought her, she got him one right back. He left a donut on her desk, and the next day she'd brought a box into work and put them in their office. It was annoyingly cute. He was half tempted to buy her flowers, just to see what she'd do about *that*. Still, even with this tit-for-tat charade they were playing, it was worth it to have her close.

Her apartment was still a mess, but she'd managed to get some belongings, and he was getting to like seeing them. Liked seeing her in his space. For once, coming home wasn't so bad. Seeing her car parked next to his in the parking lot did something to him. The simple things added up to so much in his heart.

*I'm a goner for her.*

Her sweater in the dryer. Her makeup bag in the main bathroom. The books she read, which were all from his shelf, even though she tucked them out of his sight when he was around. Every night, she went into his spare room.

Most nights, she had the dream. The one that ripped her from sleep into terror. Every time, he went to her. Reached for her and pulled her out of it, made her laugh or picked one of their little nothing fights to bring her back to herself. When she was calm, he went back to his own bed, and in the morning, they went right back to their game.

She pretended she was fine, and he pretended not to see the tension in her face, the lack of sleep showing under her eyes.

How the heck she functioned, he would never know. It took him a while to drop back off after leaving her, and he didn't have her demons or a clue how to free her from them.

Which was why he was sitting in this dingy prison visiting room on his day off, drinking crappy vending machine coffee and spilling his guts to the only other person on the planet who might be able to make sense of this whole thing.

"What do you mean, you're living together?" Denny's face was ashen. "Does she not know who you are? That's kind of messed up, Mickey. Even for Nolans, it's all levels of wrong."

Mickey pushed the rest of the cup aside, pulling a face at the brown sludge in the bottom. "Of course she knows who I am, Den. I'm not some stalker. This stuff is garbage, by the way."

"Oh, I'm sorry. Next time I'll have one of the POs do a Starbucks run. I never said you were a stalker, but you crossed paths somehow. How did that happen?"

His brother's eye roll reminded Michael of when they were younger, horsing around together. It made his eyes sting, but he pushed through it. "We work together. She's my work partner. We both run the ER on the same shift."

"You work together! How?" Denny's calm tones exploded into loud disbelief.

"Settle down, Nolan," a prison officer built like an aircraft hanger called out from across the room.

Denny shot him an apologetic look, raising his hands. "Did you get her a job or something? She's not one of your projects, Mickey. Please tell me that. What happened to her was down to me, not you. I don't want you picking up pieces for me anymore. I want you to live your own life for once. Do something for yourself, what you want."

"It's not like that." Mickey heaved a frustrated sigh, thinking of the many sides of Lauren he'd seen. And the ones he still wanted to see. "I don't know what it is, but it's not about you or me. She's...complicated. When she came to work at Seattle General, I had no idea. Her getting the job had nothing to do with me, but then she needed a place to stay, so I offered. I think we're kinda friends now."

*At least, I hope we are. Even if this is all we'll ever be, having her near...it's not about guilt. Or obligation.* He wanted her by his side because it made him feel like he was living for himself for once.

Denny nodded his head, the shell-shocked expression on his face all too familiar to Mickey. "Complicated sounds like an understatement for the pair of you. I can't believe she didn't leave immediately, never mind speak to you. I know you helped her, but being my brother? That's got to be weird for her."

"She remembers me from that night." Mickey clenched his jaw. "She knows you're my brother. She's known for a while now." *That's part of the problem*, he added silently.

Denny shook his head in disbelief. "I can't believe this. I can't believe she's actually staying with you. I thought she'd hate you."

"Oh, she does." Mickey couldn't help it; he smiled thinking of her. "Well, she did at first. I think she tolerates me now." He thought of how her lips tasted when they'd clashed that day in the washroom. And then that time on his couch, when he'd had to run to the shower to cool off before he did something stupid. Except the look on her face had given him hope that perhaps *she* didn't think it was so out of left field. He saw her reaction to his proximity, caught her watching him.

Perhaps in some ways she more than tolerated him. He'd walked around the apartment shirtless a couple of times, just to test his theory. She hadn't recoiled in horror. The night he'd gone to her side after a bad dream without a T-shirt on, she'd definitely given him the once-over. Not that he did anything to acknowledge it at the time. He'd worn a T-shirt and shorts to bed ever since, just in case. If she stayed through the summer, he was going to have to rethink that strategy or always have a go-to outfit by the bed, like a firefighter on call.

"Mickey, don't tell me you like her."

*Oops. Nice move, bro. Grinning like a dang cat in front of Denny while talking about Lauren? Way to hold your cards close to your chest.* "I do like her. She's an excellent colleague."

"You know what I mean." Denny winced. "You and her together? She'd never do it, man. Not after…" He didn't need to spell it out. Denny never needed to remind him what had happened. "Is she okay, at least? I mean, physically and mentally?"

"She's healing," he told his brother, not bothering to sugarcoat it. It wouldn't do either of them any good. "She has scars. Severe ones on her legs. She keeps them covered, but her face…. She's still getting her life back together. I think work helps." *I think I help, too.*

"You do?"

"Yes." Mickey shot his brother a half smile. "She's amazing at her job. Ripped me a new one the first day we met, and we still clash over patients, but she's relentless. A pure hellcat. Brave. Downright terrifying to be around, at times."

When he met Denny's eye again, his brother was crying. "I'm just so sorry I hurt her. I could have killed her, Mickey. I will never be able to make that right."

Mickey leaned forward to pat him on the shoulder before the guards yelled at them to separate. "I know, Den. I know. You're doing good, though, aren't you? With the program and everything?"

Wiping his eyes, Denny's shoulders dropped an inch. "Yeah, bro. It's going great. The program's helping. There are a few guys in here going through similar things. It's helped on the rough days, but you have to know that I'm done with all that. After what happened, I will never touch another drug."

"Good." Mickey sighed, feeling the tension seep from his brother right into his own muscles. "Because I told you; next time, I'm done. This is your rock bottom. No last chances. I'm gone."

"I know." Denny nodded with a sniff. "I won't waste it. I just want to do my time now. Get out and do something productive with my life for once. Have Mom and Dad been in touch?"

Another awkward subject. They wanted nothing to do with Denny now, and Mickey knew his refusal to cut ties with his brother would never be acceptable to either of their parents.

"The odd phone call, here and there. You know how they are, always traveling somewhere these days." Even when they did bother to call, the conversations were stilted. Perfunctory. Detached pleasantries, with no talk of the son they couldn't bear to mention.

Denny's lips thinned. "As long as they're still speaking to you, that's something."

"Yes, well, they should have stood by you," Mickey

started, but Denny's face stopped him. "It's complicated, you know that. They were hurt, and it affected their business. All the years of worrying about you, the rehab attempts. It took its toll on them."

"It's okay," Denny said with a sigh. "I get it. To be honest, I have no one to blame but myself. Which brings me back to your new roommate. Are you sure you know what you're doing there? You were pretty messed up, too, after. I know you looked out for her, but she's not your problem, Mickey. She's mine."

Mickey felt his whole body stiffen at his brother's words. Declaring Lauren his, even in that context, stirred something in him. Something territorial and possessive.

"She is not a problem or a burden to anyone, Den, and she's not yours, either," he blurted out, the harsh tone in his voice unmistakable.

Denny smirked.

Mickey laughed incredulously. "You said that on purpose, didn't you?"

"I just know how to push your buttons, little brother." Their matching grins faded back into seriousness all too soon. "Just be careful, won't you? I hurt the woman, and I can't take that back. I just want her to be okay, and being near you must be hard for her. I'm not sure that's something that can be overcome." He huffed out a defeated breath. "I don't want you to put yourself out there and get hurt, Mickey. I've done enough in that department. Caused a lot of pain for both of you."

Mickey wanted to tell his brother that she was okay or that she would be, but then he thought of her nightmares. Was being near him a trigger? Seeing his face every day, was that something else that hurt her all over again? It was the opposite of what he wanted for her. Being a trigger for her trauma? It was unthinkable. He'd have to walk away, and the thought of not having her in his life now cut him deeper than any weapon ever could. He'd bleed out if she left his life.

"That doesn't mean we can't be good for each other," Mickey told his brother, hoping that was true. "I want to be in her life, Denny. This thing between me and her, it's not about you. Not for me, Den. It's not pity or guilt or even obligation."

Denny looked at the security guard before standing. "I'm going to hug my brother goodbye now."

Mickey stood, and as the two brothers embraced, Denny squeezed him tight. "Just be sure of what you're doing, Mickey. God knows you've never put yourself first, but ask yourself if you're really in this for the right reasons. My mistakes are mine to bear, and it's about time that you lived your own life your way. People pleasing is all well and good, but it's draining, brother."

Mickey held him tight, wishing Denny could walk out of this place with him. That Denny could have the chance of a new life, too. He had a point, this was all so complicated, and his growing feelings for Lauren were making the waters even murkier.

He had to be sure that this was right, for all of them. There were plenty of women in the world; he could possibly be just as happy elsewhere. The trouble was, he knew it might already be too late for him. He just had to stay true to himself and listen to his heart.

"Help me! Somebody, help me! Please!"

*This is worse than the others.* Mickey's heart was pounding as he vaulted out of his bed and sprinted to her room. It wasn't the spare room in his mind anymore.

"Lor," he soothed, throwing back the covers. This time, she reached for him as fast as he did her. Like she was expecting him to come save her from this. Had gotten used to him being there. "It's okay, baby." He let the endearment slide easily from his lips on these nights now. Allowed himself that little admission. "Sshh, baby. Rest, now."

"Mickey," she huffed, her breaths short and sharp. "You came."

She was in his lap like always, but when he turned her chin to his, expecting her to still be asleep, she was looking right at him.

"You're awake," he murmured. "That was fast."

Their faces were so close now, he could see the tears in the corner of her eyes shed from the dream that tormented her. Feel her sweet breath on his face. He allowed his thumb free rein on her jaw, and she turned into it.

"You called me baby."

"You heard that, huh?" He didn't bother lying to her. He wasn't capable where Lauren Basso was concerned. "You're normally asleep."

"You call me baby a lot, do you?"

He pretended to ponder what she'd asked, grateful that the night covered the flush he could feel on his cheeks. He was pretty sure it wasn't covering the pounding of his heart. Knew she could feel it under the palm she had rested there.

"I tend to mix it up." He flashed her a toothy smile. "Baby, Satan, the usual."

She showed her teeth right back. "I have to say, Morticia was my favorite."

"Oh yeah? I am pretty proud of that one. Same dream?" he asked softly. "You in the car, right?"

She pursed her lips. "Yeah, except it's on fire, and I'm stuck like I was, but I'm alone."

"I'm not there?"

A small shake of her head brushed more of her loose locks along his arm, making his skin tingle.

"Not till I wake up." He pulled her closer, wishing he could tuck her safely into his heart. "You're always there when I wake up now."

"Good." He nodded, pressing his lips to her forehead. "I want to be there."

"I don't mind baby, either," she half whispered, and his heart danced in his chest. Till he remembered what Denny said.

"Noted, baby. Have you always had these bad dreams, since the accident?"

He wanted her to say no and yes at the same time. Hating himself for wanting to hear that her pain had existed far longer than they'd been in each other's lives.

"Not at first," she told him, making his heart thud in horror. "I think the pain meds helped keep them away the first few weeks, but after, yeah. I rarely miss a night."

The breath shuddered out of him, pain and selfish relief combined that being near him hadn't caused them. "Tonight was a bad one," he pressed, wanting to unlock the code that would stop them forever.

"I'm overtired. They get worse then." She went to sit up, but he held her still. Not ready to give her up yet. "Believe it or not, I've been better since I came to live here." Her eyes widened at her admission, and he held stock-still. Would she take it back, or say more? "Another person being in the same place, I guess. I sleep better after." A half admission, but he saw the truth of her and wanted more of it. "You'd made a pretty good security blanket, if you ever get bored of playing doctor."

Inwardly, he was preening like a peacock. *She likes*

*me wrapped around her. I am helping her.* "I can stay, if you like."

She froze in his arms, and he wanted to take it back almost as much as he wanted to hear her true answer.

"Lor, if you want me to sleep in here with you, just ask me to."

"I've already leaned on you too much, Mickey. I'm fine—"

"On your own? I know, but let me be there for you, anyway. Please?"

"Why?"

*Why? A loaded question. A million answers. Because I can't stay away from you. Because since that night, all I see is your face. Because your nightmares twist my guts every night, and I hate the damn walls between us. Because my brother broke you, and I want to be the one who helps you put yourself back together. Because having you in my arms is my favorite thing in this whole wide world.*

All true, but too much for this tentative thing growing between them. So, he went with their default banter instead.

"Because I'm exhausted from all the bed hopping, and I think we'll both sleep better in the same bed."

A truth, too, one that was just enough to show her he was serious without making her jolt from the bed.

"Bed hopping?" *Bingo.* "You make it sound dirty. Thinking about the neighbors again?"

He smiled in the moonlight that fell across the tangled sheets. "I told you, I have a reputation to uphold now."

Shaking her head, giving up a little chortle. "Just for tonight then." She slid from his lap and settled down under the covers. "So we can sleep."

"Finally," he joked, making her laugh again. Pulling the

covers over his body, he left enough space between them to make her feel comfortable and tried not to breathe in her scent as he lay there.

When her breathing grew deep and even, he felt himself settle for the first time since he'd heard her screams. These nightmares needed to stop. Whenever he came to her, she relaxed. He felt it whenever he put her on his lap. She responded to him. And tonight, she'd said his name. Had let him stay.

Piece by piece, she was starting to trust him. Let him in. Give up some of that control and hand it into his waiting arms. He just wondered where it would all end, and whether he would be the broken one left bleeding in the aftermath this time.

# CHAPTER EIGHT

"That's good, Lana. Keep breathing for me. Slow breaths, in and out. The medicine in the mask will make you feel better soon."

Lauren checked her patient's oxygen levels on the monitor again. It was still at eighty-seven percent, and the little girl was pale and wide-eyed as she breathed through the nebulizing mask. "Erin, go ahead and prep the liquid steroid for me, ten milligrams."

"Yes, Doctor," Erin nodded, leaving to get the medication.

Lana's hand grabbed for hers, and Lauren sank into the chair next to the bed. "Are you scared, sweetheart?"

Lana nodded her head frantically under the mask.

"It's okay. More medicine is coming to help you breathe more easily. Nurse Erin called your parents. They're on the way, but they asked me to help you. Look after you till they can get here themselves." Lana gripped her hand tighter at the mention of her parents, and Lauren's heart swelled. Lana Volkov was only six years old. She was scared and struggling to breathe when her nanny had brought her in after the little girl had collapsed in the park. Even worse, her nanny had left the second her shift ended, leaving the poor girl alone while she waited for her parents to get there from work. "I have other patients—"

Lana's grip tightened, and Lauren squeezed her hand back. "I'm staying with you, Lana. Don't worry. What I was going to say is that I have other patients who get scared, even grown-ups. It's okay to not feel brave right now."

When Erin had been and gone with the liquid dose of the steroid that would help Lana's struggling lungs, the girl settled down a little but still didn't let go of Lauren's hand.

"You starting to feel better now?"

A timid nod. She was the cutest little button of a girl, her long brown hair setting off her wide blue eyes.

"Good. That's great, Lana. You're doing so well. You know, I was in the hospital not that long ago, and I was scared." Lauren raised her free hand and traced the scar along her face. "I was in an accident, and I was alone, too. I know it's scary, but you're going to be fine. When your parents come, they'll think you're so brave. I do. You are officially my favorite patient."

Lana grinned from behind her mask, and Lauren's heart swelled. Her oxygen levels were coming up fast now. Whatever it was that had set her off in the park might just be a blessing. Lauren suspected the little girl had asthma, and now she'd get the treatment and medication she'd need to improve her life. A little girl like her should be running around and enjoying the outdoors, and now at least she'd be able to do it without a terrifying trip to the hospital.

When her parents dashed through the doors, frantic and stressed, Lauren met them. Explained the course of treatment and referral to the asthma clinic, made sure that Lana was better and ready for discharge. When she finally left them, the little girl was giggling, cuddling the teddy that Lauren had given her, ones that the hospital kept for young patients.

She was feeling pretty good about herself when she

headed to her office later on. She'd actually talked about her accident to a patient and not come out in a cold sweat. She'd shown her scar, willingly. She'd never thought that she'd be able to speak about her experiences at all, but she'd done it without thinking to help soothe a scared little girl.

She was practically skipping though the door when she spotted what was on her desk. Next to the lunch that she'd bought that morning for her and Mickey was a vase of flowers.

"What?" She reached for the card, running her fingers along the petals of the bright, fragrant blooms. "Who..."

The card was typed, but the moment she started reading she knew it was from Mickey.

Thanks, beautiful, for the best night's sleep I've had in a long time.
M

She turned the card over and over in her fingers. He'd sent her flowers. Thanked her for letting him be there for her.

She wanted to hate it, but it was impossible. The man was a walking green flag, and a smoking hot one to boot. She could feel the smile cracking her stoic face, the warmth of the blush on her cheeks. She wanted to hate a lot of things about Mickey Nolan, but the thing she was fast realizing was that she didn't at all.

Moving the vase nearer to her monitor so she could look at them while working, she opened her lunch. And didn't stop smiling once the whole time.

Gloria shot him a knowing look.

"What? Something on my face?" Mickey ran his hand down his jaw, shooting one of his favorite nurses a sideways glance before scanning the faces on the corridor again. He hadn't seen Lauren since she headed for the office, and he was antsy to see her.

"No, but you need to stop bouncing around the place like you lost your favorite chew toy. I swear, you have ants in your pants today. Are you waiting for something?"

"What? No!" He cleared his throat. "No, of course not. Just checking the admissions board, that's all."

"Mm-hmm." Gloria sucked through her teeth. "I might believe that, if the board was in that direction."

Nolan's face was hot. "Well, you don't miss a trick, do you, Gloria?"

"Not often, Dr. Nolan." She clicked her pen, patting him on the shoulder as she passed by. "And for the record, she looks for you, too. I like her for you."

"You don't think it's too complicated?" he blurted at her retreating back. "You know our history, right?"

Gloria eyed him over her shoulder, her expression kind. "I've done this job for thirty years, Mickey, and I've seen some things. What you learn from saving lives is that sometimes, some people are brought together in the worst ways possible, for the best reasons. Like a certain doctor who is quickly realizing that Mickey Nolan is a determined man."

"I always said you were wise, Gloria." He smiled.

She raised a brow. "That's me, and I know romance when I see it. It's about time someone was there for you."

"I wish it was that easy," he mumbled, thinking of all the ways this could end. All the ways it might never start. He was like a puppy around Lauren, just waiting to be loved on. If she ever tickled him behind the ears, he was pretty sure his tail would wag.

"Give it time, she'll see it." Someone came down the

corridor, and Gloria flashed him a wink. "Keep watching that board, Dr. Nolan."

A beat later, he heard Gloria say hi to someone, and a familiar voice say it back. When Lauren spotted him standing there, the smile that lit up her face almost knocked him on his ass. A real smile. *Oh man, she's so pretty.* "Hey."

"Hey yourself," she said, twisting her lips to one side in that adorable way he loved. "What's wrong with the board?"

Nolan cleared his throat as she brushed his shoulder with hers when she came to stand with him. It took him a minute to even register what she'd asked. "Huh?"

"Gloria said something about the board?"

*Snap out of it, Nolan. Work, remember? Practicing medicine?* "Oh right, yeah! No, it's pretty—"

Her finger crashed against his lips. "Don't say it out loud! You'll curse us."

His lips pursed together, kissing her digit. "Sorry," he murmured out of the side of his mouth. "Forgot."

Her eyes fell to his lips, and he watched her own part. *My ice queen is definitely thawing.*

She turned to the board, dropping contact and stepping away as she studied the list of patients. "I'll take the suspicious rash if you take the one in three?"

"Sure, and I discharged bed twenty. The bowel obstruction in ten just went up to the ward. I think that's it for now, although the broken pelvis you were treating is still here. Waiting for a bed to free up, but Erin is on top of his pain meds—"

"Thank you for the flowers." Her words tripped over themselves coming out of her mouth so fast. "You didn't have to, but I—"

"Somebody help me, please! I just found her, but she's not breathing!"

A man in hi-vis came running toward them, a woman in his arms, her head lolling against his shoulder.

"Put her in trauma four," Mickey called back, pointing the man to the free bed as he and Lauren ran to help. "Do you know what happened?"

The construction worker put the woman down on the gurney while Lauren checked her pulse. The woman was ashen white, dark circles and old makeup around her closed eyes.

"No, Doc, she was in the alley next to our site. God knows how long she'd been there, she's cold to the touch. I stepped away for a smoke, saw her feet sticking out from behind the dumpster. Junkies hang around there, I've seen them before."

"Pulse is weak, heartbeat slow," Lauren cut in.

Mickey opened her eyes to shine a light, hesitating for a second as he fully looked at her face. *No*, he thought. *Not now.* "Pupils are pinpricked. Check her arms."

Lauren was already cutting through her top as the nurses took the workman outside to take some details, but she knew what she was going to find before Mickey had even asked the question.

"Track marks." The woman's arms were covered in needle marks, but they were all old, bar one on her left arm. "Looks like a relapsed addiction. Get me some Narcan! Protect her airway!"

Mickey checked her airway, seeing no inflammation or obstruction as Bonnie got to cutting off her tight jeans to check her for other injuries. She had a smell of the street to her, a thin layer of dirt, grease and sweat on her clammy skin.

"Airway clear, get ready for recovery position. Can we get a patient history, please?"

Bonnie, gloves on, was carefully sifting through her clothing. "No needles or ID. She only has a few coins in her pocket. We can try to run her though the system, but I don't recognize her as a regular."

"Must be new to the area, then. Narcan in. Ready me another dose," Lauren commanded. If the first Narcan didn't work, the odds were that the overdose was severe. Sometimes they couldn't get them back at all.

She would never understand why people did this to themselves. Surely the highs were not worth all the lows. In the ER, they chased away death for a living. Seeing others hurtle headfirst toward it was hard to understand. "The other track marks are old, healing. She must have gotten clean at some point. Looks like she overdid it this time."

Seconds passed as they waited for the medication to reverse the ones already in her system, but her vitals were still tanking.

"Another Narcan?" she asked Mickey. "She's not responding."

Mickey didn't reply; he was too busy staring at the patient.

"Dr. Nolan, another Narcan!"

He snapped his eyes to hers, reaching for the additional dose. "Sorry, Narcan going in now. Bonnie, the patient's name is Angela Wilson. She's twenty-eight. We have treated her before but not in the past year. She's been in rehab a few times, upstate."

"You've treated her before?" Lauren asked, remembering the look on his face when she came in.

Mickey didn't meet her eye as they worked to save the woman. "Yeah. She gets clean every once in a while, and then she's back on the hard stuff." His lips thinned. "I really thought we'd seen the last of her."

"Ugh," Angie moaned, her eyes fluttering as she started to come around from the heavy pull of the drugs. "Get off me!"

"Angie, settle down." She stilled as Mickey spoke, his tone firmer than Lauren had heard him use before. "You're in Seattle General. What did you take? We need to know. Heroin again, right? Anything else?"

Angela's eyes flashed venom, but he stared her down till she shook her head.

"How much? A baggie, two?" When she didn't reply, Mickey leaned in close. "Answer me, Angie. Right now."

"Yeah, all right. Yeah." She lifted her hand as though to push him away, but the movement was erratic, weak.

"I can't believe this," Mickey ground out, a kind of bridled fury radiating off him that Lauren felt in her bones. The last time she'd seen him like this was with the aggressive YouTuber, but this was worse in a way. It felt personal. "I told you the last time—"

"Dr. Nolan," Lauren cut in, refocusing his attention. "You can step out now."

The team around them paused as a group, all eyes on them.

"No, I'm fine."

*Liar.* He was standing there like a powder keg just waiting to be lit. Lauren decided that she was going to be the one to defuse him. Be the person he could lean on. Or push against, if that was what he needed. "I didn't ask if you were okay. I have this patient covered. You can step out. We have other patients."

"Lauren—"

"Dr. Nolan, now."

Angie was watching the pair of them with interest now, her hazy eyes squinting between the two.

He opened his mouth to argue, but Lauren stared him down. With a huff, he snapped off his gloves and stormed out.

*I'm going to pay for that later*, she thought, thinking of the flowers with a pang. Their tentative peace treaty was fraying at the seams again.

Turning to her team, she rattled off a list of instructions. "I need a full blood panel, tox screen and a saline IV." She looked at the heart monitor. Angie's stats were stable, her blood pressure on the low side but coming up. The medication they'd given her to reverse the drugs was doing its job, but she had to rule out infection and the possibility of a dirty needle.

"Angela, do you have any drugs or drug paraphernalia on your person now? My nurses aren't going to be stuck with a needle if we check the rest of your clothing, right?"

Angela shook her head, shame and defiance warring for supremacy on her tired features. "No. I used a clean needle, I made sure of it. I don't share, and I don't take drugs."

"Well, evidence to the contrary. When was the last time you used before this?"

"Eight months. I've been in rehab. I was clean, I just…" She sighed, the fight leaving her right before Lauren's eyes. "Whatever. I'm just a junkie to you people, anyway, right? A piece of trash off the street. I saw the way he looked at me. Not worth the treatment time, not a frequent flyer like me."

"Dr. Nolan doesn't think that way," Lauren bristled,

feeling a surge of protectiveness towards him. "He treats any patient, regardless of the circumstances. It's our job."

"Whatever," Angela spat. "Like I care. I messed up, I don't need a lecture from you lot."

"That's fine." Lauren nodded. "You won't get one. Your choice, right? We can't force you to take care of yourself, and we can't police the people who come here."

"I'm not a junkie," Angela muttered. "I just… I messed up. I got stressed, made a wrong choice. That's all. I wasn't always this person."

Lauren sighed. "Yeah, well. I wasn't always the person I am, either. I'm not here to judge you, Angela. I just want to treat you if you'll let me. It's protocol to ask these questions, both for your own treatment and for the safety of our staff."

Angela's jaw clenched, but she returned Lauren's smile when she gave it.

"I note that you've had treatment before. If you've got the details for the rehab center, I can call them. Or next of kin? We can call someone to sit with you till you're well enough to be discharged."

"I don't have anyone to call. I have nothing else on me, I already used it. Mickey knows about the rehab center. Ask him."

*Mickey.* Not Dr. Nolan. None of his adult patients ever called him Mickey. Lauren wanted to ask about their connection but stopped herself. It wasn't professional, nor was it her business who they were to each other. For whatever reason, Mickey was upset that Angela was here again, and that just made Lauren want to help the woman more. To resolve the situation for him, take some of that stress off his shoulders.

Once the blood was drawn and the rest of the staff had moved on to other patients, Lauren found herself lingering.

Angela had been crying quietly to herself, looking like a shadow of a woman as she curled in on herself. She was an addict, and Lauren should feel some kind of way about that after Denny. She should be hardened to the woman's cries, but every sob that came out of her felt like a knife in the gut.

Donning fresh gloves, Lauren pointed to the chair by the bed. "Mind if I sit? Just for a moment. I could use a little break."

Angela shrugged, and when Lauren passed her a tissue, she took it with a shaky hand.

"You were lucky this time, Angela. It took a lot to get you back. Next time you might not be so fortunate."

"Fortunate?" Angie scoffed. "If this is fortunate, I should do the lottery. My ship might just come in."

"Never say never." Lauren clasped her hand. Her skin felt warm, even through the glove. "If we call the rehab center, will you go?"

"I don't need it," Angie protested.

"You do. You were found by a construction worker behind a dumpster. If he hadn't have found you, anything could have happened."

"Lecturing me on my choices? I thought we weren't doing that."

"I'm not. I'm stating the facts. Next time, it really might be the last time." Lauren absently reached for the scar on her cheek. "I don't want you to do something reckless you can't take back."

"I wasn't always like this, you know. I was a normal girl. I partied, sure, but I had college, a purpose. I just wanted a little fun to take the edge off life. So, I partied a little more and a little more. I don't know when the party stopped being fun. This shouldn't be my life. I don't want it to be. I just want to be normal."

Lauren's whole body resonated with her words. She didn't want that for herself, either. "So, make the change," she urged. "I can patch you up and give you advice, but you have to do this for yourself. You have to choose it, every day."

Angie's eyes started to well up again, and Lauren hoped her words had hit home.

She wanted to help this woman. Maybe if Denny had made a change earlier, his life wouldn't have turned out like it did. Angela was an addict. She would struggle for the rest of her life, but she had the right to that life. She was a person not too different from Lauren. Maybe if she hadn't had medicine to focus on, had that passion to point her in the right direction, she could have made some bad choices of her own. No one longed to grow up to be an addict, did they? Life shaped people, and it also broke them and bent them into different versions entirely.

Seeing this woman wrestle with her bad choices, Lauren thought of Denny. How he felt, living with what he did. Was he sober now, a person with regrets like Angela?

Lauren had built Denny Nolan up in her head, associated him with the flash of sudden headlights and the screech of retreating tires. She never saw him, never thought about how a person could be flawed but not wholly evil. He was Mickey's older brother. They'd been raised together. Could it be that Denny had made wrong turns like Angela, and no one had been able to stop him from himself? His demons? Anyone related to the kind, jovial man she'd come to know couldn't be so different in every way. Right?

She thought of Grace and her boyfriend. Of Denny and Mickey. People all hurt by drugs and their impact on a life. Lives. The anger within her was fading, being replaced by other things. Nicer emotions that didn't take such a toll on her.

*Angela is a person, just like me. A human, flawed by imperfection and wrong decisions. Shaped by the events in her life.*

Mickey, she thought with a jolt. Right now, she needed to see him. Passing Angela another tissue, she got up to leave. "I'll let you rest now. We're going to monitor you for a little longer. A nurse will come back to update you."

She had barely rounded the bed when Angela called out, "The rehab? It's called Lakeside, on Cherry Hill. Will you call them for me? Please?"

Lauren smiled, a warm feeling spreading through her. One she'd always treasured as a medical professional. The feeling that she'd helped. "Of course. I'll do it now. Good luck, Angela. No offense, but I hope I never see you again."

Angela smiled for the first time since they'd met. "I hope so, too."

# CHAPTER NINE

"See? I think that's a torso." Pointing to the image on the X-ray lit up on the viewer, Lauren leaned in closer. "And that is definitely some kind of tree."

Pediatric surgeon Dr. Rossi chuckled as he inspected the image for himself. "I swear, you think you've seen it all in this job. How much Lego did this kid eat?"

"Enough to make his mother regret not letting him stay on his Xbox, that's for sure. She was panicked when she got him here. I was hoping that we could avoid surgery, but I don't like the positioning of that tree thing."

"That's really a plastic tree? You sure?"

Lauren shrugged. "Well, I was too busy playing with my doctor's set as a girl to bother with Lego, so I'm going with an educated guess. Either way, I wouldn't like to poop it out."

"Ouch." He laughed. "Fair point. I'll speak to my team, review the films."

Mickey strode in, his face like thunder.

"Hey, Mickey!" Doctor Rossi greeted. "What do you think, Lego tree?"

Mickey ignored him, his eyes only on her. "You took my patient's X-rays? This was my consult to liaise with."

Lauren bristled, clocking the way Doug Rossi's brows dipped in Mickey's direction. "I couldn't find you, and this was an emergent case. I only passed them to Dr. Rossi because I was available."

"Right," Mickey scoffed. "Sure. I have a pager. You should have called me."

"I did," she huffed, taking a step forward. "You didn't reply. It was a two-minute consult."

"Not the point."

"Okay." Lauren folded her arms, her foot starting to tap. "So, is there a point?"

"I'll, er, leave you to it." Doug practically grabbed the X-rays and beat a hasty retreat. "I'll page you when we're ready with a plan."

"Page me," Mickey huffed. "It's my patient, so you deal with me."

Doug flashed her a *what's his problem?* look. "Of course." He closed the door behind him, and the temperature in the room dropped.

Lauren suppressed a shiver as Mickey daggered her with his eyes.

"Next time, wait for me. This wasn't an emergency."

"Perhaps not, but the patient does need the foreign objects removed, and I saw no harm in reviewing the X-rays with pediatrics. What's with you? I came looking for you after Angela—" Reaching for him, she recoiled in horror when he took a step back.

"Nothing," he snapped. "Nothing's wrong with me, I can handle my own patients. Just don't do it again."

"Fine," she snipped back, folding her arms around herself to ease the sting his distance had caused.

His gaze dropped to her arms, his throat bobbing.

The tension in the room was so thick she was choking on it. *He pulled away from my touch.* She wanted to rip her own arm off and slap herself around the head with it.

She didn't need this, this new to and fro between them. They were in role reversal right now, and she hated it. Her need to comfort him, his uncharacteristic bad mood... It felt wrong, off-kilter. A bitter taste of her own medicine. "Anything else?"

"No," he said eventually, as if it cost him to utter that one word. "I don't need anything."

"Good," she half whispered, leaving him behind. "That makes two of us."

Making a beeline for their office, she ripped the flowers out of the vase and crushed them into the bin. *Flowers are stupid anyway.*

They pulled up outside Mickey's place at the same time, but he didn't get out of his car right away. When she tapped on his driver's window, he turned to her with such sad eyes she couldn't take it.

He looked like she did for weeks after the accident. Lost. No, haunted. He was wiped out after his shift. The disturbed nights thanks to her nightmares weren't helping, either. He'd gotten through the rest of their shift, but she could tell he'd been on autopilot the whole time. He'd turned his emotions off and focused on the medicine.

Now, back home, she knew he was starting to feel it, and all she wanted to do was help him. As mad as she was at his sudden foul temper, she couldn't quite bring herself to keep ignoring him. Besides, she was staying at his place. She owed him a little bit of care, if only for that. Reaching for his car's door handle with trepidation, she couldn't stop the flood of relief she felt when it swung open his gaze not moving from hers the whole time.

"Come on, Doc. Food, shower, then bed for you."

He let her haul him out of the car, and she sent him

straight to the bathroom while she fed Tripod and settled him in for the night. She was just looking through the fridge for something to make them both when he came into the open plan lounge.

"Let's just order in. I can't be bothered to cook tonight, and you look wiped, too." He sank onto the couch, Tripod coming to snuggle up with him.

He didn't even bother to pick up a book or flick on the TV. He just sat there, stroking Tripod's fur with a faraway look on his pale face. The fire in him was a dull smolder, replaced by a melancholy she knew only too well.

That melancholy had been her shadow not too long ago. She knew when it was around now, sensed it in others. Wanted to evict it before it made itself right at home in Mickey, where it didn't belong.

"Okay, sounds good." Her voice deliberately cheery, she acted as normal as she could. Which wasn't very normal, because chirpy didn't come as easily to her as it did her suffering counterpart. "What do you fancy? Chinese, Indian, burger?" Nothing. "How about a pineapple pizza with extra pineapple, Mickey?"

"Yeah, fine by me. Whatever you fancy. I'm not really hungry."

"Well, you need to eat."

"I don't want to eat, okay? I'm fine."

"No, you're not."

His eyes snapped to hers, and they were pure cold fire. "And how would you know, huh? You're not okay, and you pretend just fine. Why don't you just leave it?"

"Because you didn't leave me! You've been up my ass ever since I came here. Looking after me, doing your stupid golden retriever thing—"

"What? Are you calling me a dog?" Tripod squawked when Mickey stood up, striding over to her.

She met him step for step till they were practically bumping noses.

"I've only tried to be there for you, to bring you out of yourself," he went on. "I was helping you or trying to. You're hard work, you know that?"

"Yeah, I know that. News flash, Lauren Basso is a prickly pear!"

"That's a nice way of putting it."

"Whatever, Mickey. Whatever you're selling, I'm not buying. You helped me when I didn't want it, so just cut it out. Let me help you for once, you stubborn idiot! Tell me what the hell is wrong with you! After we treated that patient, Angela, you were so weird, why?"

"Just leave it, Lor." He went to sidestep her but she matched him.

"No. I won't, because you are not this person. Something is going on with you, and I'm not going to let this drop. You know her, right?"

"Not your business."

"Probably not, but I'm asking anyway. She got you all riled up, so I'm guessing it's complicated. Is she an ex or something?"

Mickey laughed bitterly. "An ex? Does it look like I've had time for a love life, Lor?"

"Okay." Lauren waved her arms in surrender. "Twenty guesses, huh? That our new game? Cool. So, not a girlfriend. What else is there? Distant cousin? Or perhaps you know her from your circus days? Am I close?"

"I'm not in the mood for jokes."

"Ah, Captain Obvious just flew in again. Great. Well, whoever Angela is to you, seeing her tonight turned you into a grumpy nightmare. So tell me already, what's the deal?"

"You won't like the answer, trust me."

"I don't care. I would rather know than have you keep this to yourself. I'm leaving in two days, and—"

He stumbled back. "You're leaving? Why? Because I was moody?"

"Well, it's not the best look on you, granted. But no, I'm leaving because my place is nearly ready, and I won't need to stay here anymore."

"You never said." Was that hurt she was seeing in his eyes?

"I got the call this evening. I would have mentioned it, but you were doing your impression of a medically trained robot at the time, C-3PO."

He snorted, clamping a hand over his mouth to cover it and dragging it down his jaw. "Funny. Calling me a robot when you walk around like Spock all the damn time, pretending human emotion is an alien concept."

She gasped, then gave him the Vulcan salute, her whole body turning into molten fire. "Live long and suck it, Nolan. I'm not doing this anymore."

"Ohh! You're not doing this, huh. Whatever. Like you care, anyway."

*Well, that stings.* "I do care, actually," she admitted, not backing down when his surprised gaze flashed to hers. "We have to work together, and I... I want you to be okay when I go back to my place. This is not like you. You're the annoyingly chirpy one, remember? This, being all angry and stomping around, it's not you. Tell me what's wrong. Why did seeing Angela set you off like that?"

"Because I know her!" he boomed, the air rushing out of him. "I've known her for years. Hell, we practically grew up together, okay? She's Denny's ex. She's the one who got him hooked on drugs in the first place, okay? I hate her! I hate him sometimes, too, but I still had to save her. I am always the one doing the right thing all the time, and it's getting old! My parents barely bother to speak to me, visiting Denny depresses me, but I can't leave him alone, because he's still my brother—but I'm tired of being Mr. Perfect, all right? I am sick of saving people who mess around and hurt other people. I'm sick of being hurt, Lauren!"

He sucked in a shaky breath. "And I hate this most of all. How we met, how complicated things are. How we can't seem to decide whether we're fighting or laughing. Bonding or feuding. I'm tired of seeing you hurt. I can't take it anymore, witnessing your struggle. All I want to do is…" His jaw slammed shut like a steel trap, and he took another wide step away from her. "Just order whatever to eat, okay? I don't care. I need to get some sleep."

Utterly shocked, Lauren tried hard not to let her jaw drop. That wasn't Mickey. That man just now, she didn't recognize him. She wanted to go to him. She wanted to tell him that he didn't have to be Mr. Perfect for her or anyone else. That his job was not everything he was, either.

But he was already heading to his room. Walking away from her, so she let him be. She was only here for two more nights. It was what she wanted, right? To be back at her place, away from him? Away from all of this and everything he brought out of her.

Normally, she would have hung on. Bitten his face off for speaking to her like that, but all she felt was sorrow. He was holding the whole world on his shoulders, and she couldn't be the one to share the burden, could she? It—whatever this was, attraction, some kind of proximity bonding—it wasn't something that could actually *be* anything. Because situations like tonight were always going to come between them.

Angela had triggered him, and Mickey had thought Lauren would be upset to learn who the other woman was. She knew the second he'd said it that he'd been thinking about her, too. How treating the addict ex of Denny would affect her, as well as him.

*It didn't, though.* The voice in her head was calm and clear.

The knowledge that Angela was part of the Nolans' life should have floored her, but it hadn't. She hadn't even thought about it, not really. She'd even liked her, had wanted to help her patient come through the dark times and out the other side. She'd done her job and held herself together, while Mickey had fallen apart.

Logically, she'd known it was likely he visited Denny in prison. She didn't need to question that. She knew he was the type of man who would be there for his sibling, but he'd kept that from her, too. In every situation, he shielded her first and took the brunt of the impact.

*I would have lifted that car off you with my bare hands if I could have.*

If they were together, then would she always be seen like that by him? Someone delicate, who needed to be shielded from everything ugly? She didn't want to be that person. A burden.

*A victim.*

The second she admitted that to herself, she knew it was what she'd been. A victim. A trauma sufferer. Sure, she'd survived, but she had held herself together with pins and screws forged from hate and anger. She had let herself be the victim, regardless of how strong she'd thought she was being. She hadn't healed properly, not mentally, anyway. She was still right there in that damn car, feeling scared and helpless.

The only difference was when Mickey had reached for her hand when they met again, she didn't take it. She'd slapped it away.

Her face burned when she pictured Mickey earlier that day, recoiling from her touch. She recalled the horrible feeling in the pit of her stomach when he'd done that. Had Mickey felt like that every time she'd done it to him? She had thought that the two of them circling each other was harmless in the grand scheme of things, but right now, she wished, just for now, that they were closer.

She ordered from his favorite place and left his in containers, putting them in the fridge when they cooled in case he got hungry later.

He didn't come out of his room once. She didn't hear anything after the shower sounded in his en suite. No TV, no shuffling around. Even Tripod was subdued, sitting in his cat tree with judgmental eyes following her every move as she tiptoed around the place, setting things in order.

After she showered and got into bed, she fought sleep with everything she had. The fear of having a nightmare was too much. She knew that tonight it was probably inevitable, with her tired mind whirring in overdrive.

*Not tonight. I can't put him through that.*

He wouldn't leave her to deal with it alone. That wasn't Mickey, which was half the problem, and one of the reasons sleep was evading her in the first place.

Her head was full of all the memories of him. The clown, the joker. The doctor everyone fell in love with the minute they met him. The other side of him. The thoughtful side, the one who made food and brought her flowers.

The man who rescued a cat with three legs and nursed him back to health, gave him a home and cared for him deeply. The man who was angry and hurting because the actions of others were like scars on his body. Ruining the beauty of the kind man he was forever and causing him so much pain.

So, sleep was not an option. The risk was too great, given the certainty that a nightmare would soon follow, flapping into her head with thick, dark wings. She didn't want him to come to her again, because she knew he would, even though he was in pain himself.

It was going to be a long two days, without sleep. She couldn't even nap at work, because any colleagues witnessing her nightmares would be even worse. At this rate, she was going to have to grab a fleeting power nap in her car and hope no one witnessed her thrashing around. Even the thought of anyone seeing her so vulnerable made her feel sick.

*I have to stay awake. Somehow.*

With a frustrated grunt, she threw the covers back after another forty-five minutes of naming parts of the human anatomy in alphabetical order in her head and went in search of coffee.

Mickey's door was still closed. *Good. He'll feel better after some solid sleep, at least.*

As she rounded the corner, Mickey was there. Low-slung shorts hung from his sculpted hips, his back to her as he ate from one of the containers she'd left him.

"Oh!" She screeched to a halt, her bare feet slapping on the polished floor. "Sorry. I'll go."

He turned at the sound of her voice, his broad chest bare and muscular as he tensed up. The fork he was holding bent under the strain of his grip as his eyes narrowed.

She felt naked under his appraisal, tugging the hem of her sleep shorts down a little and hoping to everything holy that her nipples weren't showing through her white spaghetti strap top.

"No. It's okay." His voice was thick, rough. "Can't sleep?"

"Something like that." Her toes curled together as she shuffled from foot to foot. "I'll leave you alone."

"I don't want that," he pushed out, his voice low. "I'm sorry, Lor."

"Don't," she breathed. "You don't owe me an apology. It's none of my business. I overstepped."

"No, you didn't. I was just…shaken, that's all. I thought she was all better, you know? It brought some stuff up I haven't dealt with, I guess. I didn't mean to take it out on you. You didn't deserve that, and I really am sorry. I don't want to fight with you."

"Don't you?" Her lips pulled to one side, seeing a glimmer of him returning to her. "That's a shame. It's kind of our thing."

She wasn't mistaken; even in the dark, his eyes were definitely taking her in again. He could see her scars in these shorts, but he didn't look like a man who didn't enjoy what he was looking at. A shiver slipped down her spine, and she shifted to cover it up.

"Not our only thing. Is your place really going to be ready soon?"

"Yes. Tomorrow night's my last night here. Landlord says I might have to replace some bits of furniture, but it's all being plastered up and painted as we speak."

He put the container on the island, stabbing the fork into the leftover food. "Bit of a long time to go without sleep." He nodded to the coffee machine. "Even with caffeine."

*Busted.* It was so annoying, how he knew her so well. "I'll manage."

"What you're doing's not managing, Lor."

"I could say the same about you. You still look exhausted."

"I haven't slept yet." His eyes held hers. "Think I was waiting for you to need me."

His words slammed into her. *This man.* Even with everything he'd been through, he was still doing it. Still being that selfless, annoyingly cute savior for everyone. She took in his taut stance, the way his hair was ruffled. She'd thought it was from sleep, but he'd been running his fingers through it. His tell for when he was agitated.

*I know him better than I ever wanted to. I can't unknow him.* Whether she liked it or not, he was tattooed on her scarred skin.

Crossing the room, she took his hand in hers and led him to her bedroom. His fingers linked through hers without a word till they were standing at the foot of her bed.

"Lauren." His voice was barely a whisper.

"Just…" She squeezed his fingers. "Just shut up and get into bed, okay? It's late."

"Bossy," he shot back.

"Yep." She smiled, hoping he wouldn't see it in the dark.

# CHAPTER TEN

The smell of fresh paint greeted Lauren as she arrived home two days later, bags in hand. The sound of silence smacked her in the face as she took in her surroundings. No little patter of paws, no Mickey passing her a glass of wine or discussing their day. Her apartment was put back together, her things in place, for the most part.

Locking the door behind her, she dumped her bags in the bedroom and waited for the old feeling of security to wash over her. She had thought this was her oasis, once upon a time. When she was discharged from the hospital, moving into her own Oscar-free home was something she'd focused on during recovery. She didn't need anyone when she was here. It was only hers, the one place she could walk around naked if she wanted to, free from people judging her scars.

Once that door closed behind her, the mask could come off. She could be herself. Dr. Lauren Basso, independent badass.

The trouble was, she hated this apartment now. If she was honest with herself, it pretty much sucked. Hard. She didn't want to rattle around in this hidey-hole anymore. She didn't want to sit on her love seat and watch TV on her own.

She wanted to be on Mickey's huge couch, arguing over

the remote and eating from his favorite take-out place. She wanted Tripod to snuggle up on her lap while she bickered over medical procedures with her annoyingly chirpy work colleague.

By God, was he annoying. He liked ice hockey, and she didn't understand it, but for the past few weeks, she'd found herself checking the scores for his Seattle team when she was stuck at work. She hated his aftershave that clung to her clothing from being around him, meaning she smelled him the whole day long. She detested a million tiny things about him, but all she wanted was to have them back.

It had been mere weeks, but for the life of her, she couldn't remember a blessed time that Mickey hadn't been with her.

For the past two mornings, they'd woken up together. On her last night, they didn't even speak about not sharing a bed. After dinner, they'd both slipped under her sheets as if it was the most normal thing in the world. She didn't remember waking up during the night, but this morning, their last morning, she'd opened her eyes to find her head on his chest. He was still fast asleep, lying on his back, both arms wrapped around her like a human shield.

Angela had gone back to rehab. Lauren had been sure to make the arrangements herself, checking in with the rehab center directly to see if she'd settled in. She was doing well, and Lauren hoped that she would be able to make it stick this time. She'd tried to update Mickey on her move, but all she got was a nod. A nod, from the man who usually couldn't shut up to save his life. It was infuriating, but she understood his reasons.

He'd been distant at work since he discovered she was moving back home. Not unfriendly or aloof, but quieter around her. She'd heard some of the nurses commenting on it but didn't dare meet their eye in case they saw the truth written across her face.

To everyone else, Mickey was back to his usual goofy self. Cracking jokes with the patients, laughing with Jarvis and the other doctors. He didn't spar with her anymore. Didn't bite when she pushed his buttons. The only solace she could take from it was that it wasn't just her the exuberant doctor was avoiding. Whenever Dr. Rossi came into the ER, Mickey was downright glacial.

Whatever was eating him, she wasn't going to ask him. Not. A. Chance. Whatever was between him and Doug Rossi, it wasn't her business. Doctors clashed over patients all the time, and it wasn't like she hadn't been in the ring with him herself a few times.

Still, it bothered her more than she'd thought it would. As she showered off the day, hoping the hot water would release the tension in her shoulders, she tried to put it out of her mind.

It was for the best. It was what she wanted, wasn't it? From the minute she'd met Mickey again, all she'd wanted was for him to leave her alone to get on with the job in peace, and now she was out of his place, she could do that. They didn't need to be in each other's personal lives. They were quits now. He'd been there for her, but she'd been there for him when Angela had shown up. The debt was paid.

If she stayed her original course, they would be fine. Yes? This thing between them would likely fizzle out. He'd get bored, and then this silent aloofness would become the norm. Which was just what she'd wanted from that first day. So it was a good thing, surely. He'd helped her, and she'd let him. Had helped him, too. Maybe now, he would finally feel like the debt he thought he owed her was paid, and he'd fade away from her life.

Even thinking of it that way made her stomach flip, and she was having a very hard time explaining it away in her head. Lying to herself had never been easy, and it was even harder now that Mickey Nolan had shattered that hard shell of hers and left it unstable.

*Get it together, Lauren. You don't need anyone, remember?*

She just needed to settle back at home, let the weirdness of the last few weeks die down. He'd finally gotten the message she'd been trying to send since the minute they'd met. Not to quote a Taylor Swift song, but she just needed to shake it off.

It was past ten when she sat down on her lumpy couch in her favorite oversize PJs and flicked on the TV.

"This is fine." She sighed. "Home sweet home." Punching one of her sofa cushions into submission, she settled back with her favorite tub of ice cream. "Queen of my own remote control again. Mistress of my domain." Fidgeting, she gave the cushion another whack for good measure. "Hmm, perhaps the mistress needs to buy a new couch, though."

*Who am I kidding? At this rate I'm going to be trawling the highway for abandoned kittens.*

She surfed the channels, grinning when the Seattle Steelers filled the screen. "Nice, first period." Licking her spoon, she crossed her legs under her. "Come on, Bradovich! Shoot the puck!"

She'd eaten half the tub by the time they were up two. When the buzzer went off to signal the end of the first period of play, her phone beeped on the coffee table. Reaching for it, her face flushed. *Mickey.*

Just checking you've settled back in.

He'd never texted her before. She didn't even know he had her personal number. Normally, it was strictly business, work phone to work phone.

She tried not to read anything into it. This was just him doing his usual good guy thing. She could just ignore it. Pretend she'd never received it. Leave him on read and get on with her night. Her life, as it had been pre-Mickey.

But then she remembered how she'd felt that morning in his arms. All the times he'd helped her when she needed it. The way he'd protected her from the terrors that awaited her in the dark.

I'm good, she wrote. Pursing her lips before adding more. Thanks for asking.

No problem. What are you up to?

Her eyes flicked to the half-empty tub of ice cream, the hockey game on the TV.

Not much. Steelers are winning.

His reply was immediate.

You're watching the game? Thought you hated hockey.

She giggled; glad he couldn't hear it. Nothing else on, she lied.

Sure it's not growing on you? I saw you checking out Bradovich the other day in the doctor's lounge.

Can you blame me? The way he flexes his hips like that on the warm-up defies biology.

I knew it. Such a dirty perv.

He was being playful again. Teasing. Their default way of communication when they weren't tearing strips off each other. Her heart thudded.

Whatever, stalker, she typed back, not wanting the conversation to end. He must have felt the same because another message popped up at lightning speed.

Have you eaten yet?

Eyeing the rapidly melting tub in her hand, she thought of all the breakfasts he'd made. The lunches she'd bought. He was always leaving snacks in their office for her. Making sure she ate at his place.

She couldn't admit she'd gone right back to her old ways in the space of a few hours.

No, but I will.

It's getting late. You need to eat.

Okay. Who's bossy now?

She waited for him to text back, but her phone stayed silent as she watched the final moments of the game. Bradovich was back on the ice, fighting hard to push the puck toward another goal.

"That's it, work those thighs!"

The doorbell rang through the roar of the crowd. *What?*

*No-one comes here.* The super. Of course. He had mentioned that he was going to swing by at some point to pick up his tools. One eye on the TV, she slid the catch across.

"Hey, I have your stuff right here."

"Stuff?" Mickey was standing there, dressed in gray sweatpants. The hockey jersey fit well across his broad chest. In his hands was a familiar bag of take-out. "What stuff is that, and why does it involve thighs?"

"Mickey? What are you doing here? How did you know where I live?"

He shifted from foot to foot, looking unsure. "I heard you talking to your landlord. I might have begged Erin for your number, too." She waited a beat too long, and his face fell. "I just brought you some food. I'm sorry, I'll go. I didn't mean to overstep. I realize now that this is wrong of me. I didn't mean to be pushy, I really didn't."

*No. I don't want that.*

Behind them, the buzzer sounded, the crowd cheering. When his head tilted toward the sound, she grabbed Mickey and hauled him over the threshold, kicking the door shut behind him. "Who scored, did you see? I swear, those Warriors are lethal!"

"I didn't see it. Sorry. Nice place."

The game was over, the final score emblazoned on the screen, but when she turned back to him his eyes were on her.

"Thanks. They did a surprisingly good job, to be fair. Aside from the coffee table, which was water damaged, and a few trinkets." She toed the floor, nerves kicking in at him standing in her space. "Do you want to sit down? I can get plates for us."

There it was, his secret smile. "Sure, I'd like that."

\*\*\*

"Sorry we're having to eat on our laps. I never thought I'd miss the coffee table so much."

"I don't mind." Mickey grinned, taking another huge bite. "I'm so hungry I'd eat standing up."

The Ottawa hockey team was winning the game they were half watching. She hadn't bothered to turn the hockey off, and they'd settled into their old habits so easily Lauren felt like Mickey had been here before.

"You didn't eat, either, but you told me off?" She relished his wince and decided to push him further. "Sounds like it's you who needs someone to take care of them."

Mickey shifted in the love seat, his thigh brushing against hers. "Well, your tiny couch is still a little damp, and the whole place smells like paint. Did you really have to stay here tonight? Why didn't you call me?"

"It's not so bad. This is my home, I had to come back sometime."

Mickey frowned. "Maybe so, but this place isn't ready yet. You can't be comfortable here."

Pushing her plate aside, she looked again at her surroundings. Really looked. "I guess not. This was a safe place at one time. After Oscar left me, I had to get out of his apartment. I rented this so I could recover in peace, and I guess I was hiding a lot more than I thought." She sniffed the air. The smell of paint really was bad, and her couch *was* still damp, even with the throw she'd chucked over it. "It is pretty bad, isn't it? My landlord kind of sucks, but I rented this place online. I never saw it before I moved in the day I left the hospital."

Mickey's hand shot out for the remote, muting the television and turning to her till their knees bumped together. "You seriously did that, all on your own? I always hate moving, packing and shifting all the boxes. Doing it on your own must have sucked."

Lauren wanted to scoff at his question, shrug it off even, but she couldn't lie to him. He wouldn't believe it anyway.

"I didn't really have a choice." Her hand fell to his knee, and his hand covered it instantly. "I was so numb after the accident. My parents and I were close when I was younger, but then I was off at medical school and working all hours. I met Oscar and moved in, but we weren't really a couple in the ways that mattered. My parents raised me, but this is their time to enjoy their lives after everything they did for me. I couldn't bear to put them out and have them look after me. So I just got on with things, I guess. I didn't even tell them about the accident till after I'd been released, and even then I downplayed it. They were traveling, luckily, and didn't get wind of it. It's not like Oscar was around to tell them, either, not that they were ever close. He only met them once. We're not really in each other's lives now. We're not that kind of family. They raised me well in that respect, to be independent. I didn't want them to see me any differently."

She gazed around, recognizing for the first time that her place was just that. A place, not a home. Not like she felt when she was at Mickey's, with his huge couch and Tripod milling around. "I thought I was doing okay, till you."

Mickey cupped her face, his thumb stroking her cheek with such tenderness she could barely keep her eyes from fluttering closed. "I still remember the first day you came to the hospital. I couldn't believe it was you standing there. You looked so different, like the light was gone from your eyes."

"It was," she admitted. "It still is, in a way. I hate my

scars, Mickey. Every time I look at them I just remember how vulnerable I was, how helpless."

"You weren't helpless that night, Lauren. You clung to life, kept yourself alert to quell the shock, even asked me medical questions. I knew you were going to make it. You fought to be here, to be this person you are now. I think you're amazing, Lor. You amaze the hell out of me all the time. The staff told me what you did for Angie, even knowing her story. You didn't have to help her, to go beyond for her, but you did. I know you checked on her with the rehab center staff. With her connection to Denny, it must have been hard."

"It's not her fault. She wasn't driving the car that night, Denny was."

The tension between them abruptly escalated to snapping point.

"Is he always going to be a thing between us? My brother? The way we met?"

Lauren wanted to say no, but what would be the point? "You're not responsible for your brother, and I never blamed you for what happened. I know you still visit him in prison. I don't fault you for that, either, but I can't lie… It's so complicated."

She had her own demons to slay, trust issues she wasn't sure would ever completely leave her, not after Oscar's cruel desertion at her most vulnerable moment.

Should she tell Mickey that no matter how hard it was getting to push him away, it was probably for the best? It was too hard being around him; she was still broken, wasn't she? She still had far too much anger in her heart for a man like Mickey—a man dubbed Dr. Sunshine, for heaven's sake. He was the opposite of her, and her darkness would only dull his light.

It wouldn't be fair to him. He needed someone to raise him up, to meet his energy. To be there for him, to care for him and not be a burden or some obligation thrust upon him.

She couldn't even control her own nightmares. What was he supposed to do, not sleep for the rest of his life so he could chase her fears away? She wanted the best for him, to be the one who put him first for once. Even if that meant she had to break her own heart to do it. He was such a good man, he deserved all the love and light in the world. Not to spend it sitting in the dark with her.

"Don't go quiet on me now, baby. Please."

"Baby again, huh?"

He didn't take the segue into their usual banter this time. "Yes, Lauren, it is. I'm done guessing what you think about me."

"What I think? Why would you care?"

"Why do you think?" His huff was pure exasperation. "I want in on that gorgeous head of yours. I know it was a shock, seeing me at Seattle General. I mean, I was dressed as a clown for God's sake, but I still saw you. You stole the air from my lungs. I can't stop seeing you, Lor. My place was so empty when I got home tonight."

"You missed me." She meant it as a tease, but it emerged as a near breathless whisper.

"I did. I think you miss me, too." He ran his fingers down her lips, featherlight. "I need to know. What did you feel when you saw me again?" He leaned in closer, their lips almost brushing. His hand weaving through her hair. "Did you feel what I did? What I've increasingly come to feel more and more when we're together?"

His gaze dropped to her lips, and she held her breath. *I should tell him. Right now. We're not right for each other. There's too much baggage for this to ever work.* "I..."

Pulling her to him, his lips hovered a breath away from hers, and she took him in. The desperation in his eyes, the tension in the lines on his face. The way he held her, like she was something precious and beautiful.

"Tell me to stop, right now. Talk to me. Tell me that I didn't come over to see you tonight for nothing."

"Why?"

"Why?" He shook his head. "Why wouldn't I want to be near you?"

"No. Why would you want to be?" She flapped her hands. "I'm mean. Half the nurses are afraid of me. I don't play well with others."

"The nurses love you, despite what you think. They only act weird around you because their boss has been a total goon for their other boss since the second you started."

"Goon." She giggled. "Pretty sure you were like that before me."

"I was a happy guy, sure—but I never mooned in corridors or tripped over my words. I don't make breakfast every morning for anyone. I swear, I have been so aware of you at work, I doubt there's a person who hasn't noticed." His mouth tightened. "I don't know when it happened, exactly, but I feel like you're mine, Lauren."

# CHAPTER ELEVEN

He looked into her eyes, wanting her to finally understand him.

"Yours?"

"Mine," he told her. "I just want to show you how amazing you are, how capable." He risked it, kissing the side of her mouth. "How beautiful and sexy." He kissed the other side, relishing in her sharp intake of breath. He was so close. Her walls were breaking down right in front of him, and he had to resist the urge to take a sledgehammer to the rest of those bricks guarding her heart.

"When I got home tonight and you weren't there, I couldn't settle. It feels wrong now, being there without you." Grasping her wrist, he covered her hand with his, right over his heart. "Tell me to leave, and I promise I'll go. I'll never bother you again. I'll be your colleague, your friend, even. If that's what you really want."

Her gorgeous eyes were fixed on where their hands met, and for the millionth time he wished with everything he had that he could read her thoughts. To be able to tell what she was thinking, to know what was in her heart.

"So, tell me to stay, please." *Let me be here, standing between you and the nightmares.*

He held his breath, knowing that she could feel his thudding heart beating so fast in his chest for her that he could see their hands moving. Silently begging her to give him a chance. One chance was all he needed to show her they were meant to be.

"Stay."

That was all he needed. There was no double checking, no worrying that she'd run from him again.

He closed the distance he'd detested for so long and groaned when his mouth finally came down on hers. Her lips parted sweetly, and he seized the opportunity, running his hands through her hair as she wrapped her arms around his shoulders. There was barely a centimeter between them, but as they kissed the holy heck out of each other, it was still too much. He lifted her in his arms, pulling her onto his lap so that she had no choice but to straddle him. She gasped at the sudden shift, and his arms locked around her even tighter.

"I've got you," he told her in between kisses, and standing with her wrapped around him, he walked to her bedroom.

He barely registered anything but the bed he lowered them both onto. Didn't break contact from her mouth the whole time. She was warm and welcoming. The smell of her alone was driving him mad. He nuzzled into her neck, eager for more.

"Mickey," she panted, pulling back.

He moved with her, fixing her eyes on his. "Stay in the moment with me," he begged, wanting to crush the thoughts running rampant in her head. "You're beautiful." He kissed along her scar, so tenderly he hoped she felt everything he was trying to convey. "I'm obsessed with your body. Every inch."

Her smile was like looking into the sun. He was about to tell her that, but her roaming hands cut his words dead as she ran her hands down his abs. "You're not so bad yourself, Dr. Happy." She went to lift his jersey. "Off."

He obliged her, as if he'd ever do anything else. Let her undress him until he was standing before her naked. He was as hard as a rock, his member brushing his stomach as it bobbed with every touch she kissed onto his skin.

"Now you," he told her, dipping his neck to nibble on her collarbone. "There's no rush, and we don't have to do this."

He wanted to do this more than he wanted his hockey team to win. More than anything, but he wanted *her* to want it too. To be fully comfortable and present. If she regretted anything about tonight, it would kill him.

She took a step back, and his stomach dropped to the soles of his feet.

"I'm here," she murmured. Her hands shook as she started to take her clothing off. Piece by glorious piece, she disrobed in front of him.

His gorgeous woman was right here, trusting him with the most personal parts of her body, and he felt like he was flying. *How does a shmuck like me get this lucky?* She left her lower half till last, hesitating when she reached for the waistband.

He took a step closer, wanting to embolden her. To know that she wasn't alone, and he wasn't taking a moment for granted.

Reaching for his hands, she shocked the hell out of him all over again. "I want you to do it."

Lifting his hand to stroke along her scarred cheek, he nodded, dipping to lift her onto the bed. Laid out before him, he slowly pulled off her bottoms until she was utterly bare before him.

"So sexy," he told her, bending down and running his tongue along every inch of her puckered skin.

"Don't lie," she retorted, but when his eyes snapped up to hers, she was smiling.

"Oh, I wouldn't lie to you." He grinned. "And less of your sass, woman. I won't be able to talk back for the next…oh…hour."

And then he pressed his mouth to her and showed her exactly what he meant.

*Five times.* She was trying to do paperwork in her office, but every time she let her mind wander, it found Mickey. Since that night at her place, she hadn't been back there for anything other than a change of clothes.

For the past couple of months, they had spent every non-working moment wrapped around each other. Her stuff was all at Mickey's, and not in his spare room. Although they had christened that, too. And his bed, his shower and the kitchen island the other morning while they were supposed to be having breakfast before their shift. They couldn't get enough of each other, and she had never felt so beautiful. So utterly sexy. Seriously, it was like the man had never seen a naked woman before, and he wanted to conquer it for all mankind.

Five times they had reached for each other in the dark last night. Five earth-shattering, ab-filled encounters that left her utterly wrung out and boneless each time. At this point, they were both in danger of severe dehydration.

At work, they still battled each other. Pushed each other's buttons. Clashed over patients. The nursing staff were immune to it now; they didn't bat an eyelid when they were in each other's faces. When things boiled over, they took it to their office. Everything was the same, but at night they were wild.

She'd never had sex like that, even pre-accident. Compared to Mickey and his moves, Oscar was a damp mop. Just thinking about it made her blush.

Turning to the window, she smiled as she looked at the latest flowers Mickey had left her. Roses this time, bloodred with the most perfect petals. "Lauren," she giggled to herself, "you really are becoming a sap."

"A sap, huh?" Dr. Rossi was standing by the door, an amused grin on his face. "You know, talking to yourself could be considered a sign of madness. Do I need to call psych?"

"Very funny, Dr. Rossi. Actually, studies have shown that people who have conversations with themselves are often of marked higher intelligence. What brings you down to our department?"

"I got called for an incoming patient consult. A rarity from the ER these days."

*I know why that is.* Dr. Rossi noticed the flowers, stepping forward to look closer. *Thank God I've already stashed the card away.* "Roses. Nice."

Her pager went off, saving her from answering. "Thanks. I have a patient."

"I'll walk with you. I'm going that way."

*Great.* She winced. *Mickey is going to love that.* Grabbing her kit, she headed toward trauma room ten, Dr. Rossi walking alongside.

"Room ten?" he asked with a smile. "Looks like we're working together on this one."

The ambulance crew were transferring the patient onto the bed when they arrived.

"Harry, what do we have?"

"Jensen Adams, twelve. He was clipped by a car on the crossing. Blunt force trauma to the back of the head. Lacerations, embedded glass on the wounds on his upper arms, and he has two broken legs. Pupils are equal and responsive."

"Loss of consciousness?" Doug asked, shining a penlight into the patient's eyes.

He was softly groaning, his arms trying to reach out to nothing.

The paramedic nodded. "He came to in the ambulance. We've given him twenty milligrams of morphine and a tetanus booster. He's lucky he was wearing protective gear and a helmet, because this could have been a lot worse. He's alert and responsive, but the driver is pretty shaken up, too. Apparently, the kid came flying out into the road on a skateboard. The driver had no chance to stop in time. They're coming in on the next ambulance."

"The police are aware? Update them, if needed. We need the portable CT in here, stat," Lauren instructed. "Page orthopedics and neuro. Jensen, we've got you. Everything's going to be okay. Let us know how you're doing with the pain, okay? Erin, check his vitals regularly and make sure his cannula is ready for further pain relief."

"Good call," Doug said. "What's the status of his leg injuries?"

"Closed fractures, superficial lacerations. He needs a chest X-ray once the CT is done. It looks like a side impact. Breathing is clear and even, airway open, but we can't rule out broken ribs from the impact."

"Okay. Let's get his file updated. Everybody, clear out to make room for the CT."

The two doctors left the room, and Lauren was just snapping off her gloves when she felt a hand on her shoulder.

"You were great in there. A real superstar," Doug commented.

"Thanks." She flashed him a professional smile. "It's my job. I'm going to check on the other patient. Page me if you need me after the test results come in." There was nothing much else she could do right now, and Jensen had a whole team of people around him. Her staff, all rock stars in their field. "I'll be happy to talk to the parents once they're located."

"Well, I owe you. How about dinner sometime?"

*Damn. Really?* She was just thinking of a way to let him down gently and move on to the next patient when she spotted Mickey. He was leaning against the wall, talking to Gloria, his eyes right on them, watching. The set of his shoulders was tense, rigid.

"That's not necessary," she said, trying for a nonchalant brush-off. "I should get to the driver. They'll be coming in any minute."

When she went to sidestep him, he matched her and she saw Mickey's eyes flash. He started coming over to them, and Lauren's pulse picked up watching him approach. *Three, two, one.*

"Unless you're seeing someone?" Doug asked.

"Er…no." She definitely wasn't comfortable discussing whatever it was she had with Mickey with this man. She wasn't ready to put it into words herself, and seeing how Mickey was around them both when they were together, she didn't want to hurt him further or add gasoline to the fire. She was too used to protecting her private life these days. It felt alien to disclose something so close to her heart.

"Really?" Doug smirked. "Roses aren't usually something a patient sends their doctor."

"No, you're right there." Mickey said coolly, placing himself between them in one easy step. "Doug, we're pretty busy here. Any reason why you have time to hang around?"

Doug laughed. "Calm down, Dr. Nolan. I was just asking a colleague out for dinner, that's all."

"I suggest you return to your patient, Doug."

Doug raised his hands in defeat, the little crowd around them making space as he headed back into Jensen's bay.

Lauren went to meet the driver, Mickey hot on her heels.

"We need to talk," he said through gritted teeth as they went to meet the other ambulance crew in trauma room three. "Later."

"Mickey, it…" It wasn't the time, and from the look on his face that conversation wouldn't go well anyway. It definitely didn't need an audience, either. "Fine. Later."

The driver who'd hit Jensen was a really sweet middle-aged lady. She'd been driving back from the farmers market after shopping with her friends.

Mickey hadn't left Lauren's side. He wasn't speaking to her, either, but that was fine. For now. They'd made enough of a scene in the department for one day. Hell, at this point Lauren was pretty much convinced that Mickey had some kind of sway with HR, given that the recent clash of swords between the two men clearly hadn't bothered them, just like some of the exchanges Mickey and Lauren had had in front of their team. All doctors were spirited and passionate, and the ER was a high-stakes department. Tensions often rose.

Trying to hold it together while being in this pressure cooker was hard work. Even working together in stilted silence, at least she could focus on her patients and push her feelings down. Something she was skilled at doing by now.

"Jean? I'm Dr. Basso, and this is Dr. Nolan. We'll be treating you today."

She was a beautiful woman, silver-white hair haloed around her head. There was an elegance to her rumpled knitted twinset, even with the panicked state she was in. "Don't worry about me. Please, just look after that poor boy." She wiped at the tears running freely down her cheek. "He came out of nowhere. I didn't see him coming. I wasn't even driving fast."

Mickey was looking over her chart, checking her vitals. His smile was friendly, but Lauren knew from the tension in his shoulders that he was still seething underneath. "Jean, try to stay calm." His soft voice was a sharp contrast now to his angry growl mere moments ago. "Your blood pressure is a little high. Do you have any health conditions we need to know about?"

Jean wiped her tears and shook her head. "No, I keep pretty active for my age. I don't drink or smoke, I eat well. My friends and I do a pilates class twice a week." She started to sob again. "I...just can't believe it. That poor boy. The blood on the asphalt. I swear, I'll never get it out of my head." She turned to Lauren, who took her hand when she reached out. "Tell me, Doctor, do you think he'll be okay? Will he and his family ever be able to forgive me for what I did?"

Lauren looked to Mickey, but he didn't say a word. He was looking at her as if wanting the answer for himself.

"The boy is getting the best care, Jean. The police already know it was just an accident. I'm sure his family will understand that." Lauren's gaze found his again, because when was she ever looking anywhere but into his eyes? "You never meant to hurt him."

Jean's friends arrived, carrying gifts and matching expressions of concern as the trio wrapped their arms around Jean and comforted her.

"Is our friend okay?" one of them asked, and Jean nodded her consent for Lauren to fill them in.

"She's okay. A little shaken up, and her blood pressure was elevated, but we've done a full work-up, and she's in good health. She has a few cuts and bruises, but she should be fine to be discharged in the morning. We'll transfer her to a ward tonight for observation, but after the shock wears off and with rest, she'll be fine."

"And the boy?"

Lauren gave Jean's friend a sympathetic smile. "I can't divulge any information about another patient, but I can say that he is being well looked after."

The older woman's shoulders dropped in relief. "Thank you, Doctor. I just can't believe that life is so cruel sometimes, so random. We had such a normal day. Shopping, laughing. We didn't have a drink or do anything wrong."

Lauren thought of her own accident, at how she'd felt when she'd realized what had happened to her and why. "Sometimes these things just happen, whether we like it or not. The important thing is that no one died, and your friend is going to be okay. She has her friends to see her through this, right?"

For the first time, the woman didn't look so unsure or afraid. "She certainly has. We have her back."

Lauren felt the warmth of their friendship, even from here. "I thought so. I'll be back later to check on Jean. Look after each other, okay? The police already took a statement, and they have the camera footage from the crossing, so they shouldn't need anything further for now."

When she left them, Mickey was at the nurses' station, signing off on a treatment plan.

"How's Jensen doing?" she asked. "Have you heard anything?"

He ran his tongue along the inside of his cheek, not bothering to take his eyes off his paperwork. "He was lucky. He has a bad concussion, but the helmet saved him from further head trauma. He has two broken ribs, but his fractures have been treated by ortho, and the police tracked his parents. They came about a half hour ago. How's Jean?"

"Fine, physically. Mild shock, signs of stress from the accident. She has her friends with her, though. I'm pretty sure the ward will need to scare up a private room, because getting rid of them after visiting hours end isn't going to be easy."

"Fine," he said, his tone curt. "I'll let the ward staff know." She waited for him to look at her, but the stubborn idiot was doing everything he could to avoid facing her. "Is that all?"

*Wow. That stung.* "Yes, Dr. Nolan. That's all."

She spun on her heel and was halfway down the corridor when her anger and frustration got the better of her. She hated this grumpy side of him. It was like seeing herself. This closed-off demeanor wasn't him.

*You've made him this way.* Whatever this thing was between them, it clearly wasn't working out. She should never have fallen into bed with him. He was lashing out at people, at her. It was too complicated, mixing work and their personal lives, and for what? It couldn't last; eventually, just like she and Oscar had, they would get tired of each other. Mickey would realize that she wasn't any good for him, and then where would she be?

It would hurt far more than Oscar, because what she felt for Mickey was tenfold beyond whatever she'd had with her ex. She'd be stuck here, working with him, day in and day out. Seeing his happy handsome face everywhere and only getting the snarky side would be akin to torture. Or even worse, this new glimpse of him would be what he dealt with—the angry, tortured version of him that she had somehow created by coming into his life.

She was wrecking him, and that hurt her more than any scar ever would. As great as this slice of life with him had been, it was just that. A tiny slice of happiness that probably wouldn't last, and being without him would only hurt all the more down the line. *I'm not strong enough.*

Heading to her next patient, she knew what she had to do. Something she should have done a long time ago. She had to end things and stop hurting Mickey. They had a department to run, and all of this tension and stress was going to spill out and cause problems. She'd come here to work, and that was what she was going to do.

# CHAPTER TWELVE

*Where the hell is she?*

The office was empty, and Lauren had stayed out of his way for the rest of their shift. Every time he'd walked up to a patient, she'd made a swift exit. It hadn't improved his mood any. When it came time to handover to the night shift, he was desperate to get to her.

"We're expecting more supplies of PPE in the morning," Mickey told the night shift. "Gloria chased the suppliers, but I've put in another request to the other departments to give us what they can spare. Norovirus infections have risen in this area, so remember to mask up and isolate any patients coming in with those symptoms. Treat them and street them as fast as you can, because the beds are filling up faster than we can empty them. Most of the patients don't need the ER, they just need fluids and outpatient treatment. Trauma patients and emergent cases remain a priority." He flashed them one of his trademark wide smiles, one that felt like a lie on his face. "Have a great shift, people. I'll see you in the morning."

The minute the staff started to disperse, he was off in the direction of the parking lot. *She didn't even come to handover.* She should have been there, and he had a sick feeling of dread in the pit of his stomach.

He needed to talk to her. Apologize. He'd been such an

ass to her but he couldn't help it. Hearing her deny his existence to Doug Rossi, he'd struggled not to confront her about that in the middle of the department. He was losing control around her, his whole body pent up with repressing everything. He wanted to be the man she deserved, and he was failing. It hurt so much, seeing her deny this thing between them. It cut him to the quick when he was boiling over with emotion, only to see her shut down around him. Like what they had was nothing, that it didn't matter.

The trouble was that those emotions were hissing out of him in all the wrong ways. He wasn't being himself, and he hated that almost as much as not having her.

She'd been doing so well lately. She smiled more, laughed with Erin and Gloria. She'd made a friend out of Jarvis, who treated her like a little sister. Her guards were slowly coming down, but she still kept that barbed wire fence around her heart.

He needed her to see how far she'd come, how beautiful she was. Every night they weren't at work, they were together. Cooking together in his kitchen, or eating takeout on the couch in front of the TV. Tripod loved having her there, and he was pretty sure that the little cat had adopted her as his favorite person. Mickey could relate.

She was in his life. At work, in his home and in his bed. He couldn't get enough of her, and she was so open with him when they were in the dark, naked. She'd let him take her in the shower, wrapping those legs of hers around him and not freezing up when he touched her. The other night on the couch, they'd been watching a movie, and she'd put her bare legs in his lap. He'd felt like a conquering hero, and the foot rub she'd allowed had led to the best sex they'd ever had. Right there on the couch, her astride him as he thrust up into her, running his hands over every inch of her and making her moan in all the ways he loved to hear.

But there was still this emotional gulf between them. A gap that he couldn't quite close, no matter what he did. She never said yes to him taking her out in public. He'd tried movies, dinners, ice skating. She'd always refused. But every night, her car followed his home. They never spoke about it. They never had a conversation about whose bed she was going to sleep in that night.

It was driving him crazy, this thing that they were doing. Being together while not really being together. So he kept showing up in all the ways she'd let him. Devouring her every chance he got, if only to feel close with her. The full secret-boyfriend experience. The breakfasts, donuts at work. Flowers on her desk with cryptic cards. Ones that she always seem to hide, because they were never with the blooms the next time he checked. They spent their nights wrapped around each other, and the nightmares came less and less. When they did wreck her slumber, he was right there. Wrapped around her, and all it took was a touch and an "I'm here, baby" in her ear, and she was free of its clutches. Back in the bed with him.

But this secret was wrecking him. The fear of her leaving was a constant acid burn in his gut. Making him tense, angry even. The happier she got, the worse he felt that he couldn't declare her as his. She was his but only in the dark. Outside his apartment, they were colleagues. Sparring partners. It wasn't enough, and now he'd kicked off Dr Rossi and embarrassed himself and her. The one thing she didn't want was attention at work, and he'd done that with his frustrated jealousy.

*I need to get it together*, he thought as he dashed to the parking lot. *Stop messing this up, Mickey. Show her your heart, not this angry, bullish version of yourself. Make this right.* She always parked away from his, but he took note of her spot. As he dashed toward it, he saw her. Lit up by the parking lot lighting as she got into her car.

"Lauren!" he called, putting his hand on the door before she could close it on him.

"Mickey, what are you doing?"

"Where are you going? My place? Why didn't you wait for me?"

Her whole face was pinched tight, making his gut lurch. "I'm not going to yours. I'm going home."

"Home? Why?"

"Because I pay rent there, jackass." She got out and stood in front of him.

His eyes closed on a sigh. "I've annoyed you, I know. I'm sorry. Okay, I didn't mean to cause a scene back there. I was wrong, I… I keep getting things wrong when it comes to you, but I can't help it. I'll do better, I promise you. I know you hate it, and I shouldn't have behaved like that."

"So why do it? All of our staff were watching. It's already bad enough that they have to put up with us going head-to-head like wild tigers."

"I would never embarrass you on purpose, Lor. Tell me you know that. I just didn't like watching you get hit on by him, especially at work."

"Just because he asked me out doesn't mean I was going to say yes."

His pulse was hammering, frustration building within him. The thought of Lauren letting that guy take her out for dinner when she continually turned Mickey down had been incredibly difficult to hear. But not as difficult as hearing her deny that they were even together! He needed to hear it from her, something. Some admission that he wasn't out here on his own, with his bleeding heart in his hands.

*This isn't you.* He knew that; he was just so scared that she would walk away from him, though. Leave him alone again. It was driving him crazy. He'd never wanted anything or anyone more. He would unravel without her in his life. She'd haunted him for too long now to walk away without trying everything he could to prove to her that she was worthy. Of living her life, of being loved. *I just want it to be me that you choose.*

"I'm sorry, Lor. Hearing you say you were single..." he began, but she was already shaking her head, a look he'd never seen before on her face. For the first time, he knew just what she was thinking, and he tried to get out in front of it. "I would like us to be together. For real. We could take this public. Date. We could give this a real shot. No pressure, no rushing things. I just want the chance to date you."

Lauren put a hand to her mouth. "You don't mean it. Stop saying things like that." *Stop saying everything I secretly want you to say but am too scared to say yes to. I wish I'd met you before all this, Mickey. When I wasn't terrified and broken and scarred by life.*

She wished they could have just met in some normal way, two people crossing paths in a coffee shop. Liking the look of each other, dating and laughing and squabbling over medical cases. She loved fighting with Mickey, when it wasn't clouded by their not-at-all-meet-cute. The desperate, hopeful look in his eyes was killing her. Tearing her heart open valve by valve.

"I should have said it a long time ago. Lauren, we stay

together every night. I see you at work, and all I want to do is show everyone how I feel about you. How proud I am that a woman like you gives me the time of day. I want more, much more."

She could feel herself shutting down before his eyes. Her hand came up to cover her scar, and he reached for it.

"No. Don't hide from me. Please. I can't take it anymore. You know what we are to each other, but I'm done pretending."

She gazed up at him, fear and confusion swirling through her brain, paralyzing her. What should she do? She knew what she wanted, but she also knew she couldn't have it.

Mickey took the chance. Dipping his head to hers, he kissed her. He didn't care who saw them. He wanted the whole world to see what she meant to him.

She was kissing him back, letting him in. Her hand curled tight around his, and when he finally pulled back, he took the risk and told her his secret. "I love you, Lauren Basso. I think I always have. Being with you has been the best thing that ever happened to me."

The tears started falling then, but when he bent to kiss them away, she pushed him back. "I can't do this. I'm sorry. We need to end things."

*I must be hearing things. She feels this, too, I know it.* "Say that again?" he asked, his voice breaking. "I don't understand."

Bottom lip wobbling, she pushed at his chest with two firm hands.

He took a step back, despite that small distance tearing at his heart. *I'm losing her.*

"I don't love you, Mickey. I can't do this anymore. I

never should have started something with you in the first place."

"Don't say that. Don't do this, not now."

"Why not now? We can't be together, and you know it. It's too complicated. It's not even real!"

Tears welled in his eyes as he took her hand and placed it over his heart. "Does this feel real to you? My heart's beating out of my damn chest! I just told you I'm in love with you, and you're running away?"

"I'm not running away. I'm being smart. Like I should have been a lot sooner. What happened today isn't the only reason. It's everything, Mickey. I'm not right for you."

"That's my decision to make, isn't it? I want you. I've never wanted anyone or anything more."

"You don't want me. You pitied me. I was someone you needed to fix to appease your own guilt, and things got confused along the way. We mistook this weird bond we have for something else."

He huffed out a bitter laugh, releasing her hand. "This is not some ridiculous trauma bond, baby."

"Don't call me baby. And yes, it is. We went through something terrible together, and with your brother—"

"Denny has nothing to do with this. With us. He won't interfere. I already warned him not to contact you months ago."

*Wait, what?* She had received a letter from him after it had first happened. He'd asked her to consider visiting him, but she'd ignored it. He'd never gotten in touch again. *Was that down to Mickey?* "Does he know we work together?"

The sheepish look on Mickey's face spoke volumes.

"Does he know we—"

"Sleep together every night? Practically live together? No. Even you are denying that, Lor."

"But he knows, right? You've talked to him about me?"

He took a step closer, and she reached for the car door.

"Yes! Yes, okay. He knows you're important to me, but he's also fully aware that you don't want to hear from him. You never have to see him, Lauren, I promise."

"He's your brother, Mickey. He won't be in prison forever. What then eh? Are we all going to sit down and have Christmas dinner with him and our parents, like some dysfunctional family? Don't you see how wrong this is? I know you do, it's twisting you up inside. You've changed, and it's all my fault."

She jumped into the car, and he took a step forward. "Don't leave. Please. Don't drive like this, at least. Don't you see? I just want to be with you, not hide in the dark."

She slammed her hands on the steering wheel, sobbing now. "But I live in the dark! I always will! Just let me go!"

"I don't want to," he said hoarsely, feeling his heart break apart. An aortic dissection with every word she spoke. "I love you too much."

Her tearstained face looked right into his as she shook her head. "It's over, Mickey. Whatever we were, whatever we could have been… It's over. Please don't follow me. Just leave me alone."

He hiccuped a breath, too choked to speak properly. Running his hand through his hair, about ready to rip it out at the roots, he knew with a sinking heart that he wasn't going to win her over. This stubborn, beautiful and brave woman that he loved was clearly never going to feel the same way he did. She would never see past the circumstances of their first traumatic meeting, the attention that they might get being together for the world to see.

His fool heart was barely beating when he slowly nodded. "I'll go. I won't follow you. Just, please. Don't drive yet. Give yourself some time. I want you to be safe."

She wasn't even looking at him now. The tiny nod of her head as she shut the door and blocked him out of her life was the only acknowledgment he got.

Defeated and with a pain in his chest he couldn't get rid of no matter how hard he rubbed, he walked to his car on numb legs. As he pulled away from her to go back to a home that was filled with her in every corner, he gave her a last look. In the dark, he was sure he could see her crying again. He watched her through the rearview before he made the turn, and she was lost from his sight.

*I don't love you.* It rang in his head over and over on the journey home.

When he found himself sitting on the couch some time later, alone and in the dark, he couldn't even remember the drive back. Just the way her face had fallen when he'd declared himself. The way she'd run from him, just as he'd feared she might this whole time.

When Tripod came squawking onto his lap, he pulled the little furball close and dripped tears into his fur. "She's gone, little dude. She didn't want to stay with us."

Lauren didn't go into work the next day. When she still hadn't slept as the clock struck three, she rang in, letting the night shift know and left a message with HR. Every time she tried to fall asleep, all she saw was Mickey's face. Remembered everything he said to her as he begged her to stay and give them a chance. She knew he wouldn't be happy with her ending things, but she'd never expected the torrent of heartfelt words.

*He loves me.* She'd been so blindsided when she heard him utter those words, she'd almost taken back everything she'd said. She'd lost herself when he kissed her. Like she always did whenever he touched her.

When the nightmare came for her this time, it was full force.

*My legs. I can't feel my legs. Are they even still there?*

*I open my eyes, try to move but the pain. God, the pain. It's everywhere. My head feels like it's been hit by a truck. I managed to lift my arm to my face when the screech of tires made me freeze.*

*The other driver. Where's the other driver?*

*The car looks wrong. The dashboard's gone. Where the hell is my seat belt? I reach for it, but it pulls loose. Something's wrong. So very wrong. This is bad. My seat belt's been ripped from its holder.*

*"Help!" I shout, but my mouth won't work properly. The metallic taste of blood coats my tongue, and I spit, instantly regretting it when a sharp wave of pain rushes through me. I need to get help. I hear another screech of a car screaming to a stop, a car door. The driver?*

*"Hello?" A deep voice, laced with panic, calls out. "Hello! Shout if you can hear me!"*

*"Help! Please, help me!" I call, and there he is.*

*Mickey. Crawling along the asphalt, his hand reaching out to grab mine. "Don't move," he says, his eyes scanning everything. "You need to stay still, okay? I called for help. But I'm a doctor, I can help you." His eyes finally land on my face, and he takes a sharp breath in.*

*It must be bad, I think, to make even a doctor gasp.*

*"I'm...doctor...too," I say, my whole face feeling foreign to me. "How...bad..."*

*He smiles, taking my pulse and holding my hand at the same time. "You're going to be fine, I promise."*

*He promised. Doctors don't make promises to patients*

*like that. He's either certain I'm dying, or he's Superman and he can see through metal. I know now that the reason the dashboard is not there is because the car isn't on its wheels. It's a wreck, keeping me prisoner in its iron cage.*

*"I'm going to die," I tell him. My voice is oddly calm, even with the cold realization flooding through me. "I'm going to die here."*

*The man squeezes my hand, wincing as he tries to get closer and the glass cuts the underside of his arms.*

*"Don't," I try to tell him, but everything's woozy now. The pain is all consuming. My face feels wet, cold. Wrong. I can't feel my legs. Everything hurts, and the cold Seattle night is biting my skin through my meager clothing. "Get...hurt."*

*"I'm fine, don't worry about me. What's your name? I'm Mickey."*

*"Lor..." I try to say Lauren, but speech is hard.*

*"Don't try to speak," he says, dragging a medical kit up to his side. "I'm here. I won't leave you. You're not alone, Lor. I'm right here with you, and I'm not going anywhere."*

Jolting awake, Lauren reached across the bed for him. He was always there when she awoke, calling her baby, holding her tight. But this time, there was nothing. No strong arms to steady her. No deep voice to soothe her. Just her, alone, her hand splayed across the cold side of her lonely bed.

The sun was already up when she dragged herself out of bed to open her curtains. He'd be at work now, getting ready for his shift. Doing the handover. She tried to picture him smiling, laughing and making everyone's morning brighter, but all she could bring up in her mind was the way he'd looked at her last night when she smashed him apart. Turning him down so brutally he would never want to be near her again.

She'd thought it was the only way, because she was too dark for him. Too grumpy for his sunshine. Their relationship was like the Seattle weather, and she would have always been the rain that spoiled the warm days.

"It will pass. He'll soon realize he's better off without me. That I wasn't someone he should have felt he had to fix because he felt guilty."

*He still did it, though.*

She thought of all the banter, the flowers he left for her just because. His little notes that she'd kept in a box in her locked bottom drawer because she couldn't bear to part with them. She never told him that she reread them whenever work got tough. She never told him how safe she felt with him. How he challenged her and took care of her without making her feel small or weak. He respected her at work, despite their fiery clashes. She loved those, too. Almost as much as she loved the way they made up after, wrapped together in his apartment.

*Being with you has been the best time of my life.* He'd said that, too. He knew her inside and out, more than any one person ever had before. Or would again. He'd opened her up post-injury, and she knew that was special. She couldn't see herself being able to exist like that again with any other person but him.

It didn't matter now, though. She'd made her choice, right? It would hurt like hell, but she'd get through it. Someone like Mickey wouldn't be alone for long. Someone else would see his bright, beautiful eyes and be lost just like she'd been.

Her phone beeped on the nightstand. She'd turned her work phone off, not wanting to get called in.

You're not here, Mickey had written. Please, at least tell me that you got home safe.

The pang in her heart stole her breath. It was barely twenty minutes into shift. I got home safe.

The three little dots danced and stopped. Danced and stopped.

Okay. HR told me you took some time off, but you can't avoid work forever.

He'd already been to HR?

She was still thinking of something to say when the dots danced again.

I know you don't want to hear this, Lor, but I love you. I will respect your decision, but just know this. You were never a burden or an obligation to me. Guilt has never motivated me. Not once. I wanted to be there for you. I've always wanted to be there. I promised you once that you weren't alone and that I wasn't going anywhere. I would keep that promise till the day I die if you ever saw it in your heart to give us a chance.

She crumbled onto the bed, shallow breaths turning into sobs as she read his words over and over through watery eyes.

Tripod and I miss our roommate. So much. You are so much stronger than you think, and you might think you've broken me, but I am made of strong stuff, baby. I'd take everything you can throw at me just to have you with me.

When she didn't reply, too stunned to do anything but stare at the phone, a final text came through.

Nothing is too hard to get through, when we have each other. If you really have given me up, just do one last thing for me. Don't give up on yourself. To me, you are not the dark. You're the moon and the stars. The beauty that lights up the night sky with its brilliance. I love you, Lor. I always will.
Mickey xx

She read his words over and over, fresh tears rolling out of her every time. The hurt evident as he once again poured his heart out to her. Checking on her when she had ripped his heart out of his chest the night before.

That was Mickey. She had reminded herself of that fact so many times. Convincing herself that it was just his way. He was the man who looked after everyone else, because it was how he was built.

She'd been kidding herself the whole time. That she didn't need him. Or want him. She'd been pushing him away like he was the last man on earth she'd ever want to be with.

The truth was, Mickey Nolan was the only man for her. She finally realized that she was letting her anger and pain run the show, even now—and it was time to start allowing her other emotions to take center stage. To step into the light and finally be free.

# CHAPTER THIRTEEN

Lauren slid her ID into the back pocket of her purse and braced herself for what lay beyond the imposing steel doors before her.

"Just through those doors, miss. Take notice of the signs, and no touching."

Nodding mutely, she forced her legs to propel her forward. She'd thought of this moment so many times over the months of recovery, of working with Mickey. A moment that she'd never thought would ever become a reality but often envisioned. She had imagined myriad conversations the two of them might have, but with every step she took toward his table, her mind emptied. All of the questions and recriminations slid from her grasp the closer she got.

*Breathe, Lauren. Breathe. You need to do this. For yourself, for your future. For Mickey.*

Thinking of the man who'd brought her back to life, she drew a deep breath and looked into the eyes of the man who'd almost destroyed it. The man who looked something like Mickey but garnered a very different response as she neared his table.

"Hi," he said, his voice barely audible.

Folding her hands on her lap as she took a seat, she raised her gaze to Denny Nolan. "Hello," she breathed, relief flooding through her as she took him in.

Since the accident, Denny had become a monster in her mind. A ripping, snarling gargoyle, but he was just a man.

"You look better than I expected." The words came forth unbidden, and she bit at her lip before speaking again. "I mean, I...don't know what I mean."

He gave the briefest of nods, as if he could read her mind. "I'm clean. I have been since that night." He heaved a sigh, flashing her a guilty smile. "That's not what you meant, though, is it? I know I'm the villain in your story, Dr. Basso."

She didn't reply; she didn't need to. He was the villain, once upon a time. Maybe in some way he always would be, but she'd changed. Grown. She was no longer afraid to face him. The longer she sat there, looking at Denny, the more she realized that she was healing. Had healed. The broken pieces of her were not jagged anymore. They'd knitted back together, a little raggedy in places, sure, but she was almost whole now.

Almost. Which was why she needed to do this.

"Look," Denny stammered. "I know that I can never change what I did to you, but I am so glad that you're here. In the program, we are taught to make amends as part of our recovery. I hurt a lot of people, but you are the one I did the most damage to."

"You did," she said, her hand reaching up to trace her scar before she could stop herself. "I hated you for a long time for what you took from me. It wasn't just the pain or the fear from that night that hurt me. It was everything that came after. My confidence, my fearless nature. It was all just...gone."

Denny didn't say a word, he just sat there. Head hung, listening.

"But then I went back to work, in a new place. Tried

to start again, and I found another man who infuriated the heck out of me." Denny met her eye, and she couldn't help but laugh. "You have to know, Denny, that your little brother is the biggest pain in the ass. Seriously. He was just so happy all the time, I couldn't stand it. I lashed out at him, and I was angry with him, too, I guess. That night, in the car…"

"He came to rescue you, but then you found out he was there because he's my brother."

Lauren licked at her lips, her mouth dry. "Yes. You know, I thought about him often in those early days. I was so scared that night. The pain was intense, and I knew I was hurt. Badly, but I didn't know how bad. Then he was there, holding my hand and telling me he was a doctor. That I would be okay. He saved me in more ways than one, but afterward—reading the news, I couldn't help but feel betrayed, I guess."

"He never defended me, you know. After the accident, I…" Denny huffed out a ragged breath, looking every bit the stricken man, and Lauren felt something she'd never thought she would. Sympathy. Compassion. This man had suffered, too. Was paying for his mistakes, even now.

She reached out and tentatively covered her hand with his.

"No touching," the prison guard boomed, but she ignored him.

"I'm okay. It's okay."

"No touching!"

Pulling her hand back, she glared at the guard.

Denny surprised her by chuckling. "Mickey said you were fiery. He wasn't kidding."

"He talked about me like that?"

Denny pulled a face as if she'd just said the sky was

blue. "Nonstop. After the—that night, he was relentless. He came to see you in the hospital, but they refused to let him in. Then the news broke with his name, and he knew that you wouldn't want him near you after that. He never excused what I did, not once. He told me in no uncertain terms that if I didn't take responsibility for everything, we were done, that I had to make things right for hurting you. When you came to work at Seattle General, he couldn't believe it."

Lauren laughed. A free laugh tinged with tears as she realized just how long Mickey had been fighting her corner, while she sat in it, clawing and biting at him the whole time. "Neither could I. I almost quit that day, but I don't know, Denny. Fighting with your brother gave me the kick I needed to get over things."

As she wiped an errant tear away from her cheek, she saw Denny take in her scar.

"I'll never forgive myself for what I did to you, Doctor—"

"Lauren," she cut in. "Call me Lauren, please. And this—" She waved a hand over her scar, a small smile lighting her up as she remembered all the times Mickey told her she was beautiful. How he kissed and touched her scars with reverence, looking at her like she was a survivor and not a victim. "The scars are still there, but they don't define me now." She looked Denny in the eye. "No more than your mistakes define you. I forgive you for that night."

"Lauren, you don't have to say that."

"I know, but I need to. Not just for me, but for you and Mickey. I know that you did the right thing, and you're doing your time. I came here to see how I felt, whether I could get over this once and for all. Whether it was enough to keep Mickey and me apart."

"And?" Denny asked, his face tense with caution.

"And I do. I do forgive you, for everything. I know you have an addiction, but you've taken accountability for your actions. I'm better now. I am getting back to being me, and I have your brother to thank for that. He really saw me, even when I didn't see myself."

"That's Mickey," Denny smiled, the eyes so like his brother's brimming with tears. "He never gives up on what and who he cares about." He wiped at his face. "The question is, if you've forgiven me, what's stopping you from being with him?"

Lauren opened her mouth to list all the ways they shouldn't be together. How she still had a lot of work to do on herself, how their family situation was complicated, but she knew that didn't matter. Not really. Nothing mattered but her work and Mickey.

Seeing Denny was the last dragon she had to slay, and forcing herself to do it wasn't just for her. It was for Denny, too. To help him. Maybe she couldn't help the past or repair the brothers' relationship with their parents, but she could admit to herself that she'd panicked.

Mickey was steadfast, sure. Unbreakable. He was so sturdy that she'd learned to lean into him for strength without even realizing it.

*And he leaned on me, too.* They were both scarred, in their own way. They wore masks every day, but somehow, from that first time, that horrible life-changing night—they saw the truth of each other. Had always seen behind the masks they both wore, even as they fought against it.

She looked up at Denny, her tears falling unchecked. "Nothing," she laughed, and Denny smiled. "I have to go."

Denny stood, pulling her into a hug she accepted readily, despite the guard barking at them again. "Say hi to my little brother for me. Go get him, Doc."

# CHAPTER FOURTEEN

"What's eating Dr. Sunshine lately? I swear, it's like walking into Siberia down here."

Gloria sighed at Jarvis, tilting her head in Mickey's direction. "Dr. Basso took some time off. I think something happened between them. Her leave request was very sudden."

"Well, yeah," Jarvis scoffed. "They've been circling each other like cats in heat for months."

"This is different, sugar. I think she ran from him."

*No kidding*, Mickey huffed as he tried to pretend that he couldn't hear his colleagues discussing his dumpster fire of a love life. It was hard enough as it was, trying to concentrate on work. The relief ER doctor they'd brought in to cover for Lauren was terrible compared to her, and every time he saw a woman even slightly resembling her come into the hospital, his heart ground to a near halt.

The doors of the ER swished open behind him, and Mickey tuned out his colleagues to focus back on his task.

He needed to get it together. He'd hardly slept since she left. His place was so empty without her, his bed cold and lonely. He slept on the couch with Tripod and hadn't shaved in days. God knows how he was going to work here with her when and if she came back.

Not that she'd stay. He was expecting HR to tell him that she'd handed in her notice any day now. She was running from him, and he didn't have a clue how to stop her or even if he had the right to try.

Denny had been ringing him from prison, but he hadn't picked up. Couldn't, because he didn't want to take his feelings of devastation out on the one person he still had in his life. None of them could change the past, as much as they might want to. At least he could take solace in the fact that he had helped her find herself, even if he'd wrecked himself in the process of putting her back together.

"It's a real shame," Jarvis muttered close by. "I really thought that they were a perfect match."

"Are you done?" Mickey snapped, turning his full glare on them. "I've already spoken about gossiping in the workplace. Whatever is going on with Dr. Basso and me, it has nothing to do with—"

"Mickey?"

Oh great. He was even hearing her voice. *Maybe it's an impending stroke.* A quick death by aneurism didn't sound too bad right now.

"Dr. Basso!" Gloria chimed in, making his whole body tingle. "We weren't expecting you today."

"Hi, Gloria. I came to speak to Dr. Nolan."

Mickey couldn't bring himself to look at her. He knew what was coming, and he didn't want to hear it. Couldn't hear it from her mouth. If he looked at her, he was going to fall apart. This time, he was going to be the one doing the leaving.

"I'm busy with a patient. I'm sure that whatever you need to tell me, HR can pass the message on." He heard Jarvis tut and Gloria suck in a breath, but he didn't care. He couldn't bring himself to turn around and face the woman who had spun the world on its axis since the minute he'd set eyes on her. "I'll be in my office, if anyone needs me."

"Mickey," she called out, but he didn't stop walking away. "Dr. Nolan. Please wait."

He heard her footsteps behind him and sped up.

"Mickey, talk to me."

"No, Lor," he ground out, his eyes closing in pain as his name for her slipped from his damned fickle lips. "I get it, okay. It's done. You're leaving General."

His hand was on the office door. He almost had a door between them when she spoke again.

"I just went to visit Denny."

His whole body locked up so tight he nearly snapped the handle off. "Why would you do that?"

"Because he asked me to, months ago. He wrote me a letter. I never responded before, but I went today. I spoke to him."

Mickey's ragged, broken heart swelled with pride. She'd really been to see Denny? He wished to God he'd answered his calls now. His big brother had obviously been trying to give him a heads-up. "And?"

"Will you look at me? I'm not talking to your back."

Huffing out a breath, he turned to lean against the door. As always, she looked beautiful. *My love.* He took her in, not knowing whether this would be the last time. Her makeup was streaked.

"Have you been crying?" He reached for her, his hands cupping her face on instinct. "What did he say? Why did you go there?"

"I went there for you."

"What?" His thumbs ran along her skin, and she shocked the hell out of him by nuzzling closer. His hands running free along her scar, not a flinch on her face as she stared up at him. "You didn't need to do that, Lor."

"I did." She smiled, her eyes welling with fresh tears. "It was time. I needed to move on, for all of us. I'm sorry, Mickey. I was a coward."

"No, Lor. It was me, I expected too much."

"No, you expected me to be honest and not run from you. I'm so sorry, but I need to tell you. I will never run again. When you told me you wanted more, I panicked. I walked away from you, and I regret it. So much."

"You do?" He pulled her into his arms, not caring who saw them. Not caring who heard. Hell, he wanted everyone to hear his woman coming back to him.

"Of course I do. I love you, you big idiot."

"You...love me?" His smile could have given the sun a run for its money right now.

"Yes!" She laughed, and he wanted to bottle the sound and keep it forever. "I forgave Denny, Mickey. I don't want the past to hold me back anymore. Especially if that means I can't have a future with you. Ever since I came here, you were there for me."

"And you hated every minute."

"Well, you *were* dressed like a clown when I first saw you."

He groaned. "Don't remind me. I will never live that down. I couldn't believe you were there, and I was dressed like that." He dropped a kiss on her scar, breathing her in. "I never stopped thinking about you after that night. I tried to check on you, but then the news broke, and I knew you wouldn't want to see me. It felt like fate was playing some cruel trick, throwing us together again."

"I thought so, too. I was just so angry, and you annoyed the hell out of me."

"Yeah, well, you are pretty easy to wind up. I knew you were in there somewhere. The woman from that night wasn't gone forever. I just needed to show you who you were."

"You did. You showed me so much, Mickey. I'm in awe of the person you are for everyone. You always show up, go above and beyond. I just want to be the one person who is there for you, too. I want to chase away your nightmares and hold you in the dark. If you'll let me, I promise, you will never feel alone again."

"I love you, and I'm so proud of you."

They were grinning at each other like idiots, when the applause erupted.

Turning to the noise, they both blushed to see their whole team clapping in the doorway. Gloria was hugging Jarvis, and Mickey didn't miss the "I told you!" she yelled.

"I think we've been found out," Lauren smiled, not showing one iota of her old, unsure self.

Mickey took her face into his hands, his nose dipping to brush against hers. "I think the jig was up a while ago, Dr. Basso. HR is going to love this."

"Not as much as I love you." She grinned, wrapping her hands in his hair and pulling his mouth to hers.

The whole place whooped around them as he lifted her into his arms, her legs coming up to wrap around his waist as they kissed each other. Pouring all of their relief and joy at being back together into each other as their mouths collided.

"No more wasted time," she said. "No more fear. I just want to be with you. All in."

Mickey pulled away, just enough to look into her beautiful eyes that showed no fear, no recrimination. Only love. "Baby," he rumbled, pulling her ever closer. "You've had me this whole time. I just needed you to give this clown a chance."

*Two years later*

Gloria smiled at the new hire as they walked toward the joint ER doctors' office. "Welcome to Seattle General, Nurse Evans. As you have already heard, we are a level one trauma center and the best Seattle has—"

Loud voices filtered from behind the door, and Gloria started to chuckle as she gave a little knock before swinging it open.

Lauren and Mickey were toe to toe inside, glaring holes into each other.

"Dr. Nolan, I already told you, trauma two is for *my* incoming patients."

"Not a chance, Dr. Basso, I already bagged it! It's my favorite!"

Lauren huffed, poking him firmly in the chest. "Bagged it! Geez, you really are a clown. I already called it, so it's tough nuggies!"

Mickey snorted. "Tough nuggies? What are you, twelve?"

"Sure am, little piggy! Want to pull my pigtails?"

"Do they always fight like that?" the new hire asked Gloria from the corner of her open mouth.

One of the porters chuckled on his way past. "Oh, they're not fighting. Just having a discussion. They're also married. To each other. That's their love language, right, Gloria?"

"Married? Those two?" Nurse Evans balked, glancing back at her new bosses.

Gloria was still laughing as she led her over to the two warring doctors, who were still glaring at each other. "Doctors, this is Nurse Samantha Evans. The new hire."

Lauren and Mickey turned to face them, matching horrified looks on their faces as they clocked the audience they'd been oblivious to.

"Nurse Evans!" they said together. "Hi!"

"Our apologies," Mickey winced. "Gloria here must have forgotten we were in an important meeting. Right, Glor?"

Gloria's smug smile told them both in no uncertain terms that she didn't buy their bull. "Of course, Doctors. We'll be at the nurses' station when you finish your… er…meeting."

Mickey closed the door behind them, his lips twisting to one side.

"Whoops." Lauren winced as Mickey pulled her into his arms. "I think fighting with my husband might not be the best idea at work. We might have scared the new nurse off."

"I'll make it right, don't worry." He snatched a kiss before she could swat him away. "Besides, I love fighting with my wife. It's the best time I've ever had, and given that our department is at the top of the hospital rankings, I think it would be unwise to break our lucky streak, don't you?"

"Right." Lauren laughed, pulling away to take a box out of her desk drawer. "Well, remember that when I'm gone."

"Gone?" Mickey's face dropped. "What do you mean—"

"Open it."

Flashing her that sexy smile he kept only for her, he opened the lid and saw the test nestled in the paper. His jaw dropped as he gazed at it.

"You're pregnant?" His grin lit up the universe. "We're really having a baby?"

She tried not to cry, but it was a lost cause. Being with this man had cracked her wide open, and with the pregnancy hormones roiling through her, she was one big sappy mess. "We are, and I don't want this department going to hell while I'm on maternity leave, so bring that fighting spirit home, you hear me?"

Lifting her in the air, he twirled her around.

Wrapped in the arms of her husband, she had never felt happier. She was healed and loving every single minute of her life. She had a real family now. Mickey and Denny were closer than ever, and she had grown to appreciate her brother-in-law for the person he had become. She had spoken at his appeal hearing, testifying to her forgiveness and the hard work he'd done since the crash to correct his life and help others suffering from addiction in prison.

She'd even been to the prison to give a talk herself, showing them firsthand what addiction could cause…and how much a support system and going through the steps of rehabilitation could change lives.

They'd all had to recover from the event that linked them together, but she didn't hate her scars so much anymore. Mickey had made her feel beautiful even before she believed it herself, and now she knew. Her scars and her past didn't define her. And now she was starting her own family, one that would give the two brothers so much joy.

Mickey's parents were less cold toward Denny now, after Lauren and Mickey's interventions over the past few years, but the damage had been done. A grandchild might just be the bonus they all needed to mend that final scar.

Mickey was going to be the best dad ever, and Lauren couldn't wait for their new chapter to begin.

He was still holding her tight, his face so handsome and joyful it took her breath away. "Baby, I am going to fight you so hard you'll be begging me for mercy. After missing you and our little pineapple all day, the gloves will be off."

"That sounds like war, Dr. Nolan. One that I intend to win."

Mickey shook his head, pulling her back down to his lips and making her squirm. "Never surrender, babes. That's my motto."

"Well, calling our baby *pineapple* is a good way to wind up the mother of your child."

"Aww, come on!" He chuckled, running his tongue along her jaw because he knew it drove her crazy. "It's perfect, right? Cute, spiky? You know whatever child we have is going to be competitive with our DNA. I love you so much, Lor. I swear, I am going to take care of both of you for the rest of my life."

"I love you, too, Mickey." She kissed him again, and the second he put her down, she ran for the door.

"Lor! Where are you going?"

She turned in the doorway, flashing him a grin and flipping him off. "To my trauma room, bozo." She placed her hand on her belly, giving it a little pat. "We win!"

"Hey!" he yelled, hot on her heels, a cackle of laughter bursting from them both as they shot down the corridor. "No ganging up on Daddy!"

\* \* \* \* \*

*If you enjoyed this story, check out these other great reads from Rachel Dove*

One Night to Twin Surprise
Faking It with the Firefighter
A Baby to Change Their Lives
How to Resist Your Rival

*All available now!*

# MILLS & BOON®

## Coming next month

### EXPECTING IN THE ER
### Tina Beckett

They got on the elevator, and he pressed the button for the second floor, which was where Mack's office was housed, and they rode up in silence. He didn't try to indulge in small talk or anything else until they reached the confines of his office, and he firmly closed the door and gestured to one of the two seats in front of his desk.

He sat behind his desk, feeling the need to keep barriers between them, including physical ones, to get the point across that they were separate beings with separate lives, despite what had happened in Boston.

'Well, it seems I am to welcome you back to the team.'

'I'm sorry, Mack. I was pretty sure you would have said no, if I had come to you directly with a request to come back to work.'

He nodded. 'Which brings up the question of why you want to come back.'

'Do I need a reason?'

'Frankly, yes. I'm sure it's not because I'm here.'

Her teeth came down on her lower lip for a minute before she answered. 'Not entirely, but it did weigh into the equation.'

'Lainey—'

'No, stop. Before you say anything, I didn't come back in hopes that we'd get back together. That's not what either of us wants. I think we've proved that point. But there is another player in this game. One I just found out about a couple of weeks ago.'

'I don't understand.'

She put her hands in her lap and leaned forward. 'I'm pregnant, Mack.'

*Continue reading*

## EXPECTING IN THE ER
Tina Beckett

*Available next month*
millsandboon.co.uk

Copyright © 2026 Tina Beckett

# COMING SOON!

We really hope you enjoyed reading this book. If you're looking for more romance be sure to head to the shops when new books are available on

## Thursday 26th March

To see which titles are coming soon, please visit
**millsandboon.co.uk/nextmonth**

---

## MILLS & BOON

# FOUR BRAND NEW BOOKS FROM
## MILLS & BOON MODERN

Indulge in desire, drama, and breathtaking romance – where passion knows no bounds!

## OUT NOW

Eight Modern stories published every month, find them all at:

**millsandboon.co.uk**

# TWO BRAND NEW BOOKS FROM
# Love Always

Be prepared to be swept away to incredible worldwide destinations along with our strong, relatable heroines and intensely desirable heroes.

## OUT NOW

Four Love Always stories published every month, find them all at:

**millsandboon.co.uk**

# OUT NOW!

Available at
millsandboon.co.uk

MILLS & BOON

# OUT NOW!

Available at
millsandboon.co.uk

## MILLS & BOON

# LET'S TALK
## *Romance*

For exclusive extracts, competitions and special offers, find us online:

- **f** MillsandBoon
- **X** @MillsandBoon
- **◉** @MillsandBoonUK
- **♪** @MillsandBoonUK

Get in touch on 01413 063 232

For all the latest titles coming soon, visit
millsandboon.co.uk/nextmonth